MONKEY AROUND

First published 2021 by Solaris
an imprint of Rebellion Publishing Ltd,
Riverside House, Osney Mead,
Oxford, OX2 0ES, UK

www.solarisbooks.com

ISBN: 978-1-78108-920-0

Designed & typeset by Rebellion Publishing Ltd.

Printed in Denmark

MONKEY AROUND

JADIE JANG

SOLARIS

To the APAture '99 Planning Committee and the Hyphen founders: we sat around a lot of tables and planned a new world.

And to ancestor Stacey Park Milbern, who brought me back to the table.

CHAPTER ONE

TUESDAY, OCTOBER 11, 2011
CHINATOWN ROOFTOP, SAN FRANCISCO

THE GUARD LOOKED entirely human.

He wore designer jeans, knockoff Gucci loafers, a sheeny buttoned shirt, and too much hair gel. He smelled, even at a distance, of strong cologne. His skin was a taut medium brown, with faint wrinkle lines starting between his groomed eyebrows and around his cheeks. He held his cigarette between his thumb and first two fingers and blew crooked smoke rings.

He looked entirely human. That was my first clue that he wasn't.

I know, I know, if everyone who looked human wasn't, then nobody would be human (interesting thought, that ...) but that's not what I mean. There was a ... brightness to his appearance, like he was in HD while the rest of the world was a cell phone video. He was too perfectly what he appeared to be: an inevitable side effect of wearing a bought glamor. Other people's magic just doesn't sit naturally on you, and only an amateur

7

would take that sparkling, sharp visage at face value.

This guy, if Ayo's info was correct, was a bajang: a shapeshifter that had a human-like form, and a weasel-like form. The human-like form, however, wasn't entirely human. He should have had clawed hands and taloned feet. And he was entirely too tall for a bajang, being around my average human height. And bajang, apparently, don't have higher deceptive magic. Not that he'd have gotten away with it if he had. I have my own magic detector, when common sense fails, and my eyes were burning away merrily.

The only thing I couldn't tell you is why a rooftop guard would need to go to such trouble to hide who he was. I mean, he was on the *roof*.

I was at that moment in the form of a shadow at the base of the air conditioning vent. The guard had come out almost immediately after I got there to have a smoke, and gave the place I was shadowing a few hard looks. Probably saw that something was wrong with my spot (there wasn't supposed to be a shadow here) but couldn't put his finger on it. I waited.

He seemed nervous, for some reason.

Halfway through his cigarette, he decided he was done. He gave me a last hard look and flicked his cigarette into me, turning to go back through the door before it landed. The butt flew through me, bounced off the air conditioning vent, and landed, just outside my square of darkness. I gave it another minute to see if he was coming back, then transformed from a shadow into a rhesus macaque monkey. Monkey was my default animal form, and the best form from which to do what I was about to do.

I pulled a hair from my chest, set it on the bare skin of my elongated palm, and focused on it. The tip of the hair turned into something resembling a microphone,

8

and the shaft began to lengthen. The microphone nosed its way into the vent like a snake, and the hair continued elongating behind it as it slithered down the airway. The root end of the hair shaped itself into an ear bud and I put it into my right ear, even as my left hand continued feeding the shaft of the hair—now a flexible cable—into the vent.

It didn't look like any technology you've ever seen. I started out in high school trying to make real machines out of my hairs, but I didn't really understand their mechanisms, so they never worked. But when I got it through my skull that it was magic, not engineering, I just made the things look like what I wanted them to do, and then they started working like whoa.

The microphone head slid past several rooms featuring sounds appropriate to a "massage" parlor (I'll spare you any elaboration.) Without looking I reached around the vent chimney for the black patent leather crossbody purse I'd brought with me (fashionable and water resistant!) I pulled out the stone Ayo had magicked for me and cupped it over my left ear, and the conversations became understandable. I couldn't suddenly speak Chinese, mind you, despite four years of college classes. But the gist of the conversation filtered into my brain, even as I listened to words I couldn't understand. I was listening for a particular female voice—one that sounded like a warped metal door being scraped open across a rough cement floor—or for snatches of conversation about the owner of that voice. I got nothing.

I was on the hunt for Dalisay, the head of the Bay Area aswang contingent, who'd disappeared without a trace two days before. It was a fairly serious matter: leaderless aswangs would be no joke, especially when their leader was Catholic AF, kept them all living near the cemeteries of Colma, and organized raids on said cemeteries to keep her flock from stealing live babies. This was the third building belonging to the Hung For Tong I'd checked tonight, and the only one I'd found any people—or critters—in.

I pulled my cell phone out of the purse. Like the magicked stone, it didn't—couldn't—change shape with me, so I had to deal with it—irritatingly—whenever I went on an assignment like this; hence the purse, which was real, not made out of my hairs, like the rest of my clothes. One of these days I'd figure out how to make a phone from a hair, and then we'd be cooking with dynamite.

- **NOTHING SO FAR. GO FOR PLAN B.**, I typed and sent, then returned the phone to its baggie, in its hidden corner.

A minute later, I heard a phone ring through the mic. A brusque male voice answered, and I heard Ayo's tiny, tinny voice coming through his cell phone. She sounded angry and demand-y. The brusque male voice told her, apparently for the second time, that he knew nothing, and hung up. Ayo didn't call back, like she would've if this had been a real demand.

Then a softer male voice asked the brusque one the obvious question. The brusque voice said, "That woman asking about Dalisay," and the other one grunted. After some desultory talk, they turned to tale-telling that would put X-Tube to the blush. Either they didn't have Dalisay, or they were all talked out about it for the night. Without shifting its position, I changed the mic into a micro camera, and repeated the room-by-room search (I could do sight and sound at the same time, but it took a lot more focus.) This turned up nothing on Dalisay again, just stuff I would never, ever unsee. I pulled the hair camera up, turned it back into a hair, and stuck it back on my chest.

- **NOTHING.** I texted to Ayo.

– ??? She texted back. This was Ayo asking for next steps.

– TALK TOMORROW. She could ask for details at work tomorrow if she wanted to. I turned off my phone and put it away.

I turned to go, and kicked something by accident. It clattered away across the rooftop—a beer can. It hadn't been there before. I would have known; I had been the shadow it was sitting in. I looked for the half-smoked cigarette, didn't find it, and knew that I wouldn't. I should've known: the cigarette hadn't sizzled out when it hit the wet rooftop. The bajang had thrown a basic enchantment over the beer can to set it up as an alarm. Whoops.

I had just enough time to admire his crude, but effective, tactic before he yanked the rooftop door open and tumbled out. He was shorter by a lot, and his Gucci loafers had been replaced by taloned feet. A look of focused rage now marred his handsome face and his eyes glowed orange.

My rational brain was telling me to flee. But I also have a monkey brain, and Monkey loved to fight. And Monkey currently had the upper paw.

I slid into human form, expecting to gain a moment of surprise. My human form is, I'm too often told, rather young and sweet-looking: a pale-skinned girl anywhere between fifteen and twenty-five years with Asian features and long hair just this side of the blonde/brown divide. About half the folks I'd fought screeched to a complete halt at the sight of her. Me.

But this guy was good. He didn't pause, just closed on me with a fury of lighting-fast punches and kicks that left me breathless … and delighted. I shoulda just put him down, but: 1) I'd never fought a bajang before, 2) I'd been getting bored with life, and 3) this guy was *good*.

He was so fast I couldn't see his hands and feet moving. Wow. Okay, then, buddy, *Okay*! Let's see whatcha got!

I backed us up along the short length of the roof, opening up a bit to keep up with him. I even let him land a few, just to see how he'd handle it. Ooooh, he was *pretty*. Look at that form! And that speed! Maybe my sweet little face was relaxing in admiration, because he took advantage, leaping forward, sinking his claws into my shoulders, and smashing the bony crown of his head into the bridge of my nose.

... Or, at least, trying to. I turned briefly into a dragon egg, the sudden hardness of my shell thrusting his claws out of my flesh, just in time for him to smash the hard part of his skull against the hard part of my everything. I switched back to monkey, the claw-holes behind my shoulders gone as if they'd never been. He staggered away from me, pressing his paw to his crown.

I didn't think it would stop him for long; I was told bajang have hard heads. So I swung up on my knuckles to kick him in the throat, the gut, and the ... did bajang have balls? I noted that none of this had a particularly strong effect, although his throat seemed marginally more vulnerable than the other two. Fair enough: I stuck four monkey toes into his throat again for good measure. He choked, recovered ... and then it was *really* on.

He feinted a swipe from my right, then swept my legs. Or tried to. I turned to mist for a moment, then rocked back on my knucks and shoved him on the side with my feet, using his excess momentum against him. Instead of stumbling, he executed a controlled fall, which he turned into a sideways roll back up into a side kick. Damn, this guy was *good*. Moreover, I'd seen that move before. Come to think of it, I'd seen a lot of his moves before.

I switched back to human so I could speak.

"Where have I seen you?" I asked, as much to find out as to see if he was distractible. He wasn't. I had to block a 1-2 ... then a 3, even as his face opened with surprise and ... was that ...? Guess he was pissed off.

"MMA," he mumbled, as if coerced, then followed the concession with a vicious claw-swipe that would've taken out my eye, if I'd had an eye just then.

... Ooooooh, MMA! Right! This guy was Budi "Bu Bu" Budiman, Indonesia's golden boy for a few seasons—until he took some time off to recover from an injury and never came back. I could almost see what had happened to him play before my eyes like a soap opera recap: his treatments paid for by a mob boss, his recovery not as quick and complete as the business required, his debt suddenly unpayable. And now this contender was a leg-breaker. Sad, but common. The question was: why did they put what was undoubtedly their best guard on the roof? They couldn't have known I was coming.

As if reading my thoughts, Bu Bu's rictus of fury cracked open at the mouth and he asked me in a voice that sounded ... shaken, "What *are* you?"

Ugh. I hated that question.

I did wonder, for a second, if I'd hate it nearly as much if I knew the answer.

And there it was: *I* was distractible. He sensed it and took advantage of the moment to break the rhythm we'd created together. In a move I hadn't thought he'd try again, fool that I am, he feinted left, jabbed left, then swept my legs. I went straight down and he threw himself over me, using his claws and talons to encourage me into a hold.

Okay, fun and games over. He was poetry in motion, but *nobody* puts me in a hold. The monkey part of my mind shrieked at me to kill him, but was easily overruled.

I grasped his wrists and prised them away. I'd been holding back, and he didn't think I could prevail in a strength contest, so he pushed back. Not very respectful.

I yanked his wrists outward with about 50% force and felt something in the soft tissue give. He didn't cry out, but his strength fell away. I suddenly hoped I hadn't broken those golden wrists. This guy was too much of a gem to injure permanently.

I shoved him off and snapped to my feet. He rolled away and up and paused for a moment to think, his whole body projecting wary defiance. To be fair, I'd been giving him the impression that he had various split seconds here and there to think things out, but the truth was, he didn't. I simply reached in with both hands, grabbed his injured wrists above the joint (didn't wanna hurt 'im!) and used them as leverage to run up his body. At the top, I backflipped and, still holding his wrists, threw him over my head backward toward the rooftop door.

This was Monkey's favorite move: you never knew where they might land! It was like I was a bride at a wedding where I was marrying kickassery, and the opponent was my bouquet.

Oh … where is Bu Bu? I thought to myself deliciously. Where could Bu Bu be?

I whipped around, but he was already rising out of his crumpled position. What the hell? Didn't he *know* when he was beaten?

"What *are* you?" he asked again, in a wavering voice, and I looked more closely at his expression. Suddenly, I realized that he wasn't furious—he was terrified. Had been, the whole time. What? Of li'l ol' me? Weak.

I paused to consider responses. Your Daddy? The iron something in the velvet … hm. How about: *The Long Dark Night Of Your Soul, Motherfucker*? Yeah, that was good. I turned back into a shadow, for effect, thinking it probably wouldn't faze him, but would be funny.

But my punchline was preempted by a bloodcurdling scream … from Bu Bu. I focused on him. All at once he'd gone from injured-but-defiant to cringing and abject.

"You just like *him*!" he cried in a high-pitched voice. "You same … *thing*. What *are* you people? What you want?"

My brain froze. What the— what? *What* "him"? *What* "thing"? *What the fuck?*

The slippery little fucker took advantage, and turned to run. My monkey brain kicked the rest of me back into action. I turned into a giant frog, leapt, and gravitationally encouraged him by the shoulders into the ground. Then I turned back to human, rose, and grabbed him by the throat.

I shook him a little. "Did you see another one like me? Where? When? Did you see one like me? Did you?" I shook him with every question. Really, it was more monkey brain than me. Monkey didn't think a little injury should come between friends.

But Bu Bu was completely overcome. He cringed before me, holding up his injured wrists in a pathetic attempt to protect himself.

"Get ahold of yourself, Bu Bu," I commanded.

At the sound of his name, he burst into terrified sobs.

"Don't!" he cried. "Don't eat my soul! Please!" And he dissolved into blubbering.

I heaved him to his feet and shook him a few more times, but no more info fell out. Monkey would have been happy to keep shaking him until I was exhausted, but cooler parts of my mind recognized that I'd have to give him time to calm down … and maybe find a little leverage too.

I crabbed sideways, still holding him up with one hand, grabbed the bamboo tube Ayo'd given me out of my purse, and flipped the cap off with my thumb. With a "swop!" sound, the cringing Bu Bu disappeared inside. I put the cap back on.

He could just sit there for a while, until he was ready to talk. I wasn't letting this go. I'd been waiting my entire twenty-five years for some little clue about what I was, and this MMA goon was the very first one.

CHAPTER TWO

I STOOD AT the top of Portsmouth Square Park, balanced on the spine of its pagoda-roofed pavilion, and breathed the city in. At 2 am the park was empty of chess players, gossips, and smokers; the intermittent aroma of restaurant garbage alternated with fishy breaths from the Bay six blocks away. I was mostly socked in by the giant bodies of financial district skyscrapers, but in between them I could see the sparkling eyes of more distant windows, and the vague black ribbon of the water—or of a void sketched out where the heart of our region ebbed and flowed.

Since I'd moved here, whenever I stood in a high place (and being a monkey, that was more often than your average human,) I'd look out at the cityscape and feel almost like it was looking back at me: a friend, a witness, almost as if it had its own spirit … as if it could speak—although I believed without question that this was a product of my own imagination.

And these days, I thought I knew what that spirit would be saying. I'd spent high school and college under the heavy public apathy of the Bush years, and experienced how difficult it was to motivate my cohorts to any kind of action. So that fall, when word of the Occupy Wall Street protest tore through the air like lightning, and Oakland (and even San Francisco) rose up in response, I felt like something was waking up: some better angel of our nature, something militant in the spirit of the Bay. I felt like I, like *we,* were on the threshold of a new era, a new mass movement, one where life would take a huge leap forward.

The peace of late-night Chinatown overlay that excitement. I breathed them both in.

Then I texted a contact at St. James Infirmary—a local clinic for sex workers—to send their outreach team to this massage parlor. I didn't know if the "girls" were there by choice, but the St. James team would make sure they got what they needed.

Due diligence done, I headed for the wide-open sky and massive, blocky warehouses of SOMA. Jazzed by the weight of Bu Bu's bamboo container against my hip, I decided to run off some nervous energy down Folsom past Kearny Street Workshop's new location (no longer on Kearny Street—people, don't name your art gallery after its location; not in San Francisco) and stick my head in the window to see what their new exhibition looked like.

I'd done an internship at the venerable Asian American arts nonprofit while in college, hoping to connect to my non-existent roots, and it became my home away from home. The organization was also the fiscal sponsor for the magazine I helped to run, and we often held meetings there. They'd had an event tonight—a stand-up comedy showcase—which I'd wanted to go to, but had to miss for tonight's emergency search. I knew everyone would have gone home long before, but still felt like checking in. I'm a monkey; I'm social like that.

I passed a homeless person sleeping in a strange little patio area before a storefront next door, but when I reached the gallery itself, a curtain was drawn and I couldn't really see inside. While I stuck my nose to the dirty glass and tried to see through a crack in the curtain, my monkey brain noticed something else. The smell of homeless, unwashed body, which tended to hit me a little harder than humans, had come wafting to me from next door, but it smelled … off. More of my attention followed the smell back from the curtained gallery window to the strange little enclosed patio next door. The smell wasn't, in fact, of unwashed body at all. No, I'd smelled it a time or two before. It was of decomposing body. The body was dead.

Now it had my complete attention. That's why I smelled it at all. My nose isn't that good: slightly better than a human's, but nothing like the carnivore-shifters' noses. I walked back a few yards to where I could see clearly and I could now see that it was all wrong. The body wasn't huddled up, but rather splayed uncomfortably, half on his back, half on his side, his arms and legs thrown out in awkward positions. I'd thought he was covered by a blanket, but it turned out he had a sports jacket all rucked up over his head, like he had been clutching it around his face. His clothes were new, there was no cardboard lining the ground, and no bags of belongings or bedding.

Jesus, was this a body dump? I couldn't see any blood or signs of a struggle, so presumably the person hadn't been killed here. What a strange place to dump a body!

Folsom is fairly busy during the day, and—I glanced up—this storefront belonged to a catering company that did its own baking. There'd be someone here in a couple of hours.

That was enough to send me to my cell phone, but another useful habit stopped me from dialing 911 right away: Maya, my rational brain said, get your story straight! Although I hadn't done anything wrong, I could see right away that "I smelled the dead on 'im, officer" wasn't going to fly. I needed to check his pulse properly, and leave evidence that I had, before I called in a dead body.

I crouched and pulled the jacket away from his head and upper body, revealing … what must've previously been a human face with pale olive skin, but was now sprouting light-colored fur around his temples and cheeks, with his mouth distorted by elongated teeth and a snarl, his fingernails halfway grown into claws, and the barrel of his chest bowing strange and angular. His corner-folded eyes were staring amber.

I was immediately glad that I hadn't called the cops. This guy wasn't human. He was a shapeshifter.

* * *

"A WERETIGER, TO be exact," Ayo said, 20 minutes later when she arrived. I didn't see any stripes, though the poor dude was stuck forever (or until he rotted) in the moment of transformation. I was holding out for a were-beaver (not that I'd ever heard of such a thing, but a girl can hope) but almost convinced it was just a run-of-the-mill werewolf.

"How do you know it's a weretiger?"

"I've met this guy before," she said. "His name's

Wayland. He's a harimau jadian from Singapore. He runs an import/export company that—among other things—supplies a lot of the Chinese tchotchke stores on Grant. Very successful."

"Aiya! *Wayland Soh*?" I shrieked. My gut suddenly felt like lead.

"Yes," Ayo looked at me, puzzled. "Do you know him?"

"Shit shit shit …" was all I could say for a moment. I'd only met him once and I couldn't have recognized him anyway with his face all distorted. "Fuck, Ayo, we were courting him for sponsorships!"

"We" was shorthand for one of the Asian American nonprofits I was involved with: the magazine, *Inscrutable*, as well as Kearny Street Workshop. There was a lot of crossover in the personnel between the two orgs (Asian America can get kinda incestuous, especially in San Francisco.) One of the magazine's staff members, who was also a KSW board member, and I had met Wayland last week and he (Wayland) had been impressed with our youthful joie de vivre, or something, and wanted to see what kinda stuff we did. Shit, he'd probably been here for the comedy night!

Both our orgs were laboring under the funding crunch that had resulted from the economic crash of 2008. Both orgs were direly in need of new funding streams, and local sponsorships seemed the best way to go. I wasn't in charge of fundraising, but I did know that Wayland had been our first solid sponsorship prospect in a long time.

"Well, that sucks," Ayo said, sucking on her teeth and pulling out her phone. I could tell by her tone that her mind had already wandered away from the plight of San Francisco's nonprofits. I felt immediately chastened. Here was a man—okay, a … sentient creature—dead, and I was worried about funding streams!

Ayo leaned against the side of her car, holding her phone to her ear and looking like someone on hold. I looked past her and jumped a little when I realized that there was a man sitting inside her car, staring at me. He looked—as far as I could tell through the streetlight glare on the windshield— brown and classic, with a nose that belonged on either an Egyptian or Aztec god. He also looked middle-aged, Ayo's age or older, and tired. Had I interrupted a date when I called her? Was Ayo dating a man this time? It had been a while.

"Are you calling his family?"

She shook her head. "The Asian cats have a sort of benevolent society they all pay into. He heads it up and uses that position to influence the Chinatown machine. They'll want to investigate this death and handle his remains."

Inside my head, Monkey insisted that *I* was perfectly capable of investigating this myself, but my rational brain answered, faintly, that this wasn't my problem.

"I didn't even know he was a supernat!" I said out loud, as if knowing would have changed anything. "We met at a mixer at the Asian Art Museum... there were performances and, and artists everywhere!" That would've neutralized my ability to see deceit. But even if I'd seen it... I wouldn't have done anything differently tonight. Of course I wouldn't've. So... why did I feel responsible?

Someone answered Ayo's phone and she, ignoring my outburst, spoke some language into it. An irritating thing about Ayo: she speaks at least nine living languages, and reads at least five dead ones. People are always surprised when they finally meet her, because petite African-looking women aren't supposed to speak [Russian/Arabic/ Spanish/fill-in-your-own-annoyingly-useful-language- here] like a native. She can learn a new language in three

22

weeks, damn her eyes. She learned Chinese after she met me—during a vacation, mind you—while I'm still completely hopeless at the language after four solid years of college classes, plus a summer intensive. She beeped the phone off and returned to examining the body.

"It's not where he comes from that we should be concerned about," she said. "It's where he went." She took a few snaps of him with her phone and checked them out.

"What do you mean, where he went? Like to Hell, or over the Rainbow Bridge?"

Ayo flashed me a narrow-eyed look. "I mean, where did his essence go?"

"His essence? Doesn't that disappear when you die?"

She sighed the sigh of the multiply martyred. "*No*, Maya. Not right away." She studied the body for a moment more. "By 'essence' I don't mean 'soul.' If there *is* an individual soul—an ori, the spiritual seat of personality that adds an ancestor to the spirits—if there is one, it has a metaphysical reality that's beyond my perception. What I *can* perceive is the essence of a person—something you might call his emi or qi, his living energy. It's what returns to the natural world's energy at death. It maintains a certain ... personality or echo of the person, while still combining with all the other energy and ..." Here's where I started tuning her out. Once she got into lecture mode she grew increasingly obscure until only one of her ancestors could understand her. But she got irate if interrupted.

She flew outward into the cosmos, ordering it for her fellow, less knowledgeable mortals, before finally returning to the subject of: "... essence retains some of its character for a time, but mostly it just returns to the world. It's exactly like what happens to a dead body.

It lingers in its form for a while, but deteriorates until there's only a skeleton—a structure that suggests the person that was but isn't the person that was. Over time, even the bones can wear away, and all that's left is the converted mass of the body. Well, it's the same with the essence. It lingers in and around the body, holding its shape much as the body does, but deteriorating and dissipating. It can linger for weeks or months, or even years, and is where the notion of ghosts and evil dead comes from. People who are sensitive to it can 'see' it; that is, sense it, and then their brains transform that presence into an image."

"And this guy has only been dead for, what? A few hours?" His body wasn't too cold yet, although it wasn't much warm, either.

"Right. So there should be a lot of relatively inert essence lingering around his body."

"But there's not?"

"Not a shred. Not a scosh. Not an iota."

I didn't reply, but shuddered, with my whole body.

"Yeah," Ayo said, "exactly. But it's even worse than that." I raised my eyebrows. "Our essence is where we draw the energy for magic. And for shape-changers it's even more elemental. Shapeshifters' essential beings contain magic, because magical shape-changing is part of your being. That makes the magic in your essence orders of magnitude more powerful."

"Wait, what? I'm more powerful than you? Then why can't I do more magic than you?"

"Maya," she said impatiently, "this isn't a role-playing game. You *are* more powerful. You're just constrained to use your power in a particular way. Shapeshifters shapeshift. That's what the power's for. You can't really redirect it. It's inherent to your essence. The magic I use, on the other hand, is just out there in the world. I don't own it, I just use it, so I can pull different kinds of magic from different sources and slightly divert it. Any human can."

She frowned, catching herself. She'd been about to launch into another of her favorite lectures. "We've *talked* about this," she said. "You need to read those books— Maya, you need to know this stuff cold. I can't keep watch over supernatural creatures the way you can. You really *are* more powerful and you need to understand the way our differing abilities balance."

Whatever. "Okay, but if we shapeshifters have so much raw power, then why is no one after it?"

She didn't say right away. She scanned and rescanned, then finally sighed and stepped back.

"Two answers: One, it's extremely difficult to separate someone's essence from their body. Essence and body aren't really separate. Pulling away someone's essence would be like pulling away someone's arm. You'd have some arm-shaped matter, no doubt, but don't expect it to grasp or throw anything ever again."

Hmph, I thought. Dr. Frankenstein might disagree with that. But then, that's fiction, isn't it?

Ayo went on: "So even if you could do it, you couldn't make it do anything for you, because it's not yours. ..." She trailed off.

"And two?" I asked impatiently.

"Well ... It looks like someone *is* after it."

Before I could even shudder along with her, the were-cats arrived—with a vintage sixties hearse, no less!— and after the requisite thirty seconds spent sniffing in my general direction and stifling knee-jerk snarls, five of them got busy processing the scene. The sixth came to confer with Ayo in some presumably Asian language, casting me baleful glares every so often. They completely ignored the man in Ayo's car, so I assumed that meant he was human—although that was no guarantee. After a few minutes, Ayo came back over to me.

"You can go. I'll take it from here. Best you keep away if you don't want to answer uncomfortable questions about yourself."

I struggled with myself for a moment. I really wanted to find out ... no, not my business. "Who's that dude, anyway?" I pointed to her car, distracting myself.

She turned to look, as if she'd forgotten him. "He's a client," she said.

"Is he human?"

Ayo sighed demonstratively. That meant yes.

"How can he be a client if he isn't a supernat?" What I really wanted to know was what he was making of this whole scene. Ayo might have been ... *adjusting* his view of what was happening outside the car.

She sighed impatiently. "Maya, the human world and the supernatural world are inextricably linked. You know that." I knew that *tone*. "But, believe me, if there's a job for you in this, you'll be the first to know."

"There's a job for me in this?"

"He's looking for something, but doesn't want to tell me what it is." She rolled her eyes. We both knew this schtick. Humans were super tricky about the supernatural and didn't want other humans to know that they believed in it—assuming, of course, that they did. "It'll probably turn out to be—"

"Merman's penis?" This was our jokey code word for superstitious black market bullshit: you know, dried incubus dong and things like that, stuff that either didn't exist and was replaced with powdered goat horn, did exist but was entirely inefficacious, or stuff that did exist and had some function but that you'd have to kill a sentient being to get.

She nodded. I started to turn away.

"Did you get anything on Dalisay?"

I started a bit; remembering. The emergency that the evening had started with had been driven entirely from my mind. I felt the urgency of it again, but now it was warring with the urgency of a murder, and one almost literally on my doorstep.

"No, nothing at all."

"Nothing?"

"Not a shred. Not an iota. Not a scosh. He literally said 'That woman asking about Dalisay,' and that was it. No chatter, no rubbing of hench-hands while they revealed their wicked plans. And no sign of her being there, either. They either don't have her, or they're holding her somewhere else. My money is on 'don't have her.'"

Ayo frowned in concentration. "Or she's dead," she said, slowly.

I shuddered a little "How much trouble are we in, if she isn't found?" I asked.

Ayo shrugged absently, but her worried face told a less laissez faire story.

I'd been checking the buildings of the triad-affiliated Hung For Tong because they supplied her with blood plasma for her protégés, and had been the last appointment she'd gone to in her calendar. Maybe the Tong had gotten greedy and were holding her for ransom—although there hadn't been any ransom demands yet. Or maybe it wasn't them. If it was a kidnapping for ransom, it could be almost anyone. Dalisay's little aswang coterie had amassed quite a fortune over the years, a lot of it from their neat grave-robbing.

Preoccupied with the question of who else might be in the kidnap business, I tried to leave again, but Ayo stopped me with: "And the bajang?"

I frowned.

She held out her hand.

"No way, Ayo. Finders keepers." I put my hand over the pocket that held Bu Bu's bamboo tube.

She looked confused … and annoyed. "Maya …" she started.

I sighed. "He said something to me. He said something and … I think he might know what I am."

Her look narrowed. "What did he say, exactly?"

"He said I was like the other one." She waited. "He indicated that there's another one like me!"

"And you didn't ask what that meant?" she cried impatiently.

"Well, he got all freaked out and started blubbering and I couldn't get any more out of him!"

She frowned. "Why did he get freaked out?"

"Oh, I don't know. He said something about …" *OMFG* "Oh my god, Ayo, he said something about 'Please don't eat my soul'!"

In a moment of perfect understanding, Ayo and I looked at each other, then turned to look at the weretiger.

But when I turned back the moment was broken and Ayo was holding out her hand.

"Give him to me," she said, now severe.

"No, Ayo! This is my first clue … *ever*!"

"Do you know how to interrogate a bajang?"

"I figured I'd rough him up a little."

"They don't experience much pain. They have to be otherwise motivated. Do you know how?"

I could feel my chin beginning to jut out.

"Give him to me," she said again, then her voice softened a little, "and I promise I will squeeze every last mote of monkey info from him."

My stubbornness warred with Monkey's bloodthirstiness, both of which were fighting my pragmatism.

"And I'll need to interrogate him for these guys over here," she tipped her head backwards at the werecats. "If it's related, they deserve to know."

I couldn't argue with that, although it was almost impossible to make my hands move. After another brief struggle, I pulled the bamboo tube out of my pocket and handed it to her.

"Be careful with him," I said.

"And the stone."

I pulled the magicked stone out of another pocket, hardly less reluctantly.

"Now go home and get some sleep. You're working the cafe tomorrow."

I went, but with a heavy heart and a heavy gut. I'd turned over responsibility, for now, but … that certainly didn't mean I'd turned my back on it forever. In fact … I straightened my shoulders. In fact, with what I was doing tomorrow night, I'd have a chance to investigate without even going out of my way. I wasn't gonna say so, but I was still on the case.

CHAPTER THREE

WEDNESDAY, OCTOBER 12, 2011
SANC-AHH CAFÉ, OAKLAND

I SLID IMPATIENTLY into work the next morning, not looking forward to a whole day of slinging drinks before I could get back on the chase. I worked primarily as a barista for Ayo, although lately, those side gigs—like the one the previous night—had been creeping up on more and more of my spare time.

Cafe Sanc-ahh, my workplace, was three quarters full of human-looking supernats—half hipster, half demimonde—who stopped in briefly all morning to indulge in rumors about Wayland's slaying. (I hadn't heard a peep about Dalisay being missing, though. The aswangs were apparently keeping it quiet.) The killing of a supernat was unusual. Not that we didn't fight amongst ourselves—a lot. It's just that we all tended to be hard to kill; part of the reason we fought so much. And the consequences for killing one of us—a fatwa against you by every other supernat of that persuasion or cultural corner being out for your blood—made death matches a lot less fun. So a death like this, with no apparent cause and a hidden motive, was worth gossiping about. At length. I listened for a while, but didn't hear anything apropos the werecats' investigation—or my own curiosity.

Café Sanc-ahh was a play on words. Before there was decaf coffee, there was something called "Sanka" (from the French "sans caféine"): instant decaf that was the only choice you had if you wanted to sleep that night. Café Sanc-ahh served the most extensive menu of non-caffeinated brews, teas, tisanes, infusions, and ... less commonly known drinks of less acceptable substance and provenance. This was, of course, owing to Sanc-ahh's baseline mission as a sanctuary, i.e. a magically protected commons where all kinds of supernatural creatures could seek shelter and mingle without conflict or danger. If you want to keep a bunch of supernats from killing each other, the first step is not to wire them up on a stimulant; particularly a stimulant that struck some of the supes particularly hard, and some of them ... shall we say ... obliquely.

Most sanctuaries made sure to locate in out-of-the-way places, or "bad" neighborhoods, and set up aversion spells around themselves to discourage human curiosity. Some even put a glamour in the entryway to make the place look uninhabited, and closed, if a human dared enter. But Sanc-ahh was different: not only was the space open, full of windows and light, painted a soft ivory, decorated with a bright, multicultural collection of masks, kites, and dolls, and furnished with matching, mellow wood furniture—all to look as welcoming as possible—but Ayo even had an entire drinks menu posted specifically for humans. You had to ask for the supernat menu.

Of course, there were limitations on human entry. Sanc-

Ahh *was* a sanctuary after all, so during demon-hunting sweeps (when the various parochial and secular demon-hunting organizations got antsy and came after us in an organized throng) the cafe was locked down to humans. Any who came looking for Sanc-Ahh would get the distinct impression that they'd passed it already—where was it again?—and oh, by the way, they had an urgent personal errand to run elsewhere. And the sanctuary's protections *always* sent away humans who came with ill intent. But humans who came with goodwill—or even humans who came in absentmindedly—were welcome the rest of the time.

This was, very definitely, an Ayo thing. She was always saying that humans and supernats were bound together in all sorts of weird ways, and that the world was as out of balance as it was because the natural and supernatural had rejected each other during the Enlightenment and blah blah blah. It made working here more complicated than at other sanctuaries, because we all had to be careful about displaying powers and strange appearances in front of the borings.

I hadn't yet identified an upside, but I loved Sanc-Ahh like I'd never loved any sanctuaries I'd haunted before.

I'd started working at Cafe Sanc-Ahh at the beginning of my junior year at UC Berkeley, after I'd finally decided to use university resources to investigate what kind of creature I was. I bounced from department to department, with no one willing to take the time to help me, until someone finally gave me a name: Ayo Espinosa, who'd been a brilliant interdisciplinary folklore enfant terrible, with extra PhDs in anthropology and comp lit. She'd lectured savagely, armored herself with an entourage of enamored students a handful of years younger than she, refused departmental allegiance, and bullied tenure out of the university through sheer, hard-assed publication. Her star rose and fell precipitously. She started to talk about the fairy stories she studied as if they were systems of fact. Her fascinating topical mash-ups in class became simply bizarre, class attendance dropped, and it soon became necessary to avoid her at parties. When a dean approached her about "seeking help," she quit and disappeared. Ten years later, Café Sanc-ahh opened, quietly, a few miles down Telegraph Avenue, and her former colleagues—detractors and admirers alike—pretended not to know that it was Prof. Ayo flying her freak flag in Oakland.

I thought I knew what all of this meant: one of us had revealed themselves to her. I'd seen it before. They usually went a little crazy, the rationalist humans, when they found out about supernats. So I was expecting something else entirely when I stepped into the near-empty cafe one afternoon with my story already somewhat polished from use: I was working on a piece of creative writing; I had made up a supernatural creature with a set of powers and I really wanted to find out if there was an actual fairytale or myth of a creature with exactly this set of powers or something similar; have you ever heard of such a creature? I didn't even get the first word out before Ayo accosted me.

"I like the way you look. What are you?"

This was familiar, if somewhat blunt.

"Uh, I'm adopted, so I'm not sure, but I seem to be East Asian and white. Probably Chinese and European mutt. You know, hapa."

"No, no," she said impatiently. "What kind of *supernatural* creature are you? Some kind of nature demon? Hungry ancestor? Shapeshifter? That's it, isn't it? You're a shapeshifter aren't you?"

Shit, I thought, she's really persistent. But I knew the rules.

I looked around anxiously, but none of the handful of patrons seemed to be paying attention. I decided to play dumb.

"Uh, Dr. Espinosa?"

"My mother is Dr. Espinosa. I'm Ayo." She snapped her fingers at me when I looked around again. "Pay attention, kid! What kind of creature are you? Lord, maybe she's a really cute troll."

"Uh … they told me you believed in all this fairy tale stuff, but I thought they were exaggerating."

Her clear, dark eyes narrowed at me. "Don't bullshit a bullshitter, baby girl. You're wearing expensive, matching, *new* clothes two sizes too large, an elastic belt, and cheap flip-flops in January. Dead giveaway for someone who changes size and shape quickly." This was long before Ayo helped me figure out that I could make clothes out of my hairs that would shapeshift with me. "Besides, you're blaring supernatural energy like a loudspeaker. You should learn to tone it down."

I gave her my best shocked look, but the effect was ruined by the entrance of an extremely unkempt naga, who immediately started hissing at me, and kept it up for a good half-minute before she got herself under control. I completely destroyed my innocent act with a threat display: baring my teeth and hunching my shoulders. In such moments, Monkey was not to be denied.

"Now, now," Ayo said, "This is a sanctuary. You both know the rules."

A *sanctuary*? Run by a *human*? My shocked look was genuine this time.

I took a little more coaxing (mixed with her characteristic gentle bullying) but she eventually got my story (my real story) out of me. Whereupon she explained the nature of her business and offered me a job. I was a little nonplussed.

"But ... do you know what I am?" I asked, bewildered.

"Not a clue. Unless you're indigenous American—are you sure you're not indigenous? There's a Meso-American howler monkey god and there are lots of African monkey gods and spirits— but no, you're a rhesus macaque, you said. That's Asian. Asian stuff isn't my speciality. I do comparative stuff with folk tales from Africa, Europe, and the Americas. What about that job?"

"What? ... Why?"

"I said already: I like the way you look. And I have an opening. Plus, you're blaring supernatural energy like I've never seen: that means strength, which will come in handy keeping the peace around here. A sanctuary doesn't keep itself. Besides, this is your best way to find someone who might know what you are. Oakland's the fourth busiest port in the US, and we get creatures from a hundred different cultures coming through here monthly. I used to travel to find them, but I've discovered that if I sit here, they'll come to me. ... What do you say?"

Two birds; one stone? What *could* I say?

I hadn't known where the local sanctuary was until I met Ayo. Demon hunters avoided the ivory tower (I'm pretty sure it's just class snobbery,) so on campus I only had to watch out for government recruiters: spooks and crypto-military types who were always looking to weaponize supernatural powers, but had learned, over the centuries, that trying to force themselves on supernats always—sooner or later—ended in disaster for everyone.

Working at Sanc-Ahh had plunged me squarely back into contact with both the supernatural and the human underground. But working with Ayo was ... different, from what I'd previously experienced. Ayo saw the complexities in everything, and helped me to see them, too. The underground wasn't as one-sidedly wicked—

or attractive—as I'd thought as a teenager. And my place in the world might have broader horizons than I'd originally feared.

After several excruciating hours, during which I nerve-ate an entire nylon string bag full of mandarins, Ayo swept in and headed for her office, completely ignoring me. She was probably just spacing out, but it piqued me. I went invisible and flew to the office door, quickly taking on the door's shape and becoming visible again.

Ayo waved her hand at the latch and I made an unlocking sound, then she turned my handle, pulled me open, and, per her usual habit, looked around the room behind her as she went in. I don't know why she made this paranoid gesture every time she entered her office, but it made it easy for me to—

She banged her shoulder unexpectedly hard on the actual office door, which was still shut.

"Puñeta!" she cried. "Maya!"

In an instant, she was holding my hand, which had been the door handle, while I stood before her, guffawing.

"Don't do that!" she cried, shaking my hand off like a bug.

She unlocked the real office door and opened it carefully, checking to make sure the office was actually behind it. I looked around the cafe but the dampening spell she kept around her office door had held, and no one had noticed my little prank.

"What did Bu Bu say?" I asked.

"Who?"

"The bajang."

She sighed and pulled me by the arm into her office. She took her damn time going behind her desk and putting her bag away. As she did it, my eyes wandered over to the door in the back of the office, which looked like the door to a closet. A warm feeling infused me, and I felt a mild yearning toward the door, even as I felt both those feelings blocked, as if hitting a wall. I sighed.

"Maya," Ayo said. She'd been talking.

"What?"

"I said I'm sorry to have to disappoint you, but I got very little out of the bajang."

My heart dropped. "Nothing at all?"

"He indicated he'd seen some creature like you, only male, but his description was confusing, like it was two creatures, and one was a shadow—"

"I was in the form of a shadow for part of the time he saw me. Maybe the other one did that, too, or maybe he could have made a hair clone." (I can also make clones of myself out of my hairs. I know, it's weird.)

"Maybe." She didn't sound convinced. "What he said didn't make sense otherwise. He said it was two creatures, then one creature, then the shadow was a soul-sucking demon, and then he shut down and wouldn't say anything else."

"So it could be a creature like me that made a hair clone and turned into a shadow and ... sucks souls ... which I'm pretty sure I can't do, because BLEAGGHH ... or it's something like me—"

"—Connected to some shadowy soul-sucking creature. Which is what *I'm* thinking. If there's another creature like you, it's unlikely to have a major ability that you don't have. And soul-sucking is a major ability."

I tended to agree. "And that's it? Nothing about what killed Wayland? Did the shadow suck another soul?"

She shook her head. "Believe me, I tried."

"Well, give him back to me. *I'll* try." I said it through gritted teeth.

"Well, he's gone."

"*What?*"

Ayo sighed. "Maya, he asked to go and you know I couldn't hold him after that. He hasn't done anything, and we're not in the business of kidnapping."

Maybe *she* wasn't. "Where did he go?"

"I honestly don't know. The moment I released him, he jumped out the window and disappeared around a corner, and that was it." This meant she'd questioned him at home. She lived in an old warehouse in Jingletown and he wouldn't have stuck around in that neighborhood.

Dead end.

She looked at me expressionlessly and I glared back. That didn't mean this was over, though. Just because Ayo couldn't tell me where Bu Bu had gone didn't mean I couldn't find out on my own. And believe me, I was going to find out. One way or another, this soul-sucking creature was connected to something … to some*one*, like me. And the bajang knew something about it. Damned if I wasn't going to squeeze it out of him.

I waved it away. "Whatever." Her eyebrows went up. She knew me better than to think I'd truly let this drop. "How's the investigation into Wayland Soh going?"

She shrugged and said pointedly, "I don't know because I haven't asked. Not my business." A patent lie, although she believed it as she said it. Ayo was too nosy to stay out of anything in the supernat community. She was just trying to put me in my place.

"Well, it's *my* business! I knew the guy! He was part of my community! And he was probably there in the first place because I'd invited him! So …" I trailed off, not sure where I was going with my indignation. So I was going to ask about the investigation, that's what! Monkey supplied, internally. "Can't you … I dunno, ask around your Afro-Caribbean mafia or something?"

"Maya," she said crisply, "please don't call my community a 'mafia.'"

"Well, you know what I mean. The gossip network. The grapevine."

"And what, exactly, do you want me to ask the Bay Area's African Americans and Afro-Caribbeans about the death of a Singaporean harimau jadian?"

I huffed, frustrated. She was being obstructive today. She usually had about ten different avenues of gossip and information to go down at any given moment, and many of them started with her own communities, but I couldn't think of anything to say to how she'd just laid it out. I got up to go.

Oh yeah: "About Dalisay, I have a Chinatown contact I'm going to hit up tonight. They're connected to the Hung For Tong, I think. They may have info about Wayland, too."

Her eyebrows went up, again, but she didn't say what she was thinking, which was, patently, Why didn't you mention them before? Ayo hadn't stopped being frustrated by my inability to trust people with my secrets—despite the fact that Ayo knew more of my secrets than anyone—but she had learned to stop bitching about it.

"Well," she said, with studied casualness, "Let me know if that turns up anything."

With a last, yearning glance at the inner door, I stepped over a pile of unsaid things, and went back to work.

Soon after, I was facing the counter, wiping off the front side, when I felt a kind of displacement of air, or maybe a displacement of energy. Something that told me someone had entered the shop. But it was strange as well: mostly I didn't feel customers' entrances with my whole body.

I turned to see who it was and was suddenly eyes-to-chin with … Him. All six feet and muscles hands lips eyelashes of him. The grace of a dancer, the tongue of an angel, and the talent of, well, someone girls palpitated over. *Him*.

He backed up a step, surprised. I took in the full blast of him, and my eyes burned.

"Tez Varela," I murmured. It was almost a whisper.

He looked at me, frowning. He'd been about to say something.

"Hi!" he said, not quite covering the fact that he didn't recognize me. "How are you?"

I never forget a face or a name, but have realized over the years that most people do; and I know this tactic for what it is. I was embarrassed and piqued, which overcame my shock.

"You don't know me," I said.

"Oh." His confusion increased slightly, evidenced by a line appearing between his perfect eyebrows.

"I used to go to the poetry slams a lot in college." His line disappeared; perfection restored. My fangirl came out. "You're so amazing!"

"Oh," he said, looking embarrassed, "yeah, thanks … that was a while ago. … Do you write?"

It was a blatant bid to get attention off of him. He must not be writing anymore.

"No," I said. "Just a fan."

"Oh, okay … cool. Um … is Ayo around?" If he weren't so beautiful, I'd say he looked shifty.

"She's in her office. Through there." I pointed to the door to the back office.

He went, and I watched him go. *Man* did I watch him go.

I couldn't believe it. Tez Varela. Here.

Tez was one of the first people I encountered when I came out to the Bay Area to go to Cal (UC Berkeley to you.) During freshman orientation there was a lunch break, and I was sitting out on a patio outside MLK (the Student Union to you) with two Instant Best Friends eating sushi (for lunch! California!) While we tried to act bored and sophisticated, a group of older students wandered into the middle of the patio looking genuinely cool, set their bags and notebooks on the tables, and then, as if it was no big thing, started freestyling. This is what I had come to Berkeley for: beautiful, cool-looking people standing around being intensely creative.

The rhythm shifted and a boy stepped forward: such a boy! He was tall and muscular and lean, and moved like a stalking lion. Unlike the others, he didn't twitch his hands, but raised and lowered them slowly, as if he was stroking someone, or sharpening his claws. And his voice! He didn't seem to have a speaking voice, only a series of purrs, growls, and cries. He could improvise and perform with every part of his body, simultaneously. He switched seamlessly back and forth from English to Spanish, rhyming in both together, and I was so dazzled by this feat, and by his heavy-lidded eyes and perfect mouth, that I could barely pay attention to the sense of what he was saying: something brilliant, angry, and funny about wage slavery.

The little performance ended abruptly, and the group passed out flyers for an open mic night off-campus. I was scared to leave campus my first week, and couldn't get anyone to go with me, but I went anyway for a glimpse of him. From that moment until the beginning of my junior year, my head was full of Tez Varela. For two years I went to every open mic, reading, and poetry slam I could find. And when I got involved with Asian

American student organizing and saw that he performed at protests, too, it was like a sign from god that activism was the right path for me.

The crush I had was so all-encompassing, it could almost have been called love, if I had ever gotten to know him—or even, you know, *talked* to him. But I didn't. Not once in two years. It was partly because he had such a devastatingly beautiful girlfriend. But it was also, to be honest, because my eyes burned when he performed. I'd thought, for a hot minute, that meant that he was a shapeshifter. I could tell when someone was being deceptive—lying, or hiding their true shape—because my eyes flared when I saw them. It took me a minute to notice that all the other slam poets—and musicians, and actors, and writers, and dancers, etc.—that I saw performing also made my eyes burn. All artists, it turned out, are being deceptive when they produce or perform arts. They're creating worlds that don't exist and convincing you that they do exist. It's a kind of magic.

I followed him for a few weeks, thinking he was just like me, and then, when the true realization hit, I was so devastated—and embarrassed—that I couldn't bring myself to approach him. And so it stayed.

He was two years ahead of me, so he had graduated by the time I came back for my junior year. After he disappeared from my life I had a couple of starter boyfriends, and eventually, I stopped thinking about him. But it was like he'd been hovering back there, just out of sight. The Platonic ideal of a man, once again made flesh.

After half an hour in Ayo's office he came back out, Ayo following him. She gestured to me.

"Maya MacQueen, this is Tez Varela," she said.

"We've met," I said. My eyes flared again, and he saw it.

"Hi ... Maya?" he said, looking a little discomforted.

43

"Maya," Ayo barreled on, "Tez needs some help and I think you can provide it."

Tez looked even more uncomfortable. "I'd really rather *you*—"

"Maya has my complete confidence," Ayo said. "And you already know, Tez, that this isn't really a human issue. I try to keep the balance between us, but there's only so much I can do." And she walked away, abruptly, as if to underline this. Yeah, whatever. Ayo thought she was god, so this was a piece of nonsense. Wait— did that mean … ?

Tez looked doubtfully at me. I had to take the bull by the horns.

"How can I help you?" I asked, chin up, radiating confidence.

"You'll have to discuss it outside of work," Ayo called across the room. "This'll be an extra gig. Usual rate."

"Why don't we meet tonight?" I said to Tez, completely forgetting the million other things I needed to do tonight. "Where do you live?"

"In the City," he said reluctantly.

"Me too. Whereabouts?"

"Mission."

"Perfect. Let's get a drink at Zeitgeist tonight at 9:30. That work for you?"

"Uh … sure." He still looked doubtful. My monkey brain knew how to handle that.

I became him, just long enough to say, in that delicious voice, "Good. See you then." Then I turned back into myself.

He jumped back a foot, like a cat hearing a gunshot. His sleepy eyes were completely round.

I left him standing with his mouth open, and went to bus the tables, pretending to ignore him. But all I could think about was: 1) the fact that he was standing behind me, in my cafe, and 2) he'd made my eyes flare, even when he wasn't performing. Ayo's informative little speech clinched it: he *wasn't* human.

CHAPTER FOUR

AFTER MY SHIFT ended at six, I headed to Ogawa/Oscar Grant Plaza—where the Occupy encampment was—for the magazine meeting.

Inscrutable (tagline: *Asian by Occident*)—now a national glossy magazine of Asian American news and culture—had started as a project of the Berkeley Asian American Students Association where my best friend Baby Aquino and I had met. But we'd made something to be proud of with it, and, after graduation, we'd decided to take it with us out into the real world. We'd been making slow—but steady—progress ever since.

The magazine staff usually met at Kearny Street Workshop's gallery, but I'd changed our meeting location that night to a Vietnamese restaurant on Ogawa/Grant Plaza. There's always a sort of membrane in the middle of the bay between the city and Oakland that San Franciscans are very reluctant to breach. None of the staff had been to Occupy yet, but knowing my folks, once I'd gotten them down here to the encampment, they'd find it much easier to make their way back.

An empty chair at the head of the long table—cobbled together from a number of smaller tables—wore Editor-in-Chief Baby's perennial cute red hoodie, waiting for her to get back from another of her endless phone calls. Mari Hashimoto, the Publisher, in her usual self-deprecating way, sat next to her, her baby blue sweater hiding some wicked tattoos. Mari, Baby, and I were the only three founders/college friends left at the mag.

Our CFO Salli Wu, a bunch of tech people, various editors and designers, and "business" folks (all entry-level marketing people professionally, and all world-class partiers) faced off down the length of the table. Salli, a recent recruit, was a coup: a freelance accountant a touch older than the rest of us, and more professional. She was also my Chinatown contact: she consulted with the Hung For Tong's legitimate businesses on financial and accounting stuff.

Today Salli, per usual, was looking like the Halloween "sexy costume" version of a corporate warrior in her red-slash lipstick, slightly too tight pencil-skirt (revealing a rare Asian bootyliciousness,) and spike heels. She unbuttoned her suit jacket and put it on the back of her chair without getting up, accidentally (or maybe not) loosening the button holding her silk blouse closed over her breasts. I caught a glimpse of a lacy black bra before I averted my eyes. Anyway. That was Salli.

And grouped around the other end of the table sat Romeo, Han, and Todd, our arts editors. They were always together, and they were also a band. But unlike most other guy-friend-group bands, they were *good*: individually they were great, but together, they were *magic*, one of those rare instances where the group transformation created something that was genuinely greater than the sum of its parts. They made my eyes flare, *hard*, even when they weren't playing. I called them "Cerberus" behind their backs.

I stopped inside the restaurant entrance to survey the scene, figure out where to sit, and feel a flush of pride and camaraderie: this was my tribe. As a group, they were one of the faces that the spirit of the Bay Area turned toward me, and I loved them fiercely.

Baby sat down, the waitress left with our orders, and Mari spoke the ritual: "Shall we begin?"

We sped through financial and fundraising reports—which I mostly ignored—and chả giò, barely slowed down for marketing and subscriptions and bánh xèo, before we finally turned to the main course—and editorial. I underlined the importance of the magazine supporting Occupy and got everyone on board with a public statement. Then we got down to the nitty-gritty.

"Why do we suck so much at coming up with features?" Baby asked, after a fruitless half hour. "Holy-moly, do we have holes! We need one feature for fifteen, and a feature and two featurettes for sixteen."

For some reason, I was looking over at Cerberus as she said this, and at the same moment, Todd lifted his head and looked directly at me for a moment before looking down again. My eyes flashed, and it seemed … it seemed that it had to do with him only, and not with all three. WTH?

"Actually, there's something I've been wanting to do for a while," I said, as if in a dream. I had no idea what I was about to say, but then blurted out: "Shapeshifters."

Whatever instinct I was going on seemed to be correct. Todd's head came up again and he looked at me piercingly.

"What about 'em?" Todd asked, a little too forcefully.

It was the first time I'd ever seen him being forceful. First time I'd ever seen him being individual.

"Well," I said, thinking furiously, "you know we've been talking about wanting to do stuff on identity that isn't Ethnic Studies 101? I know we don't focus on Asian cultures at all, but I think it would be fascinating to look at how Asian cultures view losing your identity to western cultures. In anime and manga, I mean. Through physical transformations. Shapechangers, cyborgs, that kind of thing. Why are these hybrids so popular both in Asia and the West?"

Baby started looking interested. "Huh, a creature-feature. I like that. Would you want to write it or edit it?"

"Edit," I said, "I don't really know much about anime. I was thinking maybe Todd could pick it up. Todd?"

He narrowed his eyes. "Well, I'll talk to you about it, offline. But I'm not sure I'm really clear on what you're looking for."

"Great! We'll schedule after the meeting." And I closed my laptop with a thump before I could "instinct" myself into any more trouble. "And don't forget, the general assembly is happening *right now* just outside, so jump in if you feel up to it."

We spent the requisite quarter hour splitting the check (we were journalism Asians, not math Asians,) and I had to hold myself back from eating more than three of the orange slices the Chinese-Vietnamese restaurant owners gave us gratis. Then I ran to grab Salli as she was walking out the door.

She checked her teeth for lipstick, then gave me her thousand-watt, politician's smile (I'd said the moment I met her that she would be a City Supervisor one day) and we headed out together: she was still inches shorter than I, even slinking around on those heels.

"Hey, Salli. You were at KSW last night, right?" I asked.

"Yeah, of course! It was the *APAture* comedy night," she said. "Prime networking. Where were *you*?" She smiled to take the sting off.

"Here, remember?" I pointed the crown of my head at the encampment. "Hey, listen, you remember Wayland?" Salli had been the staffer I'd met Wayland with.

"Wayland Soh? Yeah, he was there last night, as promised. And guess what? He agreed to sponsor *APAture* next year! Score one for synergy!" She paused for my congratulations. I felt a little sick. *APAture* was KSW's annual emerging Asian American artists festival, and the event where I interned a few years ago. It's the place that really made me feel like I'd found my community, but the org had been having serious money problems, and getting a business sponsorship was really important to keeping it afloat.

"Why?" Salli asked, concerned at my silence.

"Oh. Uh, my boss is connected to his family. He, uh, he died last night, and the circumstances were a little suspicious."

"Oh my god! Oh shit!" she cried, in rapid succession. I think the "Oh my god" was for Wayland, and the "Oh shit" was for the sponsorship.

"Do you happen to know if he left KSW after the event?" I asked.

"What do you mean 'if'? ... I assume he went home or something ..."

"Um ..." Wow, this was awkward. "Actually, his body was found just outside."

"Oh my *god*! What happened?"

"So you didn't see him leave? Or see him with anyone?"

"No! No ... I mean I was the last to leave 'cause I was locking up, and I saw him outside talking on his phone.

We waved goodbye but I was carpooling with someone else and Wayland had his own car. Did he … was he … Should I be talking to the police about this?"

"Oh, no. No, the police think it's a heart attack. It's his family that is suspicious."

"So … is there a reason to think it was … foul play?"

"Oh no, no, not at all. … Did you know him well?"

"No, hardly at all. I networked him same as you at that thing last week. I mean, I'd seen him before, but I'm not sure we'd ever been actually introduced. Knew him by reputation."

"And what was his reputation? Did he have any enemies?"

Salli looked worried again. "Um, he was well respected. I never heard anything bad of him. I wouldn't know about enemies; his family should know that better than me. What's this really about, Maya?"

"It's probably nothing. I just said I'd ask and now I have. I think they were just shocked that he'd have a heart attack on the street with no one around to help him."

"Oh, that poor guy. I wish … I wish I could've known …"

"Yeah, it's so sad … Hey, Salli?"

"Hm?"

"You have some connections with the Hung For Tong, right?" I knew she did. She'd hooked us up with a source for an Asian gang story we'd done two issues ago. It was how we recruited her.

The sweet, volunteer accountant Salli vanished and was replaced by the warier, clear-eyed femme fatale who'd survived Chinatown's housing projects. I'd only seen this Salli once before.

"Why you ask, Maya?" Jeez, even her Chinatown accent was peeking out.

"Was Wayland involved with the Tong?"

"Oh, they think it's gang-related?"

"No, just asking."

"No, he wasn't … not really. I mean, he had to make nice, and they probably smoothed the way for some of his deals … for a consideration, you know." She rubbed her thumb against her first two fingers. "That's probably why I'd seen him around. I heard that he headed up some sort of secret benevolent society that might've done business with them. But I wouldn't know the details of stuff like that."

Most of that was true, but my eyes flashed deceit at her last sentence. WTF? How would Salli know the details of the Tong's bribery and smuggling deals? I knew exactly what that "secret benevolent society" was, though—the werecats' association—and was shockingly discomfited at the thought that Salli might, too.

"Do you know who Dalisay is?"

She frowned. "Why does that name sound familiar?"

"She's a middle aged Filipina, lives in Daly City. She has some business dealings with Bountiful."

"Oh, her. Yeah, I think I've met her once or twice. Screechy voice?" She really *had* met her. This gave me pause.

"Were you involved in any of her business?" I asked. I couldn't believe that Salli—

"Oh, no," she said, smiling ruefully. "That's a different vertical." My eyes flared at that. Wow, catching Salli in a lie. And a lie like that! What was she doing? Cooking the books for Bountiful? Helping them launder the Tong's money? And did she know what Dalisay was? OMG, did Salli *know*?

"Well, Ayo's a friend of her family's, too, and she's been missing for two, no, three days now. The last place they can trace her to is Bountiful's offices on Saturday night. You wouldn't happen to know anything about that, would you?"

"Oh no, that's terrible! No, I don't know anything about it. Haven't heard anything, either." She sounded very definite, but my eyes flashed.

"Hm," I said slowly, and then, very fast: "So they kidnapped her?"

Salli didn't flinch. "Wow, no! I have no idea! I'd have heard if they'd done something dramatic like that. But they're not in the kidnapping business, take it from me." That was the truth.

"So they don't have her."

"No, Maya," she said gently, "I don't think they do."

This was a blatant lie. Wow. And she was a good liar, too. I'd never have known if I didn't have magical means. So WTF? They have her but they didn't kidnap her? And how deep in this *was* Salli?

"And what about Bu Bu?"

"What about him?"

Not just shock, this time, but dread settled into my stomach. Salli knew Bu Bu. She must *know* ...

Hardly daring to breathe, I asked, "Do you know what Bu Bu is?"

Salli rolled her eyes, which I'd never seen her do before. "Yes, Maya, I've seen an enforcer before. I know what one is. No, I don't get involved in that side of the business. Not my swim lane." All of that was true. Her eyes took on a delighted gleam. "I'll tell you what, though. The rumor is that guy used to fight in the MMA." No hint of deceit. So she *didn't* know. My relief was like the opposite of a boner.

"Do you know *where* Bu Bu is?"

She frowned. "Mai, I'm not sure about these questions.

What do you want with Bu Bu? How do you even *know* him? I mean ... I know you used to ..." She trailed off.

My alarm bells were screeching. "You know I used to *what*?"

"I've heard rumors that you have—*had* connections to the Celestials at some point. I didn't know if they were true ..."

This was the first I'd heard of such rumors and I was shocked. Maybe I shouldn't've been. My brain was working frantically.

"Salli, you can't believe everything you hear."

"Well, to be honest, I didn't. But this conversation is making me rethink." That was definitely the clear-eyed, housing projects Salli speaking. Yeah, you and me both, beyotch. Time to get this convo back on track.

"Well, you know Ayo imports some stuff in the gray area?" I'd hinted as much before. This wasn't news. She nodded. "Well, Bu Bu has a connection that she needs, but he disappeared. I just wanted to see if you knew where he was."

"As it happens," she said, "I *was* at the Bountiful office today and I heard ... some people complaining that he's been out of pocket since last night. He can't have gotten far, though. I don't think he's here legally. And he owes some people some money."

That was the truth.

And suddenly, I was overwhelmed by how badly I'd been misjudging Salli this whole time. I needed to withdraw, and reset. I mumbled a quick thanks and left her with a group of *Inscrutable*rs lurking at the edges of the Occupy encampment's general assembly meeting.

The fall air cleared my head, and by the time I was on a cloud flying over the bay, I'd calmed down. No, Salli being deeper into Tong biz than I'd thought was a *good* thing (for everyone except Salli herself, maybe.) She'd been a lot more helpful than I'd expected. And she'd confirmed that there was a clear connection between Bu Bu and Wayland: the Tong. Plus, she'd connected the Tong pretty solidly to Wayland's werecat benevolent society. I made a mental note to get the werecats' number from Ayo the next day. Maybe I'd get lucky and they'd even know where Bu Bu was.

I didn't know what any of this could have to do with Dalisay, but the coincidence was starting to chafe.

CHAPTER FIVE

WEDNESDAY, OCTOBER 12, 2011
ZEITGEIST BAR, SAN FRANCISCO

RATHER THAN BE exhausted after yesterday's protest and assembly, a late-night recon/asskicking, a full day's work, a tense meeting, and an intense and discomfiting revelation about a friend, I was completely jazzed (I wonder why.) I breezed into Zeitgeist for my date with Him, high on righteousness and community spirit. (Yes, I know, it was a "meeting," but a girl can dream.)

Zeitgeist was a beer garden with almost no indoor seating. The evening temperature tonight was in the low sixties—practically tropical for SF—so the patio was packed. I scanned the crowd at a squint and got no flare, so I got a pitcher and some lime wedges (which I put all of into my own glass; the beer wasn't Corona and nobody besides me likes lime in their cheap beer,) and found a planter in a corner with enough room for two butts, the pitcher, and two glasses. Tez showed up a couple minutes later, his beauty a dark light in the nighttime crowd. He headed directly for me through the row of hipsters squinting around trying to find their friends by sight—definitely some kind of were, Tez.

After initially finding me in the crowd, he didn't look at me again, but rather leisurely side to side, like a predator on the prowl through the jungle. It looked reflexive, a habit, but even so, he was drawing all sorts of attention, even in the half-light—especially, though not exclusively, female attention. The females in question were drawing his attention, as well, and I finally got to see him smile. Left, right; this woman, that: what could only be called a cheese-eating grin was being passed out like Halloween candy, and a splay of swooning women were left in his wake.

Monkey was displeased at the performance. I wasn't happy that my first personal experience of his smile was how it was applied to other women. He was here to meet *me*.

I surreptitiously pulled out a hair and flung it at him. It spread and settled gently over his front teeth, creating the illusion of a gap: a *huge* gap where his two front teeth, and one of his canines, were missing. The missing canine was a particularly nice touch: predators would rather lose a tail than a canine. The next woman he smiled at—a particularly pretty one—recoiled and looked hurriedly away. One by one, the women in his path followed suit.

He was frowning in bewilderment by the time he reached me.

"I hope you like PBR," I said, "'cause it's a week to payday."

He sat down carefully and filled a pint glass, while I recalled the hair I'd plastered over his teeth. He barely noticed, swiping absently at his mouth with the back of his hand. He drank the beer off in one go, while I checked out his look. He was wearing the hell out of a fitted, dark grey t-shirt with a screen print of several lines in red on it.

"It's the routes of the Silk Road," he said, slitting his eyes at me.

Silk Road? Oh god. *Please* tell me this guy isn't a rice king!

"Let's get the pleasantries over with," I said. "What are you?"

He sighed reluctantly. "I'm a nagual. Do you know what that is?" He pronounced it "nah-whall." It sounded Spanish.

I grinned. "No, but I'll betcha a thousand dollars Ayo does."

He smiled a little. "Yeah, it's true. She seems to know more about it than I do. That kind of shocked me today." He shifted his torso. "The anthropologists will tell you that we're basically sorcerers or medicine men in the tradition of the Aztecs ... but really, it's a kind of magical propensity that gets passed down in bloodlines; like musicality, or u-shaped tongues. We have magic and can shapeshift, and we end up being village medicine men, you know? Really, I don't know much."

I perked up. "Weren't you raised by your parents?"

"Well, yeah, but my Dad died when I was ten and he hadn't really started teaching me stuff yet." I perked back down. Not like me, then. "My mom wasn't one, so she didn't know that much. We keep it pretty close." He looked down. "They came up from Mexico before I was born, so I didn't have a whole extended family to teach me and anyway, our family on my Dad's side was dwindling. I think I have a half-uncle or something, but no one knows where he is, and my grandparents are dead."

He hesitated, like he could expand. But then he let out a breath and leaned back against a bush.

"So … now that we have that out of the way—" I said.

"Hold up. Your turn. What are you?"

"Can't you tell?" I said snidely. He sniffed me. Yep, this is my life: hot dudes sniffing me.

"I have no idea what you are. You don't even smell like anything definite. You smell like … I don't know."

I sighed. Here we go. "Truth is, I don't know either."

"Wow. … Don't your parents—"

"Foster kid."

"But someone must have—"

"Dropped anonymously at a fire station at 2 months old."

He paused. "Really?"

"It sounds super melodrama, but it actually happens more than you'd think."

"So you're mixed blood?" He meant mixed supernat and human.

"Probably not."

He paused again and parsed this. "So … are you, like … super-badass?" Now he was looking coy. Or … something.

"Pretty badass, yeah, if that kind of thing scares you." My chin was up.

He smiled that pretty, pretty smile and—I realized suddenly—for the first time at me. My pores burned.

"*Cool*," he said. "So … what do you turn into?"

"You first."

He smiled wider. Oohh, he was pretty. "A jaguar."

He yawned and shifted his torso again, showing me that catlike grace I'd always noticed and never fully identified. "Now you."

"Well, I can turn into pretty much anything." Yeah, I'm an idiot, I wanted to impress him.

"Really?"

"But my default is monkey."

"A monkey?" He chuckled. "Monkeys are delicious!"

"Uh … you've … eaten a monkey?"

He chuckled. "Only a small one. What kind are you?" he asked.

"Oh, my default is just a standard rhesus macaque. Probably the most common monkey in Asia."

In the brief silence—and the intense gaze from him—that ensued, I realized that I wasn't sure if his interest was personal or epicurean. "… A pretty *large and aggressive* monkey, actually. But enough about me. Let's talk about what brings you here tonight."

"Oh … right." He leaned back again, his doors closing. His body language was amazingly expressive. I guessed I knew why now. "Well, um, it's my sister. I need you to get her for me."

"Okay …?"

"Um, she's the youngest, eighteen now, legally an adult, although her inner child is more outer, so I can't sic the cops on her. And she said she was moving out and I wouldn't see her again, so she's not even really missing. But she's just doing it to piss me off."

"Back up. Start at the beginning. If she's acting out to piss you off, does that mean you're the boss of her?"

"Well, apparently not anymore, but yeah. I said my Dad was killed when I was ten?"

Whoa. "Was killed" is different from "died." I nodded, and filed that away for later questioning.

"Well, Chucha was one. Then my mom died right after I graduated from Cal—she hung on two months just to get to see me walk in commencement. We had to set up a live feed so she could watch from her bed." He thought for a moment, his face blank. "Chucha was twelve. She took it the hardest."

"You have other siblings?"

"Yeah, there are four of us. I'm the oldest, then Manny, he's twenty-two now, then Pronk, ze's twenty, and Chucha." I noted the pronouns, and started to feel the sharp poke of envy in my heart. I'd always wanted siblings, and Tez had one of each kind.

"You were their guardian?"

He dropped his chin to his chest. "Yeah, well, I shared custody with Tio Carlos—my mom's younger brother who lives in Salinas. But he's got three stalks of his own and couldn't even afford the gas money to come up and see us every week. They'd take them once a month for a weekend so I could get a break, but you know...."

So many things were coming clear now. Suddenly responsible for three teenaged siblings at the age of twenty-one—no wonder he dropped out of the slam scene. He had to get a job. Maybe I shouldn't envy him, but I still did.

"So, is she staying with Manny or ... Pronk?"

"Naw, we all still live together. We got rent control. Manny just transferred to State, and Pronk is starting community college in the spring, so we have to keep expenses low." His voice was dripping with parental pride. This guy had more moods than the ocean.

"So I'm guessing that Chucha's the family black sheep?"

He flinched. "It's not like that. They all acted out and screwed up their high school transcripts. And Manny and Pronk both kicked and screamed about how college is bullshit and then got real quiet when they had to work a shit job for a couple of years. We got our Padrinos— kind of—family friends—old friends of my parents— who live and work in the neighborhood—who kept an eye on them after school so they didn't get into too much trouble. And I got them into after-school programs and stuff. But I think we just didn't worry enough about Chucha, 'cause she's the baby." He chewed his lip and rubbed his belly absently.

I stuck the shiv in quick. "And they're all naguals too."

He nodded, still absently, then realized what he'd done. He narrowed his eyes at me. "Don't tell nobody," he said, his voice full of a menace I'd never heard from him before. I shivered. Definitely more moods than the ocean.

"Do they turn into cats too?"

"Manny's a donkey and Pronk's a deer. So with Manny, you just gotta make sure he gets stubborn about the right thing, and then you can't stop him. And with Pronk, you gotta hook zem with zeir curiosity, while not scaring zem away. So once you get them both on the right path, it's all cookies and beer."

"A donkey and a deer?"

"Well … it depends on what day you're born. Not my fault." He grinned briefly to himself at this and I suspected it was something he said a lot around the house.

"And Chucha?"

"Dog," he said, heavy with meaning. I looked askance; I didn't know dogs; they didn't like me. "Well, some dogs, they're dominant, and, although they're very loyal, they think their humans belong to them and not the other way around. And they do what they want, they sit on the couch, and they steal the meat, and they poop where they want—"

"Got it. Doesn't take to authority. And you two get along like cats and dogs."

"Yeah, that's the other problem," he said quietly.

"So she left home at eighteen after you had a blowout.

Am I warm?"

"Smokin'. ... Thing is, she got all messed up without *anybody* knowing. Even the other kids didn't know, they just knew she was skipping school sometimes. It just kills me, you know? She's the brightest bulb on our string. She coulda gotten into any ivy league; she was in the GATE program until Mom died. And the pep squad. I guess I didn't realize how hard she took it."

I was getting whiplash from the whipping between proud, coy, predatory, and guilty. Boy, this dude had a lot of emotions to deal with. And looked great doing it. I stayed shut and let him get on with it. A little more guilt, an arrest, a high school expulsion, a GED, and some slacking later:

"... so I told her she had to get a job and she said she already had."

"Did she tell you what it was?"

"She's running with the San Antonios. You know, over in East Oakland. Fruitvale. That's when we had the fight. Literally—physically. ... Actually she set me back a bit."

For a moment I just looked at him uncomprehendingly, until understanding bit my brain, hard. The San Antonios were the biggest gang in Oakland, a branch of the Bones that spread from Central America, through Mexico, all the way up to the Canadian border. They were, among other things, street soldiers for the Serpiente Cartel. I'd encountered a few of the Chicago Bones crews in my misspent teenage years. That was why Ayo had pushed Tez at me. This was doubly bad news: that I'd have to connect with a Bones crew, and that Tez would, eventually, discover why Ayo thought I was the perfect person to extract his baby sister from such sinister hands.

The pause had gone on too long. "So she can take you?" I asked with a false sneer.

He looked scornful. "Did you miss the 'manipulative' part? Of course not, but she can fight me until I have to give in or really hurt her, and she doesn't hesitate. I do."

"So she can take you."

He thought for a moment. "Yeah, I guess you're right. She can." He looked up expectantly and said, as if giving me all the information I needed: "She's holing up at their HQ."

"Okay, why don't you just go get her?"

"Uh, I don't run with 23rd St. but ... there's a territory thing. Some of my friends are 23rd St. and I'm from this hood and ... well, for some kids—not me, but some—they kinda replace the traditional village structure to a certain extent, you know? ... And, well, each village would have a medicine man or priest or something, right? I mean, I'm not trained, and this isn't the village and I've been very clear about not being 23rd St.'s bitch and they know they can't make me. I mean, you know we're stronger and faster ... maybe you don't know—"

"All shapeshifters are," I said, in Ayo-mode. "The power has to go somewhere when we're not shifting. Go on."

"Okay. Well, you know, if someone from the block gets hurt or something, maybe there's something I can do about it. Somebody has some bad luck, maybe I know a trick or two. That kind of thing. You know."

From working for Ayo for five years, I did know. "And maybe they get you some woo-woo supplies, too?" I suggested slyly.

He looked disturbed. "I'm not a stereotype." Whoops, no, make that "offended."

"Come *on*, Tez. We're *all* connected to organized crime in some way. That's the breaks when you're underground. You mean to tell me they never do *you* favors?"

He sealed his lips demonstratively. Okay. I see you, tho'. I waited for a bit but he was being stubborn now. Time to shift gears.

"So does everyone in your neighborhood know about you? No secrets?"

"Nah, I didn't mean to give you that idea. It's not open. You know, some people are ... superstitious, and some people genuinely aren't. And the people who aren't simply don't believe in it and that's that. And the people who are superstitious are ... weird. Once they know what I do, they treat me like the whole thing is real and they believe it. But if somebody asked them, in all seriousness, if they believed in monsters and were-animals and the like, they'd snort and—completely sincerely, feel me?— tell that person to grow up. Only the old people—and only some of them—are up in themselves enough to just be real about it."

I shook my head. "And the gangs?"

"Those dudes are like anyone else. Well, maybe a little more vulnerable to magical thinking. They have a tendency to come from broken or divided homes, so they might have less ... stuff from their families. And if their shot-callers believe, then everybody else acts like they believe, but it's kind of a toss-up."

This was similar to what I'd experienced with Asian gangs, so I nodded. "Do all the gangs have a nagual?"

"Not even close. But they all want a supernat, if they can get one. Most of the shot-callers have seen enough to know that it's real. That's why Chucha is such a coup for the San Antonios. She can fix boo-boos and bad luck just as well as I can and she's badasser than any of them." That was a new mood: defiantly proud guilt.

"Well, if she's just doing what you're doing ..."

"That's the problem: she's not. I'm available to anyone

in the neighborhood—anyone who comes to me, really. And I have a legit job on the peninsula with medical and dental. I'm not exclusive to 23rd St., and I won't cover for them or help them with anything illegal. And I don't hurt anyone unless they come after me or mine first. Chucha, on the other hand, … she's *joined* them. She's living with them and they're paying her and she's gonna break kneecaps and guard drug shipments or whatever the fuck those dudes are doing."

"Is she really okay with all that?"

"She's really smart, but also really naive and romantic, and sometimes incredibly childish, and Juice, the shot-caller, has romanced her. I think she honestly thinks she can write her own ticket; can be a badass and not lose her soul. And I think she's setting herself up for a long, hard fall. But she's doing it partly to prove to me that she's not like me, so she wouldn't listen to me even if I could get close to her, which I can't as long as she's in Fruitvale."

"Which is where Ayo was supposed to come in."

"Yeah, but she seemed to think Chucha wouldn't listen to her."

"She's right. She's too authoritative, and knows it. And too much of a straight-arrow professor type. She'd have Chucha's back up in five seconds flat."

"And you won't, you fancy, model minority, Berkeley grad?" That was the most complicated one yet: scorn, challenge, coyness, humor, wryness, and … a bit of flirtation?

"Don't forget summa cum laude, dude." His eyebrows went up. "Let's just say … I know more about what it's like to be Chucha than you can possibly imagine." He still looked skeptical. A part of me didn't want him to know about my rough side. Let's be honest: it was the part of me that knew that boys didn't like girls who are more badass than they are. But my monkey brain didn't like being thought of as a fancy model minority type. In a fit of monkey pique, I said, "But if you don't trust me, we can just forget about it."

And then, all of a sudden, he slumped, defeated. I don't know if he just, in that moment, decided to show me, or if he couldn't hide it any longer, but right then I realized that this was a last ditch effort for him, a Hail Mary pass. He really didn't know what else to do.

"Tez," I said, trying for gentle, "I *do* know what to say to her. Or rather, I know how to say it so she'll hear me. So … what is it you want me to tell her?"

He heard me, but he didn't move. He just sat there, slumped over, staring at his hands. I wasn't sure if he was reluctant to speak, or if he didn't know what to say. This was important, so I let the silence sit.

At length, he turned to me and gave me a look that was purely pleading—the kind of look you never see on a guy like him: so confident, so practiced, so full of game.

"Tell her to come home. She can have anything she wants. I won't stand in her way. Tell her—" he broke off and slumped over even more. "Tell her she wins. Just come home."

CHAPTER SIX

THURSDAY, OCTOBER 13, 2011
SANC-AHH, OAKLAND; CHINATOWN, SAN FRANCISCO

MY TWO BUSY days caught up to me, so I slept in Thursday morning. That afternoon I scoped out Oakland's San Antonio district and found Chucha's gang's HQ, but absolutely no one was stirring. I remembered then that gangbangers tended to be nocturnal creatures. I'd been part of the daylight world so long I'd forgotten. I'd wait for night, then.

I went to work in the afternoon; I was closing Sanc-Ahh that night and this worked out well for me, since I wanted to move on finding Bu Bu before he left town—if he was planning on leaving. This meant tapping into my supernat contacts, and Thursday evening—the start of the weekend for the young and hip—was the best time to be at Sanc-Ahh.

Urban supernats broke into two unevenly sized groups. The first, and by far the larger, group, was comprised of those who acted as human as possible, both at home and abroad, and treated their supernature somewhat as an ethnicity. They took care of what they needed to take care of to satisfy their inner monsters, be it howl at the full moon, buy black market blood plasma, or take out a cow or two when the spirit so moved them. The young and hip (seeming) among us even enjoyed these things, the way your urban Chinese American hipster enjoys eating chicken feet and washing their hair before the new year. Tez and (mostly) I belonged to this group.

The second, and much smaller group, consisted of folks who chose to live as monsters. For them there was no struggle with their internal nature, no lying to their nonexistent human friends, no lying to themselves that an inner monster was just a cultural tradition. They could let it all hang out, all the time. The downside, of course, is that their life choices were extremely limited. They were watched more closely than the larger group of passers, so they could only work and spend their leisure time in supernat enclaves, sanctuaries, and the twilight world of organized crime.

I had chosen to join this group in my mid-teens, and had returned to the world of restraint, light, and opportunities a couple of years later, disgusted by many humans' tendency to wallow in the worst part of their nature, and shaken by my own willingness to enable this with violence and mayhem. Working for Ayo gave that tendency in me a safe, constructive outlet, keeping me from being a hypocrite when I returned to pass as human in the human world. This underground party was also the group Bu Bu belonged to, and the group Tez's sister Chucha had decided to join when she threw her lot in with the San Antonios. The group I was going to have to try to convince her to leave again … as soon as I found her.

And this was the group I was targeting with my

attention that evening: calling in five favors, starting to owe three more, and buying four expensive drinks. But nobody had seen Bu Bu, and those who had heard about him didn't know where he was now. The best I got was from a Churel, who had apparently outbid Bu Bu for some sort of job on the meat market the day before. She must've been really good; she looked about five years old and tapped her front-facing heels shyly as she talked to me, scrunching up the skirts of her frilly white dress in cute little hands. I suppressed an internal shudder. She wouldn't tell me what the job was or for whom, but it didn't matter, since *she* was working for them now, not Bu Bu.

She couldn't tell me where he'd gone to from there, but her answers had pacified me somewhat. At least he *was* still looking for work in the Bay Area, and not immediately looking for passage out. Maybe he was still hoping to pay off that debt. Maybe … maybe even it was *me* who had scared him off from working for the Hung For Tong. I mean, he'd apparently encountered two creatures like me on two different occasions, and somehow seen one of them accompanied by a soul-sucking shadow. Or something. Honestly, that'd be enough to dissuade just about anyone from continuing on a job. Maybe I still had time to find and pry more information from his weasely snout.

Ayo came out of her office, and I had a brief moment of warmth—as I caught a brief glimpse of the office interior and that door—before she shut the door behind her and cut off any nascent desires the sight might've aroused.

"Okay," she said, as if continuing a conversation, "they're coming in soon."

"Who?" I asked, genuinely confused.

"The werecat dudes," she said. I still felt—and evidently

looked—puzzled. "You asked me for their number last night?"

Oh, yeah, I'd texted her on my way to Zeitgeist that I wanted to call them. But one of the favors I'd gotten tonight was the address of their benevolent society office, and I'd been planning to make an uninvited visit. "Oh."

"Well, I called and they said they could come to you. I think they don't want you going to them or having their number. I have to run out now. There's a story I'm after ...." She trailed off absently as she swept up a few empties from the nearest tables.

"And?" I asked, impatiently, taking them from her to the sink.

"So I'll be out, but I'm assuming you wanted to speak to them without me, anyway."

I gave her my best inscrutable look and she rolled her eyes, then swept out the door. Yes, I did want to speak to them without her. She didn't know how to tread softly, and there was a certain freemasonry among supernats that she didn't understand how to leverage and that wouldn't apply to her anyway. She knew this, vaguely, and left me to do my thing with increasing frequency. I was ... ambivalent about that.

The rest of the evening seemed to crawl by without any sign of the werecats. I closed, and slowed my roll on the cleaning and post-close organizing, but still nothing. I damned Ayo for a close-fisted info-hoarder, and the werecats for stereotypical intramural paranoiac beast-men. I left at 2 am and flew directly over to San Francisco Chinatown.

The office of their benevolent society (an unofficial organization with no apparent name) was simply the back office of a tiny tchotchke store on Grant Ave. unfortunately located exactly opposite the much larger and more popular Peking Bazaar. Their shop didn't seem to have a name (the awning merely stated the street number) and was doing its level best to avoid attracting financial success by way of custom. The place positively screamed "front!"

My source tonight had told me Wayland actually ran the society from the comfort of his own office, but the werecat hoi polloi were to be found crammed into the seats and crevices of this shop, and at all hours. It was their, very cramped, hangout, and also where they employed new members who hadn't found their paws yet.

I arrived invisibly and set up across the street to watch. The shop was dark, closed and locked, but, unlike most of the shops on this street, had no steel security gate to pull across its vulnerable windows. Probably the locals knew better than to mess with this bunch. After watching through the windows for a few minutes with human eyes, I caught several flares, although my night vision wasn't good enough to see what deception I was tracking. I switched to cat form (housecat, mind you) and immediately clocked several shadowy human forms prowling the aisles of the shop, evidently roused by some whiff of my presence. I cursed for the thousandth time my inability to remember non-primates' sensitive noses.

Hm. How to begin? They clearly hadn't been intending to honor their promise to Ayo to come see me, which irritated me. I could wait until they settled down and then knock for admittance. But they were unlikely to open to me at this hour, especially since they refused to let me come to them and refused to come to me. No, I was going to have to get hard core on these suckers.

Monkey cheered up radically, while my rational brain urged me to reconsider. Reconsider what? Monkey wanted to know. Rational brain offered some half-baked Asian culture politeness mumbo-jumbo, but Monkey wasn't having it.

Still in Monkey-mode, still invisible, but back in human form, I unlocked their front door with a hair and watched as flares sparked all over my field of vision: one, two, three coming out from the back ... four and five coming down the aisles to the right and left ... And maybe a sixth, already waiting in the front corner. They didn't make a sound, and could see far better than I could.

Time to even the playing field.

I plucked several hairs and turned them into hot pink road flares, tossing one toward the source of each of the flashes in my eyes. I snapped my fingers, lighting them all simultaneously, and watched as six— no, seven: there had been two in the corner up front—pink-faced Asian men cried out in pain, and crouched defensively.

While they were focused on covering their eyes (one was even groaning,) I plucked another several hairs, turned them into ropes, and leapt around the store, tangling each cat in a swirl of rope—not very securely, mind you, but it would take a redneck minute for each of them to extricate themselves.

I started with the groaning guy to my left, but should've left him to last, because, by the time I got to 'em, the last two to come out of the back room had recovered and were waiting for me. And they looked like the biggest, as well. I was still invisible, but since cats rely on their noses and ears as much as their eyes, this was hardly a hindrance to them, and both of them were staring straight at me.

The last ones out of the office were likely to be the leaders, so I took a split second to consider my approach. In that second, these two—with the simple ease of people who have been fighting together for a long time—got the jump on me. With incredible speed, one seized my arm from the left, while the other swept around my right to block my exit.

I tensed, but, having located, seized, and blocked me, they stood still and made no other aggressive moves. Hmm. Monkey froze in confusion. I sensed nothing but professionalism. Interesting. Monkey wanted to fight, but now it was more out of curiosity than aggression.

Lefty, still holding my arm, demanded something in some language. It was a tonal language, that much I could tell. Something Southeast Asian, maybe?

I sighed, and became visible. I could hear Righty taking a step back in surprise, but Lefty didn't let go, only gasped a little. So they *weren't* expecting me.

"I only speak English, sorry," I said. "What did you say?"

Lefty looked over my shoulder at Righty, and they seemed to confer silently for a moment.

"You da girl from Ayo," Lefty said. It wasn't a question.

"That's right," I said, "And *you* the guy who was supposed to come talk to me tonight."

"So you break in my shop?" he asked calmly, but with a real stark undertone. What's more, he was right, damn his catty eyes.

"Were you going to let me in if I knocked?" I asked, not the only one being catty tonight.

He eye-conferred with Righty some more.

"Mr. Soh none of yoh business," he said bluntly.

Yeah, that's what I thought. Interesting that he got right to the point, though. That was definitely the cat speaking and not the Asian man. I might make more headway if I talked to the Asian. Not that I'd been raised in any Asian culture, and Spaghetti Monster knows I tended to avoid newcomers like the plague, but I'd spent enough time around Asian Americans by now to catch the drift.

I slipped out of his grasp and bobbed my head subtly.

"I don't mean to be nosy," I said, raising my pitch a register and softening my tone, "but I'm involved with Kearny Street Workshop, an organization that Mr. Soh was sponsoring. That's where he was killed, you know. He was there that night to visit the organization and confirm his sponsorship. So I feel somewhat ... responsible."

I was speaking their language on two levels: predator, and hostess. To them, KSW was my territory and Wayland was a guest who had died under my protection. I was claiming a part of the responsibility for his death.

No part of me stopped to consider why I was doing this, despite the fact that it could potentially get me in trouble—the same kind of trouble, in fact, that the Hung For Tong was facing for being the last place Dalisay was seen. Even Monkey, a firm disbeliever in responsibility, was overwhelmed with curiosity and suspense. And the rest of me ... well I couldn't quite explain my interest. Maybe "responsibility" *was* part of it. Or maybe just aggression. Maybe I *did* feel my territory had been breached.

All around us, the other five cats had extricated themselves and were rising and approaching. I was careful not to react.

The two cats exchanged a quick glance again, and Lefty seemed to give in.

"We know why he wen' dere dat night. But we still don't know who kill him, or why dey kill him."

"Did he have any enemies?"

The cat scoffed. "Of course! But dey not kill him. No opportunity." He paused. "And ..."

"And you don't think any of them know how to suck out a soul," I said bluntly.

They all seemed to flinch as one, but Lefty nodded. "Do you know what 'suck out a soul'?" he asked. "Ayo does research, so we want to know what she find out. Do you know?"

I immediately knew I didn't want to tell them that we had a lead that connected my type of creature—whatever *that* was—to a potential soul-sucker. "No, we don't know yet. But we're on it. Don't worry. If anyone can find a candidate, it'll be Ayo."

They didn't look satisfied—who would be?—but they nodded.

"She'll call you the moment she has anything. And in the meantime," I took two steps to the checkout counter and quickly wrote my cell number on a blank receipt, "call me if you find out anything else. I'm pursuing an … alternative lead, which might turn up nothing, but I'll definitely let you know if it does." As long as it doesn't implicate me, I added internally.

Lefty took the receipt and seemed to study it for a moment, then reach a decision. "Mr. Soh say somebody follow him, two night before. But he doesn't know who. He doesn't see anything, he just feels like somebody follow him so he sleep at friends' house. But next day, nothing, no following, so he go out by himself again and no more problem."

"Two nights before he died?" I asked, feeling somewhat breathless.

"Yes."

"Do you happen to know where he was when he picked up the tail?"

The cat actually pulled a top-bound notebook, like an old-fashioned reporter's notebook, out of his jacket pocket and flipped through it. "He was in Chinatown. He go to his office, den he visit Golden Gate Fortune Cookie, den he have a dinner meeting at—" here he said a word.

"Which one is that?" I interrupted.

"Great Eastern," he said. "Den he go to friends' house. But he think he is follow after he leave his office."

"So he might've picked up the tail at the fortune cookie factory?" I asked, trying to control my breathing, which was speeding up.

"Yes, he think somewhere around dere."

"Okay," I said as neutrally as possible, standing up. "Thanks. I'll definitely let you know if I find out anything."

They knew a dismissal when they heard one. They exchanged a group look again.

"You call when Ayo have information?" It sounded like a polite question, but I knew a demand when I heard one.

"You'll be the first to know," I said, and stood patiently, waiting to be let out.

Lefty frowned a bit, but I'd engaged his politeness already and he couldn't take it back. He gestured at the henchcats, who each stepped forward and handed me a rope. I pointed at the flares as well, and they went and got them for me. All the while, Righty stood behind me, blocking my way out. When I'd collected my things—ropes in one hand, a bouquet of road flares in the other—Righty led me out the door, holding the door open for me and following me out. The entire group, in fact, followed me out.

I was hoping they'd go back inside so I could take directly to the sky without being seen, but politeness cut both ways, and going invisible in front of them wasn't going to be possible at this point. Well, they'd gotten a good whiff of me by this time, and probably had a good idea of where the rope and road flares had come from. And I needed to show them some trust if they were going to trust me.

I sighed and turned the items all back into hairs and let them return to my head. One of the henchcats gasped, although Lefty and Righty didn't look surprised. I called down a cloud, and stepped onto it, and Righty said something to Lefty, who nodded. What he said sounded like "shee mm hoong" or something, but I had no idea what even language that was, much less what it meant.

I waved and took off, watching them wave below me as long as I was in sight.

The moment they were out of sight I let out all the air I'd been holding. Holy crack-monkeys!

The Golden Gate Fortune Cookie Factory was a popular tourist destination, but it wasn't Wayland's sweet tooth that had me clenching. The factory was located in Ross Alley, passing below my cloud right now, which was around the corner from the entrance to Bountiful Import/Export Co., the Hung For Tong's business headquarters. Bountiful was also the last place Dalisay had been seen.

In the crammed architecture of Chinatown, all buildings in a block essentially share a roof. Which means if you are on the roof of the Bountiful building, all you have to do is walk to the eastern side to look directly down into Ross alley, and see the entrance to Golden Gate Fortune Cookie Factory. Hovering over the Bountiful building, I was looking right at it now, an unusually clean spot— kept so for tourists—in normally grubby Chinatown alleys.

My brain started clicking overtime. Two nights before

his death was when Wayland had picked up the tail. Two nights before Wayland's death was when Dalisay disappeared. I'd met Bu Bu two nights later on the rooftop of the Tong's massage parlor several blocks southeast of the Bountiful building: far out of sight and earshot.

But placing a guard on your roof was unusual. Humans didn't typically break into buildings from the roof (which is why it was my entry of choice.) What if … what if Bu Bu had been working at the Bountiful building previously, and sighted the soul-sucking shadow creature—and its "like me" companion—*on the roof*? What if that's why they'd stationed him there on Monday?

This left a lot of questions unanswered. Such as, why, then, move Bu Bu to the massage parlor? What were the shadow and its monkey companion after? What was the link to the Hung For Tong? And what did all of this have to do with Dalisay? Did she … could she have gotten her soul sucked? But why? Who would be out to get her? Was it at the Tong's behest? Maybe even by accident? In their territory? That would certainly explain why they still had her, or her body, but hadn't kidnapped her.

But then, was the shadow/monkey after Dalisay or was she just in the wrong place at the wrong time? What would they want from her or from the Tong? And Wayland's connection with the Tong was through business, but he wasn't a close associate. So why did it go after Wayland?

I'd need to check into the connections between the Tong, Dalisay, and Wayland. And I'd have to ask Ayo if there was any way I could help expedite her research into shadow creatures. I was sure that this was no coincidence, but that was about all I was sure of.

CHAPTER SEVEN

Friday, October 14, 2011
San Antonios' HQ, Oakland

Friday I spent the morning asking around—by phone and on foot—but no one knew Bu Bu or had even heard of a bajang wandering around.

I also couldn't pick up any other leads on Dalisay, although I did fly out to Daly City late Friday morning to check out her apartment and the sweatshop, which were the last two places she'd definitely been before she met with representatives of the Tong, just in case there were any clues others had missed. There weren't, that I could see.

The aswangs who met me out there told me that as far as they knew, blood plasma was Dalisay's only connection to the Tong—well, that and the Tong had originally connected her to the fence she used to sell valuables taken during their grave-robbing. They'd never heard of Wayland, would *not* let me look at her books and papers, assured me that they had done so themselves and there were no mentions of Wayland or the Tong, and then had the audacity to look disappointed that I had nothing new. There was, however, an ominous glint in some of their eyes, that told me that situation needed a resolution soon.

I took advantage of the Occupy march on the police headquarters that afternoon to canvass a couple of activists I knew who worked at community development corporations in San Francisco. These CDCs tended to focus on elder and newcomer housing, and a lot of aswangs and other nasties ended up housed in their SROs (single-room occupancy residences.) These advocates, of course, had no idea that some of their cute, wrinkled old clients were legendary monsters, but they were deeply tied into on-site gossip, and would have heard about it if there were some interesting word on Dalisay, who organized her younger aswang cohort to volunteer at the elder community centers monthly. But there was—as I'd expected—no word. And, amidst thunderous frowning and one accusation of stereotyping (if they only knew!) no one had heard anything about Dalisay being involved with Chinatown mafia.

As for Chucha, the werecats had made me go so late I decided not to try to find her last night, but instead to get some sleep, and wait for late Friday night when, my sources told me, everyone would come back after hours to smoke up or whatever, but more importantly to report on the week's activities and prepare for the weekend. So, by the time I took my leave of the Occupy encampment that evening after the general meeting, I was full-up with frustrated mission and rarin' to go.

Oakland's San Antonio district was at once the most diverse neighborhood in the Bay Area (albeit divided up into distinct enclaves) and one of the Bay Area's classic food deserts (albeit bordered by a corridor full of restaurants from a dozen different cultures.) The San Antonio's HQ was a small three-story apartment building with six units, two on each floor—situated in the middle of a block of mostly single-family and duplex houses, in the middle of a neighborhood full of more of the same. It sat next door to an empty lot overrun with straggly grass (and one tree in the back) and right now, at around midnight, it was all lighted up inside. I changed to monkey and came in off the roof of the building to its left. The HQ roof was accessible by a wooden staircase that would let me into backroom windows. Easy.

But before I could even take stock and make an entry plan, I heard the distinct thud and crash of a fight in the yard below. Fun! my monkey brain thought, and I hunkered down for a bit of spectatorship. Squinting down past the staircase, I saw a body smack against one of the dirty garbage bins lined up along the backside of the fence. It settled into a lax sitting position on the concrete. I squinted at the fighter. He looked like he had clawed hands and feet, and a familiar, wrinkled face that might be handsome on a human. Wait, that looked like Bu Bu! Was that Bu Bu?

I waited for him to get up and get at his opponent— I'd be able to identify him from his fighting style— but he didn't move; he'd been, apparently, knocked unconscious. Bummer! I missed most of it! Where was his opponent? I looked around the yard, but didn't see any other figures.

If that was Bu Bu, what was he doing here? Had he not gone back to the Hung For Tong? Had someone else caught him, or had he sold himself to someone else on the meat market?

Looking closer, I thought for a moment that something was on fire, since I was looking at the downed fighter through a cloud of smoke. I squinted a little more, then swore and changed into a cat for the night vision. The dark scene below snapped into monochromatic high contrast, and I realized that what I thought was smoke was actually … a human-like figure, but a figure that wasn't entirely solid. I reared back for a moment, there was something so uncanny about it.

But my curiosity reasserted itself and I squinted at it again. The smoke-figure reflected no light at all, but rather created a darkness, like a shadow with no solid object to cast it. The figure was roughly human-shaped— no, maybe it was shaped like a four-legged creature—and it bent over the body of the other fighter. The creature should have blocked most of it from my view, but I could see the body through the shadow. The downed fighter suddenly became rigid and started twitching, as if the shadow figure were doing something horrible to it.

As if waking up slowly from a nap, my rational brain stretched, yawned, and mumbled something about a soul-sucking shadow creature.

What? Monkey Brain screeched.

Soul. Sucking. Shadow. Creature.

All of me woke up at that.

I switched back to monkey and dropped three times, straight down, catching my long arms and legs on the anchoring timbers of the staircase to slow my fall. The shadow figure hadn't moved since it crouched over the body, and remained in this position as I approached cautiously, having to overcome a strange reluctance with every step. Monkey was quiet, my fighting aggression almost completely calmed.

The body continued to jerk horribly, and I could hear the sound of hoarse gasps. Although I couldn't see clearly what was being done, I carried a deep certainty that the downed fighter was losing his soul. Monkey should have been up in arms, along with my anthropomorphized moral certainty. But I couldn't dredge up any feeling except dread.

Finally, I stood directly behind the figure. Up close it was more shadow than smoke, more an absence of light than a mass of something. Come on, Maya! I thought, possible fight here! but I couldn't make myself dive in. Not knowing exactly what to do, I poked at the shadow figure with my elongated fingers. The tips sank slightly into the darkness, then encountered resistance, as if pushing against rubber, although it didn't actually feel like that.

The shadow figure—and I don't know how I knew this, because it had no face—*turned* to me somehow. It was like its attention reversed, although its body— such as it was—didn't shift. Monkey shrieked in horror and retreated to the back of my mind, yelling at me to flee. I changed back to human in some bizarre reflex. My whole body shuddered for the long moment during which it studied me.

Then, without any change, it simply … extended a portion of its … shadow smoke, and … pushed me back. I didn't expect any strike, yet found myself windmilling halfway across the yard, gasping with the impact of what felt like a car hitting me at 15 miles an hour. But worse: for a moment I felt utterly humiliated and worthless— much worse than having my ass handed to me should have felt.

The … *thing* gathered itself into an amorphous shape and … floated—there's no other word for it—through the fence and away from the house. Floated fast.

I struggled to recover, both physically and psychologically. It took me a long minute to remember that I was capable of anything. Then, urged by that same reluctant alarm, I ran back and crouched over the body of the other fighter, who was gasping for breath.

It was Bu Bu, at last. And he was dying.

The door burst open, I spun around, and four human gangbangers spilled out. They stood for a moment before the foremost noticed the crumpled fighter behind me.

"Help me!" I cried at the same time as he shouted, "He got Bu Bu!"

Another guy ran out the back door and stood, taking in the scene. His stance told me he was better trained than the others, and his disgusted frown told me he was a boss—lieutenant, probably.

"What the *fuck*?" he said expressively.

I didn't care; Bu Bu was dying. My chance was *dying*. I crouched back over Bu Bu, whose pained gasps were slowing down. But it wasn't because he was recovering his breath. I put my head against his chest and heard his heart stutter, then stop. No no no no no. I pushed my head in and listened harder, but it didn't start again. His chest looked like it was deflating. Fuck fuck, no!

"Someone tell me what the fuck is going on," the lieutenant said warningly, as I started feeling around Bu Bu's chest—for what, I didn't know.

"Do you know where a bajang's heart is?" I asked frantically. He looked at me, startled, as if he hadn't noticed that I was a stranger until then, or maybe hadn't noticed I was female. He drew a gun out of his waistband and pointed it at me.

"Who the fuck are you?"

"Dude! We *so* don't have time for all that! He's *dying*. *Help me*."

He just stared at me. I gave up and pulled Bu Bu down flat to the ground to start CPR. Let him shoot me if he wanted. I didn't have *time*.

But I couldn't find a heartbeat and, though my breaths in were inflating his lungs—or whatever bajang had in place of lungs—it was clear that I was just blowing into what amounted to inanimate matter. Bu Bu was dead.

"Fuuuuuuck!!!" I screamed. I had no other words. "Goddamn motherfucking shit!" Okay, those were other words, but they weren't particularly good ones.

The henchthugs were gathered around their lieutenant when I recovered enough to look up. Goddammit, I still had a job to do. The lieutenant was still watching me, and pointing the gun, but hadn't taken the safety off. I wasn't sure if that was incompetence or overconfidence.

"He's dead," I said, and inside me something wailed with rage and frustration, but I was calm on the outside again.

"Yeah, that's what happens when you kill somebody," one of the henchbrains said.

"I didn't kill him," I said. "That shadow-thing did."

"Who sent you?" the lieutenant demanded.

"I'm here to see Chucha."

He looked confused, then shook it away. "Give the Huexotl back. Then we can talk."

I didn't understand what he'd said for a moment and had to parse out the sentence.

"The *what* you say?" I asked. The word sounded like "way-shuttle"

"The walking stick you killed Bu Bu for. No fucking around now."

I stood up and he released the safety. Not incompetence, then. I held up my hands. "Do you see anywhere I could be hiding a stick?" I turned, slowly, all the way around. He looked even more confused. "I seriously do not know what you're talking about."

"You're lying," he said, unsure. Not incompetent, but not super bright.

"Can you describe this ... stick?" I tried to keep irony out of my voice, because he might be smart enough to pick up on it.

"Bu Bu was holding it," he said to one of the henchthugs. "Go check him." Dude obliged, to no avail. I realized that they were all focused, first on me, then on the guy who was checking Bu Bu. If this all-important stick hadn't been spirited away by the shadow, then it must be lying around here somewhere. I looked around and caught a flare from the opposite corner of the yard, a shadowed spot.

"Is that it?" I asked, pointing.

The others all turned and looked, like flock of birds switching direction. But the lieutenant wasn't a sucker. "Beto, go see," he ordered not taking his eyes off me. The henchbrain went, and after a bit of awkward feeling around in the dark, returned with the stick. It was actually a cane, or, like he'd said, a walking stick, about three and a half feet long with a knob shaped like an animal head at the top, carved entirely out of a single length of wood. Unremarkable, except for the fact that it was making my eyes flare so hard I'd soon be crying fire.

The henchbrain held it up. "Good thing we came when we did, or she mighta gotten away with it."

Oh. My. God. This dude was unbelievable. The lieutenant was experienced enough to be watching my torso for signs of an attack, so instead I turned my body to rubber, stretched my still upraised wrist across the seven or so feet separating us and switched the safety back on his gun. Then I detached it from his hand with a simple twist and drew my hand back to its original shape. While he was still scrambling about himself to grab the gun back, I popped the magazine, then the one in the chamber, and tossed the gun back to the shocked lieutenant, who fumbled, but caught it at last.

"If I'd wanted to 'get away with' anything, I would have. I'm not here to steal your little stick. I'm here to see Chucha." I thumbed the rounds out of the mag as I spoke and tossed them one by one into the corner where the stick had rolled. When the mag was empty, I tossed that as well. "Enough bullshit. Take me to your leader, or whatever. Or just take me to Chucha. I have a message for her."

CHAPTER EIGHT

FRIDAY, OCTOBER 14, 2011
SAN ANTONIOS' HQ, OAKLAND

I KNEW IT was her because … well, imagine a female version of Tez: a bit rounder about the features with eyes wider-set and a subtly smaller jaw (but still jutting and somehow, more stubborn than Tez's), a bit shorter, considerably more hourglass-shaped, but still tall, strong, full-lipped, and stunning. She didn't have his languid grace. She moved more energetically, holding herself square from her hips and shoulders, and her face wore a snarl that was no less menacing for being attractive. Plus, she was fast.

I found that last bit out the hard way.

See, when I said I knew what to say to Chucha, I really meant that I knew not to say anything to her, at least not at first. Predators respect physical power. All predators, no matter how small, have to have a physical reckoning of some kind (be it only butt-sniffing) before settling down to be social. And Chucha, with that name and that job and Tez's description, wouldn't stop at sniffing my butt.

Tez, a cat, should have known this, but he was also a poet, and college educated, and human-passing, and never truly a part of this world. My plan was to come in hot, take her down quick, then deliver my message. She'd hear me then.

That was the plan anyway.

She stood stage left of an ancient naugahyde recliner, clearly a throne, in which sat the shot-caller. The shot-caller had a generic kind of charisma, and a general sort of handsomeness that may have explained how she placed her loyalty. If you like Brazilian futbol stars (and let's be honest, who doesn't?), this dude might be a close enough approximation to get you off.

A side table to the left of his throne held a collection of empty beer cans and ... some books? I could see "Aztecs" and "Meso-America" and "shaman" in the titles. Hey, this guy was reading up on the same stuff I was! I knew I was being snobbish, but my respect for him increased 1000% once I knew he read—and once I knew he was reading up on his new girlfriend/bodyguard.

Okay, the shot caller was not a lightweight. Was Chucha?

I smiled and deliberately flared my eyes at her. She immediately went into a standing crouch, and snarled like a startled weedwhacker. I grinned as insolently as I could, pulled easily out of my escorts' hold, and, using the glass-inlaid wooden coffee table as a launch pad—with Monkey screeching my fool head off from the inside—jumped her.

Or, at least, I meant to jump her. She simply stepped aside and, while I was gaping and windmilling past her, drove a roundhouse into my kidneys. (That's punch, not kick, and I'm glad of it.) I revised my estimate (seriously, ten years of crappy fighters and suddenly I'm up against two good ones in a single week?) just in time for her to jump onto me, and it was on. I was hampered by my decision not to change shape in front of civilians (at least not in an obvious way. After that first punch, I turned into silly putty wherever I saw a fist or foot coming. I'm not a masochist. But still, human-shaped silly putty. I doubt they noticed.)

She didn't seem to be hampered by anything. I'd never encountered a fighter so purely aggressive. There was no defense in her game. She took every hit, didn't dodge a single blow, just kept coming through whatever I threw at her, trying to land her own punches. After her initial success, I didn't let her land too many, but she kept me so busy playing defense, I didn't land many myself.

The shot-caller had leapt up almost immediately and shoved the coffee table out of the way—I guess he liked it—which made a little room for us to fight in. (I noticed that no one tried to interfere; not that we gave them a chance: we were both too fast.) I took advantage to throw her down and see how she grappled. Turns out, she grappled just fine, and just as aggressively and disregarding of hurt as she boxed. When I pinned an arm, a leg, or a neck, she would squirm so violently that I was forced to either back off or break it, and then she'd turn the same move back on me, with no such compunction. I finally started understanding what Tez had told me about her fighting style. She was just too fast and too aggressive. It was true, I couldn't win this one without hurting her. And she wasn't dumb. She'd figured out already that I was trying to avoid hurting her and she was using it against me.

Time to find out if the courtesy was mutual.

I jackhammered her off me with both feet, then lay back in the submissive pose I'd seen taken by defeated werewolves, crying "Uncle! I give!" I guess she hadn't been a thug for very long because she managed to stop her dive back onto me by snapping out her arms like wings, then falling to her knees gaping at me. She had picked up that I wasn't a pushover, and she wasn't expecting me to give in. My chin was tilted away from her so she could see my throat. I whimpered a little for good measure, but she immediately looked suspicious, so I gave in and grinned again.

"What the fuck, Chucha? Who is this?" the lieutenant cried. The shot caller was projecting "confused," but was cool enough not to let it show on his face. He let the lieutenant do the talking.

"I have no fucking clue," Chucha said.

I flipped up and everyone started. Chucha jumped up almost the same moment. The lieutenant, idiot that he was, pointed his gun again, the gun that I'd unloaded for him. I grinned with what I thought might be disarmingness, although from the tense response, it probably wasn't.

"Look," I said, "I'm just here to talk to Chucha, okay?" She looked skeptical, to say the least.

"Why'd you attack me, then?" She asked, reasonably enough, damn her.

I sucked my teeth. "You were growling at me! I thought you were going to attack!"

She rolled her eyes. "Whatever." Geez, how old was she? I thought they were over the snottiness at eighteen.

"No," the lieutenant said, "Juice, she's lying. She's after the Huexotl. She killed Bu Bu."

My whole body clenched at the reminder of what I'd lost. I forced myself to relax again, and sighed theatrically. "Seriously? Guys, if I'm so badass I can kill Bu Bu so easily"—I am, but they didn't need to know that—"why wouldn't I just take your little stick and run off with it? And why would I want your stick anyway? I'm sure it's magic, but I don't know anything about it."

The shot-caller—Juice?—sat back down in his lounger. "Talk," he said to the room.

"We heard fighting and came out back and found her handling Bu Bu. He was dying."

"Yeah, and tell him where you found the stick, dumbass," I said.

The lieutenant looked confused.

"That's right, all the way across the yard from me. And you can tell him about my trying CPR on Bu Bu, too."

Juice raised his eyebrows at his lieutenant, who nodded confusedly.

"Where's Bu Bu now?" Juice asked.

"Still out back. Squirrel's guarding him."

"Bring him in here," Juice said, getting up and moving out of the room. We followed him into the dining room, with its long farm table, while the henchmen brought the body in. In the light, unmoving, Bu Bu's body looked tiny and shrunken, his clawed hands and feet curled up like a dead bird's. My heart clutched again for a moment.

"How did he die?" Juice asked.

There was a silence. None of us knew.

"Ask her, jefe," one of the henchthugs said, pointing at me.

"I have no fucking clue," I said, in Chucha's voice. She started, then snarled at me, but nobody else noticed.

Juice stepped around the table and felt the key points of Bu Bu's body: his neck, his head, his spine, his ribs. "There's no blood," he said, "and nothing feels broken." He looked at me. "So what do *you* think happened?" He was looking at me intently. Maybe not just a thug, this one. He had real pull.

"I came down from the roof and he was already fighting with that shadow thing."

"What shadow thing?"

I described it, and the fight, and the fact that it disappeared just before the henchthugs came out, which made them scoff. But Juice looked thoughtful.

"Maybe it's something about the Huexotl," he said.

"Or maybe she made it up," the lieutenant said.

"Seriously? Are we still on this? If I killed Bu Bu then how did I do it?" I waited. The henchthugs had taken my minor transformations in the dark in their stride. Was it because they couldn't really see what I was doing, or because they were, as Tez put it, superstitious? Bu Bu was lying here right in front of us in all his off-color, clawed glory. But I noticed none of the henchthugs was looking directly at him. What did these humans see when they looked at him? At Chucha?

"I don't know," the lieutenant said, finally. "Maybe he had a heart attack or something?"

"Maybe she took a shot at his throat and it choked him?" one suggested.

"Maybe she's got those kung-fu moves like in *Kill Bill*, where you hit a guy the right way and his heart explodes?" offered another.

Juice closed his eyes briefly in what was apparently a prayer for patience. Chucha just rolled hers.

"Look," I said, "I don't know who connected you with Bu Bu, but I'm the one who captured him in the first place. You know Ayo?"

Juice and Chucha exchanged a glance. "Yeah," Juice said. "You caught him?" He sounded slightly admiring.

I nodded.

"Well, we've only had him for a few days, but he was worth every dime. Next time you catch something like that, take it directly to me. I'll pay top dollar for a fighter like that. Cut out the middleman and everybody wins."

He smiled charmingly and, in that moment, I realized that I'd started to admire Juice, because my admiration just flew right out the window. I didn't yell at him about using the meat market middleman, or about supernat slavery, though; partly because Chucha didn't react to his statement (did she think his ideas about supernats didn't apply to her? How had he gotten her, anyway? Didn't she go through the meat market?) and partly because I wasn't here to give lectures on equal rights.

"Look, I really didn't kill Bu Bu. I'm just here to talk to Chucha." Juice nodded imperceptibly. He believed. And my mention of Ayo had probably decided it. Typical.

"Is this family, social, or business?" Juice asked me.

"Family," I said.

"You can use the back room," he said to her, pointing with the crown of his head. "Take care of this and get her out of here. We still got things to do tonight."

Chucha led the way, stance tight. As soon as I shut the door behind me she asked, "Is anyone hurt?"

"No, no, everyone's okay." She relaxed slightly. "Your brother wants to talk to you."

"Which one?" I had a momentary stab of envy again. Oh, to have so many brothers you didn't know which wanted to talk to you!

"Tez."

She rolled her eyes. "Whatever. How do you know Tez?"

"We went to Cal together." Well, that was technically true, anyway

"What are you, anyway? I can't really smell anything weird but … what are you?"

"I don't know. That's not the issue."

"You don't know?"

"Left on a doorstep. Fostered. Not the issue, okay?"

"No, I mean, like what do you turn into? You turn into stuff, right? I felt your skin getting all weird ..."

I sighed. I realized we would have to do me first, so I sat down on the bed. "I can turn into anything, really. Animal or object or person. But I default to monkey pretty easily."

"Monkey?"

"It's what's for dinner."

"And you can really turn into anything?"

"Pretty much. I mean, some things are harder—"

"And you really don't know what you are or where you come from?"

"Really truly."

"Wow ... like you could be a *princess* or something. Like, a really badass princess!" She hitched herself up onto the dresser, and her eyes gleamed when she said "princess" in a way that told me that a part of her was still twelve years old. I knew which part of her.

"Yeah," I said, "or I could also be the daughter of the devil or something super evil. It's less romantic than scary if you really think about it." And I'd really been trying hard not to think about it since Monday night.

She sighed, "But the possibilities are all there. And you *are* really badass. You were holding back." She said the last with a little pout, like I'd denied her a treat by not breaking her limbs.

"I don't think being a nagual is anything to sneeze at. And you're pretty badass yourself. I couldn't have taken you without really hurting you."

She snorted. "Being a nagual is all bullshit ritual and math and dealing with people's fuckups. It's all being 'responsible,' like my brother. Bo-ring. The only good parts are changing and being strong and fast."

"Don't forget the healing factor ... and the enhanced senses."

"Yeah, that too ... except when you're living with a bunch of guys."

"Tell me about it. If gangs were run by women we'd be 'just saying no' to black market perfume."

She sneered at me, little girl gone and teenage rebel back. "What do you know about *gangs*? Aren't you one of Tez's little college girlfriends?"

Well, now *that* was interesting. Was it just a figure of speech or did he have a harem? This was not unheard of among people who turned into animals. I filed the question away for later gnawing.

"Oh," I said breezily, "I used to ride with the Celestials back in the day. Before I went to college. And seriously? More than anything it was the smell that got me moving on. I lived in a women-only dorm at Cal."

The New York Celestials had been in the news recently for general ruthlessness, and I could tell from her expression she'd heard about it. I let her take that in for a second. Yes, Princess, I was in a badass gang and I left and went to college. And I can *still* set you back.

"Really?" she asked, looking at her knees as if she didn't care (but I could see her ghosty dog ears pricked towards me.) "Were you, like, somebody's girlfriend or something?"

I blew out an exaggerated scorn-breath, skipping over my on/off dalliance with the Celestials' version of Juice: "Yeah, right: *those* losers? Nah, I ran security for a while, then I got sick of it."

She was turned entirely towards me again, not hiding her interest. Dogs were so obvious. "Dude, how old were you? You can't be much older than me!"

"Actually, I'm closer to your brother's age. I'm twenty-five; I just look younger. It's the Asian thing. But I was, like, fifteen when I started with the Celestials, and sixteen when

I became head of security for the whole Chicago branch. I bailed pretty quickly after that, though."

"Why?" she asked. I had been planning to say something smartass about the smell, but she asked so simply and honestly that I couldn't help being honest back.

"I didn't like what I was turning into. I hurt some people, and I was starting to really not care. Then they wanted me to kill some people, and I was starting to not care about that, either. It was really time to get out."

Chucha blew scorn at me. "You couldn't deal. I get it."

I cocked an eyebrow. "And you can? How many people have *you* killed?"

"How many have *you*?" she countered. She wasn't taking this seriously.

Should I—?

I felt challenged, for the first time in a while. But I also felt ... weird, I know, but I felt responsible for her. And I wasn't getting through to her.

I deliberately remembered—decompartmentalized— the person who allowed herself to kill. She was part "me" and part "monkey". I let that girl out of her cage for a moment. She was calm ... I was calm, looking around the room for weapons and cooly evaluating Chucha for easy ways to put her down.

"Three," I said, my voice pleasanter, lower. "One by accident." I looked at Chucha with that person's eyes. I let her fill in the blanks. I could almost hear her hackles rising. She swallowed audibly and jumped herself down from the dresser.

"Did you have a message for me or not?" Her sudden aggressiveness told me she was probably spilling fear-smell. It wasn't really reaching me but it was doubtless making her even more nervous. Hm. Now was not the time to give her Tez's plea. She was on the defensive, and would take any sign of weakness, even at second hand, as a cue to attack. No, I needed to stay in the dominant position I'd gained.

"Tez wants to meet with you," I said.

"I have nothing to say to him." That sounded ... equivocating.

I stood up, and grew my body with the upward motion until I was taller than she was. The effect of this, I knew from experience, was chilling. She shrank back, ever so slightly, but still showed her teeth. "Are you saying 'no'?" I asked, bleeding a little more monster into my eyes.

"I don't see what the point would be," she replied, stalling. "We've said all there is to say."

"Maybe not." I put gravity into the two words, and let them sit. I didn't move otherwise.

We stood like that—an enforcer and an unknown, slightly larger, monster—staring at each other, for a full minute. She looked panicked and cornered, defiant and rebellious. But she also started to look ... what was it? Relieved? As if perhaps here was a way out?

"Fine," she said finally. "Where and when?"

"Why don't we three meet at the Sanctuary on Monday, early evening, say, six?" I knew Tez was free. We'd arranged this time in case she'd been amenable.

"Fine," she said again, as if saying more would reveal something. She got up and put her hand on the doorknob.

"Oh, and I want to talk to your shot-caller again. What's his name, Juice?"

"Why?" she asked, suspicious.

"I want Bu Bu back."

She just stared at me. "Why?"

I considered what to say to her. "He's part of an investigation Ayo and I are pursuing. I've been looking for him all week, actually. It's just a coincidence that he ended up here."

"What kind of investigation?" she asked, all excitable little girl again. She was almost salivating.

I gave her my patented "inscrutable" look, which worked a lot better than it should in Obama's America. "Did he talk at all about where he was working before he came to you?"

She grimaced in disgust. "No, not at all. He was an arrogant pig and bragged constantly and wouldn't take orders."

"Maybe he told one of the guys?"

"No, he was even worse to them, and he freaked them out anyway. I was the only one he'd talk to. He was one of *those*, you know." Yeah, I knew. Supernats who despised anyone without superpowers. We all had those tendencies and I had to struggle harder than most to keep mine in check. "I was the only one who worked closely with him, so he would've hardly had the time to talk to anyone else. I kept him out back most of the time. He didn't sleep much, so he was at least useful that way."

"What did he brag about?"

"MMA fights, exclusively. It was interesting, for five minutes."

Another dead end. I tried to keep the disappointment off my face.

"Well, Ayo will want to study him to see what exactly killed him."

"Okay," she said, easily. She opened a drawer in her bureau and pulled out a bamboo tube, similar to the one Ayo had given me to catch Bu Bu in. I guessed the meat market middleman had had one to keep Bu Bu in when he went to them. Can't say those fuckers don't know what they're doing.

Chucha went out the door, gesturing for me to follow.

"It'll save us the trouble of disposing of the body."

I followed her, but *really* didn't like how easy it was for her to talk about body disposal. For a moment, this gig felt personal: I had to get this girl out of here.

CHAPTER NINE

I SLAMMED MY front door behind me, and The Damned Book fell off the shelf. I whipped around and glared at it.

My apartment, an illegal sublet where I'd been living for three years, was a studio composed out of what had once been the dining room and part of the kitchen of a second-story, two-bedroom, Mission district flat. The dining room, which was the main room of my studio, had the remains of a Victorian plate rail lining one short wall: a four-inch-deep shelf set at about head height for the purpose of displaying china, which most San Francisco hipsters now used for books or artwork. Of course, I did too, using my heaviest book—one that could stand up on its own—as a bookend. It only stayed put if I didn't slam my front door when coming in.

And of course, my thickest tome was a secondhand, jacketless, clothbound, unabridged translation of *Journey to the West*, cursed be its name and bindings. I'd dug this one up in a used bookstore to use in my classic Chinese literature class right at the beginning of my sophomore year of college, and thought I'd scored. What I hadn't quite figured out was that you needed to buy the right edition of a book for class, so you had the same translation and page numbers and so on. When I couldn't figure out my first reading assignment, I took the book with me to my prof's office hours.

The prof, who was handsome in what I thought was a fatherly way, and very Chinese looking—exactly what I wanted—had looked stony faced at my sophomoric enthusiasm and confusion. Then he'd told me that— well I don't know if I remember what he *actually* told me. What I heard was that I wasn't really Chinese and didn't really belong in his class, and was too stupid to understand the reading material anyway. Thinking back, there's no doubt in my mind that whatever he said exactly wasn't about me at all, but about whatever had put him in such a vicious mood.

But at the time, it had devastated me. I'd come out to Berkeley hoping to connect with an Asian community in some way—to find my roots—but I felt like such a fraud that I went through all of freshman year nearly failing my Chinese language classes, and not daring to sign up for a Chinese studies class—or to talk to an Asian-looking person. But I'd won enough courage by sophomore year to sign up for the prof's class ... a courage that was the thinnest crust of ice, shattered at a touch. If I hadn't met Baby that same day, I probably would have dropped out and gone back to Chicago. As it was, I *did* drop that class, and my plans to major in Chinese studies. In fact, I never afterwards looked anything Chinese up in books, and avoided asking Chinese people anything (which, of course, put a crimp in my identity search, but I'd get panicky and short of breath anytime I tried any of these things so …) I still thought of that episode as a sort of earthquake in my life; a cataclysm. A disaster.

The book still stood for everything that was holding me back: the humiliation, the hurt, the impostor syndrome, the failure, the fear that everyone could see what an outsider I was—all being made real by that horrible prof. I told myself that someday I would surmount that book, someday I'd read that fucker end to end and *own* it; and once I did, the whole world of Chinese culture would welcome me in and I'd know everything. But I hadn't yet, not in six years. Hadn't even cracked it, nor any of the other books on Asian folklore Ayo pointed me at and I pretended I'd read. So whenever I came home in a mood, it would jump off the shelf and display its fraying, blank, blue cover at my feet, an accusation from the universe, an eternal, sneering question: what have you done to know yourself? What have you done, to improve yourself?

I kicked it against the wall, swearing for the thousandth time to throw it away.

It was of a piece with my mood.

Of course Bu Bu would die just when I'd found him again. *Of course* he didn't talk to anyone, didn't tell anyone about his previous (possible) encounter with a soul-sucking shadow creature, or with something like me. *Of course* the person I was depending on for clues about *me* was a total asshole. A total *dead* asshole.

I went and kicked *Journey to the West* one more time for good measure.

Then I speed-dialed Ayo, who generally stayed up late, and preferred information to sleep.

"Mmm?" she asked, in her "you interrupted me," not her "you woke me," voice.

"Bu Bu's dead," I said shortly, knowing I'd get her

divided attention better that way.

"… who?" she asked, fully alert, but not sure if she was needed to comfort me or not.

"The bajang."

"Oh. … Oh! What? How did that happen?"

I gave her a quick rundown.

"Jesu Christi! Don't go anywhere! I'm on my way!"

I started to protest—it was nearly 3 am, after all—but she had already hung up.

At least this time of night there'd be no traffic. Given her propensity to drive recklessly, she could potentially be here in 20 minutes.

It actually took only ten before she was knocking at my door. I hadn't even heard her climbing the creaky stairs, which meant, I was absolutely sure, that she'd used some sort of magic to get over here so fast. But she blew in like a whirlwind, giving me no time to ask questions—Ayo tended to be the one asking questions—tossing her bag and implements everywhere, grabbing Bu Bu's bamboo tube from where it sat on my table, and tossing his body out of it onto the floor. Ew, that was my yoga mat. Yeah, I was gonna be needing a new one of those.

As I tamped down her blizzard of questions, she didn't even glance at me once; she was too fascinated with Bu Bu.

"What … what is it?" I asked after a long pause. I knew what she saw, though. "His soul is gone, isn't it?"

Ayo blew out a windy sigh. "Essence. Yes. It is. How long?"

"No more than two hours."

"Yeah, this is similar to Wayland. The remains should still be surrounded by inert essence for days yet. But there's very little left."

"Very little?"

"There's a bit left. Much less than there should be for a shapeshifter. It seems you interrupted this ... shadow creature, you said? Looks like you stopped it before it got all of the essence." She stood up from her crouch. "Well, I'll take the body home with me and examine it. Maybe I can figure out what kind of creature did this."

"Your research hasn't turned up anything?"

"Nothing specific so far." She eyed me. "How about you? I know you've been investigating ..." She let it dangle.

"Well, it's not nothing, but I don't know what to make of it."

"What is it?"

I ran down the facts I had so far: Bu Bu seeing a shadow creature at some point, possibly Saturday night; the Tong people having seen Dalisay more recently than Saturday night; the contradiction of them not having kidnapped her, but having her all the same; and the coincidence of Wayland feeling as if he'd picked up a tail the same night, and at the same location, that Dalisay had last been seen. I also wondered aloud if Dalisay hadn't maybe been the shadow's first victim, even if only by accident.

"But I don't know what club Bu Bu, Dalisay, and Wayland all belong to besides the Hung For Tong fan club. And Wayland's connect with them is pretty minuscule. So is Dalisay's, actually. If one of them were to be killed by accident, I'd have thought it would be Wayland. But he was pretty clearly stalked and deliberately killed."

"It's true, that connection may be a bit tenuous," Ayo said, thoughtfully. "I do, I think, see one more connection among those three, though."

"Really? What's that?"

"Well, we usually think of aswang as vampiric beings, but they are also, legitimately, shapeshifters."

That struck me rather hard, and we both stopped to consider it. I remembered the shadow turning to *look* at me, and shivered.

"I have to say, it's all rather discomfiting. ... Maya, you should keep an eye out for any reason something would be attacking shapeshifters."

"Well, there was that stick ..."

"What stick?" Ayo asked sharply.

"Oh, I forgot to tell you. Bu Bu here was guarding a sort of magical walking stick for the San Antonios. When I first got there, they accused me of trying to steal it. But I wasn't really focused on it and I guess they got that pretty quickly, so they put it away and I forgot about it. It made my eyes burn like the Embarcadero on the Fourth of July, though, so maybe it had a glamour on it or something. Maybe it wasn't really a walking stick."

"What did it look like?" she asked, still sharp.

"It was about a meter or so long, made entirely of what looked like tropical wood with ivory, red, and brown striations, probably oil-polished but not stained or varnished, with a knob carved into the top depicting a stylized animal head: maybe canine or feline." This was Ayo's training: she sent me after rare objects all the time and I'd learned to be very specific in my descriptions. "They also had a name for it. It sounded like 'way-shot' or 'way-shuttle' or something."

"Could it have been 'Huexotl'?" She pronounced the word pretty much exactly the way Beto had.

"That sounds like it, yeah."

"Did you recognize the style?"

I shrugged. "Could've been Polynesian, Meso-American, Iron-Age whatever ... you know I'm bad with visual culture."

"That's ... very interesting," Ayo said. "Very

interesting." She tapped her chin in thought, then looked up decidedly. "You're in touch now with that Chucha nagual girl, yes?"

"Yeeees …"

"See if you can find out from her where the San Antonios got this 'Huexotl' from and how long they've had it. Maybe our weretiger friend was involved with it before. Maybe it came through the Tong. Maybe that's what this shadow creature was after." She nodded, as if she'd solved that problem. And I had to admit, it made sense, especially for three in the morning. Her abstraction took advantage of my exhaustion and she'd nearly wandered out the door before I thought to ask:

"Can you connect me with the werecats again, tomorrow?"

"What for?"

"Well, I was thinking earlier we should look through his books. Maybe he and the Tongs are BFFs and we just can't see it. And maybe even Wayland was involved with getting the stick—"

"Say no more, I'll call them in the morning."

CHAPTER TEN

SATURDAY, OCTOBER 15, 2011
SANC-AHH CAFÉ, OAKLAND

SATURDAY DAYTIME WAS too quiet, with our usual clientele off having brunch elsewhere—yes, *all day long*. I was still disturbed by the fight with the shadow last night. Add that to my intense frustration at losing Bu Bu, and my inability to just haul off and tear Wayland's office apart (for one thing, I didn't know where it was; I was waiting for Ayo to get back to me, but she was out after stories,) and I was in a fine state of agitation when the door jingled open.

Sending a momentary flare to my eyes and a slight fizz of electricity to my nerves, Todd walked in. I stared at him for a moment; it was the first time I'd ever seen him without Han and Romeo, his bandmates and co-arts-editors. Then I realized I'd forgotten about our appointment, and I *so* was not in the mood to deal with anyone.

Todd must've picked up on that, because he hesitated a few yards from the counter.

"Hi Todd," I said, making an effort.

His eyes widened and he pantomimed looking over his shoulder and then pointing to himself. I rolled my eyes. Not *that* much of an effort.

He saw this and put on an exaggerated concerned look. He dropped his messenger bag, somehow managing to grab his ukulele case from inside it, then whipping the uke out of its case all in one smooth gesture. Without taking his eyes off of me, or putting his uke strap on, he launched into a complicated introductory set of arpeggios. As annoying as I found male clowning (you know, the kind that *insists* that you pay attention and laugh,) I couldn't help but be impressed with this. He was really freakin' good.

He paused dramatically, waggled his eyebrows at me, and then dove into a bright, plucky melody that sounded familiar, but didn't reveal itself until he reached the chorus: "It's My Party And I'll Cry If I Want To."

I grinned, in spite of myself. Message received. He seemed to think that constituted a detente, because he finally approached the bar, still playing the song—only now it was relaxing into a reggae beat—and kicking his bag with the case on top of it ahead of him. If you were only watching for the goofy content, you might just miss how incredibly graceful one would have to be to pull all that off. I didn't miss it, but I wasn't entirely having it. Yet.

"What kin I do you fer?" Monkey drawled, trying to take control of the situation back.

He slung his hips over the bar stool. "Wayll thar, missy," he drawled back, locking eyes with me, and holstering his uke, "I guess I'll take one-a them thar 'Blood Rains.'" I raised my eyebrows. A Blood Rain was a house specialty drink, a strong blood detoxifying cleanse that was aimed at a certain type of supernat. We didn't list it on the human menu, because it sometimes caused humans to faint, although it certainly made them feel cleansed afterwards. Todd knowing about it could mean a number of things. I reconsidered my initial eye-flare when he walked in. Maybe ...

"Blood Rain, huh?" I asked. I pulled the dried mixture out from the shelves behind me, without looking. "You've been in here before, I take it." I yanked several bottles of red juice out of one of the half-fridges, and spun them, one by one, as I set them on the counter. I'd been a fan of the movie "Cocktail" as a little kid, and spiced up my shifts with a little flair bartending, learned at the fancy hostess bar below the Celestials' HQ in Chicago. My own contribution to Sanc-Ahh's infrastructure was putting the juices in liquor bottles with chrome pour spouts. Ayo had paid for the addition, since I'd broken up more than one ugly mood in the sanctuary with a distracting performance.

"Haven't been in a while," Todd said. "Probably about five or six years. Since I moved into the city. But when it first opened I was in Oakland. I practically lived here."

He watched in obviously impressed silence as I spun the bottles over my forearms again before knocking whacks of each into the cocktail shaker. I finished with a bump to a long stall (that's a flip over the shoulder, bump off the elbow, landing on the back of my hand and just sitting there for what seemed like forever) and then a simple pour after that, a cheeky move that always got a laugh.

He laughed. Now *that* looked good on him. He had a strangely long, but triangular face, with slanting eyes, a long, straight nose, and a small mouth that stretched into a very wide grin. In repose, his face could be considered classically handsome, but I'd almost never seen his face in repose. Mostly, I'd seen him talking with, or for, Cerberus, and making goofy faces, grinning, mugging, generally being a funny dudebro. But this smile was a genuine one, I realized. Was it just me, or was he handsomer than usual? And was that why I was suddenly so busy trying to impress him?

I set his drink out. "On me," I said, waving his wallet off. "Are you from the Bay Area? … I can't believe I've never asked you that before. But you must be from here, to be such a social justice warrior."

He laughed that genuine, good-looking laugh again. "No, not really. More central coast. Watsonville, actually."

"Oh, wow, a real Californian." He bowed. "I don't know anything about the central coast."

"It's a place, like any other. Maybe more relaxed, in some ways. More uptight in others. And I was a pretty ordinary kid. But then my family got interned—" he paused as if he had been about to say something else, "… and when I found out about that whole history I was pretty shocked. So I started studying up on it and it got me more involved in Asian American stuff."

"Who was that? Your grandparents?"

He looked at me for a second. "Yeah, my grandparents." My eyes suddenly flared. Wait, what?

"What camp?" I asked, trying to stuff down my suspicion.

"Tule Lake." Not a lie.

"Wow, heavy," I said. Tule Lake was for the real go-getters, the ones who'd objected to being deprived of liberty without due process. "Were your grandparents community leaders?"

"Yeah." My eyes burned again. "Not in any kind of official capacity, but folks in the community kind of

116

looked to them. Not everybody liked them, and they were denounced, which is how they ended up there." None of that last bit was false, which means that he was telling a true story, but just lying about it being his grandparents. What the hell?

He sipped his drink and I wiped the counter, trying to think of what to say next.

"So," he said, "should we talk about the—"

"Yes! Yes we should." I put the damp cloth down, grabbed an apple out of the fridge, and came around to sit next to him. "What do you think about the shapeshifter thing?"

"It's an interesting idea. But Asians, especially the Japanese—for manga and anime—really don't think about hybridity or transnationality the same way that we do. In anime and manga most shapeshifting transformations are animal transformations. Then probably the next most common is gender transformations—which is a big thing in Asian mythologies, with demons changing genders to entrap people 'n' stuff."

"Whoa! Freudian much? Are there mangas like that? Or depictions of foreigners living in Japan? Or Japanese living abroad?"

He tapped his fingers on his knee, thinking. "For the living abroad thing there's *Ranma 1/2*. This father and son go to China and are cursed with transformation there. And for transnationality there's *Ghost in the Shell* where the protagonist is a cyborg in this really multinational future city." He gave me a long, and frankly geeky description of each of these, which I might have found a snooze if anyone else had been telling me, but was fascinating coming from him. "And I can dig up one or two more, I suppose. There's some new stuff I've been meaning to watch. How long do I have?"

"I can give you to the end of the month. I know you write quickly."

"But think slowly." He demonstrated, tapping his leg again. It was a nice-looking leg, I had to admit, encased as it was in slightly worn skinny jeans. "I'm trying to connect this to mythology, but it doesn't really connect. I mean, there are shapeshifter legends in all major cultures. But they're mostly human-to-animal or animal-to-human. The transformations just have to do with basic human wonders and fears and weird hankerings for their pets. Also: desire for magical solutions to their problems."

"For example ..."

"Oh, uh ... well, the most well-known one in East Asia is the fox spirit. It's called the kitsune in Japanese, huli jing in Chinese, and kumiho in Korean. It's an ordinary fox that, if it lives to a certain number of years, acquires the ability to change into human form—usually a beautiful young woman, for the purpose of luring men, of course. In Japanese legend it's a hundred years, but in Korean it's a thousand. And generally the fox spirit is ambiguous, both good and bad. The Koreans, though, think they're all bad, because they're just like that."

"Paranoid, the lot of 'em. Not that it isn't justified, when it comes to you all." I waved at him indicating he represented Japanese people everywhere.

He chuckled. "Too true. But the fox spirits are basically blamed for a variety of things, or credited with a variety of things: most commonly, I think, men's wandering eyes. And there's a lot of Little-Mermaid-type stuff in Chinese legend, like a white snake spirit who turns into a beautiful woman when she falls in love with a human man. And animal spirits and demons who have to learn religion or magic to a certain extent to be able to transform into human form; like humanity is for extra credit. There's a lot of that; transformation into human form is a reward for perseverance and learning."

"That must be why I'm human. I studied really hard at Cal," I said.

He grinned.

"You really know a lot about this stuff." I got up and went back around the counter to toss my apple core.

Todd's eyes followed me and he sat forward to lean over the counter, as if trying to maintain contact. "Well, that's sort of my thing. Folklore and sci-fi and fantasy. They all go hand in hand in the nerd world. It's why I used to hang here: Ayo is a font of knowledge about all the traditions I don't know about."

Which reminded me. "Hey, do you know anything about shadow creatures?" He looked confused. "Oh, I was just thinking that that would be an interesting metaphor for immigrants and sojourners. You know, the invisible subaltern."

"Oh. Well. ... You know ... you'd think they'd be everywhere, but actually, they aren't. Native Americans have a few sort of death creatures that can take the form of a shadow, but other than that, shadows only show up in European tradition as ghosts, mostly. Dead people. 'Shades' you know. Also Sprockets. At least, as far as I know. They don't really show up in Asian mythology."

"Guess I'll have to ask Ayo. What about essence-sucking creatures?"

He looked even more confused. "As a sort of ... you mean like ... a metaphor for deracination or something?"

"Yeah."

"Uh ... well, in Japan there's a flowering tree that sucks out your soul. And there's also a dude named Wanyudo who was condemned to wander around as a flaming cart wheel, stealing the souls of whoever looks at him.

Like the illicit result of an orgy among Medusa, St. Catherine, and the Wandering Jew. But I don't think that's what you're looking for."

"I guess not. I was thinking more of a shadow creature that sucks out your soul, kind of thing."

"That would probably be in the Native American realm. You'd have to ask Ayo."

"Figures," I said.

I wasn't facing the cafe door when I heard the bell jingle and felt a displacement of air, almost like being struck in the chest and losing your breath. "Tez," I thought immediately, proving that I could habituate myself to anything, as long as it involved a hot, lippy jaguar-boy. Todd, who had been rhapsodizing about Ayo's breadth of knowledge, frowned at me and looked over his shoulder. He must have seen me stiffen. Argh. If Todd saw it, no doubt Tez saw it too. He was an ambush predator, after all.

"Maya," Tez said in his creamy chocolate voice. Was it possible to lick the sound of someone's voice? I turned my head—slowly because I wanted to savor the sight of him.

"Hey, Tez," I said, as slowly as I could. I didn't have a luscious voice, and Monkey had me compensate by slowing down. "How's it going?"

He raised his eyebrows right about the time that Todd raised his. Okay, maybe it was too slow. Tez looked from me to Todd.

"Oh, uh, Tez Varela, meet Todd Wakahisa. Todd's one of *Inscrutable*'s editors. We were just talking shop." Shut up, Monkey said. He doesn't need to know that this actually quite good-looking guy isn't in play. Also: isn't he?

"Hey," Tez said, giving one of those uber-guyish chin

tips. God, it looked good on him, though.

"Hey," Todd said, with a new, slightly lopsided, wicked smile the likes of which I'd never seen on his face. My god. Why didn't he *lead* with that smile? He'd have the world at his freakin' feet.

He held out his hand, which Tez clearly wasn't expecting. Tez hesitated for a moment, then took Todd's hand. It was the first time I'd seen him acting awkwardly. I guess that was the point of the exercise.

They stood there, hands locked, for a moment that seemed to last forever, and I got to take a good look at both of them. They were an illustration of contrasts, with Tez cool and unsmiling and tough, wearing a fitted black t-shirt with a fashionable light-grey screen print of swooping lines on it; Todd grinning wickedly and looking like he was trapped for a moment in a state of suspended animation, wearing a white shirt printed with foxes, rabbits, and hedgehogs, over maroon skinny jeans. They both had black hair, but Todd's was a shiny blue-black, straight, and swooped up into a faux hawk; Tez's was so dark brown it was actually black, and curly, as far as I could tell, but cropped so short that it barely swerved.

Todd, likely the older of the two, looked five years younger, with his shorter stature, triangular face, and small mouth. He nearly vibrated with energy, always moving some part of his body, tapping fingers, jiggling legs, stretching his neck. Tez's square, jutting jaw— with its perennial shroud of stubble—had made him look like a man even when he was nineteen, and his broad shoulders and indefinable magnetism gave him a gravitas rarely felt in anyone, much less someone so young. The height didn't hurt, either. As the moment stretched slightly beyond what was normal and social,

Tez seemed to loom over Todd, who was still seated on a high stool. Somehow, Todd didn't seem lessened by it. Todd was bright where Tez was dark. No, that wasn't right—Todd was a funhouse mirror and Tez, a glass darkly. Or something—

And the moment was broken. They released each other.

"Cool shirt," Todd said. "Is that the route of Magellan?"

I looked again. The screen print went all the way around the shirt and was a stylized map of the world, with route lines.

Tez looked impressed. "Yeah," he said. "Good eye."

And both turned to me.

"You have anything for me?" Tez asked.

"Yeah. Excuse us for a second, Todd," I said. I came back around and led Tez to the other end of the counter, away from Todd. I didn't look at him until I thought we were far enough away for privacy. But suddenly looking up at him was a bad idea. His closeness, and his intense attention nearly took my breath away again. Cool it, Maya.

"Okay, it's all set up. She'll meet us here on Monday evening at six pm. Our evening traffic doesn't start coming in until about seven, so that gives us some time for conversation."

"Maya, I appreciate your help contacting her, but I'm not sure you should—"

I cut him off. I'd been expecting the objection. "Look, Tez, I realize this is a family matter, but you called in help because keeping it in the family wasn't possible anymore and, believe it or not, I know this fight extremely well. And if you meet with her, just the two of you, it'll go down exactly like it did the last time, or the last 50 times. You need a referee, and maybe a translator."

That last thought must have gotten through to him

somehow, or maybe he'd already come in a receptive mood, because he looked thoughtful, rather than stubborn.

"Translator, huh?"

"I speak Tough Cookie fluently."

"'Tough Cookie'?"

"Don't hate."

He smiled in spite of himself. "So ... How was she?"

"She was ... good, I think. She clearly has the respect of the boys, and seems to be working well with Juice, you know the—"

"I know who he is," Tez said darkly.

"Well, he's no common thug, that guy, and he seems to be treating her well. She was well dressed. No dark clouds around her head. For now, prying her away might be more of a job than you can manage. However—"

"What?" he asked quickly.

"Well, I got a teeny tiny impression that a very small part of her isn't entirely down with the situation and would be glad of a way out."

"Of course! She's not stupid." He huffed in frustration. "Where is all this coming from anyway? How are *you* getting through to her?"

I was grateful he hadn't asked before. I'd always worried Tez might be a bit of a straight arrow and I didn't want to look like a loser or a thug in front of him. But the question, and the revelation, was inevitable.

"Tez, I was in a very similar situation, about ten years ago. I got mixed up with some bad people and my foster dad came after me and tried to reason with me. And part of me wanted to go home, but I had left home to prove myself to him in the first place, among other things, and his coming after me may have actually kept me from coming home a half year longer."

"Chucha isn't you," he said stubbornly.

"People are people," I said. "And any creature with a human aspect has human psychology. You know that. Chucha and I are both tomboys who lost a mother, lived for a while with male authority figures with sticks up their asses, and then fled into a world of toxic masculinity and violence to prove ourselves. It's not rocket science, Tez."

"I don't have a stick up my ass." Well, at least he picked up on that right away.

I stepped around him and took a good look. His head followed, but he let me.

"As fine an ass as that is, you have a huge stick up it with Chucha's name written all over it. Here, let me get that for you."

I reached for him, not really sure what I intended to do if he didn't react, but he huffed a surprised laugh and grabbed my wrist.

"Thanks, but if my ass is that fine, maybe I should keep it." He shook my wrist, but didn't let it go.

"A joke? From Tez Varela? Maybe I should look at your ass more often."

He grinned slowly, not letting go of my wrist. "Any time, Monkey girl. Any time."

I smiled back.

I didn't quite realize we were having a moment until Todd, whose existence I'd completely forgotten, stomped on it.

"Hey, are you done with your conspiracy for world domination yet? We should finish up here."

I'd thought we were finished, but Monkey kept me from saying so.

Tez, still holding my wrist, looked as if he wanted to say something else, but swallowed it. "Six pm on Monday?" he asked.

"With bells."

With one more look, he dropped my hand, chin-tipped Todd, and whooshed out of the cafe, taking my breath with him. I stood, looking out the door a while after he disappeared.

"Hot date?" Todd broke my breathless reverie again. He was a real buzzkill.

"Cold date," I said flatly.

"Tonight?" He looked a little anxious, and frankly, I *was* annoyed with him for interrupting my moment with Big Cat.

"Nope." I went back behind the counter and started wiping the already spotlessly clean counter.

"Busy tonight then?" A smiling note in his voice made me look up. He was smiling that wicked, lopsided smile again. Whew. I didn't know if I had any more impressed to give anyone today, but damn, that was a good smile.

"Well," I said, no longer flatly, "I'm helping with an antiracism training at Occupy, as soon as Stoney relieves me here, then joining the protest at rush hour, then going to the general assembly."

"Of course," he said, with exaggerated thoughtfulness, "I should be going with you, being a badass social justice warrior and all."

"You have to keep up your end."

"And after that?"

I shrugged. It depended on Ayo getting ahold of the werecats, which might not happen tonight.

"My band is playing tonight at 10. Wanna come?"

"Maybe."

"Guess what our new band name is. Just guess."

"No idea."

He looked even more wicked. "Cerberus."

My heart stopped. "'Cerberus'?" I squeaked. "You're

calling your band 'Cerberus' now?"

He laughed. "Baby told me that's what you call the three of us. It's so much better a name than the last five we came up with, so we took it. Tonight will be our debut as Cerberus. So, you have to come, and drink champagne. I'll put you on the guest list. Plus one, if you wanna bring Baby."

How could I say no to that?

CHAPTER ELEVEN

SATURDAY, OCTOBER 15, 2011
STARRY PLOUGH BAR, BERKELEY

"SO YOU THINK he was gonna ask you out?" Baby asked. Baby's enthusiasm for my Tez-crush had never waned, part of the reason I loved her. About the current situation I'd told her only that Tez had some family connection with Ayo; the rest of the story was more or less Baby-safe. Baby knew about (and was fascinated by) my history with the Celestials (although, of course, she merely thought I was an expert martial artist; she had no idea about my supernatural abilities), so she understood why Ayo would think I was a good choice for the job. I wavered between feeling guilty and feeling delicious about the secrets I kept from Baby.

"I don't know. But we were having a moment," I said, exaggerating my frustration. "Damn, why did Todd have to be there?"

"You think Todd's into you?"

"I have no idea. I mean, he was flirting with me, but—"

"But he flirts with everyone," Baby agreed.

Really? That hadn't been what I was about to say, and I realized in that moment that Todd had never flirted with me before. Why not, if he flirted with everyone? "You know, I've known Todd for three years or so, but until today, I didn't know anything about him. Did you?"

She shrugged. "Not much. I mean he's from the central coast, he's a demon on the uke, and he writes like a motherfucker. What else do I need to know?" She thought for a moment. "But he *is* cute, I guess, now that you mention it"—I hadn't, but didn't say—"so I'm gonna pay more attention to him tonight, see what's up."

Baby was the boy-craziest lesbian I'd ever met, although she was focusing especially hard on my nonexistent love life right now because she was taking a six-month "celibacy break." (Don't ask.) She'd taught me how to be girl-crazy out loud (I did occasionally date women, although I hadn't yet progressed to a relationship with one; Baby called me a LUG to tease me, but I wasn't sure she was wrong,) but she hadn't at all needed me to reciprocate since she had a low-stakes, fun, flirtatious way with men, and she genuinely enjoyed their company, whereas *my* enjoyment of them often tended to be in indirect proportion to how attractive I found them. Come to think of it, Baby had taught me a lot about relating to boys, too.

"You do that," I mumbled, adjusting my bra. My clothes were all made from my own hairs, but I still wasn't good at nice lingerie, and when we went out I liked to wear the lacy stuff, even though it was considerably less comfortable than my usual. I don't disparage my powers, but they aren't *all* they're cracked up to be.

I'd met Baby (and Todd, and a handful of other *Inscrutable* staff) at the protest that afternoon, and we'd changed at Baby's temporary pad (don't ask) in downtown

Oakland. Ayo hadn't gotten back to me, nor responded to my texts, so now we were exiting the Ashby BART station and walking to mural-adorned nightclub The Starry Plough, ahead on the corner. The Starry Plough was right next door to much-crazier-mural-adorned La Peña Cultural Center, just north of where Oakland turns into Berkeley. I'd spent most of my weekends freshman and sophomore year at places like La Peña, places that hosted open mic nights and other literary and performance offerings—at first in stalk of Tez, but increasingly because that was where I found my peeps. After Tez graduated we'd moved next door to the Starry Plough to see bands, and my musical taste had broadened considerably. Half of my college social life had taken place on this very block, and I loved it fiercely.

In fact, we'd met and recruited Cerberus for the magazine right here, the year we graduated. And tonight, the place was packed for them. Cerberus had an unusually large following for a local indie band, and their not-infrequent shows were always packed, despite the fact that they changed their name every six months or so. For the first time I wondered if magic had anything to do with that.

We arrived just in time; Asian time, that is: half an hour after they were supposed to start. They were all on stage, fussing with their equipment, making my eyes burn, when Baby and I took our beer bottles from the bar and went to join the crowd, (Baby grabbing a napkin and wiping down the sides and mouth of the bottle I handed her even though, after a massive fight, I hadn't pranked her *at all* in well over two years.) Todd looked up as we approached the stage, and gave me his wicked grin. He was learning, this one.

"Damn," Baby said, a little breathlessly. "He's not just cute, he's *electro*cute. How come I never noticed before?"

His eyes flicked to her and his grin grew wider. Had he heard her? The only way he'd heard her speaking low in my ear, from 15 feet away, over the canned music and the audience noise, was if he were—

Han's drums interrupted my thought and the noise. Todd slung his uke strap over his head and hooked it on. Romeo stepped up to his stand-up bass and took firm hold. Fire washed over my eyes as, without looking at each other, they launched, in perfect sync, into their first song. What they played was rock 'n' roll, if rock music had polyrhythms, insanely tangled bass lines, and the bright, plucky, pseudo-Spanish-guitarness of a lead ukulele. You could hear Hawai'ian slack-key guitar mixed in, and occasionally the plucking of a koto, and the ghosts of jazz, blues, bluegrass, punk rock, and Romani music were seated approvingly behind.

You've never heard anything like this, and you've never seen anything like it, either. Romeo kept his head down, and his body bowed out like a bracket, but his instrument spun and spat like a strung tiger. Han played his drum kit like Muppet Animal on meth, frequently dropping his sticks and leaping into the neighboring circle of his percussion instruments like, well, like me in monkey mode. And Todd writhed and jumped and slid before them like any lead singer, only there were no vocals, and, although his body moved in every direction, his face remained perfectly still, albeit smiling.

Instrumental-only music usually made me itch, but these guys kept whole crowds absolutely still—or completely wild, depending on their mood—without any trouble, including, and especially, me. To be honest, I wasn't really sure if I *wanted* Todd to be interested in me, because I didn't entirely want to get behind the music to see the flaws in the man. The music was too unique, too special.

After nearly an hour, everyone in the place was bathed in sweat and the band took a break, to much hooting and applause ... from me most of all. I had eleven years of intense musical training under my belt, but didn't seem to have a single creative bone in my body. So I absolutely melted hearing true artists play—and these guys were true artists; not merely able to compose their own music, and not just practiced and incredibly tight, but also able to make a completely unique sound, and one that expressed who they were, and where and what they came from, perfectly.

"Thanks," Todd said, when I had awkwardly expressed this to him and the guys and tried to buy them a beer (they got free drinks when they played.) He seemed genuinely pleased, although Romeo and Han gave me and Todd funny looks.

"Yeah, thanks," Romeo said. "Haven't seen you at any of our shows recently. It's good to see you out and about again." This seemed to be invested with more meaning than it deserved.

"Oh, well, actually, I've been neglecting everybody and everything except the magazine, and now, Occupy, because I've been taking a lot of extra hours at work."

"Saving up for something?" Todd asked. Romeo and Han exchanged a glance with each other, then with Baby. All three moved away as one.

"A '65 Mustang," I said, "or a life."

"Well, I don't know about the 'stang, but you're getting a good start on the life part right here."

"Drinking a beer in a bar is getting a life?"

"Drinking a beer in a bar with a handsome and talented musician is getting a life."

"Don't forget 'modest'."

"I didn't."

I laughed, and as the break went on, laughed more in 20 minutes than I probably had the entire previous month. I'd never been very good at flirting—I simply can't laugh at jokes that aren't funny, and I can't express an admiration that I don't feel; there are downsides to being a smart woman, especially if the hottie trying to flirt with you isn't as smart as you are. But Todd made it easy: he was genuinely funny, and I did genuinely admire his playing ... and his writing, and his editing skills ... and his looks ... I didn't have to fake anything. He was the one who was good at flirting, not I, but he was so good at it, that I didn't notice that I wasn't.

"I should've taken a picture of you two to upload to Wikipedia under 'hook up'," Baby said as the boys returned to the stage to fuss again with their equipment. "That was more of a 'shook up,' though."

"We were just talking, Baby."

"That was to talking what chocolate covered strawberries are to fruit."

And then the music took us again, only better this time, because my mood had heightened, and I felt ... seen.

Nevertheless, I was yanked out of the magic sometime later by a strong flare I saw out of the corner of my eye in the crowd. I turned to look and saw a South Asian hipster dude who looked somewhat familiar. He saw me looking and nodded, and I recognized him. We'd met a few years back when Ayo sent me to talk to his father. He and his family were vanaras, Indian monkey-shifters, and Ayo thought maybe I could be related to them in some way. But, although they were very cool (legendary warriors with kickass moves and great senses of humor), they were nowhere near as powerful as I was, and couldn't do most of the stuff I could do. Plus, they weren't rhesus macaques, but a kind of larger monkey breed of their own that sort of descended from macaques. The dude ... Aahil, I think his name was, Aahil invited me to go tree climbing with him and his cousins some weekend in the redwoods, and I said I'd go, but I was so disappointed that I didn't belong to them that I never went. He came to a few *Inscrutable* parties with his friends, but then that was it, and I hadn't seen him in nearly two years.

I considered going over to him to say hi, but then remembered Todd. Was I Todd's ... date tonight? That was stupid. I was Todd's friend. And even if I was Todd's date, that didn't preclude me talking to other guys. Especially if I wasn't interested in them. Although ... Aahil was pretty cute, too. Jeez, I was turning more boy crazy than Baby!

After way too much thinking about it, I decided it would be not only stupid, but rude not to go say hi to Aahil. But when I turned back in his direction, he was no longer standing where he'd been. Confused, I scanned the crowd and caught no flare. Huh? Had he left already? I looked again, more closely this time, and saw ... what was that? Was it a ... shadow? I caught just a glimpse of something dark and shadowy near the door before it disappeared and I was left wondering if I'd actually seen anything at all.

I stood too long like an idiot before my rationality got through to me and I bolted out the door. There it was, that strange shadow-figure, floating rapidly down the sidewalk past the group of smokers outside La Peña, who were too involved in their conversation to notice. I took off after it, albeit somewhat slowly, still hobbled by the same indescribable reluctance I'd felt in the San Antonios' backyard. Once past the smokers, I quickly shifted into a large dog, feeling a bit safer that way.

The shadow kept pace 50 yards ahead of me for a block, but then folded itself into a mini-copse of trees in someone's yard and disappeared. I switched to monkey and swung over the fence into the yard, but it was too dark and full of tree-shadows for me to be able to see anything. I stood looking around for a few minutes, hoping to see movement, but all I saw was an obese cat, trying to sneak away without my noticing.

I tried to force myself into the yard. What was I afraid of? I was Monkey! I was afraid of nothing! But the reluctance dragged at my legs like mud, and Ayo's voice, saying the shadow's victims were all shapeshifters, spoke in my head.

I returned to the street and looked around, nonplused. How to find a shadow at night? It was worse than a needle in a haystack.

And anyway, what the *hell* had it come here for? Clearly not me, I'm not sure it even saw me following it. Or maybe ... maybe it *had* been looking for me, thinking I had the stick? Wait, that was reasonable, actually. The last time it had seen the stick, I was interfering between it and its attempt to take the stick. It had fled when the San Antonio boys had come out, presumably because they-plus-I were too many for it. Maybe it assumed I'd taken the stick and came after me, only to realize I didn't have it.

But the stick was still with the San Antonios, wasn't it? Wouldn't it check there first? Maybe ... maybe not. Who knows what kind of logic animates a creature like this?

But, if I was right, that was extra evidence that it was after the stick, and that meant ... that meant that Wayland would have *had* to have something to do with it. That meant ... sigh ... exactly the same thing it had meant earlier that day: I had to wait to hear back from the werecats about getting into Wayland's office.

But—and I stopped dead—this meant Chucha was in the line of fire. I'd have to warn her … and Juice too, probably. I thought for a moment and then determined to swing by the San Antonios' house before I went home to put a word in some ears. I shoulda gotten their phone numbers.

I changed into a hound and loped back the few blocks to where the La Peña smokers were re-entering the building. I skidded to a stop next to the mural just in time to see Baby come out the door, concern on her face. She stared at me, and I stared back for a split instant, before Monkey turned me back human.

"… the fuck?" Baby whispered.

"Hey Baby," I said, as nonchalantly as I could.

" … the FUCK?" Baby said.

"What?" I asked. "I was just breathing second hand fumes. And just for a second. I swear. I didn't come out to smoke. Believe it or not, I came out for fresh air."

"But … but …" she pointed at me, at a very rare loss for words.

"What, Baby? What is it?"

"You were … you looked like …"

"I swear. To. God. I was not smoking. No matter what it looked like." It was a stretch, I realize. The smokers had already reentered by the time Baby came out. I was hoping enough of the smoke smell had lingered to give me my alibi. But it was Baby who was my self-appointed non-smoking guardian, a role she took very seriously. If anything could distract her, it would be the prospect of my recidivism. Truth was, I'd never smoked, but back when I'd had trouble dealing with crowds and left events often for a quick flight to clear my head, I'd needed an excuse for going outside frequently. Ironically enough, since I couldn't stand smoke.

I put on an innocence-injured face, to underline it and give her a chance to think.

She did. That's right, Baby. You didn't just see your best friend transform from a dog into a human because *that would be crazy, wouldn't it*?

"Uh," she said, scrambling for a footing. "Did you just see a dog around here somewhere? I thought I saw a dog."

"A dog?" I asked, putting on confused face. "Look, do you wanna go back in? We're missing the ending. I didn't wanna leave but it just got really stuffy after a while."

"Yeah, right," Baby said, recovering, sarcasm first. "Fresh air my ass. Let's go back in." She even sniffed me as I passed her, smelling for smoke. I wasn't sure whether to feel guilty for manipulating her, or triumphant, for manipulating her successfully. But I followed obediently, even smiling.

CHAPTER TWELVE

MONDAY, OCTOBER 17, 2011
SANC-AHH CAFÉ, OAKLAND

I DIDN'T SEE Chucha again on Saturday night. She wasn't home, so I passed my word of warning along to the henchbrain on duty and left, still worried that nobody would take it seriously. And Sunday didn't yield any results. Ayo didn't get permission from the werecats to go through Wayland's stuff, but she had his office address, and was ready to turn a blind eye to whatever I had planned. So I broke in and went through every freakin' receipt in the place, as well as all the spreadsheets on his desktop computer (the password was on a post-it stuck to the bottom of his top drawer, and he didn't use any database software, just simple excel spreadsheets) but nothing looked weird or out of order, every item was a huge lot on a huge pallet, and there were no walking-stick-sized packages anywhere.

Granted, if he was doing any black market deals, he probably wouldn't record them in the same spreadsheets the IRS might be auditing. So I also looked through the entire office, including both the obvious wall safe, and the less obvious floor safe under his very heavy desk (it looked like heavy rosewood, apparently had a core of iron, and only a shapeshifter could have moved it by themselves,) but found nothing. Actually, the floor safe was suspiciously empty and I suspected his werecat next-of-kin, or whoever his trusted second would be, had already cleared it out.

I made a mental note to get Ayo to figure out who this person was and ask them, but she didn't show up at work Sunday, or all day Monday—or answer my texts—so I was shit out of luck and starting to grow anxious again.

Todd showed up at Sanc-ahh on Monday evening about when I was expecting Tez and Chucha. Dude had the worst timing ... or maybe the best, depending on what he was trying to do. If it was "annoy the hell out of Maya" I'd call it good. I plucked a hair and threw it surreptitiously down onto the stool facing me.

Todd greeted me cheerily and sat down enthusiastically, right where I'd planned. With a loud rip, a farting noise tore out from his seat. He looked down, startled, then looked up, as the noise continued. His cheeks pinkened. It went on. We both waited. It was really long. Heads came up all over the cafe. The note held for a fraction of forever ... Then the sound trailed off into something that sounded suspiciously like a raspberry. Todd's face was a study of embarrassment, surprise, and ... awakening delight.

He jumped up again and looked at the seat, then picked up the black-seat-colored whoopee cushion between two fingers. "That is *damned* impressive, Maya. Where did you find it?"

I snatched it back from him and stuffed it in my pocket. "Trade secret."

Gazing at me delightedly, Todd sat back down, but before he could order and I could be rude to him, Chucha swept in the door and made a beeline for me.

"Hey Maya!" she said, in a bright, almost girly voice that I wouldn't have expected from her. She was smiling ear to ear.

"Hey Chucha," I said, glad, but puzzled. "How are you doing?"

"Gassed!" she cried, and then laughed. No, she *giggled*. She plopped herself down next to Todd, who was looking at her in some alarm, and pulled her backpack around to sit in her lap. Then she did a double take at Todd, her smile fading, sniffed him, and wrinkled her nose in a half-snarl.

"Uhhh …" I said, "Chucha, this is Todd."

Chucha sniffed again and burred a small, ambivalent-sounding growl. Todd started up from his stool and bolted for the door. For just an instant I thought I saw a bunch of … was that reddish hair? … but he was gone too quickly for me to take another look.

"What the hell?" I asked the room.

"Figures," Chucha grunted.

I stared at her for a second. I wanted to ask her what she'd smelled, or if she had something against Todd, but it was against Sanctuary rules for any supernat to out another, or to bring their beefs into the Sanctuary. I'd just have to ask Todd himself the next time I saw him.

"Want something to drink?" I asked her. At my recommendation she ordered a Seven League Cleanse, which was supposed to increase your running speed, but more importantly, couldn't hurt you. Some of our house mixes could strike people in weird ways.

I gave Chucha an extended version of my Cocktail show. I thought it might annoy and impress her in equal measure, but she was wholly delighted. She even clapped when I pulled off a particularly gruesome spinning shadow pass (behind and over the shoulder with a spin.) Her inner twelve-year-old was on full display this evening. She was even wearing a ponytail. It struck me as a little strange, but what did I know? She was used to being the baby of a fairly large family and I'd pulled rank on her last time we talked. Maybe she'd accepted her role, and that signaled her to act like a little girl. It worked, too; I found her attitude ... cute, god help me.

After she'd tried out her drink and pronounced it "Bomb!" she leaned in confidentially and grin-whispered "Wanna see something?"

"Sure."

She unzipped the top of her pack and, with a bit of a flourish, pulled out the walking stick.

I was struck speechless for a moment. I'd been pretty sure the San Antonios still had it, which put Chucha in the line of fire, but I hadn't figured on her being entirely in charge of it now. Goddammit, this didn't just put her in the line of fire; this made her the shadow's target.

My eyes burned and burned as I looked at it. Strange: now that she was holding the thing out, it was the length I'd remembered: roughly three and a half feet. But a moment ago it had been entirely enclosed in a backpack that was no more than two feet long, and I hadn't seen any pointy bulges. The stick had definitely not been sticking out. Magical indeed.

I reached out in a daze to touch it, but she snatched it back from me.

"Mine!" she snarled, then looked startled at herself. I was startled too, and I moved my hand back. She calmed. "Look. Don't touch," she said, demonstrating by looking lovingly at the stick.

"You pull guard duty?" I asked, as casually as I could.

"Hunh? Oh. Um. Yeah. Juice got Bu Bu mostly to guard this"—she raised the stick briefly—"but when he bit it I had to take over. It's supposed to be temporary, but I think I'll hang on to it. Don't want another lightweight like Bu Bu losing it again." She looked up. "Juice says to say thanks, by the way. If you hadn't shown up, that … thing—whatever it was—would've gotten away with the Huexotl."

She said the name like a prayer.

I frowned. Bu Bu wasn't a lightweight; not by a long shot. Evidently she hadn't sparred with him, because he could've taken her, no question. Even worse: they seemed to agree with Ayo and me that the stick—the way … the Huexotl—was what the shadow creature was after.

"Chucha, did you get my message?"

"About what?" She looked more perky now. So: no.

"Bu Bu wasn't a lightweight, and you know I'm not either, but that shadow thing *really* set me back, and it *killed* him. You need to be careful, because you'll be directly in its way now."

She rolled her eyes. "Whatever," she said.

"No, *not* 'whatever,' Chucha! Be careful with the shadow thing and don't try to take it on yourself!"

"Just because *you* couldn't take it, doesn't mean *I* can't."

Oh, how soon they forget. But I could see I wasn't getting through to her. Maybe Juice would be more rational about it. I made a mental note to get his phone number from her before she left. And now it was time to "collect intel," as Ayo would put it.

"So, where did Juice get that thing?"

"Dunno. Before my time." She was cradling it in her left arm now, and began stroking it with her right. Weird.

"Do you know *who* he got it from?" I was having to rein myself in hard from assuming that Juice *must've* gotten it from Wayland. There was a whole world of possibilities out there. Just because him getting it from Wayland would've been neat and clean didn't mean it was the truth.

"Nope," she said simply. Sigh.

I thought for a moment; she'd been with the San Antonios only a few weeks, but they couldn't have acquired Bu Bu any earlier than this past Tuesday, so ... "Who was guarding it before Bu Bu?"

"Oh, they had this werewolf kid doing security for a stretch. Almost out of control and no experience, but all they could find. Then Juice got the Huexotl and things started going better and that's when he found me. So I started doing security and Justin—that's the werewolf—was just responsible for guarding the Huexotl, but he got killed, so then Juice found Bu Bu—"

"Wait, he got killed?" My thoughts were whirling. "When did this happen?"

"Sometime really early ... um ... Tuesday morning, I think? Yeah, Tuesday."

"You saw this?"

"No, I was out. I never saw that shadow thing. Nobody did, in fact. Nobody except you." She sat up a little straighter and looked ... sober ... for the first time. "You know, they're taking your word for it. *I* know you're telling the truth, but you better not give *them* a reason to doubt you."

No doubt she meant she could hear my heartbeat, the way all other predator shifters could. Walking lie detectors, the lot of 'em. I found my own lie detecting ability more elegant—and more reliable. It was easy enough for me to turn into a—literally—heartless creature and lie that way.

"So then Bu Bu took over watching It." Jesus, she could even capitalize Its pronouns. "But he didn't even last as long as that kid." She stroked the stick. She was really starting to wig me out.

"Where's his body?"

She acted as if she didn't hear me for a moment, then looked up. "Oh. Uh … He's tucked off." She looked chagrined for a moment.

"Where?"

She rubbed her face against the stick for a moment, eyes closed. "I'm not allowed to say." She sounded chastened, and looked as if she were now drawing comfort from the stick. A ha! A loose thread. I decided to pull.

"Chucha," I said. She didn't open her eyes, but I could see her invisible ears prick up and turn towards me. "Chucha, did you-all inform his pack? You know the wolves tend to be pretty touchy about their remains. His people will want to handle his body."

This was true. They were extremely control-freaky about their physical leavings (hair, nails, etc.) and insisted on cremating and scattering themselves, lest witches get ahold of their parts and gain control of a whole pack through one of its members. (Probably also to keep the government from getting proof of their existence, but nobody talked about that.)

However, if a barely controlled young wolf was allowed to work security for a gang, he was without a doubt packless, and that made him a pariah with whom they wouldn't concern themselves (except to kill him first chance they got and burn his remains. You know, as you do. Did I mention that I don't like werewolves?) But if Chucha didn't already know that, I didn't mind guilting her a little. I'm Machiavellian that way.

"No," she whispered, pressing her forehead into the

stick. "Juice said nobody could know where he's at."

"Well," I said quietly. "Bummer for Justin."

She squeezed her eyes shut tighter. "He was an asshole anyway. Couldn't keep his paws to himself. Always cattin' off."

I decided to let that stand. Once they started to justify their own bad behavior, there was no more guilting them. If I let her get away with it, though, the guilt would grow on its own. I should know.

"Well, if you change your mind, you can tell Ayo where to find him. She could possibly help you guys by telling you how he died. That might help you figure out who got him."

She didn't say anything. I felt a strange satisfaction. She was feeling it. Good.

"So … what's it for, anyway?" I asked gesturing at the stick.

"It's magic!" she said brightly. She nuzzled it with her nose, like a baby. Creepy. "It gives you power." Okay, now she really sounded high. "Can't you hear it? It … sings."

I listened dutifully, and of course, heard nothing. "Chucha, let me touch it for a moment. I won't take it from you. I just wanna hear the singing."

She jerked her head up and glared at me.

"Honestly, it's really rude of you to go on about how wonderful it is and ask me why I can't feel or hear it, and then not let me feel or hear it."

She looked chagrined again. "Okay … but just one finger."

I leaned over the bar and ostentatiously placed my right index finger against the stick. She didn't make it any easier, still cradling it in her arm and holding it in a death grip with her other hand. The moment my finger connected,

I felt it, but it was very faint. The closest I could come to describing it would be if you were sitting on an inner tube in a river's eddy, and you pushed out into the center of the river. It felt—very faintly—like the main current of the river seizing you and moving you along. I felt more awake. More able. Yes, I'd definitely call that "power," no matter how faint it was.

I removed my finger, thoroughly creeped out. Once I detached from it, the current felt a bit … wrong … somehow. Or maybe just alien. It didn't feel like me. And I didn't know why, but the thing was affecting her much more strongly than me. Maybe it was prolonged exposure. Or maybe something about what she was responded more strongly to the stick. I wished I could test her power, see if it had actually made some sort of change.

"So, it just … gives you power? That's all it does? Are you sure?"

"Well," she said dreamily, "I ain't seen the instructions, so I don't know, but I can feel the power …"

I chuckled at her "instructions" line, but she didn't smile back. She was serious?

"Wait, Chucha, what do you mean by 'instructions'? Are there … actual instructions?"

She nodded, eyes closed again, clearly listening to the humming.

"Chucha … *where did he get the instructions from?*"

Her eyes opened again at the intensity in my voice. She looked puzzled. "He got 'em from Ayo, of course."

WTF?

At that moment I'd've been willing to bet my tail that Ayo'd had no idea what she was selling.

"Chucha, what do these instructions look like? A book? A scroll?"

"Oh! No, just a piece of paper. You know, like torn

out of a spiral notebook. College ruled. Written with pen, I think." More WTF??? did the macarena across the landscape of my mind.

"And what do they say?"

"Juice won't show them to anyone. Doesn't matter. I know what to do with it."

"How do you know what to do with it, Chucha?" I asked, trying to keep my creeped-out-ness out of my voice.

"It tells me. It tells me what I should do with it."

Holy Oktoberfest, that wasn't scary at all.

"Chucha, why don't you put it away for now? Tez will be here any minute." I didn't say that he might want to take it away from her—I didn't want to put ideas in her head—but she must have thought the same thing, because she put it obediently away. Instantly, she seemed soberer, although she still smiled that beatific smile, and still exuded a good mood.

We were silent for a while.

"So seriously, why do you hate your brother so much?" I asked.

"I don't *hate* him. I just can't live with him anymore. He's so uptight."

"Yeah, I guess he is a little. Can't really blame him. Responsible for three kids at the age of twenty-one."

"Yeah, and he totally holds that over our heads! Not that he ever says anything about it. He just gets this uptight look on his face whenever you don't do what he says and you know he's thinking about how he should be out partying and not taking care of us." The sudden bitterness startled me—almost as much as the admiration clearly mixed in with it. She and Tez were two of a kind, all right: their moods shifted just as fast, and were just as complex.

"He's never struck me as the partying type."

"Well … he used to be kinda rebellious and more laid back … when I was really little."

After a brief silence, I asked what I really wanted to know, "Why is your sibling called 'Pronk'?"

She laughed. "Ze saw a nature show on tv about springboks. You know, the African gazelle-type things that jump in the air? The jumping is called 'pronking.' Ze loooved them and ended up becoming obsessed with them. So when ze started changing form, ze turned into a springbok."

"Whoa, ze's a springbok? I thought ze was a deer!"

"Yeah, ze was always gonna be a deer. Actually, springboks aren't deer, they're bovidae, not cervidae. But close enough. I mean, magic doesn't really give a shit about taxonomy. Anyway, the type of animal is determined by when you're born. But to be able to change you have to kinda go on this vision-questy thing and find your tonal—like your spirit animal. And that gets very specific, you know. Like I can't turn into just any kind of dog. I'm a Doberman."

"Of course you are. Why not a pit bull?"

"Because they're ugly! Dobies are beautiful!"

Since she seemed so expansive, I asked her more about her siblings and she told me some stories. Like Manny, who was born to turn into a donkey, became a huge— "like, Budweiser Clydesdale size"—black-spotted white mule: something he'd seen in a fair in the Central Valley sometime. I didn't focus on Tez, but managed to get more dope on him than if I had. He turned into a black panther, actually, which she explained to me at some length was just a jaguar with very dark coloring, i.e. the spots were still there, you just couldn't see them.

"How about you?" she asked, finally. "You have any siblings? I mean, like foster siblings."

"No. I guess I was too much of a handful. My foster parents decided not to take on any others."

"And they never adopted you?"

"They did, of course. But I got into the habit of calling them my foster parents and it just stuck."

"How long were you with them?"

"From eight onwards. They adopted me officially when I was thirteen. It was kind of difficult, since my birth parents' rights never got terminated. Nobody ever found them."

"Wait, if you were in the system since you were a baby, how come you didn't get adopted right away?"

"Huh. Imagine you look in your cute little foster baby's crib and find a baby rhesus monkey."

"Whoa, really?"

"It kept happening. I'd just sort of turn into a monkey every once in a while, and the foster parents would return me to the system without telling anyone why. I'm pretty sure they all thought no one would believe them. Thank god, because if anyone had reported it, I'd probably still be living in some government 'hospital', getting experimented on." I shuddered at the thought, as I always did. Chucha shivered as well.

"I think I went through ten families by the time I turned 3, at which point I figured out how to control it ... to a certain extent. But after that, the mommies always asked me what I was being so secretive about—you know, you can trust me, and we love you, and we only want the best for you. So—three times, mind you—I eventually gave in and showed them. Finally, when I was eight, I realized I couldn't show anybody. Ever. And that's when I found a family that stuck."

"Are they ... good ones?"

"They were. My foster mom's dead. And my dad ...

They did their best. It wasn't their fault that I was totally fucked up by the time I got to them. They straightened me out a lot."

"I'm sorry—about your mom, I mean. How did she die, if you don't mind my asking?"

"Breast cancer."

"Really? My mom, too. God that really sucks. And your dad is still around?"

"Yeah." Yeah, I didn't want to talk about my dad. "If you don't mind my asking, how did your dad die?"

Her face got that tough look back on, the one I'd last seen at the gang HQ when she was still trying to intimidate me. "Oh, he was killed."

"Really? How?"

"Mission Mob."

"He was involved with gangs? As a nagual, you mean?" That shocked the look off her face for a moment.

"No! My dad would never—No. He was the nagual for the neighborhood, like Tez. No, the Mission Mob, they said this dude owed them some guap, and the dude came to my dad for help. So my dad tried to negotiate with them and they broke into our house and stole a bunch of our stuff. So when my dad went to ask for it back, they shot him." She looked blank.

"You remember this?"

"No! No, I was only one at the time. My Padrino— kinda like an uncle but not really..." I nodded. "He told me about it." She grinned suddenly. "But my mom was a total badass and got them to back off. Amo said she looked just like Wonder Woman back then. He'n't have to lift a finger to help. She did it all herself." Her eyes filled with stars.

"So ... your mom fought gangbangers, your dad was killed by them, and now you *are* one." I shook my head in demonstrative wonder. I just barely held myself back from wondering aloud what her parents would think of that if they knew. I suspected Tez had already hit that button and didn't want to break it.

I was rewarded by a brief, stricken look, followed by her hard face again.

"Anyway, I don't think Tez is coming and I gotta bounce," she said briskly.

I checked the clock. It was ten to seven. "Is this unusual?"

"Nah. It's part of what sucks about being a nagual. Probably some neighborhood emergency."

"Okay, I'll call Tez and make a new appointment. Give me your number."

She hesitated. "I'm in the middle of switching phones"—a lie, but whatever—"so give me yours and I'll call you."

I did, and even managed to get Juice's number from her (or so I thought; I tried it later and there was no answer and no voice mail, so I have no idea whose number it actually was.) She was all business, right up until she left two minutes later. Was it just me, or was she disappointed that Tez didn't show up? This might all work out better than I had thought.

CHAPTER THIRTEEN

Ayo arrived at seven on the dot, and seated herself on Chucha's recently vacated seat at the counter. I filled her in on Wayland's office, and she promised to ask about who might have any of Wayland's outstanding personal papers. I tried to persuade her to give me her contact with the werecats so I wouldn't have to keep going through her or wait for them to call me, but she said, "They're too old-fashioned," and left it at that. I assumed she meant you had to know them for years to have any of their trust, and, although I wasn't sure she was right, I had to trust her on this one.

"How's the Tez situation?" she asked,

"He didn't show up. Chucha said he'd probably had a neighborhood emergency. She didn't seem fazed."

Ayo nodded. "Did you ask her about that Huexotl?"

"Oh, not only that!" I told her about the instructions and she was thunderstruck.

"What do you think about that?" I prompted, after a

long, speechless moment.

She still didn't say anything. She had her "thinking furiously" look on. Then, without a word to me, she got up and headed for her office. Oh, no, she wasn't getting away with *that*.

I sped around her, invisibly, and appeared in front of her, a tactic I only used when I didn't mind irritating her. But she barely noticed, and simply tried to walk around me. I grabbed her by both shoulders and shook her until she focused on my face.

"Ayo, you *have* to tell me what's going on."

She shook her head, not in denial, but as if to clear it. "Mai, I have no idea what's going on. It's just, those ... 'instructions' did you call them? Yes, I got something in a flat envelope for Juice in trade for some ... stuff." She meant both stories and merman's penis; if it had just been the former, she'd have said so. "When was that? Maybe two or three weeks ago? Shit, my memory has gotten bad."

"But who did you get the envelope *from*?"

She looked at me in surprise. "That's the thing, Mai, I got it from Wayland."

I jumped up and down in place for a moment. "That's *it*, Ayo! That's the connection! So the shadow *is* going after supernats who are connected to the stick! I can't prove that Wayland had the stick before the San Antonios, but if he got the instructions for them—through you, of course—then it's reasonable to think he might have gotten the stick for them—more directly, of course. You'll have to find out who Wayland's next of kin, or any kind of assistant is, and maybe you can question them ..."

My mind began spinning again. I'd have to ask Juice where he got the stick from when I called him later. I put that on my to-do list. Tomorrow. I'd get in touch with Tez to rearrange a meeting, then I'd go to talk to Chucha.

"But what *is* this Huexotl?" Ayo asked, almost helplessly.

"Oh, I was just going to tell you ..." And I told her about Chucha holding the stick, and her strange reaction to it. She frowned furiously. Clearly, she liked it even less than I had. "Ayo, I got a really bad feeling about it. Do you think the stick is ... I dunno ..."

"Evil?" She asked. Her tone told me a lot.

"Yeah, I know, I know, there's no good magic and evil magic, no good creatures and evil creatures, just what we do with them."

"Exactly," she said, satisfied teacher all over.

"But I didn't like what the stick did to her."

"Well," she admitted, "I'm not liking what you're telling me, either. But it does explain why a named walking stick might be worth killing over. I mean, if it makes you *feel* good, as well as giving you power ..."

"Yeah, I know. Like a drug."

"Exactly."

We both thought for a few moments.

"Huexotl ..." Ayo said. "I thought it might be Indigenous. I've been asking local Ohlone to no avail ... But ... 'Huexotl' is Nahuatl and I thought it was just an affectation by a Chicano gang ... But maybe the name goes back farther than that. I mean, Chucha *is* a nagual. Maybe she's more susceptible to its power because she comes from the same cultural realm. ... How long have they had it, did you say?"

I told her.

"A lone werewolf, eh? Justin? He came through here. Damn. *I* was the one who referred him to the San Antonios."

"*What?*"

She sighed. "The kid had done some bad things, Mai. He was being hunted and came to me looking for a way out of the Bay Area. I didn't want to put him on a ship or a bus with a bunch of humans." No, I could see why not. An uncontrolled and already blooded werewolf trapped in a tin can with a bunch of helpless humans? Nope. Double nope. "I thought maybe running around with a gang would drain some of his energy. Maybe they could find a safer way to get him out of the country. It's not like a werewolf is any deadlier than an AK. And I couldn't just give him up to be killed."

No, she couldn't. If he'd killed, even without intending to, the local pack would be after him. Sometimes, having human morals and ethics was a huge burden.

"He was killed." I told her. "They didn't see by whom, but I'm thinking it was probably the same shadow creature. They ran in after he was dead, but before the killer could locate the stick."

"And the body?"

"Dumped. Chucha wouldn't say where. If you wanna know, ask Juice."

She sighed, heavily. "Well. I suppose that was a nearly inevitable end for that kid. Poor little lobo. He was turned against his will, you know." She sighed again.

She was about to say something else, when the front door opened and she looked up. A man walked in, middle-aged and stocky. He looked familiar. His wide face was a warm medium brown, with a dramatic nose that made him look ... got it! He was the guy I'd seen in Ayo's car the night I found the weretiger. The guy who wanted a Merman's penis. My inner (and possibly outer) eyebrows went up.

He looked around, saw her and nodded. She nodded back and got up.

"I don't need to tell you to keep an eye on Chucha," she said.

"Is there a job for me there?" I asked, tipping a chin at the man.

She rolled her eyes. "Too close-mouthed. I bet he's got stories though ..." she looked greedy for a moment. "He's looking for a paper document, but absolutely refuses to tell me what's on it."

"A piece of paper? You mean, like a scroll or a parchment?" My hairs went on end, but I wouldn't assume. Scrolls and parchments were fairly common commodities in magic-users' lives.

"College ruled, single sheet, paper. I'm about to tell him to go away, so don't worry about it."

My whole body went all over needles and pins.

"Ayo," I said, pawing at her arm nervelessly. "Ayo, Chucha said the instructions were on a piece of paper ripped out of a spiral notebook. College ruled."

Her eyes narrowed and she lasered in on the man. "Play it cool, Maya. Leave it to me."

She led him into her office.

I watched them do it and felt a yearning ... to go into her office, and the room behind it— but that thought was snapped off at its root as the door shut. And all that was left was my curiosity and titillation and frustration, and her closed office door.

They stayed in there longer than I expected, and he didn't leave looking as frustrated as I felt after Ayo came back out and told me he'd bound her to secrecy.

"Well, what *can* you tell me?" I cried. "Ayo, if this were just my idle curiosity—"

"I'd say I know something, but not anything that can help you with what you fundamentally want to know. I don't think the part he wants kept secret has any bearing on … any of this. I don't know any more about the Huexotl. I don't know if he knows about It. And I don't know what the instructions say. I don't even know if *he* knows what the instructions say, only that he wants the paper. That's all. I'd also say you *know* when you're on the right track and you need to follow your gut." And she went back into her office, looking as if she needed to shut herself away from her desire to tell me all.

She reopened the door again a second later. "But keep away from that damned stick, Maya, and warn Chucha again. I don't know about the Huexotl, but that shadow creature is bad news." And she shut the door again.

Damn Ayo's ethics! Seemed I was always waiting on her for something. But if I saw that mystery dude again, I wasn't letting him get away until I found out what he knew.

CHAPTER FOURTEEN

TUESDAY, OCTOBER 18, 2011
PETGLOBE; OGAWA/GRANT PLAZA;
SANC-AHH CAFÉ, OAKLAND

I GOT UP early Tuesday morning to head down to Oakland Chinatown, where I stuck my head into the Formosa Herbal Co.'s warehouse in case Dalisay had more than one source for blood plasma (they were in competition with Bountiful Trading Co. because more than just traditional Chinese medicine was being "traded.") But nobody seemed to know anything, and no one recognized Dalisay's picture, either. Oh well, it was a Hail Mary pass at best.

I had the day off but had to work in the evening. I was itching to go back into the city and dig up something at the werecat association ... or do ... *something*. But I couldn't think of what, and the stress was giving me a headache. Maybe a break would help. Maybe I should head for Occupy and live in stinky utopia for a while ...

But I decided to treat myself first. I ran as a large pit bull trailing a leash (the pittie kept people from approaching me, and the leash from calling animal control) up the fifteen blocks into the parking lot of Pet Globe, a ginormous pet food supermarket that had a specialty organic section frequented by humans who loved their puppies and kitties waaaaaay too much.

Inside the store, and back in human form, I headed back to where my favorite cat treats were kept. (I'm usually a fruit-snack gal, but a qori ismaris who tried to date me—he was cute, but I just can't with hyenas; that *laugh*!—introduced me to cat treats and I'd been hooked ever since.) The aisles in this store went all the way up to the ceiling, it seemed, so I didn't see Chucha until I turned the corner and came face to face with her.

"Maya!" she cried, looking shocked and guilty. I looked at her hands. She was clutching five bags of Critterganic cat treats, my favorite. Oho!

"*Cat* treats, Chucha? What does that say about your big bad doggie self?"

Her lower lip pushed out. "Cat treats taste better than dog treats! They're richer and have less filler!" She looked suddenly embarrassed. "I mean, I … read that somewhere. Better for your … cats."

She knew I wasn't buying it. I let her dangle in my pitiless gaze for a couple more seconds, and then laughed and smacked her shoulder.

"Dude. Why do you think *I'm* here?"

"I thought you were following me."

I raised my eyebrows. "You really don't have a very high opinion of your brother, do you? No, I'm here for the"—and I plucked two bags out of her hands—"Critterganics."

"You eat those too?" I raised my eyebrows. "… Orrr, wait, do you have a cat? 'Cause I have a cat."

I laughed. "You *so* do not have a cat, and neither do I. These are my favorites." I tore a bag open and stuck a treat in my mouth. Then I offered it to her. She watched suspiciously as I chewed and swallowed the treat, then tentatively took one. Then I took one. Then she took another one. Pretty soon we had killed half the bag.

"Maybe we should buy these first," I suggested, eyes still locked.

And just like that, we went from a chance meeting in a store, to two people being in the store together. We paid together, and left together.

"So," Chucha said outside, "you going to work?"

"Nah," I said. "This is my day off. I don't have to be at work until evening. I was thinking of spending the day hanging out at the encampment. You wanna come?"

"What's this 'encampment'?"

I stared at her. "The Occupy Oakland encampment?"

She shrugged. "I don't know that."

"Haven't you heard about Occupy Wall Street?"

"Sure. Those white hippies pissed about being suddenly broke camping out where that bronze bull is."

That gave me pause, although the description was close enough. "Well, it's in Oakland now, since last week. They're occupying Ogawa Plaza—they renamed it 'Oscar Grant Plaza'."

"And you're involved with this? I didn't know you were a hippie!"

"I'm an activist—actually, there are a lot of people of color involved here in Oakland, and we're trying to get it renamed 'Decolonize Oakland' rather than 'Occupy,' because of the bad history of occupation."

She shrugged. "Okay. ... So, how are we gonna get there?"

"I usually run as a dog. Let's do that."

"Oh ... uh ... I can't just change like that ... can you?"

I turned into my usual pit-bull-with-leash to show her, then back.

"Fuckin A! I can't do that! God, I wish I could."

"I thought you could—"

"No, not during the day, and there's this whole … No I can't. So how are we gonna do this if you're a dog and I'm not?"

"Oh," I said slyly. "I don't have to go as a *dog*!"

Fifteen minutes later Chucha slid awkwardly, breathlessly out of my saddle in a little parking lot a block away from the plaza. She'd shrieked and laughed like a small child all the way—and bounced around like a sack of potatoes. I neighed at her for effect and blew a bit of spittle into her ear. She shrieked again and then collapsed into giggles.

I changed back before anyone wandered by.

"That. Was. Bomb!" Chucha cried. "You should do that *all the time*. You should, like, charge money."

I held out my hand and waggled my fingers at her.

"Oh," she said, and took my bag of cat treats out of her backpack, where I got a glimpse of the stick. Still with her, even on her day off. It made me glad we'd be together today; if attacked, surely the two of us would be too much for that shadow …? Then I shuddered, as I did involuntarily every time I thought of the shadow-thing.

I led her down across the street and down the sidewalk to the plaza, where we were greeted with the sound of recorded music and the murmur, and musky, sour-meat smell of a couple hundred people hanging out for a full week without showers.

I introduced Chucha to a few people, and after a while we gravitated towards Children's Village.

"I wanna help out here for a while," she said.

"I didn't know you liked kids."

"Well, I don't really. They're just … they're just really …"

"Refreshingly direct?"

"And straight up, yeah." She shook her head, and I was reminded that the reasons I liked working with kids were probably similar to hers, although my ability to read bullshit came from a slightly different source.

"Well," I said, "not necessarily *honest*, but definitely transparent liars."

We both laughed and I decided to volunteer my services as well. I hadn't signed up for anything today, wanting to keep the day open, so we spelled the current volunteers. Chucha proved talented at coming up with ideas to keep munchkins busy, and we played a few games before settling down to a series of drawing challenges. Turned out, Chucha could draw as well. She helped out one whiny kid with a drawing of a dragon, and pretty soon all the kids insisted on her drawing a dragon—or a giant snake, or a vampire—on their papers, too.

As afternoon deepened, I could see her patience starting to flag. This was why I, too, hadn't made a career out of working with kids. I enjoyed them ... until I didn't. And I wondered if this was a common shapeshifter affliction. Other volunteers had joined us, so we could leave whenever we wanted to.

Chucha came with me readily when I crinkled my Petglobe bag and suggested we find a place to hang out and eat.

"Do you mind?" I asked, gesturing at the steps that led up to the greenspace where the encampment was.

"What? You mean the sun? No. What about you? You're hella light-skinned. Don't you burn?"

"No, actually. It's a monkey perk," I said with my mouth full. "Monkeys don't sunburn."

"Really? That's actually kinda dope."

The sun was shining through shredded, patchy clouds; it was the kind of cool, bright day the Bay Area was famous for, year round. I relaxed into the space, and the moment. The encampment—the movement—moved me because I'd been feeling an aspect of the personality of the Bay strongly here. Even though we were in the heart of Oakland, it was the same personality, the same Bay that I felt from the rooftops of Chinatown, or from the peak of Dolores Park, or from the beach on Alameda. Only, in gritty Oakland, what I felt was less the bright invitation of the San Francisco view, and more a visceral anger, as bright and clear as the sunlight streaming through the square. But it was also the promise of a cleansing fire.

I could see Chucha breathing it in, taking it on, too. It was a light and energy that relaxed as much as it electrified. We talked about Chucha's childhood and her neighborhood, her school and her family, my education, and the magazine. I could feel a tension I didn't know I'd been carrying leave my shoulders and chest.

"Much respect," Chucha said, "like, y'all just decided to do something like that, and then did it. I would have no idea how to start a magazine. But I guess that's the kind of thing you learn in college." She shook her head with the admiration of someone completely unthreatened by your accomplishments—because they were so far out of reach she'd never imagine wanting them.

"Not really. We had no idea how to start a magazine, either, but because there were a bunch of us, we felt comfortable just doing it. We basically learned by doing, and by making a shit-ton of mistakes. ... But it's true, in college there are a lot of opportunities to get together with other people and learn shit by being stupid. It gives you the confidence to do stuff you don't know how to do."

Chucha looked thoughtful. "Well, I'm glad I didn't have to go."

"Why?"

She shrugged, but then seemed to really think about it. "Well ... I guess it's not so much the schoolwork. I'm okay with that and there's stuff I'd like to learn more about, although I can learn just fine from the library. ... I guess it's more the kind of people who go to college. I can't stand them. You know, the douchebags, who think they know everything and act all better than you. I wouldn't want to spend four years being around people like that."

"People like this?" I asked, gesturing around us. She turned around in her seat to face the encampment.

"Well, I mean, I wouldn't want to spend four years around a bunch of hippies, either."

"People like me?"

She looked startled. "Well, no, but, I mean, you did stuff before you went to college. You know how things are."

"Yeah," I said. "I know how things are. And after a year and a half of learning 'how things are,' I couldn't get to college fast enough. You know, a lot of the people here come from low income backgrounds, and *they* are deeply into debt going to college. That's what a lot of them are protesting, not the going to college part, but the deeply in debt part. But they go anyway. Because 'how things are' *sucks*, Chucha. College gives you a little more power to make the life you want. Maybe not much, but enough to get started with."

"Says the barista."

"Come on, Chucha. I think you must be aware by now that the cafe is the less interesting half of what I do for Ayo— "

"Yeah, taking shit jobs on the side, like talking to me."

"That's not a shit job!" I cried, just arguing, but her eyes widened when I said it. "I got to meet you, which is excellent. I never get to meet anybody who's like me, but you kind of are."

This was true. She looked down, half-smiling, half-grimacing.

"And now your brother owes me a favor, and I don't know if you've noticed, but he is *smoking* hot."

She laughed "Ewwwwww! Whatever! But straight up, how much college education do you need to talk to an 'estranged' sister?" She said "estranged" with a bit of a faux French accent, mispronouncing it the way people do who get their vocabulary from reading, not hearing, it.

"Well, I need street skills and supernat abilities, sure, but I'm actually doing a lot of investigation and research for Ayo as well." My skin and heart warmed at the thought of "research" and I thought of the door in Ayo's office that looked like it enclosed a closet before something slammed the door on that thought. "I'm part art historian, part folklorist, part curator, part travel agent, part administrator, part forensic accountant, part private eye, part hacker ... and that doesn't even cover all of it. I use something I learned in college pretty much every day, and it's always something weird and random that I never would have thought was applicable."

I paused, waiting for pushback. I didn't get it. She was looking intently at the ground, a slash of lawn golden with—and her face and arms spotted by—sunlight now coming down on us through the leaves of a tree.

"You're 'the woman clothed in sun!'" I said, on an impulse, not knowing I was going to.

"Huh?"

"Oh... it's from this poem by Barbara Jane Reyes. From *Poeta en San Francisco*... it's about the Bay and... other things. There's a, sort of... prophecy?... in this one part, and a woman clothed in sun, like you, right now, with the sunlight."

I pointed. She turned a hand and looked at the sun dapples on her skin.

"How's it go?" she asked.

"Um, well, this piece starts:

dear love, we make plans, and we rescind. stars fall as figs in the wind."

As if called up, a wind whirled up inside me, from the base of my gut to my ears. My words slowed, and drew weight, from the conversational to the declamatory. As if the wind were speaking through me.

"call to the mountains, four winds held by angels. call to land and sea, so let it be. praise be to blood of lambs, tearless, opening silence in heaven. offer hands of fire to bitter rivers. eagles lament locusts with human faces, lions' teeth, sulfur breastplates, scorpion tails."

The wind paused, and I watched Chucha. Her eyes were closed and her breathing was speeding up with the tumbling images. I remembered that her older brother was a poet. She must have grown up going to poetry readings. The wind spoke again:

"dear love, abysmal angel, for sightless idols robed in cloud. even prophets' words can sour. great city streets lined by the fallen for all to gaze upon before breath collapses, glorifies. the woman clothed in sun births a serpent's feast. earth opens its mouth to swallow the serpent's river. miracles and signs, boombox and bling bling."

My diaphragm seized a deep breath.

"dear love, this calls for wisdom."

She had stopped breathing entirely. She held her silence for a moment after I ended. She opened her eyes on the sea of tents, and turned them to what I realized was my also sun-wreathed face. An utterly sweet and perfect smile dawned: the dream of a little sister you never had. I thought that maybe Tez was not only worried but also jealous; jealous of the San Antonios and their access to that smile.

"Lemme guess," she said, chuckling. "You learned that one in college."

I laughed with her, and we sat together at the camp's edge for the rest of the afternoon.

* * *

THE GOLDEN AFTERNOON feeling carried me through most of the evening, which was a quiet one in the cafe. Tez swept in unexpectedly around nine, but I didn't feel surprised; why wouldn't I see everyone I wanted to see on such a perfect day?

"Maya—" he said, looking tense.

"Teeeezzzzz," I drawled back, smiling and feeling beatific.

"You're in a good mood," he said, smiling uncertainly.

I pulled a bag of Critterganics out of my purse under the counter and offered it to him. "Have some! I ran into Chucha at PetGlobe. We agreed that beef and salmon are the best, but they were all out." He helped himself to a handful and I grabbed a couple, too, before putting them away.

"Hey, I'm sorry about missing our appointment. There was an emergency … this guy—anyway, I couldn't come or call just then."

"It's fine, Tez. That's what we figured happened. Chucha wasn't upset. She knows how these things go with people like you guys."

"People like us guys?" he asked incredulously.

"You know," I leaned in, "naguals." He relaxed. What had he thought I meant? "You two are like mini-Ayos."

"She's a mini-thug."

"Well, she's not mini-you, that's for sure. But you might have a little more respect for what she does. The San Antonios sure do."

"They should. She's about fifty times as smart as any of them, not that you'd know it from how she's behaving now—"

"Hey, do you know what time it is?"

"Uh ..." he scrambled for his phone.

I leaned in. "It's time for you to lay off Chucha."

He stopped fumbling and dropped his chin to glare at me.

"I'm serious. It doesn't help, and it's actually hurting. Stop it. You need to treat her like an adult, no matter how little girly she acts sometimes. She's making adult decisions, so you really don't have any choice in the matter."

He blew out some air. "Whatever," he said, which sounded ... vaguely ambivalent. Maybe he was listening. "Look, I never got your phone number so why don't we trade, and then you can set up another appointment for us, okay? Here is fine. I'm open any day this week."

Well, I'd've preferred he ask for my phone number for more ambiguous reasons, but I'd take it. "Gimme yours," I said, and typed it into my phone. I called him, then sneakily snapped a pic of him while he was distracted. He was hottest when he was frowning a little in concentration.

"Hey," he said, "let me see that." I showed him. "Ugh, take another. At least give me a chance to smile."

I held up my camera for him to mug at. "Say 'shit-eating grin'," I said.

"'Unnecessary selfie'!" he said, with his teeth bared. I showed him the pic. He groaned and I held up my phone again.

"Try actually smiling this time." He gave me a baleful look and I snapped that.

"Stop it!" he cried. "Wait, wait!" as I snapped again twice. He sighed in exaggerated distress. I snapped another. "Okay, okay ... how's this?"

I ended up attaching a very cheesy grin to his contact profile. But seeing him grin like that whenever he called wasn't a bad thing. Not at all. Nor were all the photos I had just taken of him: frowning, teeth bared, groaning, baleful, distressed ... Too bad his shirt was on.

"I'm giving you 'Eye of the Tiger' as your ringtone," I said, searching for it.

"Um ... why do you even *have* an 'Eye of the Tiger' ringtone?"

" ... You just don't know. I've been waiting for *years* to meet someone whose ringtone was appropriately 'Eye of the Tiger'."

He sighed heavily.

"Just a man and his will to survive," I agreed.

"Now you," he said. "I know better than to risk my ass taking a bad pic of a chick, so go ahead, arrange yourself."

"'Arrange myself'? '*Chick*'?"

He chuckled as he snapped the picture.

"Wait! I wasn't ready!"

"Payback's a bitch, chula." He showed me the pic. I had a horrible, snarly look on my face. He chuckled again. "Smokin'."

"You have to take another one!"

"Nope. Nope. This is the one." He hit 'save' and pocketed the phone.

"Fine, if you want me glaring at you every time I call …" I wiped the perfectly clean counter.

"As long as you call …"

I looked at him, startled, and he winked.

"Gotta bounce," he said, and did.

CHAPTER FIFTEEN

Tuesday, October 18, 2011
San Antonios' HQ, Oakland

CHUCHA DIDN'T CALL that night—why would she? I'd just seen her that day—and I wanted to move things along while she was still liking me and vulnerable to my ... er ... persuasions, so I headed over to the San Antonios' house after closing. I only saw one window lighted, but I thought Chucha might be taking a nighttime security shift. I'd chance it.

Just as I was turning off the sidewalk towards the house, I saw a shadow appear to my right. It seemed to materialize in the vacant lot next to the house and to see me an instant after I saw it. It paused, facing me without a face, and then floated away, fast. I hesitated for a moment, caught by that now-familiar reluctance, then took off down the street after it, changing into dog form as I went.

It seemed to notice me following, crossed the street double-time, and then faded through a cinder block fence. I switched quickly to monkey and went up over the fence and into a tree. The yard before me was paved except where four or five trees were planted. I stopped in the first tree, looking around. The shadows beneath me moved with the slow swaying of branches adjusting to my weight, but there was no other movement. I talked myself out of cowardice, then swung down and waded, hands and feet, through the yard, swinging out in every direction, hoping to hit something that shouldn't've been there. But there was nothing.

Finally, I gave up. If it was still here, it wasn't going to move until I left. And it might be gone already.

I dropped down to the street, changed, and crossed back over to the San Antonios' HQ, which, in the past 20 minutes or so, had lighted up like a Christmas tree.

There was no doorbell, but a cute little brass knocker in the shape of a Chihuahua. As I knocked, I heard a commotion behind the door. I had to knock several times, and finally, feeling strangely desperate, bang on the door with my fist.

The dude named Beto yanked the door open. He gaped at me.

"You!" he shouted.

I was so shocked that when he grabbed me and yanked me inside, I didn't resist.

"Juice!" he cried. "Juice! I got her! It's that crazy bitch who came for her the other night! I got her!"

Inside was pandemonium. Four dudes were coming into the hallway shoving magazines into pistols and yelling "Fuck! Fuck!" and other such imprecations. Two other dudes were carrying an unconscious third from the hallway into the dining room, and one of the carriers was bawling like a baby. In another room I could hear Juice ripping a chunk off of one of his men, who, presumably, was the one yelling back "It was that shadow thing! I swear to god!" In the living room another guy I'd never seen before was yelling something about "Fuckin' 70s bitches" into his phone.

"Juice!" Beto screamed. "I got 'er! Juice!" I had no idea what was going on, and was too confused to decide on any course of action. Beto hollered a few more times before his voice cut through the noise and Juice joined the circus in the hallway.

"WHAT?" Juice screamed at him. The dude looked seriously awry. He had bedhead up one side and down the other, his t-shirt was on backwards with the tag sticking out, and his handsome, confident face was half-snarling, half-shocked.

The hallway went quiet. Beto stared at Juice for a moment, and I realized that he was in shock, too. Beto lifted the handful of my t-shirt he had hold of, like he was lifting a bag of burgers. "I got 'er, man. She was just outside."

Everyone looked at me. Suddenly, my confusion turned to dread.

"What happened?" I asked. It came out in a whisper.

Beto looked at me, bewildered.

"They got Chucha," Juice said. "She's dead."

Then I understood the scene. The unconscious guy they'd been carrying hadn't been unconscious, or a guy. I pulled away from Beto, pushed past the phone guy, and went into the dining room. One dude was leaning against the wall, his foot up, hands rubbing his face, like he was tired; the other was sitting in a chair head in hands, still sobbing. Juice came in behind me, and the rest gathered in the two doorways. I looked around at all of them in turn, trying to find a reason not to look at the body on the table, but they were all just looking back at me, like I could contribute something of value.

She didn't look like anything in particular. She looked like Chucha; she looked dead. There was none of the soft light of the sleeper in her face. It was all gone. She was all gone.

"Oh God, I'm gonna have to tell Tez I got his baby sister killed," I cried before I could stop myself.

Juice took my upper arm, hard. "What do you mean?" he asked urgently. "How did you get her killed?"

I looked at him and my face felt fevered. "I was supposed to get her out of here. I was supposed to get her to go home."

His face fell, and his hand loosened. The sobbing boy on the chair looked up. "I wish you did," the boy said. "She shouldn't'a been here."

"It shouldn't'a gone down like this," Juice said. "And we're gonna make 'em pay."

I saw an image of a funeral in my head. "We have to call the cops."

Juice stepped back. "No way. This is magic stuff."

"Chucha's human … as far as they know. She has records. She went to school."

"No way. There's no way we can explain this shit."

"She has a family. They'll want to bury her. They can't do that without a death certificate, and that means cops."

Juice just shook his head, but the sobbing boy stopped sobbing for a moment. "Juice, she deserves a decent burial," he said, his face tracked over with tears. Juice stared at him. "Come on. We owe her that, man. She was our nagual."

Juice was silent. The sobbing boy looked around. There was a murmur and Beto spoke up. "He's right, man. We gotta let 'em bury her."

"They'll blame us for her murder," Juice said.

I looked at her again. "How did she die? I don't see

any blood."

The no-longer-sobbing-boy spoke up: "There wasn't any. No sign of trauma, either." I did a double take at him. No sign of trauma? He watched too much *CSI*, apparently.

"It's just like with Bu Bu," Beto said.

Another dude spoke up. "It's like I told you man. It was that shadow thing she saw. I saw it too." Another murmur went up.

"So did I," I said. Everyone looked at me. "Just now. I saw it … float … out of the yard as I walked up. I followed it across the street, but it disappeared. I looked around for a while but …" I shrugged.

"See?" the dude said, growing excited. "It's just like I said. It was that shadow thing. It took her soul!" The boys started talking amongst themselves and the noise grew. Some were arguing, but it looked like the number of gangbangers in this household who believed was growing.

"So maybe we should call Ayo," Juice said.

"No, not yet," I said. "If you call her in on this now, it'll delay us even more, and make it even harder to turn it over to the authorities." Which was true, but really I just didn't want Ayo taking over. Chucha wasn't … hers. I didn't need Ayo to examine her; I already knew what she would find. And I didn't want her looking at Chucha like she did Bu Bu. Not now. Not yet. "You gotta decide: is this a human thing or a supernat thing? If you want to bury Chucha properly, it has to be a human thing, and you gotta call the cops."

Juice seemed to really be considering this. Opinions were starting to really fly in the room as the guys argued with one another. And Juice seemed perfectly comfortable standing and thinking, at length, in front of everyone.

"Okay," Juice said, finally, and the noise diminished. He pointed at two guys. "Get her into the car and be careful with her. Beto, just take her to emergency. You guys were on a pizza run. That's all." They all nodded. Juice took a step toward the kitchen.

"Wait. What about Tez?" I asked, before he could go. Tez needed to be informed, now, and he would want to be involved. He would never forgive me if I kept him from this. "He'll want to see her, want to see what happened here. He can definitely help you guys figure out who did this. He's as powerful as she ... was. More."

"We know who did it," Juice said, looking stubborn.

"Who?" I asked.

Juice set his jaw, but the voluble Sobbing Boy answered me "It was 70s Arroyo. They been after the Huexotl. They got it." Juice took two steps and smacked him on the side of the head. "Shut your mouth," he snarled. He looked around the room. "Nobody talks about the Huexotl. Got it?" General nods. He looked at me. "That means you too."

"You ain't the boss of me—" his chin went up, "but I got no reason to advertise this around." He frowned at me, but said nothing. "Now, you say the 70s killed Chucha and took the stick, but if it was them, they did it through this shadow thing. Maybe they have the stick, maybe they don't, but you gotta find the shadow thing, and for that, you need a good nose. Literally. And the only one I can think of who would be willing to lend his nose to you for this purpose is Tez." I looked at him slyly. "Unless you have another line on a werewolf after you got the first one killed."

"What about you?" he asked cooly.

"What *about* me?" I said, lowering my head and my voice. He didn't take the warning. And he was right about me. I could easily have taken another shape, one with a good nose, and gotten everything there was to get from the crime scene myself. But long experience told me to keep what I was from guys like this, and I wasn't switching policy now.

"You somethin'... 'woo woo', too, ain'tcha?"

I lowered my voice even more and looked at him through my eyebrows. "Don't you worry yourself about me, little alpha. Worry about your own problems. You gonna let Tez in on this, or not?"

We played eye-chicken for a long moment, then he pointed at me with his chin. "Call 'im. But tell 'im he's got safe passage for this only. Don't tell him about the Huexotl. And when that shadow thing is found, It comes back to me."

CHAPTER SIXTEEN

THAT LEFT US with at least half an hour to wait for Tez to arrive. Most of the guys seemed to get creeped out by Chucha's body, so they left the dining room to have a council of war in the kitchen. The Sobbing Boy—now quiet—stayed with me.

I wondered if my announcement to Tez on the phone had been too abrupt. There was a reason people beat around the bush when giving bad news, wasn't there? I'd always hated that, hated the way the doctors had thrown piles of words at me before telling me that Mom was going to die, was dying, was dead. So I hadn't prepared him much—just: "Tez, something awful has happened." And then "Chucha is dead." Everything after that was just the logistics of getting him here quickly. Maybe that wasn't enough. Maybe I should've called Ayo and had her break it to him. But no, Ayo didn't care— at least, not the way I did. Ayo wasn't a—

Wasn't a what? A friend? And what was I? Tez's

stalker? Ayo wasn't Tez's stalker? Could I claim to be Chucha's friend when I had only met her ... four days ago? When I'd only met Tez himself—officially—a week ago? Could I claim to be his friend? Anymore, I mean, now that Chucha was dead?

Oh. My. God. Was that all I was worried about? That some cute guy wouldn't pay attention to me because he'd just lost his baby sister? Jesus, what was wrong with me? I needed to stop thinking ...

Sobbing Boy's after-sobbing hiccups had evened out to normal breathing. He couldn't have been more than fourteen years old, this kid, grown suddenly tall and skinny and looking as if his fashionably sagging pants were a genuine hand-me-down accident. He was going to be good looking, but hadn't quite figured it out yet.

"What's your name?" I asked.

"Jimmy. You?"

"Maya."

"Why you even here, Maya?"

"Chucha had a fight with her older brother; that's why she came here. And he hired us—Ayo and me—to talk her into coming home."

"Oh," he said, as if he understood something deeply. "I didn't know she had beef with her brother."

"You know something about pain-in-the-ass older brothers?" I asked, half-smiling in invitation.

"Well, you saw the way he is with me. Always smacking me around." He looked discontentedly at his hands. Smacking him around—Juice? Juice was his brother? I looked more closely at him. Yeah ... yep, I could definitely see it.

"She was really nice, you know? Not like most of the bitches come around just to get sexed up, think they so bad. Or tease me for being little." He hadn't quite caught up to the fact of his recent growth, apparently. I suspected there was more eyeing and less condescension these days. But his sexual resentment was something I was used to from my days with the Celestials—and had no time for.

"Maybe if you don't act like they only exist to have sex with you."

"That's what she said," he pointed at her with his chin.

I turned to look at her, for a moment thinking that she was there, ready to back me up in this argument. Then I saw her hand dangling limply over the edge of the table, drained of all her quivering, rubber-taut energy, and tears sprang to my eyes. She was never going to grow into a true badass, never figure out that Juice wasn't the answer, never going to see if Jimmy beat the odds and developed respect for women, never getting the chance to teach him respect.

Juice called to Jimmy from the kitchen and he lurched off.

I forced myself to look at Chucha—at her body, knowing I was going to have to when Tez came. I needed to be ... useful ... to him. I needed to be of help to him, because god knows he was going to have trouble with this. I got up and walked over to the table and forced myself to look down at her, all of her, to scan her body for evidence, but somehow I couldn't quite see the whole, couldn't quite take it in.

I scarcely noticed when Jimmy came back in.

"Don't worry," he said. "I'll get the little bitch that did this."

I looked over at him and my vision cleared again. "It was a supernat, Jimmy. You're not equipped."

His face was the clouded sky on a windy day. "Not that shadow thing," he said. "The bitches who ordered the hit. We're gonna get 'em, tonight. We're heading out as soon as Tez gets here."

He shouldn't've been telling me about any of it. I knew the rules as well as anyone. He shouldn't've been crying earlier, either. Even little ones, seven or eight years old, get smacked when they cry. His mouth was twitching between what might be a smile or a grimace, and an attempted snarl. He looked proud one second, and terrified the next. Juice must've been coddling him, but after his sobfest earlier, I guessed that Jimmy was finally going to be forced to toughen up.

"Don't go, Jimmy," I said impulsively.

He looked at me like I was stupid, then shrugged. "We can't let them get away with that." He nodded to Chucha again and walked out.

He'd been checking in with me. Somehow, in the past half hour or so, I'd become someone he checked in with. I knew why; knew whom I was replacing.

I turned to go after him, but Tez walked in. I hadn't heard the door.

Tez didn't look at me, acted like he didn't even see me. Where I couldn't quite look at Chucha, he couldn't look at anything else. He looked like himself, but ... blank.

"I want to know all of it," he said. Was there a slight faintness to his voice?

I didn't speak right away. I hadn't told him anything about the stick or the shadow creature; not because I was being careful but because both of us had been focusing on him and Chucha. What should I tell him, and what shouldn't I?

"*All* of it," he said, more firmly. His voice jolted my brain into action, and all at once, I gave it over. This was his business, not mine. I moved around the table to his side, so I could speak quietly. I told him everything in chronological order: about the San Antonios getting the stick somewhere, about Justin and Bu Bu, both killed guarding it, about my encounter with the shadow in front of La Peña, about Chucha finally being tasked with guarding the thing and how it affected her, about pursuing the shadow tonight, and then coming in to find her dead.

"Juice is very touchy about the stick, though, so you'd better act like I didn't tell you about it. You don't want beef with him."

He nodded, just as Juice came in. They didn't quite look at each other.

Tez looked at me. Right. I was still go-between. "Juice," I said in my most respectful voice, "Tez would like to know how his sister died."

Juice complied, looking at me as he talked, but clearly talking to Tez. "They got her outside somehow. I dunno. Everybody was asleep but Chucha was on watch in the back, Beto in the front. He saw her step out the back door and then heard her open the backyard gate. So he waited for five minutes or so, then he went out back to see what was up. He found her under the tree next door and called for help, and then he saw some guys running off down the street and definitely recognized one of them as this 70s dude from Arroyo Park." I filled in the blanks: Beto had seen the guys running away with the stick. "So we brought her inside. Creeper was asleep in his room, but he swears he looked out and saw that shadow thing floating away."

"I saw it, too," I said. "I didn't see the 70s guys, but I wasn't looking." I looked at Tez. "So I can't confirm that the other guys were there or had anything to do with her death. The Shadow was alone the other two times I saw it."

"So," said Juice, after a moment. "We cool? Can we get her off to the hospital now? We can't wait much longer ..."

Tez looked down at Chucha again blankly. He reached out and tried stroking her hair, but then withdrew his hand again immediately, as if burned.

"You'll see her again soon," Juice said, then bit his lip and looked as if he regretted speaking.

Tez stepped back and nodded, still looking down. Two guys stepped forward and picked her up carefully, following Beto out of the dining room. Juice waited until they'd cleared the hallway and gone out the front door, then waved Tez and me to follow him.

He led us out the back through the yard into the lot next door, with a couple of his guys following, probably equally out of caution and curiosity. We halted under a tree.

"Beto found her here," Juice said.

Tez crouched on the ground. I noted, half blankly, half sensually, that he could squat with his feet flat on the ground. He lifted his upper lip and sucked air in through his teeth. He closed his eyes and did it again.

"What's he doing?" Juice asked in a whisper you could have heard a mile away.

"He's flehming," I said, as much to myself as to them. "Smelling through his mouth. It's an animal thing. Humans don't do it."

"Shut up," Tez said, and everyone did.

Tez's order didn't just shut my mouth. It also shut off the hamster wheel inside my head. My brain went quiet and just watched him as he samurai-walked around the crime scene, drawing in the air at about crotch-height and again at ground height. It was weird, but also weirdly graceful. Jesus, could I maybe shut off my libido at a time like this? I've never much been one for shame; it's my animal nature, I think that simply doesn't understand shame. But I felt ashamed tonight, every time I thought something sensual about Tez. The poor guy had just lost his sister, and I was throwing pheromones at him.

That thought distracted me while Tez finished his examination, ranging in circles around the spot under the tree until he reached the far side of the lot where the gangbangers had presumably run off.

"Anything?" I asked as he came back over.

"Well, I've got the scent of the 70s dudes. Three of 'em. They didn't touch Chucha, just came close here"—he pointed at a spot near the tree—"and then took off. I've caught the shadow creature's scent, too. Only it touched her. Then it went off there." He pointed in the direction the shadow had floated off. I read between the lines. The gangbangers hadn't been involved in the actual killing. They'd waited until the shadow had distracted her and grabbed the stick.

"Okay," Juice said, reasserting his authority. "Vamonos."

Tez and I exchanged glances. I spoke for both of us. "Juice, are you sure you want a war with the 70s? Something feels off about this."

He showed his quality as a leader yet again, by not scoffing. "What do you mean?" he asked calmly.

"Why didn't the shadow thing leave with them? If it were changing tactics this time—luring Chucha off so it could kill her without being interrupted—why would it need to bring backup?"

"You don't think it was working with the 70s?" Juice was skeptical.

"I don't know. Something else is going on here, and I'm not sure what it is."

I stopped to think for a moment, and then took Juice by the elbow and led him a few yards off, far enough to keep his boys from hearing, but not Tez, with his cat hearing. He seemed surprised, but amenable, and in this I saw Chucha's influence—he'd become used to dealing with smart young women. The thought gave me satisfaction ... then a sudden stabbing feeling in my heart.

"Juice," I said, "maybe don't mention this to anyone yet, but Ayo and I have been investigating a series of killings." His eyebrows went up, but he didn't interrupt. "All shapeshifters, and most of them have been in touch with the stick, but not all."

He nodded. "Justin, Bu Bu, and now Chucha—" he started.

"But Justin wasn't the first," I said, interrupting before he could claim jurisdiction. "There was one killing, as well as a disappearance well before Justin was killed. We can't confirm yet that the disappearance is related, but the killing was definitely done by the same shadow creature. So can you tell me where you got the stick from?"

He suddenly looked menacing. "No. *You* tell *me* who was killed first."

I'd been trying to avoid this, but at least I'd know if he lied. "It was a dude from SF Chinatown called Wayland Soh. Had ties to the Hung For Tong." I looked at him expectantly, but he was already shaking his head.

"No," he said, "that's not who we got it from."

I debated telling him that Wayland was the one who got the instructions to Ayo, but figured, given how close and secretive he'd been about the instructions, that he'd just get more paranoid and menacing if I did.

"Your contact—did they have any connections

with Hung For or Chinatown, or the Asians ... any connections at all?"

He was already shaking his head halfway through my questions.

"No. I'm not gonna tell you who, but I know how they got it, and there's no connection to any of those dudes. At all. Going back months, even years. I know that for a fact."

His voice sounded insincere, like he was trying to direct me away from the stick. But I had a better lie detector, and he wasn't lying about any of it.

"What does that do to your investigation?" he asked.

I shrugged, then shook my head. "Not your problem," I said. "But Juice, can you guys maybe hold off on your vendetta until Tez and I have gotten a chance to investigate *this*? They're gonna be on high alert as it is and if you come rolling up, they'll never relax enough for us to eavesdrop. And what we find out from them could be key to answering both questions. I mean, maybe they're not working with the shadow thing. Maybe it was just a coincidence they were here at the same time."

I didn't mention that I hoped that, by delaying Juice, he might reconsider involving Jimmy. He'd obviously been keeping the boy out of more serious action, his need to protect probably warring with his need for his brother to harden up and not embarrass him. This might give his protective instincts a chance to win out.

Juice gave me a hard look. "I have a stake here," he said, his voice full of meaning.

"I understand," I said. "We won't interfere with your interests. Just give us tonight."

He stepped back. "Tonight. I want you to be in touch by 10 tomorrow morning."

I hesitated. Who knew what would happen, or what

trail we'd be on the next morning? "If possible," I said finally. "If you haven't heard from me, there will be a good reason."

He raised an eyebrow. "And if we roll without hearing from you, there will be a good reason."

Well okay then.

CHAPTER SEVENTEEN

TUESDAY, OCTOBER 18, 2011
70s ARROYO TERRITORY, OAKLAND

WE TOOK TEZ'S car (a ten-year-old black Civic) but, beyond strategizing, didn't make any conversation on our way over to the park.

The Arroyo Park branch of the 70s Mad Dogs was headquartered in a small house on the park, off of 78th Ave., where the shot-caller lived, but the place was dark and quiet. We headed into the park itself and found a few young men hanging out—they didn't see us; Tez had thrown some sort of invisibility glamor over us—and hit a couple of other likely places we'd been told about, but Tez didn't smell our three suspects.

The last place we were told to look was a fast food joint on International with a patio, a holdover from mid-century when the neighborhood was friendlier. We parked away from the boulevard and approached on foot from downwind, through a low, wide plateau of auto shops. Tez stiffened as he got a good whiff of the six or seven young men draped across the plastic picnic tables.

Tez must have still been hiding us, because we got no reaction as we approached, even though we were the only moving objects for miles. One of the guys was white, a lean, twitchy type, and he kept getting up and restlessly pacing around the patio, then sitting down and quickly demolishing a section of a huge pile of chicken and fries, then getting up again. He made my eyes burn. Tez said "werewolf" low into my ear. The werewolf twitched a little more and looked in our direction—I guess Tez couldn't dampen sound—but looked away again and downed another handful of wings, bones and all. What was with all the lone wolves being hired by gangs? Was somewolf out there turning people and selling them? I'd have to remember to talk to Ayo about it.

Once my eye got past the werewolf and his tics, I noticed that the other six guys were sitting in a loose circle, ignoring their food and focusing on—yep, that was Chucha's magic stick all right. It had shrunk to about two feet long, although the knob at its top end had stayed the same size. The bottom end was now a bit wider and knobbier, and the thing looked overall like a cheerleader's baton, except more "ethnic." In fact, to a mundane eye it would have looked more like a different stick from the same set as Chucha's stick—same design, different use—only I felt an absolute certainty in my soul that this was the same stick, shrunk down. Even if I hadn't known, deep in my soul somehow, that this was the thing, the fact that these guys were sitting right out in the open playing with a valuable magical artifact they had just stolen from a bunch of guys with cars and guns would have told me that this thing was having a—let's say—*deleterious* effect on them.

"Shall we get closer and listen in?" I breathe-whispered into Tez's ear.

He didn't seem to hear me. I took ahold of his arm (so solid! So warm!) and led him in closer. An older guy with a dark braid under each ear was holding the stick; maybe he was the shot caller; it was hard to tell, since all of them had equivalent looks of excitement and wonder on their faces. Every few seconds he would switch the stick from one hand to the other, as if it was hot, or unpleasant to hold. The other guys took turns leaning in and rubbing it, grinning, snatching their hands away, and leaning back out, exclaiming, "It tingles!" and "It's like an electric shock!" and the like.

After a few minutes, the shot-caller handed the stick off to the dude next to him and rubbed his hands. The stick went around the circle, with everybody wanting to hold it, and nobody wanting to hold it for more than a few seconds. Not everyone got a turn, though, because after a few minutes, the shot-caller snatched it back and started up his hand-to-hand shuffle again. I guess this explained why the San Antonios had had to hire supernats to guard the stick. I wondered what good the stick would do for humans if they couldn't even hold it.

I sighed internally at their raptness. We weren't going to get any info from eavesdropping on them. Not for a while. We'd have to hunker down and wait out their initial delight. Maybe follow them home and listen in on any immediate future planning. I'd done this many times before.

I grasped Tez's arm again (not gonna lie, this was a perk) and tried to draw him away for a consultation but he had taken root in the ground and wouldn't budge. I pulled again, and again he wouldn't budge. I could have easily picked him up and carried him away, but long experience had taught me that guys didn't like it when girls did that, so I only did it with guys whose bones I didn't want to jump. Also, it would have made too much noise. We were only two or three yards away from the group at this point, standing a foot or two back from the werewolf's pacing perimeter, and I couldn't say anything to Tez without the werewolf, and probably the rest, hearing me.

I'd had a bunch of suggestions prepared, hoping to keep Tez from touching that thing. I didn't care if the San Antonios got it, as long as Tez didn't get possessive and start beefing with them. Whatever else was going on, this beef that had—apparently—killed three supernats so far wasn't something Tez needed in his life.

But it looked like it was too late now, and there was nothing I could do to communicate with him. For a moment, I had no idea what to do. My grip on his arm slackened, and, as if I had signaled to him, Tez jumped forward with a deep, growling scream, and reached for the stick.

He must have dropped his hiding spell or glamour or whatever it was as he leapt. The werewolf reacted unbelievably fast, vaulting over a table and grabbing Tez around the waist before he reached the center of the 70s' intent circle. He thrust Tez away from the others and displayed his teeth. Tez shrieked again—a chesty, coughing sound, but terrifying—claws sprouted from his thickening hands, and he swiped the werewolf across the face and chest. Four slices opened across his arm's trajectory, and the werewolf yelped.

After a moment of shock—I'd been learning to think of Tez as somewhat retiring and cautious—I took up a guard position between Tez and the rest of the 70s. They'd also had their moment of shock, combined with a human inability to react that fast, and were just now scrambling to their feet and looking to protect their spoils. I, somewhat belatedly, went invisible, stretched my arms out to either side, and stepped quickly forward, crowding the six of them in towards each other against a picnic table, and none too gently.

"What the hell?" one of them cried.

"Did you see that girl?"

"What girl?"

"Where'd she go?"

"Someone's pushing me!"

Since the guys had been in a rough circle to begin with, I easily collected them into a tighter one, with the presumed shot caller and the stick in the center. Then I pushed the two closest to me over, causing them to fall into the other four, and entangling them all for a few key moments. If I was lucky, they would start fighting each other and, in the chaos, I could extricate Tez.

I turned to address Tez's situation and saw that he didn't need my help, at all. The werewolf was a latticework of red stripes from Tez's claws, his shirt in bloody ribbons. He'd be bleeding out right about now if he hadn't had his accelerated healing. Tez was moving too fast and too aggressively for the wolf to respond adequately. I didn't see more than a scratch or two on Tez, and, as I watched, Tez grabbed the wolf's wrist, and, in a reversal of his arc-leap, whipped the wolf in a wide arc over his head across the sidewalk and into the street.

He didn't stop to see what had happened to the werewolf, but dove immediately into the gangster scrum, his face one huge snarl. I knew he was after the stick, and, again, I didn't know what to do, so I stood by like an idiot while he knocked 70s every which way and wrested the stick from the shot-caller.

Suddenly, everything went quiet, and I realized that most of the movement had come from Tez throwing people around. He stood in the center of a crater of fallen 70s, holding the stick and staring around at one face after another, as if trying to decide how best to kill them. Tez's claws had shrunk back into his hands, but the stick was growing in his grip. It was back to the walking-stick length it had taken with Chucha, but was, if I was seeing right, growing thicker, more cudgel-like.

Behind me, I heard the werewolf recover its wind and get up. Werewolves are always more aggression than sense, and this idiot sped past me straight at Tez. I reached out to grab him as he went past, but Tez swung his cudgel at the same time and, somehow, it was faster than me. The stick connected with the werewolf's chest and I felt a shockwave radiate out from that point that had nothing to do with physics. The wolf flew backwards 20 yards into the middle of the boulevard and lay still. As if following the wolf's contrail, Tez, his face now so mobilized with snarling that it looked like a Francis Bacon painting, jumped after him, raising his stick—no, his club—over his head.

Somehow, in the same way I knew the stick for what it was, I just knew that if Tez struck the wolf again with that thing, the wolf would die. I didn't care about the wolf: like I said, werewolves annoy me. But, without even thinking about it, I knew that Tez himself would not be okay with killing someone ... when he was back to his usual self, I mean. Almost on reflex, I changed into an Anzu and shrieked.

The arc of Tez's fantastic leap would have taken him to the middle of the boulevard after the wolf, but my Anzu's shriek dropped him directly down onto the sidewalk from the top of his arc. The sidewalk added a few extra cracks, as did all the shaking buildings around me. Wow. I wasn't even shrieking at top volume! Anzus rock!

Tez turned to look at me, momentarily confused. The 70s lay like bowling pins, holding their heads and their ears and groaning.

"Let's go!" I cried and ran across the boulevard.

"No!" Tez shrieked, recovering his snarl. "They have to die! They *all* have to die!"

Hoo boy. I don't know how we went from recon to mayhem to *they all have to die!*, but I was sure the stick was screwing with his poor, shocked, grieving head. I had to get him out of here. By the fastest means necessary.

"No, Tez!" I cried, as if in anguish. "They'll take the stick back from you! We have to run! We have to get away from them!"

Tez's entire body reacted immediately, by curving protectively around the stick. His face was a mess, a cubist confusion of alarm and rage. I waved him towards me again, then turned and, as dramatically, yet slowly, as I could, loped off down a side street, turning every other stride to wave him to me.

After a moment, Tez followed.

He could run fast. And with the werewolf out of commission, there was no one there to catch us up. Tez got out ahead of me and the distance between us grew, so I changed into a dog and sped up. I assumed he was taking us in a roundabout way back to the car we had left behind us on the other side of the boulevard, so I stayed a few yards behind him, letting him lead. But after several blocks I realized that he was just running on panic or adrenaline ... or maybe he was really feeling the stick. I put on an extra burst of speed to get out ahead of him and get him to stop.

He saw me and stopped on a dime—no few staggering steps to throw off his momentum: just stopped. His face opened, like a flower. The look he gave me was so full of

hope and joy and wonder that I took a step back. Wha—
then I looked down at my paws and realized they weren't
the thick grubby white of my usual pit bull. They were
long and elegant and ... tan, changing to black halfway
up my legs. I had changed into a doberman, without
being aware of it.

I had never seen Chucha in her dog form, but of course
I knew she turned into a doberman. It must have been
... something in my subconscious. Oh god, what did I
do? I snapped back to human form in my horror, and
watched Tez's face crumple, then immediately go blank.
He turned away from me and started stumbling back the
way we had come.

"Oh, Tez, I'm so sorry! I didn't mean ... it wasn't what
I was trying to ... I didn't know I was ... it must have
been subconscious ..." I babbled for a few moments as
he walked away, but then recollected myself.

"Tez!" I cried commandingly. He stopped. I walked to
him quickly. He didn't look at me, but straight ahead.
"Where are you taking us?"

He dropped his head, then, in a strange, but graceful,
movement, raised the stick to scratch his forehead, as if
it were merely an extension of his hand. After a moment,
he noticed the stick in his hand and raised his head to
look at it. His blank face filled again with wonder, but
not the joyful wonder of a moment ago. This, rather,
was a kind of terrible, grieving wonder, as at something
beautiful that was not what you asked for.

"Tez?" I asked, carefully.

He looked at me with that awful wonder and said
"Isn't it amazing?"

Carefully I asked, "What is it ... saying to you?"

He chuckled without real humor. "Saying? Maya, it's
a stick." He stroked it with his other hand. "It's a very

powerful stick." He chuckled again, but the laugh was a little richer this time. "Very powerful. A tree ... a branch ... Huexotl ..."

I started a bit, hearing its name coming from Tez. Had I told him its name? I scrabbled through my memory of tonight but couldn't find the moment I'd actually said the word. Huh.

He continued communing with and stroking the stick. The unwelcome thought intruded that the stick, which had retained its thickened cudgel shape for Tez, was actually uncomfortably phallic. Jesus, what was with me throwing sex thoughts around Tez at the most inappropriate moments?

"What does it do?" I asked, trying to distract us both, then felt my face heat up as a flurry of images of things I could do with Tez's stick blew through my traitorous mind.

He chuckled again, richer now, with more abandon, as if he knew exactly what I was thinking. "How the hell do I know?" he said, and then laughed outright.

"Well, we should probably get it back to its rightful owners then," I said briskly, and he stopped laughing. Giving me an angry look, he turned and walked again in the opposite direction, i.e.: where we were running to in the first place.

"Tez!" I called, and hurried after him, "We're going the wrong way!"

"What is the right way?" he said, not stopping.

"Tez! The car is back there!" I pointed back in its general direction, somewhere behind and to the right of us. He looked over his shoulder in the direction my arm was pointing, but didn't stop walking.

"Then we'll loop back," he said reasonably, and turned right at the next street.

I relaxed a little, but not entirely. I was going to have to keep him on track.

We walked on a few blocks, parallel to International, then, when I judged we were about level with where we parked the car, I turned us right again to head back. I would prompt him to hide us if there was any sign of pursuit, but he was acting weird, stroking the stick and, every now and again, chuckling for no apparent reason. So magic later. For now, I needed his attention.

"So," I said finally, "how are we going to get that stick back to Juice?"

Tez stiffened, but didn't say anything, and didn't stop stroking the stick.

"It's his," I pointed out. "Or it's the San Antonios'. And you don't want beef with them. Not now."

Tez's stroking motion turned into a hard two-handed grip. "It's not theirs."

"It is," I said. "It's theirs."

"No, It's *not*!" He shouted the last word.

"Whose is it, then?" I knew better than to argue with him, but I couldn't help myself. This weird possessiveness everyone felt was getting on my nerves. ... And why didn't *I* feel it?

He looked at it and smiled. "It makes me feel good," he said. "Why should I let that go?"

"Because you needed me to remind you that you had a car and to get you back to that car. You're acting drunk. Please, just give me the stick to hold until we get it back to Juice."

He took a step back, his face showing horror. "You! You want to take It from me! I trusted you!"

"Jesus, Tez! I don't want the damned stick! I just want it away from you!"

"That's why you tried to trick me by turning into

Chucha! You're trying to ... to confuse me!" He kept backing away.

"Tez, that's the kind of crazy talk that's making me really wary of the stick. Come on!" Plus, Monkey put in, if I wanted to trick you, you wouldn't have noticed.

"No!" he cried. "No, you can't have It!"

And he turned and ran as if all the legions of hell were after him.

I chased him a few yards, but quickly realized that that would only make things worse. He needed to cool off, and to put the stick down, get some perspective.

I turned into a dog—a pittie this time, I was careful—then went invisible. I ran back to the car and waited there, human, invisible, for Tez to come to his senses and remember where he parked. The 70s cruised by twice, obviously looking for us, but they had no reason to recognize the car.

After three hours I realized that Tez probably wasn't coming back tonight. I pulled out a hair, turned it into slim jim, and broke into Tez's car. Then I turned the same hair into a somewhat unformed key, fitted it to the ignition lock, and started it.

I drove around for a while looking for Tez, but he was gone, or gone invisible, making it harder for me to find him (I'd have to go entirely by eye-flare.) I told myself that he'd probably run all the way back to San Francisco, if my suspicion about the stick giving him energy was correct. But the truth was, I was exhausted, and cranky, and the sun was coming up. Monkey had passed out in the back of my head and the rest of me was not long to follow. He could handle himself for a few hours. I was going to bed.

CHAPTER EIGHTEEN

WEDNESDAY/THURSDAY, OCTOBER 19/20, 2011
MAYA'S APARTMENT, SAN FRANCISCO; GREG BROWN PARK,
BERKELEY

I DIDN'T GET home until nearly seven in the morning. There was no point in calling Juice. We hadn't done any of the things we'd said we would—find the shadow, spy on the 70s— and we'd done the one thing he'd said not to do. Maybe over the next few days I could reason with Tez and pry that damned stick away from him, but deep down, I doubted it. And that meant that Tez, and possibly the 23rd St. outfit, if they chose to get involved, was now going to war against the San Antonios.

Fuck.

I called in sick and let myself sleep for most of the day, but when I woke up late in the afternoon, Tez still hadn't answered any of my messages. My monkey brain pouted, but my rational brain, which had been on silent since Tez had showed up last night, finally poked me and asked what the hell I thought I was doing. I was supposed to pass messages between Tez and Chucha, that was it. I had extended my own charge to encompass facilitating between the two because I knew I would be useful at it, and, let's be honest, so I could spend more time with Tez. Well, let's be perfectly honest, also, eventually, so I could steal Tez's little sister away from him, a little bit.

Chucha. Oh no.

I had been thinking of her, for a moment, as still alive. The knowledge of her death filled me yet again, and I felt my heart pulled down like it had turned to lead. My loud downstairs neighbor came home from work and, as usual, slammed the entryway door too hard. *Journey to the West* fell off its precarious spot on the shelf and lay face up on the floor, staring at me, where I sat at the table with the remnants of a strawberry Pop Tart breakfast and a phone with no new messages.

Seriously, what was I doing? Who did I think I was, acting like this was some kind of mission for me? I should have made a final report back to Ayo long before now, so I could be shot of this damned gig and get paid. I wasn't really a part of this tragedy, and—let's be brutally honest here—Tez was going to associate me with his baby sister's death forever now. I had no chance with him, even though I was, apparently, self absorbed enough to make that a consideration at a time like this. Tez deserved some peace and quiet to be with his family and deal with his grief. And I was gonna give him that. And it wasn't like I didn't have a lot on my plate, what with Dalisay still missing and, and Wayland dead and the shadow creature running around, although I couldn't think just now what my next move was, but there was also ... also me trying to find out what I was ... although I was weary of that question right now ... and what else? ... So much ...

But ... my brain immediately switched sides, as it often did, to point out that peace and quiet were exactly not what Tez was about to get, with at least two different gangs after the magical artifact he wouldn't give up. And his extreme behavior of last night was no doubt a result of mixing grief and anger with the giddiness of the stick's power. Its influence was certainly not going to abate as long as he was in possession of it, and he wasn't going to want to give it up as long as he had it. Which meant that the only way to get it away from him ...

I stood up. My mind was made up in an instant. There was no way I was gonna let anyone kill him for a stupid magic stick.

I sat back down and pulled my laptop towards me. A little way down on SF Gate's home page I found it: "Oakland Drive-by Shooting Wounds Three/ Cops Suspect Gang War." Truce over.

I spent the remainder of the afternoon prowling the Mission in Tez's car and leaving Tez message after message. He wasn't home, but something told me he wasn't at work, either. Maybe I'd run across him tending to his duties. My mind was a hot, confused swirl of Tez, stick, Chucha, gangs, shadows, dead bodies, the encampment, general assemblies, Dalisay, Wayland, the magazine, Baby, Salli ... and the confusion only grew. A distant part of me realized this was my own grief, but since I didn't think I had a right to such grief for someone I barely knew, I ignored it. I kept trying to reason, trying to separate the different items from each other, and not succeeding.

I didn't check in with Ayo, like I should have. She would have asked me why I was still fussing with Tez, and despite my decision today, I really didn't have an articulateable reason, not even in my heart of hearts. "I have a crush on him" didn't quite cover it. "I liked his sister" didn't either. "I feel responsible" wasn't ...

I took a break to go to the general assembly, which I found out later was an unusually contentious one, but couldn't say what happened as I'd been so distracted. Afterwards I staked out the San Antonios' HQ in the dark for a few hours, as well as the Starry Plough, both places where I'd seen the shadow before. I even checked out the spot on Folsom next to Kearny Street Workshop, where I'd found the first body. But no shadow.

As I sat parked Folsom Street, watching the nighttime lighten into blue dawn, I reflected slowly on Wayland, and why he would be the shadow's first victim, assuming that he was. Now that I had a stretch of hours to really think about it, the instructions for the stick, assuming that's what they actually were, weren't enough. The shadow creature felt ... *elemental* to me, somehow. Not sophisticated or subtle. I could be wrong, but it felt to me like it was going after the stick—assuming it *was* going after the stick—for its power, plain and simple.

But I had to stop making assumptions. I assumed Juice had *had* to get the stick from Wayland, but he definitely hadn't. And, besides, the timing was wrong on that. Justin had had the stick for weeks before he was killed. Wayland was killed the same night that I caught Bu Bu—actually, the night before Justin was killed, wasn't it? That was sometime *after* Wayland had already handed the instructions over to Ayo. I paused to put everything in order:

First, Justin joined the San Antonios, a few months ago.

Then Juice got ahold of the stick, weeks ago, at least, if not months ago, from someone not associated with Wayland or Chinatown.

Then Juice recruited Chucha.

Then Juice got the instructions from Ayo, two or three

weeks ago, maybe, around the same time as Chucha came to him. I should maybe find out which came first.

But Wayland had never had the stick, and he no longer had the instructions, so ... *why* had he been stalked and killed again?

No, this didn't make any sense. Wayland's involvement with the stick was peripheral, at best. Unless ... unless the shadow creature wasn't after the stick at all, but rather ... knowledge about the stick? No, that didn't make any sense, either. Why kill everyone who holds the stick but not take the stick? If you're trying to bury knowledge of the stick, what better way to do that than to make off with the stick itself? No, it *had* to do with the power the stick itself held ...

... Unless it wasn't about the stick at all.

My mind did a little inversion, and a memory fired off: Ayo's voice saying "I do, I think, see one more connection among those three, though. ... we usually think of aswang as vampiric beings, but they are also, legitimately, shapeshifters."

Dalisay, Wayland, Justin, Bu Bu, Chucha ... yes, there were potentially five victims now, and all of them were shapeshifters. This was the direction Ayo had started to think in before I told her about the stick and we'd both decided the stick was what the creature was after.

But again, I didn't know what had happened to Dalisay. And, despite the tenuousness of Wayland's connection to the stick, all four of the shadow's confirmed victims were connected to the stick. Like I said, I didn't like coincidences, didn't believe in them.

Ayo. I had to ask her. ... When I woke up, I decided, driving home. I'd tell her everything then.

Instead, she woke me at 10 Thursday morning.

"Maya, are you able to get out to Berkeley quickly?"

"Why?"

"Stoney isn't coming in for another couple of hours so I'm alone here. I don't want to have to close up."

"What's going on?"

"A friend called me about a dead body. She said it might be a supernat. Can you check it out for me and just have her call the cops if it's human?" It was one of those moments I knew Ayo and I were thinking the same thing: what if it was Dalisay? I ignored the fact that the body was in Berkeley, across the Bay from where she'd last been seen. I almost forgot to say "yes," in my hurry to hang up and rush over.

Half an hour later, I found myself slowing down along the stretch of Shattuck I had run down the other night after the shadow, the same stretch I had surveilled last night, up near the Starry Plough and La Peña. My hackles went up as my smart phone GPS instructed me to turn down the first street past the yard the shadow had disappeared into that night—the yard where I'd lost track of the creature and given up.

I drove three blocks in, and stopped near a very small park whose entrance was a gate between two private yards. I leapt over the gate and hurried in through the strip of park to a more open grassy area shaded by trees. A woman leaning casually against a tree straightened when she saw me. I didn't see anything near her, but as I approached, I was suddenly assaulted, through the green smell of foliage, by the powerful stench of dead body.

"Did Ayo send you?" she asked. She was about Ayo's age, taller than me, curvy, and dressed like a suburban mom. Her hair was straightened but undyed, and had silver running through it. I got no flare when looking at her, and no hint of any deception, not that that meant no magic. She could be like Ayo, a human who used ambient magic.

"Yeah," I said. "Where's the body?"

She turned around and pointed towards a small, but thick growth of bushes against the park's fence. "He's under there," she said. "I didn't move him, except to look closer. I had to roll him over, actually. If we have to call the cops, I'll take the blame for that and you can take off."

I took note of the "him." Not Dalisay. The smell was growing stronger even as I stood there. He had to have been dead a few days at least. Well, he wasn't going to get any fresher. I drew in a deep breath, paused to regret it, then went to the bushes and parted them.

His body was angled in towards the fence so that his face was the first thing I saw. Even upside down, even past the bloating that was distorting his flesh and the whitish discoloration of his once-beautiful brown skin, I recognized him. Aahil. Aahil, the cute monkey shifter, whom I'd last seen Saturday night at Starry Plough, a few blocks from here. Aahil, whom I'd last seen right before I saw the shadow creature floating away. Aahil. Oh my god.

"Call Ayo," I told the woman, and she did.

It took Ayo only 20 minutes to shoo out customers, close up, and drive here. She must've been on high alert. I made good use of the time by sitting on the curb near the park's entrance, as far away from the body as I could get, and staring blankly at a hair I'd plucked and was rolling between my forefinger and thumb.

"Maya!" Ayo cried, in a voice that indicated that she'd called to me before, and I hadn't heard. She was standing before me, in the street, looking her usual exasperated self.

"It's Aahil. The vanara kid," I said. Then a thought occurred to me. "We're gonna have to call the police."

Aahil was heavily embedded in the human world. There were definitely legal threads that would have to be pulled. I felt very detached thinking about it.

Ayo sighed heavily. "I was afraid of that."

"What do you mean?" I asked startled. I hadn't talked about seeing Aahil Saturday night with her.

"His father called me Tuesday night. He told me that Aahil was missing and they'd just put in a missing persons report with the police. He wanted to know if I knew anything."

"Missing since when?" I asked, but I knew.

"He went out to a show Saturday night and his roommate said he never came home."

"You should go look at him," I said, flatly.

She frowned. "You think this is another—"

"Go look at him," I said, and looked back down at the hair in my hands.

I'd only just managed to shape it into a guitar pick by the time Ayo came back. She stood before me again. I didn't look up.

"His essence is completely gone. Just like the others," she said after a pause. I didn't speak, just twiddled the pick. My mind was mostly blank, although I could vaguely hear Monkey screeching something as if through a fog of sound.

"What do you know?" she asked quietly, after a moment.

I pointed behind me. "We were both at the Starry Plough Saturday night. It was that uke band whose CD I play at Sanc-Ahhh sometimes, Todd Wakahisa's band. We saw each other and waved, but by the time I went to speak with him, he'd disappeared. That's when I saw the shadow creature sneaking out of the bar so I followed it. I didn't see Aahil after he disappeared, but I followed the shadow thing across Shattuck and into a yard on the corner of Shattuck and 65th. I lost it there. I didn't connect the two things. Why would I?"

We both let it sink in. If I had only made the connection. If I had only *looked*—

"Aahil didn't have anything to do with the stick," I said. It wasn't a question, but she answered it anyway.

"I can't imagine how he'd even know about it. There's literally no scuttlebutt about the Huexotl around, even with all the deaths linked to it. And Aahil was a coder, not a gangster. His dad told me he'd just gotten VC money for a new app."

We let that sink in.

"Well," Ayo said briskly, her voice catching a little, "we're going to have to rethink. Maybe this has nothing to do with that stick after all. Which is good news for Chucha. How is that going, by the way? Did she and Tez finally meet?"

I felt my numb blankness being drawn downwards, like water down a drain, flowing into and weighting my already leaden heart.

"Chucha is dead. The shadow thing killed her last— ... on Tuesday night, and another gang stole the stick while it was happening."

"... Tuesday night? Why didn't you tell me?"

I felt a flash of anger and looked up, accusingly, only to realize that I wasn't angry at Ayo. Something broke and crumbled inside my head and I was numb again.

"Just like you said," I mumbled. "All shapeshifters."

Ayo crouched down and put a hand on my shoulder. If I'd been less numb I would've started. She wasn't very demonstrative, usually.

"Go on to the sanctuary," she said, gently. "You can open again now and then leave early for the general assembly. I'll be back in a few hours."

I stood up mechanically.

"Maya," Ayo said.

I stopped.

"It's not your fault—"

I practically ran back to the car.

I ignored the stretch of road where I'd chased the shadow as I turned back on to Shattuck, and drove on autopilot back into Oakland.

It was somewhere in the middle of putting my apron on that Monkey shook free of the fog and shrieked with rage. The rage suffused my entire body, starting with my belly and setting fire to my heart and my brain and my thighs and my hands. I was gonna kill somebody … some*thing*. I was gonna *kill* that thing until it was not just dead, but in fifty million shadowy pieces.

CHAPTER NINETEEN

THURSDAY, OCTOBER 20, 2011
OGAWA/GRANT PLAZA, OAKLAND

ALTHOUGH MY RAGE settled down to a simmer, my overall mood only got worse throughout the day, as I called Tez four more times, and left four more messages, but didn't hear back. I was really tired of being shut out of ... things ... and if I had to push my way back into some sort of justice in my world, so be it.

This was definitely not the best mood in which to meet Baby when we rendezvoused at the plaza for our monthly *Inscrutable* editorial check-in. These one-on-one meetings were professionally sacred, but had also become personally sacred as well. They could be short, as long as we got all our business done, but they were also sort of our BFF date night, so we usually went out for drinks afterwards. I'd been the one to suggest we meet at the encampment, since Baby hadn't had time to come down and see it so far, even during our last staff meeting.

Baby seemed preoccupied while I steered her to a set

of benches away from the tents, and I had to make an effort not to be cutting about … everything. It took her a long time to wake up to my mood, and we were through our extremely short and to-the-point meeting before she finally took me to task.

"Dude, what is *up* with you? You're like, strictly prickly today."

I remembered in that instant that she didn't know about Chucha, and was knocked breathless. How could she not know? It seemed like the whole world was wearing mourning colors. Even the sky was … I looked up, but the sky was clear and we were headed for our usual pink/golden sunset.

"Maya?" Baby asked, annoyed, but a little concerned.

"Chucha's dead, Baby. She died on Tuesday." I couldn't quite look at her and fiddled with my laptop.

"Oh my god. I can't believe it! That poor girl! Poor Tez!" This was classic Baby. She had never met Chucha, nor Tez, beyond seeing him perform now and then, but her heart immediately filled their images with humanity, and she always led with her empathy. "How's he handling it?"

"Not well. I got him safe passage to talk to the San Antonios and then he freaked out, ran off and disappeared somewhere in Fruitvale. I still have his car. He won't return my calls." I paused to think. "We drove by the 70s before that to see what was up with them and he acted like he was gonna start a beef with them. I think he might be in trouble."

"What?" Baby cried. "You said he wasn't involved in gangs!"

"He isn't. But he grew up in his neighborhood and some of his neighbors are involved in them. And the Fruitvale gangs associate him with 23rd St. So … I think he's in trouble. I really need to talk to him."

We sat in silence for a moment.

"Why do you have to talk to him?" she asked in an ominously quiet voice.

My irritation had no idea what to do with this. "What the hell are you trying to say, Baby?" I knew exactly what she was trying to say, and it was all the more annoying because I'd just said it to myself this morning.

She sighed. "Maya, I know you're not in the mood for this, but you're never in the mood to hear negative things that you need to hear. So can you please refrain from biting my head off after I say this?"

I pressed my lips together.

She sighed again. "Look, I know, better than anyone, how long you've had a thing for Tez. And I'm thrilled that you've finally gotten a little one-on-one with him. But this isn't the fun, flirty, getting-to-blow-you-type situation that I wanted for you. This is serious. And it's serious in a way that you can't afford to get involved in. I didn't know that Tez had a ... violent side—" I started to protest, but she held up her hand. "Regardless of how understandable he is in his grief, it's not good for you to be in the middle of a potential gang war."

"I can handle a 'gang war'," I said rolling my eyes.

"Can you? You're like an addict when it comes to violence. Your words not mine! But I've seen it, Mai, you know I have. Your eyes get all bright and weird and you start to get itchy to join in. You get scary when there's violence in the air. You don't need it."

I didn't say anything. This was unfair ... and yet, I couldn't entirely dispute it. I hated fighting people weaker than me—but when someone could give me a good fight? Or a group of assholes? Yeah, I loved it. But that's not the same thing as ...

"And, honestly, Mai, this whole situation is none of your business. The job you were hired for is done. Really, what's in all this for you? Tez? Do you think getting involved in this will lead to romance?"

My teeth were fully gritted. I was counting to ten. I wasn't going to bite her head off. Two. Three. We'd agreed on that. Six. Seven. I wasn't going to bite her head off. Nine. Ten.

"Just because it scares you doesn't mean it's wrong."

That hadn't been what I was going to say.

I could see Baby counting to ten as well (she was the one who taught me that,) but she went on as if I hadn't spoken. "'Cause, as I said, I see two answers, Mai. One: Tez. You want to be where Tez is, no matter how bad, or inappropriate. And two: you love this shit. A chance to mix it up? A chance to beat on people? Mayhem? Chaos? Tell me I'm wrong."

And then, on her last sentence, there was a tone in her voice, something like despair, or resignation, combined with genuine fear. For me. I'd heard that tone before, just … never from Baby. An electric current shot through me.

"You forgot number three: I feel responsible."

She started to speak and I interrupted her. "No, Baby, you're right, as usual. But just because this freaks you out doesn't mean I'm going to … doesn't mean I can stop being involved. I'm involved now."

"Doesn't he have some sort of older relative or authority figure who can talk to him?"

I thought about this. "I don't really know. Maybe, but I don't know them. I guess I'll ask Ayo."

"Yeah. 'Cause maybe … maybe … Maybe if you can find somebody who's *really* responsible for him, maybe you can leave it to them, huh?"

I managed not to yell at her, although I didn't respond.

What I'd said was true, that it felt like my responsibility, but that wasn't all it was. I still couldn't articulate it and I didn't want to—not to Baby.

"Because," she said after a moment, "it's been really hard at the magazine the past six months and you haven't been helping. I know you don't have time and you have your own jobs to do, but I see you getting involved in Ayo's shit, whatever it is—"

"Ayo's 'shit,' Baby? Are you kidding me? That's my *job*! 'Ayo's shit.' Blow me."

She lost her temper again. "No, bitch, blow *me*. I wasn't gonna say anything, but I *know* your girl is selling fake superstitious shit. What did you call it? 'Merman's penis'? She's selling that shit and I *know* it. Do *you*?"

I did know that, in general, Ayo sometimes dealt in some sketchy shit, but none of it was fake and all of it was ethically sourced, as far as she could tell. And all of it was beyond Baby to understand. "What are you even *talking about, Baby*?" I practically screeched.

She stood up, practically yelling herself now. "I had a meeting with Salli! And she was talking to somebody on the phone, really angry! And she told me you were asking her about the Hung For Tong! And that she heard that they were offering to sell two *aswang wings after you talked to her*!! Did you set that up, Maya? *Did you*??"

I didn't respond. I was in shock. *Aswang wings*? Oh. My. God.

Baby went on without looking at me, pacing back and forth in front of the bench. "I can't *believe* you would play on people's ignorance and superstition that way!! What is *wrong* with you?!?" She finally stopped, and looked up, and must've seen the shocked look on my face ... and completely misunderstood it.

"Oh, it wasn't you," she said, suddenly calm again.

"Oh, Maya, I'm sorry, I shouldn't have assumed—"

I still couldn't respond. I had suspected that the Hung For people might have Dalisay's body, but ... I didn't realize how much I'd been hoping she was alive. If they were offering her wings, there was no way Dalisay was still breathing. Salli must've taken the opportunity to pass along a message to me ... instead of calling me? Because ... because ... oh my god, she hadn't mentioned Dalisay to Baby, just the aswang wings. *She knew*. That's why she didn't want to tell me directly. She was telling me that she *knew*.

We were both silent for a while, but when Baby spoke again, it was more hard than apologetic. "Okay," she said, "I can see I was hasty in assuming ... things. But seriously, Maya, you can't exactly blame me for not wanting to see you getting involved in Chinese gangs again. And I see you getting involved in this *other* gang thing with Tez that's taking up so much of your time, but is most definitely *not* your responsibility, and spending all your extra time *here*" she gestured at the encampment, "and you have no time or patience for your own magazine, which *is* your responsibility. I mean, we're in deep shit, financially, and it's like you don't even *care*."

We sat on opposite sides of the bench, not speaking or looking at each other. Some perverse wind brought the smell of her unscented beeswax lip balm to my nose, a smell I always associated with her, but it gave me nothing today. I hoped she would take herself off before somebody said the wrong thing and we fell back into fighting again.

But she just looked at me.

I tried to remember my conflict resolution training, but my mind was in too much chaos.

"*Okay*, Baby, I heard you."

She waited another moment, then stood up. "I hope you did. I think we'll skip drinks tonight. See you later." And she walked off, if not in a huff, then definitely in somewhat of a raspberry.

Fortunately, Ayo called soon after and gave me something to focus my distress on. She was just checking in, worried about me after my reaction to Aahil's death today. Truth be told, I'd forgotten about Aahil as soon as Baby showed up. Maybe I just didn't have the wherewithal to explain two deaths to her ... no, make that three ... four ... though with Justin, that was five ...

I told Ayo about Hung For and the rumor that they had aswang's wings for sale. Ayo's voice got hard—a reaction that I rarely heard, and never messed with when I heard it.

"Okay, that's it. I'm gonna handle this now," she said.

"What are you gonna do?"

"I'll arrange a sit-down—no, I'll *make* a sit-down happen. And I'll *make* them tell us what happened. Best stay out of this and drop the Dalisay issue now, Maya. Focus on trying to find that shadow creature."

I agreed to do what she said and, for once, I meant it. Maybe by playing hardball she'd pry some real answers out of those idiots, but as for me: I was done up and done in. All of my specific questions had been answered, but I was still no closer to knowing, for certain, what had happened to Dalisay. And I had no new ideas.

Maybe it was the "new ideas" thought that got me going, because sometime that night—probably closer to morning, since I'd spent several hours between the general assembly and going to bed in another fruitless search for the shadow—I sat up in bed, going fully awake from complete sleep, but remembering no internal dream or external noise that had awakened me. I awoke with a fully developed thought: the stick.

The thought broke down like this:

First, I realized that I'd been assuming the stick was passive—I mean, just being handed around—but was it, really? I'd had a feeling of distant power from the stick, plus a flare of magic from it, which I'd assumed meant "transformation," ... but it also could have meant "deceit." And Chucha said the stick talked to her. Did it? Was the stick ... *making* things happen?

Second, Tez and Chucha were affected strongly by the stick; I wasn't; humans were affected but couldn't handle it; and I had no idea how a werewolf or a bajang were affected, if at all. Somehow, I'd been assuming that I was the only one unaffected by it, but really, I had no idea how it affected other supernats. Could it be that *only* Tez and Chucha were that strongly affected by it?

Which led me to: if only Tez and Chucha were made weird and giddy by the stick, was that a family issue? A nagual issue? Something else?

Then I remembered the stick's name: Huexotl. Ayo had said it was a Nahuatl word, and that maybe it affected Chucha and Tez more strongly because it was from the same cultural realm. What if it wasn't just from the same cultural realm but ... but what? What if its magic *matched* theirs somehow? But how? I wasn't sure what question to ask, but there was something there.

I needed to know: to know what role the stick *really* played in all this.

I shook my head, trying to move my thinking forward. That was how I noticed that I was still sleep-groggy, after all. I lay back down and went almost immediately back to sleep. "Almost," because one more thought went through my head before blackness descended: time to start looking into the Varelas directly. Maybe I could find their "family friends" tomorrow ... And maybe I could find Tez before the pile-up of villains started piling up on him.

CHAPTER TWENTY

Friday, October 21, 2011
Tez's House, San Francisco

According to his car registration, Tez lived in one of a row of grand old three-story, wedding-cake Victorians, of which there was a surfeit in the Mission. The houses on either end of the row were fully restored and painted in faintingly precise, six-color detail, their driveways newly re-cemented in a fashionable grey and fresh asphalt. The one on the right was framed by new, young Japanese maples; the one on the left had created a public "parklet" in the parking space in front of their house, complete with a cement mini-maze of benches and a bamboo-boxed succulent and cactus garden.

Tez's house was one of three in the middle that were each painted one cheap color with monochromatic trim: terra cotta, olive green, steel blue. Like the sisters who married for love in a Jane Austen novel, their resemblance to their wealthy sisters made the difference in their condition all the more poignant: their fine details rotted or torn away, and their driveway cement, devoid of greenery, cracked and pitted. And like those poorer sisters, they were overrun with offspring.

Although the lovely parklet was clean and empty, the garage in the blue house to the left of Tez's was spilling over with boxes and half-glimpsed men working on an engine. One of the terra cotta doors to the right of his house opened, and a young woman came out with a baby bound to her chest, hidden entirely behind a trailing blanket. And the central staircase leading to Tez's olive green doorway seemed packed with what were really only three men: middle-aged, work-clothed, eating. As I parked and got out, they watched, silently, six eyes that turned the whole street into a panopticon.

"Hey," one of them said, as I walked up. "Whatchu doing with Tez's car?"

I had bet myself that I could find someone hanging around on his block who could point me in the direction of old family friends, and this was about as promising as you could get. I looked more closely at him: wide face, dramatic nose ... wait a minute! He was Ayo's client, the guy I'd seen in her car, who had come to see her at Sanc-Ahh the other day. The guy who wanted—probably, Ayo wouldn't confirm—the instructions to the stick. Okay. And he apparently knew Tez. Maybe was even ... probably was one of his neighborhood ... what did he call them? Padrinos? A few things clicked vaguely in my mind.

He obviously recognized me, but wasn't saying anything about it in front of his buddies—another mind-click—so I decided to follow suit.

"Trying to return it to him. Is he home?"

The client merely raised his goateed chin, but the other two exchanged a glance.

"Why'd he give you his car?" the client asked again.

"He didn't. He freaked out and left it behind."

The client frowned and the other two looked at each other again.

"When was this?" one of the others, wearing a Kangol duckbilled cap, asked.

"Tuesday," I said. They looked meaningfully at each other. "Yes, the night Chucha died." All three looked at me. "I was there." They just stared. "He was freaking out. I kept the car because I was afraid he was gonna go back to Fruitvale and pick a fight …" I noticed I was babbling a lot of info without confirming these were the guys I was looking for. "Are you friends of the family? … Or maybe you're family? No, he said he didn't have any family left in the city."

The client seemed to have an entire conversation with his buddies without speaking. But they seemed to decide in my favor.

"Well, the closest thing they've got right now. It's true they don't have any family left nearby, so we look out for them." Tez's Padrinos, check. Maybe they were hanging out on his steps waiting for him as well. Ayo's client got up, came the rest of the way down the steps, and held out his hand. "I'm Amoxtli."

I took his hand and held it as a lifeline. Incomprehensible names made me nervous. "Amosh … ti?"

"Aahh-Mosh-Tuh-Lee, but you say the last part all together, like 'tlee'."

"Amoxtli."

"Perfect."

I shook his hand finally and let go. "Maya."

"You his new girlfriend?" Kangol hat asked. Amoxtli shot a look of annoyance at him. "New" girlfriend? Did he actually have a new girlfriend that they knew about and hadn't met yet, or were they just guessing at me? …

223

Focus, Maya.

"Nope. I went to Cal with Tez."

"That's Jaime," Amoxtli said, Jaime touched his hat, "and that's Mike," the third man waved and I waved back. "Tez isn't home yet," Amoxtli said. "He hasn't been back to work this week, but, he hasn't been home much, either." He paused. "He asked to borrow my car, wouldn't tell me what happened to his, but I made an excuse. He ... did seem to be looking for a fight." He paused again.

"What's your interest in Tez?" Jaime asked, and Amoxtli shot him another annoyed look. Jaime was unrepentant.

I sighed and leaned against the cracked plinth supporting the base of the staircase's hand rail. Amoxtli sat down again. I told them the sanitized version of the story: that I worked for a sort of spiritual leader in Oakland whom Tez knew and I had gone through similar trouble in my youth, and that was why I was asked to talk to Chucha. They seemed aware that Tez was ... er, "interested in alternative spiritualities."

"Yeah," Amoxtli told his friends casually, "Ayo's that Iyalawo I've been talking to. I was trying to get that book from her." This was news to me.

"What book?" Mike asked. Yeah, dude, what book?

"You know how Tez was all interested in nagualism?" Amoxtli said, still very casual. Wait, what?

Mike rolled his eyes and Jaime grinned.

"I can't believe you're encouraging him with that New Age shit," Mike said.

"Better than *some* trouble he could get up to," reasoned Jaime, with amusement.

Well that cleared up where Mike and Jaime were on the belief scale.

"Whatever," Amoxtli said, slightly huffily. "You know he's into that stuff. And true nagualism is syncretic anyway, a product of colonization." Oh, *really*?

Jaime grinned wider. "You sound like Tez now."

"Well, he's onto something. Anyway, I was trying to get ahold of a first edition of this book this white dude in the 19th century wrote about it, you know, for his birthday, and Ayo was gonna help me with that." He turned to me suddenly. "You know if she's gotten ahold of it yet?"

It took a moment for me to pierce my own confusion enough to notice that my eyes had been flaring throughout this whole interaction. He was lying about the book, although I knew exactly which book he meant; I'd read it this week on Project Gutenberg. I looked at him more closely and he was giving me what I thought might be his meaningful look. Oh. *Oh*. He meant the instructions!

"I think you're out of luck, dude," I said, narrowing my eyes at him. "She sold that book a *while* ago."

Amoxtli looked deflated. Hadn't Ayo told him that? Of course she had. He didn't want to believe her and was hoping I'd tell him otherwise. Well, two could play that game.

"Ayo told me you were a bit of an expert on nagualism yourself," I said, making it up as I went along.

I was rewarded by a shocked looked from all three, although I think Amoxtli was more shocked that Ayo had betrayed him. She hadn't, but he didn't need to know that.

"I've read a couple of books ..." he said, confusedly.

"Are there any shadow monsters in Meso American mythology?"

He looked relieved. "Ayo asked me the same thing. Not really. I mean, the god Tezcatlipoca, whom Tez is named after, is a god of darkness, but not specifically of shadow. There are darkness gods and darkness creatures—"

I interrupted. "How about magic sticks?"

Amoxtli went dead silent. Jaime and Mike looked at each other; Mike with disdain, and Jaime with continuing amusement. But Amoxtli's eyes were narrowing at me in a menacing way, and I realized that this dude might be a little more formidable than I had anticipated. He probably thought Ayo had looked at the instructions before she'd sold them … *if* she'd sold them at all.

"The Aztecs didn't put magic *into* objects," he said, shortly. That was … weirdly specific. My mind clicked again. I *needed* to get this guy alone.

He took a deep breath. "Now … can you … tell me what happened? To Chucha?"

Oh, yeah, I should probably let him change the subject. I told them the sanitized version of Tuesday night, rearranging some facts to let them know that Chucha had been guarding something (I didn't know what, but hinted that it was some sort of commodity) that belonged to the San Antonios and I suspected that Tez now had it and was being stubborn and vengeful and not wanting to give it back.

"So you don't know if the 70s actually killed her?" Amoxtli asked.

"Nobody does. There wasn't a mark on her but, like I said, they saw the guys running away from where she fell. So nobody's gonna know until the autopsy is done. … They *are* doing an autopsy, right?"

Amoxtli shrugged. "Tez isn't really saying much about anything."

"Is this how he gets when there's trouble?" I asked. Amoxtli looked askance at me. "We're acquaintances, not friends. I don't know him well enough to know how he deals with things like this." I hesitated. Time to start drawing them out. "I know there's been a lot of tragedy in his family …"

Amoxtli sighed and the other two men shook their heads in sympathy. "Nothing but bad luck since they moved up here," he said.

I asked how long he'd known them, and that seemed the key to unlocking Amoxtli's tongue. Boy, was the guy a hot, fluent raconteur, once you got him going, and he spent the next hour filling me in on the Varela family back story through dramatic epics and funny anecdotes.

Turns out, Amoxtli was an *old* family friend. He had gone to elementary school in Mexico with Tez's dad, Ome, and their families had emigrated together when the boys were twelve. Amoxtli's parents brought him along, but Ome's parents left him behind with a half-uncle, planning to settle in and find permanent jobs before bringing their son up. Unfortunately Ome's parents died in an accident less than a year after they arrived, so they never brought Ome to the States.

My eyes started to flare up now and again, but it seemed it was at small, unimportant details in the story. I just chalked it up to Amoxtli's artfulness as a storyteller: adding in not-strictly-factual details to spice up the narrative.

"I didn't see him again until we were 20. I'd gotten big, from all that American food, and he'd gotten handsome, I guess from good genes. I'm not sure which of us was luckier." Ome came to the US after marrying Tez's mother, Pilar, and they did seasonal work back and forth between the Central Coast and San Francisco before they found permanent jobs in the city and started their family. Things seemed to be going well for them for several years. Ome was a sort of leader in the community: mature before his time, wise and able to resolve conflicts; men twice his age would come to him for help and advice. Each of these hints caused a bit of a flare in my eyes and

I revised my notion of Amoxtli's lies as pure artistry. Perhaps he *did* know about the whole nagual thing. I was gonna have to get Amoxtli alone, sooner rather than later.

"But," Amoxtli said. "It was *because* things were going well for them that trouble found them." Ome and Pilar emigrated in the early 80s, in the middle of a period when the Mission Mob were stepping up their activities. Ome's leadership in the community painted a target on him. People would come to him for help and he'd go and speak to the shot callers for them, and his prestige in the community was resented. After a few years, some guy on his block got into debt with the Mission Mob and the shot caller, a vindictive man who didn't last long, made Ome responsible for this man's debt. When he refused to pay, the shot caller had Mob members invade their house and steal some stuff. So Ome went down to the shot caller's house and demanded his stuff back. A fight broke out, and then Ome was shot. He died a few days later.

(My eyes were popping off flares throughout this story. Hmm. Clearly there was something nagual-y and secret about the manner of Ome's death. I also couldn't help but wonder about a man supposedly so wise and capable, hauling off and confronting a gang leader in front of his people. That practically guarantees you'll be killed, or that you'll have to kill somebody.)

That vindictive shot caller tried to make Pilar responsible for the debt. But Pilar, who was not to be messed with, told the head of the nascent 23rd St. exactly who had stolen a drug shipment a few weeks before. It hadn't, in point of fact, been the vicious Mission Mob shot caller, but he found it hard to prove a negative, especially when the whole neighborhood supported Pilar's story. A brief gang war later, he was dead and the Mob's new head had learned: a) not to be so mean that his neighbors rose up against him and b) to leave the Varelas alone. (This conclusion left my eyes flaring as well, a fact I couldn't account for. It wasn't the part about Pilar looking like Wonder Woman. He'd told the truth on that one, by his lights.)

Pilar suddenly found herself the sole breadwinner for four children under ten. She was scraping and scrapping and barely making ends meet for years, but the kids always got fed, and she never let Tez get a job during the school year. No, it was college for him, and every penny he made during the summers (and he started babysitting at eleven, house painting around the neighborhood at fifteen) went into a savings account. They were so thrifty he only ever had to work part time when he was in college (although he couch surfed most of his college career, to avoid rent and transportation costs.)

"That's amazing!" I said. "There's no way a family of five could get by in the Mission on one income these days."

"Tez is making more in his one IT job than both of his parents together ever made, with all of their jobs. But it's only because they have rent control that the boys can go to school, and they *still* have to work," Jaime said.

We all paused to marvel at what had become of San Francisco.

Anyway, Amoxtli was certain that it was the stress of four jobs, and scraping and keeping four kids in line that got Pilar sick. She fell ill the fall Tez started college and he insisted on quitting and getting a job.

"That was the one time I saw Pilar strike him. She chased him around the house and out onto the sidewalk with a broomstick yelling, 'You Go To The College!'"

She plugged on for another three years, but by Tez's last year of school she was failing visibly and could only work intermittently. Tez was about to quit school again, so Amoxtli—unmarried, childless, apparently perennially itinerant—moved in with them to help out through the end of the school year. Tez had had plans to intern at Google that summer, but he had to give that up. The first few years he had to work two and three jobs to clear her medical and funeral costs, and was still paying down the last of that debt.

Which brought us up to date. We all sat silent, everyone no doubt as dazed as I was by all the information and stories. I felt like I'd been dipped in a bath of the Varela family, and was now in the inner circle. It was great background for the conversation I needed to have now, with Amoxtli, regarding a certain magic stick.

It was a strange moment for Tez to walk into.

CHAPTER TWENTY-ONE

Friday, October 21, 2011
Tez's House, San Francisco

ONE MOMENT HE wasn't there, and the next, he was standing on the sidewalk directly in front of the house staring at us in open surprise. He was, at least, wearing different clothes than he had on last Tuesday, but his hair was as unkempt as hair that short could get, and his usual facial scruff was turning into a full-fledged beard. He was also clutching the strap of a worn backpack over one shoulder. I had no doubt what was in it.

For a moment, I felt almost as if Tez had turned transparent as a baked onion and I could see through layers and layers of him. I realized that, at this place in time, I was the only person in the world who knew exactly what was going on with him. Even his siblings must've been left out of the loop. I could see it in his protective caregiver layer: he wouldn't want them involved in any vengeance he had planned. If Tez was the center of this whirlwind, I was his anchor. It was precisely *because* he didn't know me, and stakes were so low between us, that he could allow me to play this role.

Monkey screeched "run!" at me, and I almost bolted. Baby was right: a healthy, normal person would not get involved in something like this. But I felt the pull: of Tez, of this position, of the story ... I didn't know what.

Tez grinned wide. "Heeeey, look!"

His grin was too goofy. Amoxtli exchanged concerned looks with Jaime and Mike, and even with me. Shit. Tez had had three days to get used to the effects of the stick. If he was still this giddy—

"Just what I need to come home to! A pretty lady and some old farts!" He laughed loudly. I looked at the Padrinos again, wondering what they thought. Probably that he was on drugs. Not that this was much different.

"Heeey! Why so glum everybody? It's a beautiful evening!"

Amoxtli looked at me meaningfully. Too bad I didn't know him well enough to know what his looks meant. I assumed he meant: *do something*.

I grabbed Tez by the arm, unable to suppress a little fizz of excitement at the touch. "Can I talk to you? *Inside*?" I pulled and started hustling him up the stairs as the older men scooted out of the way.

"Hey, hey, no rush! There's plenty of me to go around!" Tez laughed again. He was getting loopier by the second. God only knew what he'd been doing out there all day.

This was *not* going to be fun.

The Varelas' apartment was on the top floor, and Tez grinned and flirted at me all the way up the stairs. He led me down a long, dark hallway into a bright, bay-windowed living room full of worn eighties furniture, homey tchotchkes, and a younger, skinnier version of Tez, with a dollop of Chucha thrown in. This Varela version—wearing a chocolate brown jumpsuit my inner Rachel Zoe was already taking notes on—looked up with alarm from a battered gaming console, took me in, took Tez's goofy grin on board, and dropped the game controller like it was on fire. Ze shot down the hall and out of sight. I heard a door shut. Tez showed no indication of having noticed his sibling at all. These were all not good signs.

I sat down and Tez leaned against the entertainment center, ignoring the tattered remains of his sibling's first-person-shooter game behind him, and the imminent death of an Allied soldier. The breakfront was the only new furniture in the place. He let the backpack slide off his shoulder onto a shelf. Good. Close by, but at least not touching him.

"Tez," I said, interrupting what was meant to be a sly comment about a fly coming into a spider's sitting room, "Where have you been the past few days?"

"Why? Did you miss me?" Geez, if I'd met Tez when he was acting like this, I would've heartbrokenly written him off as a sleazebag.

"I've been very worried. You were a little ... murderous ... last time I saw you. And I've had your car for four days."

"Oh yeah, thanks for bringing that back! I'm gonna need to go back to work next week." And yes, I *did* notice that he picked the most innocuous part of my statement to respond to.

"Oh, did they give you the rest of the week off?"

"Yeah. I've got 'till the ..." and his lighthearted mood seemed to catch up with him "... funeral." He looked blankly at the floor for a moment, then up at me. "It's tomorrow at four at Sullivan's, if you want to go."

"Thanks," I said. "I'd like to."

"It'll be an open casket," he said, neutrally, but with all the signs of social awareness. "Just FYI. In case that sort of thing bothers you."

"No, I prefer that. My mom had an open casket. It's better if you see."

He nodded. I decided to strike fast.

"Did they do an autopsy?" I asked, just as blank as he.

He frowned. I couldn't tell if he was confused, or annoyed. "Uh ... yeah, yeah they did."

"And?"

"And they couldn't find anything. They called it 'heart failure,' but they might as well have called it 'brain failure' or 'lung failure' or even 'skin failure,' 'cause all those things fail when you just *die*." He stopped being blank on the last word.

"Did Ayo see ... her?"

"Yeah." He shuddered. "Yeah, she did. She said all of Chucha's essence was completely gone. It was definitely that shadow thing. ... That fucking shadow thing ..."

"So it *wasn't* the 70s."

His eyes narrowed. "What is your *deal* with the 70s, Maya? Why are you so anxious to let them off the hook?"

"I'm anxious that you don't get into a war with a *gang* ferfuckssake, Tez!"

"Even if they didn't kill her themselves, they sicced that fucking *thing* on her!"

"I'm not so sure they did, Tez."

"What do you mean?"

"Tez, that thing has killed five shapeshifters so far—possibly six. Each one was a different kind: A werewolf, a harimau jadian, a bajang, a vanara, ... a nagual dog. And maybe an aswang. The werewolf, the bajang, and the— and Chucha, were all working for the San Antonios, but the weretiger, the vanara, and the aswang were not.

Tez, I don't think this thing is working for the 70s, and I don't think it's got stealing on its mind."

"That doesn't mean that the 70s didn't turn it on to the shapeshifters working for the San Antonios."

"No, it doesn't mean that, but that wouldn't really make that much sense, either." You could almost hear the clicking in my mind as I gave voice to suspicions that had been brimming since last night. "How would the 70s find out about, or get in touch with a shadow creature like that? Only through the meat market: and Ayo and I would have heard if a creature like that came through. We've been asking around for over a week now and there hasn't been a peep. No. It makes a lot more sense to imagine that it was the stick—"

"What about It?" He was, suddenly, aggressive again.

"It enhances your power. Doesn't it?"

He looked at the floor, jaw set.

"It clearly does. It made Chucha giddy and giggly, and it does the same to you, except when it makes you super aggro. And I don't know about your strength without the stick, but I'm imagining it isn't much more than proportional to your animal's strength." He shrugged. "Tez, you barely *touched* that werewolf with the stick and he went *flying*. The stick enhances your power!" He didn't respond. "Well, is it that hard to imagine that if it enhances your power, it'll enhance your supernatural energy ... uh, signature? I mean, that the stick makes you easier to spot? If the shadow is running around eating shapeshifter essences, won't it go to where the shapeshifter energy is the loudest?"

"But it didn't attack that werewolf the 70s had."

"Well, god, it barely had a chance before you came along and laid him out."

"Well ... maybe."

"Not maybe! Tez, it could be coming after you next!"
He scoffed.

"I'm serious, Tez! You're in a lot of danger, and not
just from that shadow thing! The 70s *saw* you take
the stick and they'll be after you. And I'm sure the San
Antonios have heard all about it by now, and they'll be
pretty pissed, too. You need to get rid of that thing! Give
it back to the San Antonios. Let *them* deal with the 70s!"

"No!" He reached behind him and grabbed the
backpack.

"Tez! Please! Just put the stick down! I promise I won't
try to take it from you. But you get really irrational when
you're holding—"

"DON'T TELL ME WHAT TO DO!" He stood,
towering over me on the couch, holding the stick through
the backpack bunched around it, nearly brandishing it at
me. I stood up slowly, I couldn't help it. I couldn't have
him standing over me like that. He raised the stick.

"What, are you going to hit me?" I asked sarcastically.
But underneath I was really disturbed.

That seemed to shake him.

"It's time for you to leave," and he grasped my arm,
almost exactly the way I had grasped his, and hustled me
to the door.

"Tez, you have to listen to me!" I cried, as he dragged
me down the stairs. His hand seemed glued to my arm;
as if he couldn't let go until I was properly out.

"No, I *don't*," he said, more to himself than me.

The Padrinos were still on the stairs and jumped up in
surprise as we came out. Tez push-pulled me down the
front stairs and all the way out to the sidewalk, where he
finally released me.

"Go on now," he said, with a little push. "Go."

I just stood there, shocked, my confusion echoed in

the older men's faces. Behind me Monkey noted the muscular sound of a souped-up car engine approaching, but I was too involved with looking through the layers on Tez's face, trying to find some welcome, or friendship, or even rationality, to even notice.

And that's when they opened fire.

CHAPTER TWENTY-TWO

CHAPTER TWENTY-TWO

TIME DIDN'T SLOW down, like it does in the movies. Everything happened too fast for my awareness to catch up with my instincts, but Tez and I reacted the same way. Almost before we heard the first gunshots, we had grabbed ahold of each other and yanked/fallen to the ground. After a moment of shock, I looked to see who had shot us, but Tez's forearm was blocking my face. I was partway underneath him, he was partly behind me (I have no idea how we managed to land that way), and my second thought was that my upper arm and shoulder, which is what I landed on, were going to hurt a lot in a moment.

Don't let them get away, Monkey said.

I performed a quick comedy of errors disentangling myself from Tez (who'd ever imagine I would want to do that?), getting up, and immediately tripping over the strap of his backpack, but it only slowed me down a few seconds. I left Tez still getting his bearings and hauled ass down the block in the direction of the car—a breathtaking iridescent green '67 Mustang—which had screeched off like a getaway car should, but then inexplicably stopped in the middle of the next block.

As I neared the car I saw the problem: a sweet lowrider—50s Detroit steel and curves; turquoise, the size of a house—was stopped coming the opposite direction, thus blocking the left hand lane, and both cars were waiting for an unexpectedly enormous Porsche Cayenne SUV to back out of its tiny driveway. The mustang was laying on the horn and the SUV driver was taking the time to lean out his window to yell back. One of the guys in the back seat turned to see if anyone was giving chase, saw me, saw me seeing him, and saluted with his gun. Then he turned around, no doubt certain that that would be enough to stop any thoughtless Asian-girl heroics I'd been contemplating.

Yeah, I was gonna get him first.

But *how*? Baby's voice intruded on me: count to ten when you're angry and then think about what you *really* want. I wanted to beat them all to shit. I wanted to *hurt* them for coming into my neighborhood and causing violence on such a beautiful evening. I wanted to *kill* something I ... I wanted ... Tez. I wanted them to leave Tez alone. That's what I really wanted. I wanted Tez to come out of this nightmare whole and sane and not in jail. Monkey screeched in disapproval. Monkey wanted blood and guts. Too bad.

I needed a hammer ... a mallet ... a *sledge*hammer. I plucked out a hair and made it so, just in time to wrench the passenger door open, yank out the passenger and send him flying into a parked car, the thunk of his body against metal satisfying Monkey somewhat. I then dragged my backseat thug into the street behind the car—all with my left hand. I let go the backseater and he struggled to find his feet, apparently forgetting the Ruger he was holding. Still in human form I swung my weight onto the knuckles of the fist holding the sledgehammer and, using my body as an axle, grabbed the backseater's upper torso between my legs and flipped him to the ground. The gun skittered out of his hand and a few feet down the street.

I stood back up facing the passenger, who was sitting on the hood of the parked car, scrabbling at his lower back for, presumably, another gun. I grinned, took two steps, grabbed him by the ankle with my free hand, and swung him like a dead cat into an air spin over the tail of the beeyootiful 'stang. He throwing-starred a half turn before landing on the backseater.

As they lay stunned I kicked the passenger, who was on top, over onto his stomach and snagged his weapon, another Ruger; maybe the 70s had gotten a special deal. I retrieved the backseater's dropped gun, and headed for the driver's side door.

All of this had taken about ten seconds, just enough time for the driver to get all tangled up in conflicting intentions: putting the car into park, or releasing his seat belt, or getting out of the car, or pulling his gun. He was still strapped in when I yanked his door open. I was holding the two guns in one hand, and the sledgehammer under one arm, which made it impossible for me to fire, but he was too shocked to think this through. He raised his hands in surrender and I got him to unbuckle and get out. I checked him for weapons with the head of my sledgehammer, but all it encountered was flesh and clothes. He must've given his gun to one of his companions and forgotten that he'd done it.

I gestured him to the other side of the car, the stretch of road where I'd left his buddies piled up. They were just starting to extricate themselves when I pushed him over on top of them with my foot.

One by one I released the mags and tossed them into the street. Then I popped the chambered rounds, caught them, and tossed them into the pile of gangbanger I'd built. Finally, I stacked the pistols carefully on the ground, on their sides, one on top of the other. I paused for effect; I really was talented at the theater of violence. When I was good and ready, and they were starting uncertainly to try and get up, I swung the sledgehammer over my head in a perfect arc, and smashed the two guns to smithereens.

I had driven the hammer with so much force, it hadn't even bounced, but rather stuck into a new dent in the asphalt it had created. I yanked the sledgehammer back out of the road and admired my handiwork. The handles of both pistols had taken the brunt of the strike, the crook of each gun having warped into the asphalt in the negative shape of the hammer head. The barrels had bent upwards and the mechanisms had split, spewing springs and broken rods and bits of smashed plastic from the handles.

Kick 'em for good measure! Monkey shrieked. I resisted. The sledgehammer was a pure show of strength, and the 70s had taken the lesson; well, that and me throwing the passenger one-handed. They stared at me in shock and I nodded once.

"Now get the *fuck* outta my neighborhood," I said, and turned my back. The human in me did not like turning my back on assholes, but Monkey insisted on it as a show of dominance. A *monkey* show of dominance. Not that humans aren't primates, but, ya know. Monkey.

It would've been a perfect display, too. Even the SUV and low rider drivers—who couldn't see clearly what I was doing behind the 'Stang—had frozen, staring at me through their side window and windshield, respectively. But just as I started to walk away, in slow mo, mission accomplished, a Tez-flavored blur whizzed past me and arc-leapt at the belatedly sorting pile of 70s.

"No, Tez!" I cried, "I dealt with them! Let them go!"

He may not have heard me. All I saw was a flurry of fists and feet, and … was that a backpack? He looked like a murderous schoolboy. All at once, various 70s legs and heads and torsos were being punched and kicked this way and that. He was *really fast*. I couldn't get in there. I stood frozen for too many moments, looking for that opening that Tez wouldn't allow.

While I was trying to figure out what to do—the only way to wade in and not get knocked sideways was to turn into something really hard, and then Tez might break his hand against me by accident—Tez chose a primary target: the passenger. I guessed he'd been the shooter and smelled of burnt gunpowder, because Tez hauled him out of the pile to focus his ire more effectively. The two he left behind weren't unconscious, but were bloody and beaten and dazed. I chose the less dazed one; the backseater, who'd been somewhat protected from the brunt of the pile-beating by the dudes on top of him.

"Get up!" I yelled, shaking him. "Get up and get your friends and get outta here!" He looked at me confused for a moment, and then got up to comply.

Tez was standing in the middle of the road, holding the shooter up with one hand around his throat, and hammering his face to a pulp with the other. A look of such wild, lost savagery wore his face, that he must have terrified his audience. The lowrider squealed backwards out of its position, and the SUV clipped a parked car on its three point turn and screamed off after it.

I lifted my hand, and noticed I still had my sledgehammer in it. I turned the head to soft rubber.

"Tez!" I screamed. He paused for a fraction, and looked around at me, but his eyes were yellow, afire, and he couldn't really see. Instantly, he returned to his savagery. Well, I tried.

Two wide steps and I was in striking distance. I grabbed his backpack and yanked it away from his back to get his attention. He dropped the passenger with a snarl, spun around, and swiped at me, but I was ready for him. I aimed the rubber hammerhead at his soft tissue—it would heal faster than broken bones—and lifted him gracefully away from me with a one-handed swing. He flew backwards over the parked cars and landed on his back on the sidewalk.

I leapt after him and stood him down, one foot on each wrist. He was slightly dazed from the impact and his eyes were empty. I crouched and shook his shoulder.

"Tez!" I cried. "Tez! Snap out of it! Tez!" I slapped his face.

His eyes focused on me. They were dark brown, and confused.

"What the fu—?"

"Tez! Talk to me. Who am I?"

"Maya? What's going— what are you doing? Are you *standing* on me?"

Behind us, hidden by the row of parked cars, I heard the 'Stang's tires squeal as the three 70s finally made their getaway. Tez's eyes glowed for a moment. He jerked.

"They're getting away!"

"Let them!" He looked at me incredulously, eyes focusing again. "Look, you know who they are now, and they're all beaten to a pulp. You can send the cops after them later if you want."

I stepped carefully off of him and hauled him to his feet. He was still too confused to notice how strong I was. Good thing. Probably.

"Beaten to a ... pulp?" He looked at his hands, the backsides of which were split and bloody, although already starting to heal. "I ... did that?"

I grasped his chin, hard, and made him look at me.

"Tez, you were completely out of control. *Completely*." He looked at me and his mind seemed to sharpen all at once.

"I smashed that guy's face in."

"Yes, you did. Over and over."

"That's ... that's never happened to me before."

I paused and let go of his chin, letting my knuckles rasp against the scruff for a too-brief moment.

"Yes, Tez, it has." He frowned at me in puzzlement. "In Fruitvale on Tuesday night, when we found the stick. You went off on the 70s dudes and almost killed their werewolf."

He shook his head, to clear it rather than to deny. "I don't— I barely remember that ..."

"Tez, it's the walking stick. That damned stick is doing this to you. You're full of crazy emotions right now and the stick is just ... heightening it all. It's making you giddy ... and violent."

He shook his head, but not in denial. "I can feel it. It's so powerful. It's starting to scare me. I can't control it ..." He swung away from me and slid the pack off of his back. He grasped and held the stick, through the bag, in two hands, his head bowed over it.

"Tez, you *have* to give it back to them—or to the San Antonios."

"No!" He shouted, suddenly. "Can't you *see*? It belongs to *me*!" He turned to look at me again. He gestured toward me with the stick, then pulled it back in to his chest. He looked at me, part rage, part pleading. "Can't you see it? It's *mine*! It was *always* mine!"

He was really starting to freak me out. That *thing* was really freaking me out. But I knew when not to push ... sort of.

"Fine then. Do you want to call the cops or not?"

He looked struck, then horrified.

"Ambulance!" he cried. "I was supposed to call an ambulance!"

Now I was confused. "Ambulance ... for who ...?" But he was already running back to his house, digging in his pack for his phone.

When I ran up, a few frozen seconds behind him, Amoxtli was laid out on the walkway, blood seeping out of his belly. My god, what an asshole I was. I hadn't even stopped to see if anyone was hurt. Jaime was kneeling over him, putting pressure on the wound, and Mike was on the phone with emergency dispatch.

We all heard a siren.

"You have to go!" Tez turned to me. "We can't explain why you're here! You have to *go*!"

The men looked at him, startled, then at me, for an explanation I couldn't give them.

"Okay, I'll go," I said, knowing that Tez meant he couldn't explain the reality of our association to anyone; he didn't know I'd already made up a plausible story, and now wasn't the time to clarify. Mike started to protest but I cut him off. "It's better this way," I said, not explaining, but got his number so I could check in later. Then, with a last look at Tez, completely absorbed by staring—and surreptitiously sniffing—at Amoxtli, I went to Tez's Civic like it was nothing, started it with a hair, and drove off.

I couldn't resist looking in the rearview. Tez hadn't even noticed, but Mike and Jaime were watching me drive off with their mouths hanging open. Tez still had the backpack on his back and it wouldn't be long before his Padrinos realized that there was something really wrong with him. And then they'd understand why I'd taken his car. Again.

And *damn* it: the one thing I'd tried to prevent—a gang war—had reached Tez's door. It seemed, as I drove off, that I'd accomplished nothing in the past couple of hours: I still had the car, and still *hadn't* found out anything about the stick.

… But hadn't I? I'd connected Amoxtli to the Varelas, and Amoxtli to the stick (given his menacing response when I mentioned "magic sticks," he knew *something*,) which meant his search for the stick's instructions reinforced last night's idea that the Varelas might have a special relationship with the stick. And, of course, just as I'd made that connection, Amoxtli had taken a bullet. Shit, was I about to lose another clue? Fuck, was Tez about to lose another family member?

I hit the steering wheel again and it made a complainy banging noise.

Everything in Tez's life, from his Padrino to this ten-year-old steering wheel, was more fragile and endangered than I'd thought. Tez himself was in danger, and I didn't even know yet what to wish for, for him.

I'd just have to check in at the hospital tomorrow, and hope Tez's family was in for some long overdue good luck.

CHAPTER TWENTY-THREE

SATURDAY, OCTOBER 22, 2011
SANC-AHH CAFÉ, OAKLAND

CHUCHA'S FUNERAL SATURDAY was hell.

It's awful to be genuinely grieving for someone you feel you have no right to grieve, and to have to do it alone, among legitimate mourners, most of whom are strangers to you. Just exactly how distant I was from the family was made clear to me when I arrived at the funeral home, and couldn't find Chucha's viewing room at first, because I didn't know her real name, which was Jesus Xochitl, of all things. I only found it by last name.

Then I went in and, not wanting to have to explain who I was to them, had to avoid Tez's siblings, who seemed to be everywhere.

Tez, Jaime, and Mike, plus another middle-aged couple—I assumed Tez's Uncle Carlos and wife—hovered protectively over the siblings—one of whom was absurdly larger than all of his elders. I just nodded at them from a distance, not even sure if they'd seen me.

In the casket Chucha looked waxy and made-up. That

was the only relief: the dissociation from the corpse that I remembered from my foster mother's funeral, that let you start to realize that your person was really dead.

I decided to skip the reception at their apartment that afternoon. Tez hadn't bothered to come over and ask me for the car. I took this as a bad sign, so I kept it, reasoning that once he was clear enough in the head to remember the damned car and come find me, it would be safe to give it to him. I was probably also wanting at least one more chance to see him before being shut out.

There was another march planned for that day, but I couldn't bear marching and protesting, so I spent the rest of the day at the Occupy encampment, at the kids' activity tent, helping kids to draw flowers, and thinking of nothing.

That evening Tez showed up at Sanc-Ahh. I heard the door bells jingle and felt that whoosh of pressure, so I knew he'd come in. But there was no accompanying excitement in my chest, just a sense of dread. It took something for me to turn around. Apparently, Tez was feeling the same way, because I found him still hovering next to the door, as if he might want to just walk right back out.

I waved him over and he came, reluctantly, hangdog.

"You knew what I wanted the car for. That's why you took it." He spoke as if continuing a conversation we'd just been having. I realized that we sort of had been having that conversation, right after Amoxtli was shot.

"Oh really? What was that?" I said, suddenly full of pepper. He needed to tell me this time.

"You know. I was gonna take it directly over to Fruitvale and bash some heads."

"'Bash some heads'? Or kill someone?"

That stopped him for a second.

"I don't know," he said so low it was almost a whisper. He didn't say anything for a while, and I was bursting with things to say. But I kept quiet.

"I tried to hide It," he said finally. I glanced over his shoulder and saw that he still had the backpack with him. "Tried to," not "succeeded." "You were right. It's messing with my head. I can't really control It. I thought if I could walk away from It, maybe It wouldn't affect me so much. But it didn't really work."

He looked up at me. "Even when I left It behind my head was all over the place. I can't stop thinking about It. It's calling to me, telling me that it belongs to me, that I should go get It and use It to kill my enemies and gather my … tribe, I guess. I think I'm going crazy, but I can't let It go. It's mine."

"It's … talking to you?"

"No, not exactly. I just … feel this pull to It. And I … feel those things. It's not in words. I just feel things and feel this pull, so I know all this is coming from It."

"That's unusual," Ayo said, and we both jumped. I hadn't seen her come in, and she'd probably used magic to approach us invisibly … to eavesdrop.

Tonight, this didn't bother me. In fact, I was relieved. Tez admitting that he was out of control was … a little terrifying.

"Nagualism isn't big on power objects," she continued, as if we hadn't just given her startled-face. "That's much more of a European influence. What is this thing supposed to do?"

I shrugged, and Tez furrowed his brow.

"I don't know what It's supposed to do," Tez admitted, "but what It's doing is making me stronger and faster—especially when I'm holding It—and It's trying to get me to … I dunno. It wants me to … consume It? It wants me to use It as a power base. It wants me to root in the soil. It wants me to be the land."

His eyes glowed amber now. I was freaked out.

"Ayo," I said breathlessly. "It's trying to possess him."

"I'm not getting that hit at all," she said calmly, examining Tez with her entire attention. "I think, rather, It wants him to possess It."

Tez's glowing eyes turned to her. "Yes," he said. "It wants me to possess It entirely."

"And how is that not 'one ring to rule them all'?" I cried.

"I don't know," Tez answered, his eyes dimming again. "Shit. Maybe you're right. Maybe I have to find Its Mount Doom. Maybe It has to be destroyed." He looked so distraught at this, that I almost reached out to him.

Ayo straightened, completing her survey of Tez. "Let's not jump the gun, shall we? I take it that"—she pointed at his backpack—"is the Huexotl in question?" Tez looked surprised for a moment, as if he'd forgotten that anyone else could see the damned thing, but then he nodded. "Well, then. Maya, take him to the back and show him around. See if you can find anything about magic sticks in the ... you know. I'll call Stoney in to take over here and join you when he comes."

She waved a hand casually at the door to the office, as if she was just gesturing at it, but I felt my eyes flare slightly as her magic unlocked ... and then I "remembered" what was back there, and felt a flush of pleasure.

I turned to Tez, smiling, and grabbed his hand. "Come on!" I said, feeling like a child about to show her new best friend around her room.

As I opened the door to Ayo's office, it felt like light streamed out of it, although it was only the usual single fluorescent bulb. But the door at the back of the office, which looked like it led to a closet most times, was slightly ajar, unlocked by Ayo's casual handwave. She'd also unlocked the wards around it for us, so that I'd remember what was back there and so we could both enter. I shivered, this time with a familiar delight.

That door actually led to a much larger space behind. This was Ayo's real office space, her inner sanctum, and the place where she did—and kept—most of her research. It expanded out to encompass the entire width of the building, taking up the back half of both of the building's storefronts—the cafe on the right and the rapidly changing business (right now a discount craft store) on the left—although Ayo's wards prevented anyone from noticing that the two stores were yards shorter than they should be. Or maybe her magic made this space larger inside than it was outside. I'd never really decided which.

Tez's eyes grew wide as we entered. No one knew the space existed except Ayo, Stoney, and me. Not even the short-term employees she hired now and again had access. The place was spelled for protection. Part of that protection was a spell that discouraged us from talking—or even thinking—about the sanctum when we weren't in it.

The room was lighted by halogen bulbs in soft white globes and painted in shades of amber, so it looked like the sun was always rising or setting inside. But you couldn't see much of the walls because the top third was absolutely covered in artwork—masks, implements, items of dress, paintings, scrolls—from cultures and traditions all over Europe, Africa, the Caribbean, and the Americas. And the bottom two thirds were lined with card catalogues.

Yes, that's right: Ayo had rescued some old library card

catalogue cabinets—the really beautiful ones, made from exotic woods with brass hardware—and made them the primary furniture in the heart of her sanctuary. They lined three walls, with the fourth holding equally elegant filing cabinets, including a large flat file for artwork and maps. The center of the room, carpeted by a gorgeous Navajo rug, contained a beautiful, long, wooden library table, and a couple of comfy armchairs with a side table between them.

The cafe and bookstore outside were pleasant enough, especially with the peacekeeping spells woven into them, but they looked bare and rough compared to this room, which was the heart and hearth of the sanctuary—the place from which all the peace and communion of the outer gathering places flowed.

"What is this place?" Tez asked, breathless. The energy of the place was rather breathtaking, especially when you were new to it.

"This is … to oversimplify, where Ayo keeps her research."

"In card catalogues?" he asked, still puzzled.

"Yes, and files," I said, pointing those out.

"But where are the books?" He asked.

"What books?"

"The books … or, or … documents … where she keeps her research?"

"Tez: her research is, basically, stories. And they're kept here on the cards or in files."

"But … where does all this information come from? Is she just transferring this from books? Because, why not just keep the books? Or photocopy them?"

I looked at him incredulously. "Do you not know how Ayo works?"

He looked confused, and shrugged.

"Tez, none of this information can be found in books. It's all data—stories, tales, experiences—collected by Ayo directly from the source."

He still looked puzzled.

"You made a deal with Ayo to get my help. What did you promise her?"

He looked blank for a moment, and then his face opened in realization. "I promised to get her some … thing, but I also promised to tell her a story from my family. I hadn't thought that part was important." He looked around. "This is what she does with the stories?"

"The story is the most important part of your deal with Ayo, not the least. This is her life's work." I swept the whole room with my hands. "This is how she connects us and helps us. The stories we tell are where folklore comes from. The stories passed down to us are our history. This is the intersection between human history, human folklore, and supernatural history. Ayo has collected these into a database, and here's the database."

He absorbed this for a moment.

I walked over to the card catalogues. "The information—the stories are on the cards," I explained in my best hall monitor voice. "They're organized by region" I pointed to one wall, "and by cultural tradition." I pointed to the other two. Then I opened a drawer and pulled out a card at random. Like most of the others, it was filled with tiny handwriting. "For example, this one is a story from a bouda and the story itself is a variant of the Egyptian Rhodopis story. So it's located in East Africa, and cross referenced with"—I pointed to the letter symbols at the bottom of the card—"Ethiopian folklore, Egyptian folklore, Greek history, and European fairytales, because the Rhodopis story is considered an early version of Cinderella."

I looked more closely at the card. "This card contains

all the information. But some of the stories contained on the cards are longer, so the card will have a summary of the story and its significance, the cross-reference material, and then here"—I flipped through a drawer for an example—"at the bottom right will be an inventory number which will point to a longer document on paper in the filing cabinet." I pointed to the cabinets.

"So the Rhodopis story will have a similar card in Ethiopian folklore, etc.?"

"Yes, or a more general card that points to several stories on several different cards in a different section."

"How are they organized within the drawers? Alphabetically?" He looked doubtful.

I laughed. "Unfortunately, no. There's no system for naming the stories, so you just have to look through according to region or cultural tradition, and look for key words. The key words are usually underlined on the cards, but not always. When you find something you think might be useful, pull it and bring it over to the table."

"How will you know where to put it back?"

"We put it back in the front of the drawer that makes the most sense. So the cards move around the system a lot, and the cards at the front of the drawers are the ones that have gotten the most use. Which means we should start at the back, because Ayo has already pulled all the ones she can think of that have relevance."

"How do you find anything here?" he cried, throwing up his hands.

"Magic!" I cried, then laughed again. "I don't know what kind. It works somehow. Stoney and I are sort of like … extensions of Ayo's mind when we're in here, and we all understand how and where to place things. It's a very mild kind of magic that draws from the power of books and paper and … stories themselves. It'll make sense as you get into it."

"Why— " he began, and I finished in sync with him "isn't it digitized?"

"The magic here comes from keeping the information in ink, on paper, in wooden containers. There's something about physically handling the words and ideas that puts you into a kind of frame of mind. It makes you … receptive. Being in this room, being around these papers and cards and objects somehow … enhances your ability to … use this information—find information, understand information … in a way that you can … I dunno, I guess serve the clients of the sanctuary. Did that make any sense?"

He shook his head, not in denial, but in awe.

I always knew the room was there; it was a warm place in my heart, and it drew me in. I'd spent many happy hours in Ayo's room, doing research for her, or looking for stories about myself. It meant so much to me to share this room with Tez.

Tez, unconscious of the effect his presence had on me, decided to start with the geographic files, which worked well for me because I liked to go through the cultural tradition files. He started with Mexico, and I started with the Aztecs. He started out reading everything and moving slowly, but quickly caught on to the system and eventually nearly matched my speed. We each pulled out several cards we thought might be relevant, and eventually collected a small stack on the table; but direct references to sticks, walking sticks, staffs, cudgels, or other power objects in that cultural realm eluded us.

After some time I noticed that Ayo had come in. She was standing at the table looking over the cards we'd pulled. A moment later, Tez also noticed the change in the room's continuum and looked up. Ayo smiled at him and held out her hand.

"Let me see the Huexotl."

I could hear the power in her voice, and I saw Tez struggle for a moment; but he generally was not in a resistant mood, and he handed the stick over to her relatively smoothly. It was cane-sized again, and Ayo's eyes seemed to come to life as she handled it. But after a few moments, without any appearance of discomfort, she placed it carefully on the table and withdrew her hand. Huh.

"What does it do?" she asked him, power in her voice again.

"Really?" I asked her, exasperated in spite of my feelings of well-being in this space. "You're the one who had the instructions!"

The utterly blank look Tez gave me now reminded me that I'd never told him—

"I told you," Ayo said. "I got the package, which was just a sealed envelope, and gave it to him. I didn't look inside."

"What instructions? Why didn't you tell me It had instructions?" Tez demanded, truly bewildered.

"Are you kidding me, Laughing Boy? I wanted you away from that thing, not bound closer to it!" Tez looked angry and chagrined at the same time. I took the fact that there was any chagrin in the mix as a win.

"Where are they now?"

"I got them for Juice," Ayo said quietly, which calmed him down somewhat.

"How did you know about them in the first place?" Tez asked me, already knowing the answer. But he had a look on his face ... he wanted to hear someone talk about her. He broke my heart.

"Chucha told me about it," I said gently. "She didn't get to see them either, but she said she didn't need to because the … Huexotl … told her what to do with it."

"So, Tez?" Ayo asked. "What does it do?"

"I … don't really know. It makes me stronger and faster. It … calls to me. It makes me feel … powerful and … happy—no, not happy. It makes me feel … high, I guess."

"It also changes size and shape a bit," I put in, "depending on who is holding it, maybe? Or what use they want to put it to?"

"What does it do for you, Maya?"

"Not much," I said, and Tez looked at me in surprise. I guess he really had thought I wanted it for myself. "Not that I've had much of a chance to play with it. Chucha barely even let me put a finger on it. It makes—made—them both super-possessive. And … it makes Tez extra aggressive." He winced. "I don't know if it did the same for Chucha."

I thought for a moment.

"I can feel its power, though. When I touch it I get a distant sense of being connected to a much larger source of power. But it feels alien to me. Not wrong, exactly. Just … not of me."

Tez shook his head, a rueful smile appearing briefly on his lips. "Wow," he said. "It's the complete opposite for me. It feels like … home, to the nth degree, like … like driving west over the Bay Bridge at sunset, after a long road trip … like … as long as I have it, wherever I go, I'm home. That connection to the larger source of power? It's not a connection, the source is right there for me, right under my feet, right in my hands. I don't know how to use it, exactly, but it's there. I'm like … drowning in pool of it … no, not a pool, an ocean."

Ayo stared at it some more. We all did.

Then she looked up. "Well? Keep researching! I'm just looking. If anything interesting happens, you'll be the first to know." She waved us off and we went willingly back to the cards. After a while, the energy in the room shifted slightly again, and I knew that Ayo had joined us in looking through the cards, also in the geographical section. Clearly Ayo and Tez were thinking along the same lines. But Ayo knew to range further afield. It was often creatures—people—from very different cultural traditions who heard the stories that you were looking for in this cultural realm (since she got these stories all from real people, who often met other real people in their travels.) And, in fact, after several hours of hard searching, that's where Ayo found a real clue.

"Look at this," she said suddenly, and her voice held a controlled excitement. "This is a story about a stick from an Aziza who dwelt in Oakland for many years, but had also traveled through Latin America and central Asia for decades. He told me many many stories. Problem with Azizas is that they don't have a good sense of space or geography. Where they are is where they are, so he couldn't identify places very well. So in this story he said he met a shaman or medicine man who was tied to the earth through a magical staff. It made the man more powerful, but he couldn't leave his territory."

Tez rushed over to look at the document over her shoulder. Apparently, he discovered that it wasn't written in a language he could read. He huffed and walked away like an offended cat, and stood at the bank of card catalogue drawers, but didn't open any.

She swished through pages of the document for a few moments, and Tez grew restless.

"When was this?" he asked, testily.

"Azizas aren't too good with time, either. I'm guessing

this was about at the turn of the 19th to the 20th century, but it could have been much earlier or much later. This guy was an absolute font of good stories—all he asked in return was really pure tobacco and occasionally a foot rub—but the stories came out in a jumble, and for some of them I have no idea when or where they took place."

She flipped through the pages and held one up. "These are just notes, mind you. It says Ritual for binding medicine man to earth. Wouldn't specify details of. Something about alignment of stars. Made staff of wood from tree from original home. Enabled them to draw power from land wherever they went. Partner—apparently the medicine man or shaman or whatever he was had a partner from within the clan, a ceremonial position. This partner seems to have been a storyteller, a keeper of the histories of the clan, and I think this means the storyteller was also responsible for memorizing the form of the rituals and passing them on to the next generation. This dude was the medicine man's advisor, and he was expected to confer with the storyteller before making any major decisions. And that's pretty much it. This is all from questions I asked about the storyteller, not the story itself."

"What's the story itself?" I asked. Well someone had to.

"Oh, just about ill luck that happened when the shaman didn't confer with the storyteller/consigliere guy, and some humorous havoc that ensued. I'll write out a translation for you, Tez, but I don't think it's relevant. He might have been talking about naguals. He might not have been."

We both looked at Tez and only then noticed that he was frozen in shock.

"What is it?" I asked.

"Amoxtli," Tez whispered.

"Amoxtli?" Ayo said. "That's Nahuatl for 'codex' or 'book.' Are you thinking of the storyteller role? Yes, it's true, it might have been a codex, or a series of codices, instead of a man. They kept the years and seasons, the days and feasts, the dreams and omens, the naming of children, and the marriage rites. Maybe this medicine man conferred with codices instead of another person."

"No, Ayo, Amoxtli, Tez's family friend, is a person. That's his name. You know him."

She shook her head.

"He referred me to you," Tez said, just as I was saying: "He's the one who was asking for the stick's ..." I trailed off as I heard what Tez had said. "... instructions ..." I finished, realizing. He'd referred Tez to Ayo. And instantly I knew that was the "secret" he'd made Ayo keep from me. Dammit!

"Oh, you mean Amo? I didn't know that was his full name. That's ... interesting ..."

"You kept his connection to Tez a secret from me, Ayo. But didn't it occur to you that Amo asked for the instructions because the Varelas are connected to the stick?"

"No, I didn't, because he gave me a good cover story." Which she couldn't tell me, even now, being sworn to silence. Sigh.

"Wait a minute," Tez said, "What did you say about the stick's instructions?"

I was still combing through my tangled thoughts. "Your ... uh ... Amoxtli came in and asked Ayo to find him a particular piece of writing, written in ballpoint pen on a sheet of torn out notebook paper. He didn't say what was on it, but Chucha had just told me that same day that Juice had instructions for the stick written in ballpoint on a sheet of notebook paper, and Ayo told me she'd been the one to get the instructions for Juice. We assumed it was the same thing, and I was going to ask him about it but ..."

Tez nodded absently and chewed his lip. "Where did you get the instructions from, Ayo?"

She shook her head. "We're way ahead of you. I got it from a Chinatown contact in no way connected."

There was more silence, as we all churned this over.

"He's a storyteller," Tez said, finally, in a wondering tone. I knew he meant Amoxtli. I could see Ayo narrowing her brows, almost see her grind her teeth in frustration at the stories she hadn't gotten from him. "He's a fucking bookshelf. He knows all the stories of our family. My dad told me once that he was a distant relative, that we were the same clan. Maya!" he turned to me, "My dad never made any big decisions without talking to Amoxtli first!"

"And he told me the history of your family while I was waiting for you yesterday. And he referred you to us. And he was asking for the stick's instructions. And ..." I said, emphatically, "I asked about magic sticks before you came back the other day and he gave me a look."

Tez looked shocked for a second, and then his look hardened.

"If there's really nothing more in that story," he looked sternly at Ayo, who shook her head, "then I know where to go now."

CHAPTER TWENTY-FOUR

Saturday, October 22, 2011
Outside Sanc-Ahh Café, Oakland

Tez's determined look stayed on his face, even as he was offering me a ride home.

He went out to start the car while I finished closing (the cafe had closed while we were in the back) and got my things. But when I stepped outside, I didn't immediately see him: his Civic was sitting there, dark and quiet. I looked down the sidewalk, but no one Tez-shaped was nearby. Then I looked in the other direction—

Tez was lying flat out on the sidewalk in the darkness between two streetlamps, a few dozen yards away. He was twitching and jerking and ... something was crouched over him ... it looked like a black panther ... no it was a shadow ... It was the shadow creature! *Eating* him!

My monkey brain took over and I slid into monkey form just in time to slam into the shadow creature, which I was ... relieved? to discover was solid enough to slam into. That meant: solid enough to take a beating, although its solidity felt like a brick shithouse had decided to grow foam rubber skin. It gave a little, and then it didn't, much to the detriment of my shoulder joint. Whatever it had been doing to Tez, it stopped, and, although, as before, I couldn't see a head or any features on it, I felt its attention turn entirely to me.

I couldn't suppress a shudder, although Monkey was in charge and calculating while screeching in fear. I checked its legs—it didn't have any. In fact, I couldn't tell if it was anchored to the ground, or floating, or—

WHAM! It hit me in the face with its ... I don't know what it hit me with, it felt like a shockwave, not any body part, but I took it full in the face and flipped 360 degrees backwards, landing flat on my back.

Was it just me, or was it hitting me harder than it had the last time? Or was I just weaker? Yes, I was weaker, I was weak. I was ...

The creature seemed to come closer to me—it was hard to tell, since it was all shadow and smoke, and transparency. But I could feel it hovering over me, and the hairs rose all over my body.

I reached up to grasp it and pull myself up onto its body—one of my signature moves that never failed to disorient an opponent—but, although it was more solid than air and pushed back against my fingers, I couldn't find any contours to grab a hold of. I couldn't get my elongated fingers around any part of it. It was like trying to grab a jellyfish. A really *hard* jellyfish. It pressed me down all along my upper body, although, again, I couldn't feel any hands or body parts, only irresistible pressure.

Then it seemed to go still, with its entire bulk *looking* at me, and I knew, with my entire self, that it was preparing to eat me.

Monkey had never been anyone's prey, and wasn't

about to start now. I screeched like the death of a banshee, turned into water, and flowed out from under the shadow. I streamed across the few feet of sidewalk between my position and Tez's, and then under the crevices of Tez's body. He was gasping for breath, but the sensation of water seemed to wake him, and he started sitting up, still gasping.

I came up on the other side of him, deliberately using him as a shield, (What? I was really freaked out) and reconstituted as a minotaur, my favorite muscle-form. The shadow seemed to ignore Tez, flowing over him without stopping, to get to me.

I took several rapid steps back, wound up, and roundhoused the center of the shadow's mass as it got close enough. It was a serious wallop. Almost as serious as I got. And it only stopped the shadow's forward momentum for a second. It didn't move it back an inch.

Monkey was screaming bloody murder in my head. I came at it with the two, pretty much all my punching power there. It stopped again, more completely this time. But no movement back. What the hell? My all-out roundhouse had never failed to knock an opponent out; in fact, I rarely went all out for fear of killing someone.

Starting to panic, I unleashed a rapid succession of punches and kicks at the mass of shadow, Monkey calculating angle, trajectory, and power in my head while screeching in harmony with my totally freaked out human brain. Whatthefuckwhatthefuckwhatthefuck. The shadow didn't move forward, but I seemed to have no other impact on it.

When I stopped for a moment, utterly frustrated, it walloped me again with its shock wave, but I was ready this time. I let it spin me around 360 degrees backward, landing on my feet ... mostly ... well, there was one knee on the— it was awkward, but I wasn't laid out, okay?

"All right, Slim Shady," I muttered, retreating again. "I see you. How do you feel about THIS?"

I turned into a freestanding jet engine, already running at top speed, and blasted him.

Slim Shady did not react much, but I had stopped him again.

I was tempted to be frustrated and switch tactics again, but had already learned my lesson. If Ol' Shady was gonna act like solid smoke, he'd better damn well *act* like solid smoke. Maybe it would take time to blow him all away. Well, I had nothin' *but* time.

I blasted and blasted, imagining myself as a sand blaster, as a desert storm, as a pounding ocean. I eked every bit of power I could out of my … whatever it was that power came from. And finally, after what seemed like hours, but was probably only a fraction of a minute, I started to see the edges of his shadow … move? A little? Backwards? Yay?

If I was seeing right, I was finally having an impact. But. I was also starting to get a little—just a little—tired, and I didn't know how long I could keep this up at full blast. And the main part of him hadn't moved yet at all.

"Maya?"

I didn't let up, but I could see Tez vaguely through the shadow. He was standing, but not looking very stable. Maybe that was my fault. Shady didn't seem to be blocking all the jet stream. He needed to get out of my blasting path. I couldn't call to him—jet engines have no mouths—and I was starting to regret not having telepathy. (Can you imagine? Ugh!)

Instead of using his common sense, though, Tez just attacked. He performed what I was starting to recognize as *his* signature move, a high-jump-with-overhead-punch, and I could somehow see ... or feel ... Shady's attention reverse around his smoky form, to focus on Tez.

Perfect.

I reached deep and found a little extra sumpin' sumpin' and *blasted* Shady into Tez's distinctly hairier-looking fist. The dark cloud bowed around Tez's arm. Shady *turned to look at me*—auuurrggghh—and then broke off from both of us and flew away at a speed I hadn't ever seen from him.

I did *not* try to follow. Let it never be said that I don't learn my lessons.

As soon as Shady was out of sight, Tez collapsed almost to the ground, and I had to help him into the car. I got in the drivers seat.

He was panting like a dog in labor and holding himself around the middle.

"What's the matter? Are you hurt?"

He didn't respond.

"Did he hurt you?" Jeebus Iced. He'd had part of his essence sucked out. What even was I supposed to do?!

"Who?"

"The shadow guy!"

"Oh, did you decide it was a guy? I decided it was a girl." He sounded weak, but not out of it. Maybe he was just tired. I started calming down.

"I'm calling him Slim Shady, or Shady for short."

"Shady the smoky lady."

Okay, he was still panting, still holding himself. But he was also joking. Which he didn't do much of. So that was good, right?

"Are you hurt?"

"No ... yes ... kind of. In a weird way." He panted a little more. "I feel ... just ... weak. Not sick or injured. Just weak. Like ... *diminished* ... like, a phone with a drained battery." Oh shit.

"Does your stomach hurt?" I asked, anxious again.

"No. It feels … empty. Not like hungry empty. Like … plastic bag empty."

"How can I … help?"

"There's nothing you can do. Just get me the Huexotl."

"I'm not sure you should be touching it."

"No, I need it. It knows I'm diminished, and it's calling to me. It'll revive me."

My confused brain cast about for a moment, but then I remembered seeing the bag with the stick lying a few yards away from where Tez had been downed. I lurched back out of the driver's seat and a few yards back down the sidewalk to where the stick and bag were. I hefted the walking stick, with its bag bunched around it. I could almost feel its power buzzing through the cloth of the bag. Was it getting … *stronger*? Good thing this stretch of Telegraph was mostly empty after midnight, even on a Saturday, because I'd completely forgotten about our things. I looked around and saw that I'd left my own purse and jacket in a heap near the cafe door.

Still entirely unsure I should be giving the damned thing to Tez, I went for my own things and walked bang into the man himself. He'd somehow dragged his own ass out of the car and down the sidewalk to me—or rather, to the stick—although he'd barely been able to move without assistance a moment ago.

He grabbed the stick, with the bag bunched around it, from me. As I watched, Tez held the still-bagged stick, and strength flowed almost visibly into him. He stood up straighter, the exhausted look left his face, his body began glowing with vitality again. I could almost have sworn that the color came back into his face as well, but it was impossible to tell in the orange street light.

Using the stick, he swept an elaborate bow. "My chariot awaits, milady." Oh god, he was all goofy and high again. I was so relieved that he had recovered that I almost didn't mind. Almost.

CHAPTER TWENTY-FIVE

SUNDAY, OCTOBER 23, 2011
SAN FRANCISCO GENERAL HOSPITAL, SAN FRANCISCO

TEZ INSISTED HE didn't need me to come talk to Amoxtli the next morning and I didn't argue. I was sure he'd prefer keeping the whole thing a secret, but that was just a bummer for him. Tez had been in Ayo's—*my*—inner sanctum, and had used its resources. This was no longer just about *him*. Let's be honest: it hadn't been for a while now.

So I was waiting for Tez by the elevator when he stepped off. He was startled, but not surprised. And he didn't try to argue with me, either. I guess we'd both learned a little about each other.

Amoxtli was very pale and looked like he'd lost about twenty pounds in a day and a half —an impossibility for a human, barring liposuction. But he was alert and sitting up when we came in.

"See?" he said to us both, as if continuing a conversation. "I'm fine. I'm in a normal room. They say I'll be outta here in two or three days."

"Yeah," Tez muttered, "I'm gonna wait to talk to your doctor." He said to me: "He's always a bit overoptimistic about his own health."

Amoxtli didn't, I noticed, object to the idea of Tez—not even a blood relative, and much younger—insisting on talking to his doctor. Was this a nagual thing? A "family" thing? Or were they really ... "partners" already, like in Ayo's story?

"How are the boy— Manny and Pronk? How'd they get through yesterday?"

Tez just nodded, then tilted his head. This seemed to be enough answer for Amoxtli.

"Pronk's coming this evening after ze gets off work. Manny will swing by with your clothes and stuff this afternoon."

"*You* okay?" Amo asked softly.

Tez nodded, more firmly, at the ground. Amoxtli nodded at his own feet.

"So," Tez said. "I have a shit-ton of questions for you."

Amoxtli looked wary. "About what?"

"Well," Tez said, opening his backpack and pulling the stick out, "about *this*, for one thing."

I had thought Amoxtli was pale before, but all the color drained from his face until he was positively grey. His face became drawn and furrowed, and he looked old, old, old for a moment. I had a horrible feeling that I'd been right about the stick, and I shouldn't have let it get its hooks into Tez.

But then, in the next instant, Amoxtli's face flushed again, and filled with wonder. He sat up straighter and reached out a hand to touch it.

"My God, mijo. My God. Cómo …Where did you find It?" And his eyes filled with tears.

He touched the stick gently for a moment, but didn't

try to take it from Tez. Tez, for his part, didn't seem at all discomfited by Amoxtli touching it.

"You know. You *know*," Tez murmured. "Why didn't you tell me?"

They were almost talking over each other, as if each knew what the other was going to say. "I couldn't have helped you. It was lost. It was gone. And then your father ... I didn't want you to feel as if you had lost so much. I didn't want you to know ... It was gone ..."

"You should have told me. You could've helped me. I could've gone looking ..."

"I didn't think you'd ever find It. I didn't think you'd ever become complete. I didn't want you to know ..."

"I could've found it. Wherever It was, if you had just told me ..."

They went on in this vein for a while, not really arguing, just communing over the stick and mooning over each other—until I got tired of it.

"Okay!" I cried, interrupting their flow. "What the hell?"

They both looked at me, and Amoxtli dropped his hand, smiling wryly a little.

"Sorry, Maya, I guess this all seems very weird to you."

"What is that ... thing? Is it evil or good? 'Cause I was coming down on the side of evil."

"No, no, it's nothing like that. It's not evil *or* good, It's just ..." He sighed. "You'd better sit down."

Tez and I exchanged glances, and both pulled up chairs.

I expected him to wind up into storytelling mode, but he went on in the same, very practical-information vein. "The Huexotl goes back to the time when the Spaniards came, Tenochtitlan fell, and our people scattered. There's a whole story I won't go into detail about right now ... but anyway, our clan's nagual encountered a Spanish sorcerer traveling with the missionaries as a servant, and secretly studying the magic of the Nahua in the hope of increasing his own power. The nagual made a deal to exchange knowledge of magic with the sorcerer: European for Mexican magic. But the nagual made sure he got the better of the deal, and that the Spanish wouldn't walk away with any more treasures that didn't belong to them.

"The sorcerer taught the nagual how to capture power and contain it in an object. And the nagual chose the most simple object: his walking stick, carved from a branch of a tree in his old compound, before the world changed. His new, mixed magic was successful beyond his wildest dreams: the stick tied the clan to that piece of earth, where they were living, made them belong. Their clan became prestigious in that village, and their nagual, with his walking stick drawing power from the very earth beneath their feet, became the guardian of and speaker for their land."

He began to fall into the cadence of a story.

"The nagual had two sons: one from his own loins, an ocelotl, and one he adopted, with the gift of memory and flowers. So he transferred the power of his walking stick to his nagual son, and made his gifted son the living amoxtli of the clan's story and the ritual of the walking stick. The two brothers were very close, and did everything together. And when they had sons of their own, they each taught one of their sons about the walking stick: one a nagual, and one a storyteller, and those two moved forward together in life, and brought the clan with them.

"After many generations, the clan was driven from their home by a famine, and they wandered again. And they found a home, again, through the magic of the walking stick. And so it went. Whenever the clan was endangered, they moved, and took the power of the earth and stars with them. Until the time of your grandparents, when the danger wasn't war or disease or famine, but poverty."

His voice became conversational again.

"And it was the same in our time. None of our clan would go north without their nagual, so your grandparents went with a small group, including my parents. My father was the storyteller, so he had to go, too. And they went to, you know, case the joint. If they decided to settle here, the rest of the clan would follow. Your grandparents met with terrible luck, and my father thought it was an omen that they should all go home. But by that time, he and my mom were making good enough money that no one wanted them to come home."

"So, what happened with the walking stick?" I asked. "Did Ome have it with him, or did his father take it?"

"Tez's grandfather Luis left It with Ome. Luis wasn't sure he was going to move the clan, and the Huexotl was better left on its home turf. If disconnected, It will yearn for a new home and push Its holder to put down roots wherever he spends a lot of time. Luis wanted a clear head, although apparently it was very hard for him to leave the Huexotl—and the village—behind. He had to disconnect from them magically, and that leaves a big, psychological hole."

"So Ome brought it up here with him?"

"It had become very clear that the village was dying—economically speaking—and they'd have to move. And since my folks and I were well established in the Bay Area, the decision was made to move the clan up here in stages. Ome and Pilar came up, bringing the Huexotl with them, and he didn't perform the ritual for many years; partly because they were migrating back and forth all up and down the coast, seasonally, and he wasn't sure where they would land; and partly because the clan was still moving up here, and he wanted to wait until everyone was established."

Amoxtli looked down.

"I'm not being completely honest, though. My Papa wanted Ome to do the ritual as soon as he could. But Ome was tasting freedom for the first time in his life, and he couldn't bring himself to tie himself down just then. And I was selfish; I was young too, and wanted Ome and Pilar to be free to wander with me. We were the three musketeers in those years. And … I think, as reasonable as it was for him to wait when he first arrived, being here for so long without bonding with the Huexotl made him unstable and his decisions became rather irrational."

"What do you mean, 'freedom'?" Tez asked, looking spooked. "Why wouldn't he have been able to wander with you?"

Amoxtli looked at him, and his face was sad, and compassionate.

"There's no power without a price," he said. "The price of nagualism is a responsibility for your people. You know that already. But the Huexotl is … so much more. The power It gives you is incredible. So the responsibility is also … so much more. You become responsible for the land you draw power from. And … and you can't leave it."

"What … never?" I asked.

"No, not ever. You physically cannot leave. Not for a single moment."

"But Abuelo was able to leave!" Tez cried.

"Only by breaking his bond with the Huexotl and the land. That comes at a terrible, psychological cost.

I believe that's why Luis died. He was lost without the connection, and everyone said he was clumsy and absent-minded, and his power was severely diminished. If he'd reconnected immediately, he would have bonded with the land here, the way the Huexotl was meant to be used, and his presence would have led his clan to follow him. But he was trying to be rational about it, trying to find the right place. It was a mistake."

"But Ome *had* the stick!" I cried, hating the sick look on Tez's face. "He had access to the power of it. I've seen it! I've seen how strong it makes Tez! Why couldn't he have used it without bonding with it?"

Amoxtli shook his head in disgust at himself. "I should've seen it. I should've known it wasn't drugs. Drugs probably don't work well on you, hijo. Maya, you saw how It affected him. How was it? Did he seem stable to you?"

"Well … no. But his sister just died!" I said, then regretted it immediately when both of them winced.

"You thought the Huexotl was evil because of the effect It had on him. Access to that much power, without the connection to the land, the guardianship of the land, to balance it out, leads to severe instability—psychological instability, extremes of emotion, bouts of giddiness and paranoia, irrationality, and ultimately, violence. You saw it, didn't you?"

"Yes," I admitted. "You mean he'd be like that even if … nothing bad had happened?"

"Yes," Amoxtli said. "I'm sorry, Tez, but that's how it is. Luis hid the Huexotl before he left, and Ome had Pilar take It and go to the Bay Area ahead of him, and hide It. And It *still* affected him. In the end, it became clear that he needed to bond with It, because he was becoming paranoid and irrational."

"I don't remember that!" Tez protested.

"Pilar and I kept it away from you. By the end, we were *begging* him to go through the ritual. He'd become paranoid about it, thought we were trying to 'tie him down,' as if a wife and four kids weren't tie enough. But he'd finally seen the light and agreed to it, and we were preparing for the ritual, when Bergara, that's that shotcaller I told you about, Maya, stole the Huexotl."

"What?" Tez cried. "*That's* what he stole? How did he even know about it?"

"Somebody told him— it doesn't matter who, Tez. Moving the clan up here, without the anchor of that bond to the earth, made all of us feel lost. Some of the kids were finding what connections they could, riding with 23rd St. and the Mission Mob. One of them made a mistake. I advised Ome to keep cool about it. We could've found other ways to get It back. But he was out of his mind. And he marched right over there and demanded It back, in front of a bunch of people, who wouldn't have heard about It if he'd stayed cool and kept his mouth shut. And he tried to call Bergara out, but that asshole wasn't fool enough to fight him. So he sent some guys out and, when it looked like Ome was gonna beat them in to the ground, shot his crazy ass."

Amoxtli shook his head. "It was my fault. I was a terrible advisor to him. Papa had died shortly after he'd arrived and, without Papa's advice, we were just flying by the seat of our pants. After that, the Huexotl just passed from hand to hand, I guess. It would be good luck for a while and then the dude holding It would get unstable— nowhere near as bad as a nagual would get, mind you, because they just can't access that much power—but they'd get greedy and paranoid and someone would take them down or steal It from them ... after a while I lost track of who had It and thought maybe It had gone back down south."

"But Padrino," Tez cried, distressed, "Que paso? Why didn't you ever tell me any of this? We could have used your help! We were so lost! Where *were* you?"

Amoxtli bowed his head.

"I'm so sorry, Tez. I'm so, so sorry. I see now what a mistake that was. ... I was ashamed. I was too ashamed to look you in the eye and tell you that every adult in your life had failed you, and now all the responsibilities would come down on your shoulders. I didn't think it was fair. And your mother and I agreed that it was better to let you ...

"Oh, but that's not true, either. She agreed, but she wasn't in on it. She didn't know all the secrets, and she was grieving and not thinking straight. She tried to get me to change my mind later, when she was dying, but at that time I knew it would have been wrong to load you up with so much when you suddenly had all the kids to look after. And then it just got too hard to tell you ... too hard." He looked down again, and I really felt for him.

"Whatever," Tez said, shortly. I understood his anger, too. I wasn't gonna get between them. "That's not important just now. What I need to know is, what do I do now?"

Amoxtli sighed deeply. "Tez, we're currently in the last trecena—or thirteen-day week—of the sacred year. This trecena is when great changes need to be made. In two days will come the day for becoming and transmutation, the day of Xolotl, the dog, the shapeshifter. In two days you will need to bond with the Huexotl."

"Or what?" Tez asked.

"Or someone else will."

"What do you mean?" I asked. "Surely humans can't bond with the stick? They can't even *hold* it for more than a few seconds!"

"They can hold It if they are bonded to the stick," Amoxtli answered, but to Tez. "Haven't you guessed? That original nagual, who made the Huexotl—he put part of himself in It, part of his own soul."

I started physically. There's *soul* in that stick? Essence? No wonder ...

"That's why your family line has such an affinity to the Huexotl; it's a blood tie; a spirit tie. But it also means that a human, who has no magic of his own, could bond with It—easily, in fact—and take on the magic of a nagual. That shot caller from the San Antonios, Juice? He's ready. And possibly one of the guys from the 70s as well. They'll take It back from you, and they'll go through the ritual if you don't."

"But wait," I said, "how is that possible? Aren't you the only one who knows the ritual, and the timing?"

Amoxtli hung his head even further.

"Amoxtli," Tez said sternly. "How do those fucking *thugs* know so much?"

"The 'instructions'," I murmured, realizing. "You wrote down the instructions, didn't you? That's why you were visiting Ayo. You were trying to find these things because you knew the date was coming up and you heard rumors that someone was going to do the ritual." A thought struck me. "Oh my god. Oh my god, that's why Chucha went to the San Antonios in the first place, isn't it? She was drawn there by the stick!"

Tez looked thunderstruck.

Amoxtli took a while to answer. He wouldn't look up. He finally whispered, "He threatened her. He threatened your mother, and you, and the babies. Your mother was so proud of herself for standing up to Bergara, and she thought it was over. But it's never over. There's always some pendejo behind the one you've just knocked over who'll come at you twice as hard. He came to me and said he knew what Pilar had done to Bergara, and she and your family owed the Mission Mob a blood debt. But he would let it go if I gave him the ritual to bond with the Huexotl."

He finally looked up, anguished. "I wrote a calendar of possible dates, all a long ways off. I knew he wouldn't survive that long without bonding to It. And he didn't. So It got passed along, and the ritual instructions got passed around, too. And somehow, we got lucky. Nobody's timing was quite right, nobody got to do the ritual before the Huexotl was taken away from them. And later, I heard even better news: the instructions had been lost, separated from It. That's when It disappeared, and that's when I stopped worrying about it."

"But Juice," I said, thinking out loud. "He's smart, Tez. Way smarter than you give him credit for. He must've found out about the instructions and brought the two together."

Tez looked ten years older. "What happens if somebody like Juice bonds with the Huexotl?"

Amoxtli looked like he and Tez were having a race to see who could age faster. "He's not a nagual. He doesn't have the power to reach through to the earth, and become a guardian. He won't hear the earth calling to him, but he'll receive much of its power. He'll become much stronger."

"But with none of the responsibility, and none of the stability," Tez finished for him. "And there'll be nothing I can do about it."

Amoxtli's look was the only confirmation we needed.

"What are his other options?" I asked. Tez looked at me with such hope, I realized he was becoming desperate.

"I don't know, really," Amoxtli said. "I suppose you can take It out of the Bay Area and hide It somewhere. You've had extended contact with It so I don't know if you can stay away. This is all unprecedented. But Juice has also had prolonged contact with It. I don't really know how It interacts with people who don't have a nagual's abilities, but," he gestured at his bandaged torso, "it looks like they've had pretty good luck following It so far."

"Can I destroy It?" Tez asked.

Amoxtli looked miserable. "All I know is that if the Huexotl is damaged or destroyed, some sort of doom is promised. It could be an environmental catastrophe, or it might be simply that the clan will be scattered, which would have been seen as a horrible fate back then. It's pretty much already happened, though, so …"

"All right," Tez said. "I get it."

"Tez, mijo" Amoxtli said, desperately, "I'm so sorry. You don't have to do anything you don't want to do. But you *do* have to make your decision quickly, act quickly."

"Enough," Tez said, holding his hand up. "Enough." And he walked out.

I gave Amoxtli my most sympathetic/irritated look, and ran out after Tez.

CHAPTER TWENTY-SIX

SUNDAY, OCTOBER 23, 2011
SAN FRANCISCO; OAKLAND

I DIDN'T HAVE to run, though. He was waiting at the elevator for me, pulling on his hair.

"I don't want to think, or talk, right now," he said, but didn't make any move away from me. Clearly he wanted company.

"Okay. I'm headed across to the Occupy Oakland encampment. Gonna hang out, do some work, maybe attend the general assembly later. You wanna come?

"Oh, right. ... Yeah, okay."

Without waiting for permission, I took the backpack carrying the stick in it from his shoulder, and, after a moment of resistance, he let me.

It was a beautiful day with a few high, passing clouds. On an impulse, I suggested that we fly. Tez was unexpectedly up for it, and made us both invisible while I called down a cloud. I'd never done this before—didn't know, in fact, if it could be done—but Tez stepped right onto the cloud with me and we went up.

"It doesn't ... *feel* like anything!" he said, looking at his feet.

"It's water vapor. What should it feel like?"

"It should feel soft! Or ... squishy. Or something. It should feel like we're being held up by water vapor!"

"We're not. We're being held up by magic." But I couldn't help smiling back at his surprise. Twenty-seven was two years older than I was, but I had to admit, it was still pretty young. That struck me in my heart, as both tragic and hopeful: tragic for him to have lost so much, so young; hopeful that he could still bounce back.

We didn't really talk on the way over the Bay, but I did speed up, and swoop a bit for Tez's benefit. He chuckled nervously, then laughed outright. No languid felinity here. Seeing the Bay from a bird's eye view for the first time must've really been something. The water sparkled, and we were low enough to occasionally see the shadows of fairly large creatures underwater: either whales or some of the Bay's supernatural water-breathers. The air was as fresh as air gets, and the sky was, as usual, more blue when I was in it than when looking at it from the ground.

All too soon we were passing over the massive cranes of the port, then the tangle of the freeway interchange, and descending into the street behind Ogawa/Grant Plaza.

As we walked into the encampment, I began to feel a little anxious. "Let me know if this all gets to be too much and you want to leave," I said.

He saluted with two fingers as Baby ran up to me. I was a little jolted. The magazine staff had all signed up to help out the Brooms Collective today, but after her little speech on Thursday, I wasn't sure she'd show up. I looked around quickly, but Salli wasn't there, which relieved me. I was pretty sure she *knew* about me, and didn't want to put her tete a tete with another supernat.

"Maiiiii! You're late!" Baby didn't sound accusing, though; rather, glad to see me. Considering how we left each other last time, I was pretty sure the enthusiasm wasn't about me. And sure enough, Baby's eyes cut right over to Tez after greeting me. To avoid deep embarrassment, I hurried to introduce them.

"Tez, this is Baby. Baby, Tez."

"Tez!" Baby cried, giving him a hug. "I feel like I know you already!"

Tez froze. I plotted murder.

Pulling back, she saw the blank look on his face. "Didn't Maya tell you? We used to go to the poetry slams all the time at Cal. And I saw you spit at a lot of marches, too. Man, you were on *fire*!" She knuckled his arm with her fist.

Tez looked uncomfortable, but relaxed a bit. I decided to hold off on the murdering.

"Thanks," he said.

"Listen," Baby said, taking his hand (only Baby could get away with this,) "I'd offer you condolences, but I can tell you don't want them from strangers. But I'm hereby relieving you of any social responsibilities for the afternoon. You can hang out as long as you like, leave when you like, talk or be silent as you like, and make no apologies. I got your back."

With a final squeeze, she let go of his hand and made good on her promise. I knew that for the rest of the day, she'd be keeping an eye on him and cockblocking anyone's attempts to get anything from him he didn't want to give. He was being Baby-ed. He looked a little bewildered, but also relieved.

"She's, like, the anti-Maya," he said, smiling. I chose not to take it amiss.

"She does make me possible," I said.

He laughed, a genuine one. I introduced him to the rest of my crew, including Mari and about half the staff of *Inscrutable* ... plus about half the crowd. Yes, I know everyone: what can I say? Monkeys are social creatures. Tez was friendly, but not particularly open, and that appeared to be okay with the group. Some recognized him from protests of yore; but even those who didn't seemed to regard him with a certain amount of awe. It gave me a new perspective on Tez. Was it the nagual in him? Was it the stick's proximity? Or was it Tez himself? Was he just born with this much charisma?

Speaking of charisma, just as I was starting to relax, Todd showed up. He looked blank when he saw me with Tez, then put on his goofiest smile and came over to greet us. I reintroduced him to Tez and saw them tense up at each other. Yes, definitely tension. I told myself I didn't need to make anything of it, though; it was just awkwardness—while Monkey screeched with delight. What was I gonna do now? I'd brought Tez here to take his mind off of his troubles, not to cause a cockfight ... or whatever this was.

But then Baby, bless her soul, came over and grabbed Todd's arm.

"I need you to help me with these supplies," she said, and led him away before he could protest. I knew she'd fill him in on the tragedies of the week and keep him away from Tez. Thank god for Baby.

And it worked. Todd glanced over at Tez and me throughout the afternoon, and periodically gave me his goofy smile, which I returned with double goofiness, but he kept his distance. I refused to think about how Baby might be helping me string him along ... as Monkey screeched laughter again.

As for Tez, I—or the afternoon and the crowd, or the

simple work of cleaning up—seemed to be having a good effect on him. Underneath his stoic outer face I could see he still looked worn to the bone, and desperately sad. But, as his latex-gloved hands picked up some truly disgusting bits of plastic, glass, and paper, the small muscles around his eyes, which had been tight the whole time I'd known him, finally relaxed. And he was smiling and even laughing at the occasional jokes the crew was throwing around.

Then, just as I was starting to get irritated by the crowd, as if synced, Tez and I turned to each other with the clear intention to leave. We handed off our garbage bags, and Baby's intervention allowed us to go without a fuss, walking quickly, leisurely, out of downtown and across the freeway, chatting about nothing. Soon, we lost track of time and space and found ourselves deep in West Oakland's residential neighborhoods.

Then, from one moment to the next, my monkey brain heard something and began screeching. I stopped, and caught up a few seconds later. It was the engine sound from the 70s' Mustang! Where—? Tez reacted to something behind me. I spun to look where he was looking, down the street, where the iridescent green 'Stang was just rolling up. Wow, the call of that damned stick was really powerful!

The next moment, I heard a shout behind me: "Hey, China!"

Uh, did that mean me? It usually meant me. I spun back around and saw a large black SUV approaching from the opposite direction. The passenger window was down and … Juice was calling through it: "Hey! I thought we had a deal!"

Shit. Both of them.

Tez's face went fierce. I felt a momentary fumbling at

my back, and then he lifted the stick and bent his legs. Uh oh. A short highlight reel of the next two hours rolled before my eyes: Tez beating San Antonios bloody; Tez beating 70s bloody; somebody playing the fool and getting killed; me shrieking like a kettle; an audience spilling out of the nearby houses and onto the street; somebody calling the police and shooting smart phone videos; us arrested, or possibly Tez getting shot terrifying the cops and resisting arrest; the whole thing winding up on YouTube.

"Run!" I shrieked. "No fighting! We have to get away!"

He was already off the sidewalk and into the street, but turned on a dime and headed away from both cars. Hm. Good boy. I grabbed his free hand and yanked him after me and we leapt together over a fence and into someone's yard. From there I called down a cloud and Tez made us invisible, and a moment later we were high in the air and speeding back over the Port of Oakland to the Bay.

CHAPTER TWENTY-SEVEN

As we stood on the sidewalk in front of his house, looking at the door, I opened my mouth to ask if Tez wanted me to keep the stick for him, but he spoke first.

"Do you want to come up and eat something? I'm starving, and I have some beef marinating. We could have tacos."

He didn't look at me, trying to look cool, I guess, but it made him look more anxious. He definitely had something on his mind.

"Sure! Beef tacos sound great."

In his apartment—which was completely quiet; his siblings weren't home—he led me down the hall and into the bathroom, where he showed me a hidden cupboard in the wall behind the vanity. I put the stick in, bag and all. He didn't touch it, hadn't touched it since he'd handed it back over after the near-fight.

We were mostly silent through the excellent meal; beast shifters tend to be serious about food. But finally, our bellies full and our minds as well, Tez led me to the living room and we sat next to each other on the couch.

"Okay," he said. "What do you think about this whole bonding-with-the-Huexotl thing?"

My heart beat faster. It sounded like he was putting weight on what I had to say. But then, who else would he ask?

Maybe his siblings ... but how could he ask his siblings when they were so dependent on him, so used to him being in charge? They didn't sound like they were much for bucking authority, and Tez *was* authority to them. I didn't imagine that the idea of Tez—who was already in charge of their neighborhood—taking over the whole city would seem like much of a stretch to them.

Ironically, the only person in his family or inner circle who might be able to advise him with a relatively clear head and without a personal agenda was Chucha. But then ... that's what I was doing here in the first place, wasn't it? First I was Chucha's conscience, and now that she was dead, I was Chucha's proxy.

The idea filled me with a sort of relief, combined with a terrible fear and guilt. But I had no choice. I had to do right by Chucha, and that meant being totally honest.

Tez was waiting patiently, watching my face, which, I'm sure, showed every emotion through my monkey grimaces and pink flushes. "I have no idea what to think. The whole idea is so crazy ... and so new. And it all sounds so ..."

"That's the thing! Every other second, I see it, like, from outside the window, and it looks awfully random and crazy. But then every other *other* second, I see it from inside the ball of yarn, and it sounds completely right, completely woven together. ... I mean, from the moment I first saw that thing"—he pointed directly, through the walls, toward where it was hidden in the apartment, without hesitating or looking—"I knew It belonged to me in some fundamental way. And I had this horrible feeling from the very first that if I let someone take It from me, the sky would fall ... on me and just ... in general. That's where the paranoia comes from, you know."

"Tez, it sounds like you're answering your own question. Or, at least, talking yourself around to it. Maybe we should be a little more programmatic here. Lay out the pros and cons."

"Okay. Pros: the power. Jesus, Maya, you have no idea. I can feel it already, although I don't even know the extent of it. It's calling to me through a floodgate. It's ... pulling at me, like undertow, but I don't know what it will be like when I'm swimming in it. ... Or drowning in it."

"Okay, that's a con: possibly too much power to handle. Could be overwhelmed."

"But better me than Juice, or that shot caller from the 70s. I don't have much training, but what I have is in responsibility, and balance, and taking care of people. If someone's going to be swimming in too much power, better it be me, a trained lifeguard."

"Okay, then let's call that a pro for everyone *but* you."

"And I get the feeling that it's tied to the earth, somehow. That I would have the power to affect things that are tied to the earth. That could be pretty extensive."

"How far would its reach be, do you think?"

"I have no idea. Maybe the entire city. Maybe the entire Bay Area."

"Maybe you could reverse gentrification?" I joked.

He chuckled, then stopped. Then looked thoughtful.

"Let's call anti-gentrification power a possible pro," I said.

We sat for a few minutes in silence, turning the situation over.

"Tez?" I asked, "How ... *bad* is it? Not having the stick?"

He thought for a moment. "My sibling Pronk is claustrophobic, but, ze says, ze can handle being in a small space as long as ze has access to an exit. It's control over getting out of the space that's the real issue. It's like that for me. I'm thinking about and feeling that thing all the time, and more so when I'm not holding It. But I think as long as I can get my hands on It easily, and no one is getting between me and It, I can be fine, like I am now. I *could* live like this for a while, for a long time, even, but I don't know if I would want to; just like Pronk wouldn't want to rent an apartment with a really small bathroom."

"Would the pressure lessen if the stick was farther away? Say, if someone like me were in charge of it—"

"NO!" he shouted, his face suddenly red and contorted. It took all my self control, but I didn't respond in any way. I just watched, as blankly as I could, as he realized what had happened, and crumpled in on himself.

He covered his face with his hands and then, to my horror, I heard a gasp that sounded suspiciously like a sob.

"I can't stand this, Maya. I can't stand it," he said, amidst more sobbing gasps. "My Dad always emphasized control and I've never ..." He stopped and breathed through more gasps, until his breath slowed down. "I've always known I was capable of violence, but I've always been able to control it before. Just now, I wanted to hurt you. I really really wanted to ..."

I slid over and put an arm around his shoulders. Under any other circumstances, I'd have been delighted by the fact that his shoulders were too broad and muscular to make this easy. But just now, making him feel held was my only concern, and that was a problem. I slid my hand up to his neck and just held the back of his neck with my hand. Somehow, that had always made me feel better. It seemed to work on him, too.

"Should we call that a pro?" I asked, as gently as I could. "Making this instability go away?"

He nodded, and wiped his eyes.

"Okay, maybe we should focus on cons."

He nodded again. I didn't say anything. He was still upset and he needed to be the one to say these things. I waited, and stroked his neck. His skin was incredibly smooth and silky, and he was very warm. I could feel his whole body's warmth radiating towards me— Okay, Maya, eyes on the prize here.

He got up abruptly, and walked rapidly out of the room. Damn, was I giving him too much of a pheromone bath? Damn, Maya, did you *have* to smear your hormones all over this situation?

But after a few moments of banging doors and drawers down the hall, Tez came right back in and sat down next to me—if possible, even closer this time. He spread a map out on the coffee table, and stacked another few maps next to it. It was a map of the world, all marked up, with routes and notes in six or eight different colors of ink.

"When I was a kid, there was this British guy named Michael Palin on the BBC and he did this amazing travel show called *Pole to Pole* where he chose a longitude, and then traveled from the north pole to the south pole along that longitude, all on the surface of the earth, no flying. It hit Scandinavia and Eastern Europe and Eastern Africa—including this incredible stop in Sudan. My

Padrino Mike taped it for me, and I watched it about a hundred times. It was my … what's the opposite of a security blanket?

"Ever since, I've been wanting to do that: pick a latitude, or a longitude, and travel around the world along it. I got several routes." He pointed to the stacked maps. "But this one," he gestured to the map laid out in front of me, "is the one. The one I finished in college, before my mom died. I haven't changed it since then, not because I haven't had time, but because it's perfect."

He pointed at a red line that meandered pretty far north and south, but tended inexorably east. "You see, right here, in San Francisco, we're almost exactly between 30 and 45 degrees north. And this whole route goes back and forth in the zone between those latitudes. And, I mean, talk about the garden path! Most of the interesting stuff we learn about in history classes— because they skip over the sub-Saharan African and Latin American stuff of course, which is a lot—happens in this zone: the North American nations, the American revolution, the entire Mediterranean rim, including the Iberian Peninsula—the Spanish Civil War!—Carthage, Rome, Greece, the Ottoman Empire, Palestine, Egypt, Iraq, Iran, the Black Sea, the Caspian Sea, the Suez Canal, the tip of the Persian Gulf, all the 'stans—you know, the Great Game!—the Himalayas, pretty much the entire Silk Road, the Mongol hordes! China, Korea, Japan … it's all here! I mean, there are so many other routes and places, but if I had to choose only one, this is the one!"

His voice had gotten louder and warmer throughout.

"The original plan was to finish college, work for five years to build college funds for the kids, and then spend two or three years on the hoof. I planned that during the dot com boom, and I was absolutely positive that I'd graduate, work for five years, and then sell my dot com for a few hundred million dollars and be set for life. But I did have a contingency plan." He looked at me ruefully. "I would sell my stock options in the dot com I *worked for* for a couple of million and send the kids to school and go traveling for a few years."

I smiled at him, it felt like, with my whole body. He looked around the room. "I was supposed to be cruising by now. Manny would be starting his last year at State. Pronk would be in zeir second year somewhere—maybe Cal. Chucha would have graduated early and taken a year off to intern for some Chicano state politician, and would now be getting ready to go, full ride, to Yale ... or Brown.

"I'd leave the kids in the city to take care of Mom with their summer jobs and internships, and Chucha and I would fly off in the car—I'd have some fancy Detroit muscle car by now, of course—and we'd get our kicks on Route 66, you know. Of course, we'd argue the whole way, but that would be the fun of it. Then I'd drop her off at school, ivy in her hair, with the car to take care of—did you know she's—she *was*—a great mechanic? She would study systems engineering and art; she can—could—draw too. Or maybe poli-sci. Then I'd fly out of New York like fucking Superman and she'd see me off."

My whole smiling body ached with longing for this alternate version of reality, even if it was one in which I had never met him, never met Chucha.

He leaned back against the couch and closed his eyes. "I was with this girl in college, Tiana. We met sophomore year and I was just, you know, 'awake forever in a sweet unrest,' for the next three years, right? We were, like ... I couldn't go 24 hours without seeing her." He didn't seem aware that he'd been half of an "it couple," although I was pretty sure Tiana had been. I felt the smile leave my body; not just at the mention of that beautiful young woman I could never compare to, but at his tone: that something bad was coming.

"I spun a lot of fucking cotton candy about our future together, but for some reason, I never showed her the maps. After Mom died, and I blew away enough fog to figure out that I'd be years repaying the medical debts, not to mention raising the kids and saving up for their futures, Tiana thought we should get married, and she'd get a job to help pay off all our debts and get the kids into school. And it would have been, like, the one light in that whole, dark time. I think Chucha would have done a lot better if Tiana had been there, in the house, for her, keeping an eye on her and giving her a role model. The kids *loved* Tiana." And his face contorted for a second.

"All I had to do was flip the switch. But I told her that I wouldn't let her give up her dreams for me. I told her that we'd end up resenting each other, and rightfully so. That it was inegalitarian for a man to expect a woman to do all this, blah blah blah. She found it all very moving, and we broke up in a storm of tears, and she went off to New York and dances for Alvin Ailey like fucking Kali, like a goddess of growth and destruction. And she tells all her friends what a great guy I am and how I'm the one that got away."

I braced myself.

"But the real reason I dumped her was that I knew if we got married she'd just get pregnant earlier than planned and I'd be stuck here forever. As if she were a block of hardening concrete, and not the fucking love of my life. Even after Mom died, I still knew I could go fly. It would just take longer. It took me two years to go on a date again, and I haven't had a serious relationship since— but... she didn't care about freedom, and my freedom took precedence."

I wasn't surprised, but still couldn't say anything for a moment. I refused to parse the "love of my life" comment.

"That's one hell of a con, Tez," I said, finally.

"I can *still* go," he said. "Manny's at State and can finish in two years—two and a half realistically. Pronk's only just starting, but once Manny finishes and gets a real job ...I don't have to wait for Pronk to launch. I'll be thirty, but I can just *go*."

"It sounds totally doable."

He sighed deeply, and let his head slide onto my shoulder. "You ever think about traveling?"

I sighed too. "It's different for me, Tez. I didn't ever have anywhere I belonged. I was always being pushed out. So my childhood dream was to be in one place, a place that belonged to me." I leaned my head against his. "I was a restless teenager, but I was never moving to *get* anywhere. I just needed to feel the air rushing past me, to feel my legs or my wings working. I needed the *feeling* of freedom. But the meaning of the places I went to, their history, the stories behind them, I never thought about that. I always felt like I could just keep going and going, if I wasn't so afraid of losing contact with my parents, or losing touch with the human world—losing my chance at a place that belonged to me."

I settled in more comfortably, and let my neck relax.

"Maybe you should go with me, preciosa," he murmured.

"Maybe I should," I said, with a little shiver. "I'd be in charge of transportation. Oh my god, imagine the thermals over the Himalayas! That would blow your cloud up! And you'd be in charge of touristy things once we got to where we were going."

"I know all the great hostels," he said. "I keep up with them. I have a list."

"And we could mostly go hunting to feed ourselves, so we could save money on food, and only eat at terrific restaurants."

"We could sleep in fur, actually, save money on hostels."

"We could go on forever that way."

"Forever."

CHAPTER TWENTY-EIGHT

SUNDAY, OCTOBER 23, 2011
MISSION BAY, SAN FRANCISCO

WE WERE AWAKENED somewhat slowly by the sound of "Ooh Child" by the Five Stairsteps. It took me a moment to realize that I was lying, half-length, on top of Tez, who was lying full-length underneath me. I lifted my head from his chest, then immediately regretted it, because the movement woke him and he began to sit up ... before noticing me splayed out all over him, and freezing in place.

I sat up quickly and fumbled around in my purse for my phone. The time said 7:12. I was hyper-aware of Tez, mostly behind me, but with legs on either side of me (how had that happened?), and his musky man/cat smell all around me. He stayed prone, and I felt him watching me. I had let myself fall asleep on him. No one is *that* unaware. But then I had really really slept. Oh god, did I drool on his shirt?

I managed to hit "answer" before we stopped walking in the rays of a beautiful sun.

"What is it, Ayo?" I asked, more for Tez's benefit than hers.

"There's been another killing," she said.

I glanced at Tez, and he nodded to say he had heard.

"Did you ever meet Maral?" she asked.

"Maybe …?"

"She was that Armenian Nhang? Lived in Mission Creek and led the community there?"

I grunted; I remembered her.

"She was working in the city planning office and getting her masters. She came to me for potions to help her control her blood lust. She was doing really well …"

"Was it the shadow thing again?"

"Probably. I haven't seen the body yet. Can you get down there and secure the area?"

She told me the address and we hung up. I was sitting in an awkward position and couldn't get to my feet without putting a hand down for leverage, but everywhere I was surrounded by Tez. Not looking at him, I put my hand on his chest to push myself up … but he grasped my wrist, gently, and held my hand to his heart for a moment. I felt his hand with my whole body.

I couldn't look at him, but couldn't not. His eyes were so dark, I couldn't see a thing in them. His heart was beating slightly fast into my palm, and his chest rose and fell faster than it had. I felt a little dizzy.

Then, as if moved by the same impulse, he let go my wrist and I pushed myself up.

Tez drove me there without us discussing it.

The body had been found in the garden at Mission Bay, a green strip next to the anchorage for a line of houseboats that lived on Mission Creek. Most of the river was underground, but it came out around 7th St. and flowed past the ball park to empty out in the Bay. These houseboats were the last of their kind in the city, and I knew most of them were inhabited by supernats. How else would they have convinced city officials to protect their little community: on a waterfront, in a gentrifying part of San Francisco, where high-rise, luxury condos with a view of the Bay were being built? It was one of those contradiction-in-terms neighborhoods where the pressure of change made the Spirit of the Bay feel particularly squeezed. It felt like the Bay was in the houseboats, and the construction sites were an interloper; it felt like the Bay was a child, being hugged by a noxious uncle, and looking at me for release.

We parked in the labyrinth of blocked streets, empty lots, and construction fencing spreading from the creekside outward. Gareth, a mostly mild-mannered selkie with very red hair and a very red face was waiting for us. Gareth was a *decades*-long member of the houseboat community and hung out at Sanc-Ahh a lot. I thought he had a crush on Ayo—not that it wasn't a fairly common affliction. But I also thought that the otherwise ordinary-looking Gareth kinda slayed her with his thick Scots accent. He kinda slayed me, too.

"Hi, Gareth," I said, as we came up.

"Ah, Maya, look at this. It's a very sad day."

I introduced Tez to a distracted Gareth, who led us over to the garden. Maral was lying in a jerry-rigged flower bed. Gareth, always considerate, had put some long, golden, giant kelp leaves over her face. She was almost entirely in human form, except for some wicked looking crocodile teeth poking through the leaves and distorting her lips; and she was entirely naked. (Most beast shifters don't have the same ideas about modesty that humans do, and Gareth probably hadn't thought of covering her body.)

303

"Where did you find her? Here, or in the water?"

"Oh, no, here, not in the water. Nothing could kill her in the water. She only came on land for the workday. She shared my boat, you know, and those of a couple of others: just for storage space and the shower. She slept in the water. We all have dinner together, you see."

I recognized the disjointed logic of shock and decided to let him be. If I remembered correctly, Gareth and the rest of the supernats in the houseboat community were poly. I'd met one of his partners before, and chances were that Maral—sharing his houseboat and dinners—was another partner. Poor Gareth!

Her nakedness meant she'd probably been in animal form right before she was killed. I could easily imagine Shady getting her attention the same way it had gotten mine—and probably Chucha's, and Aahil's—luring her ashore so it could pin her down and suck her essence out.

Ayo arrived soon after. Her examination of the body was quick.

"Yes," she said to my unasked question. "Completely gone."

"What is?" Gareth asked.

"Her essence," she told Gareth gently. "She was killed by the same creature that's been killing shapeshifters the past couple of weeks. Maral makes the sixth such killing."

"Gareth," I said, with a renewed thrill of horror. "Gareth, you have to be careful, you and all the others. I think this thing is … collecting."

Tez protested, but Ayo said, over him, "Do you really think so?"

"Every victim so far has been a different kind of shapeshifter. A harimau jadian—"

"Weretiger," Ayo put in, for Gareth's benefit. He nodded.

"And then a werewolf, a bajang, a vanara, a nagual dog, and now a nhang."

"Soooo …" Ayo said, "You don't think it has anything to do with the—"

"Ayo," Tez broke in, hurriedly. "Maybe we should talk about this in private."

Ayo looked startled for a moment, then nodded. Wow, how out of it did she have to be to almost out Tez in front of Gareth? I looked closer and saw faint shadows under her eyes, and remembered that Maral had been a friend of hers, too. Shock all around, then.

I watched as she negotiated with Gareth over the disposal of Maral's body, Ayo convincing him that Maral wanted her body returned to Armenia in time for an elaborate funeral three days after her death. She warned Gareth again about the shadow creature and elicited a promise from him to pass the warning on. Then Gareth took his leave of us, picked up Maral, and headed back to his houseboat.

Tez and I looked at each other, and then at Ayo, who plunked herself down at a picnic table overlooking Mission Creek, or the empty lot/construction site behind us, depending on which side you sat on.

"So," Ayo said, picking up our debate right where we left off, "Maya, you don't think the killings have *anything* to do with the Huexotl?"

I sat down across from her. "I really don't, now, no."

"You think this shadow thing is collecting shapeshifter essences? What for?"

"Hang on," Tez said, sitting down next to me, "I'm still not convinced that it has nothing to do with the Huexotl. It has attacked everyone holding It—"

"Except for the 70s' werewolf—"

"Because he didn't have it long enough; we took it

from him—"

"And except for you," Ayo put in.

We both stared at her, then looked at each other, frozen.

"We never got a chance to tell her," I said.

"Last night was a bag of cats," he said.

"Wait, are you saying that thing *attacked* you?" she almost shrieked. "Where? When?"

"Right outside Sanc-Ahh last night when we left."

"Are you all right?" she cried. She scanned me with her magic night vision goggles or whatever but apparently couldn't see any ozone depletion.

"You should check Tez out, actually," I said. "He's the one who got sucked on." Monkey immediately gave me a more pleasant visual for that and my face got hot, but Ayo turned her gimlet eye on Tez and neither of them noticed.

"You look fine, Tez," she said, calming down immediately. "But you're right, all that does maybe put the kibosh on Maya's collector theory, since he'd already taken a nagual."

"Uh, actually ..." Tez said, sounding cagey.

"What?" I asked.

"Well, I didn't want to flip you out, which is why I didn't say anything, but I think that thing was actually going after *you*. Or maybe somebody else in the cafe. But probably you."

"*What*?" Ayo and I said at the same time.

"Well, I was waiting for you outside and it just came floating up, and it kind of ... *looked* at me ... I don't know how I knew it was looking at me because it has no face," he shuddered, "but it looked at me and then it looked through the window and—again, I don't know how I know this—it was looking at you. Then you went behind the counter and it started to phase into the cafe, and I got the distinct impression that it was on your case.

"So I blocked it, and it tried to get around, but I started whaling on it, and it threw me down the street. It was about to go after you again, so I yelled to it that it had to deal with me first because I was just going to follow it inside. So ... *that's* what was happening when it came outside. It was dealing with me first. I wasn't its target, though, Maya. I'm pretty sure *you* were."

I felt my guts flip over. I'd shaken off the horror of the creature's killing capabilities because there had simply been too much else to worry about, even after it attacked me last night. But the thought that it could come after me, could take away *my* life, *my* power, *my* essence ... I shuddered down to my soul.

"So," Ayo said, thinking, "the shadow *did* attack every holder of the Huexotl since it started killing shapeshifters, but apparently it wasn't trying to collect you, Tez, so you don't actually count."

His eyebrows went up, but he didn't protest.

"And it did kill the harimau jadian first," she continued, "although he wasn't holding the Huexotl and didn't have anything to do with it, except for passing on the instructions. Then it killed the werewolf and then the bajang, both of whom were holding It. But then it diverged again and killed the vanara, who also had nothing to do with It. Then it killed your sister ..." we both winced again "who *was* holding the stick. But then Maral had nothing to do with It, either. It's too random, Tez. I have to agree with Maya. I don't think this thing is after the Huexotl."

"But it's too much of a coincidence that it went after three stick-holders in a row," Tez insisted.

"It doesn't have to *be* a coincidence," Ayo said. "All the supernats it went after who *weren't* holding the

Huexotl were prominent both in their supernatural communities and in their human ones. Wayland, the harimau jadian, was a prominent businessman and local political bagman, as well as the head of the Asian were-cat benevolent society. Aahil, the vanara, was the CEO of a very promising start-up, and the heir to the chieftainship of his clan."

"I didn't know that," I said faintly.

"And Maral was the leader of the Mission Bay houseboat community and a rising local government official."

"So, what's your point?" Tez said.

"My point is, the shadow creature was drawn to power, to creatures who were at least somewhat in the public eye, and who had taken on leadership positions. Doing that, placing yourself in the center of a network of people, or creatures, and taking on responsibility for them, actually enhances your essence to a certain extent, makes it … brighter, more visible to those who can see. Aside from the direct power thing, it's part of why people take on those roles; because it feels good and makes you a stronger soul."

"What about Maya?" Tez asked.

Ayo looked at him, eyebrows raised. She looked genuinely offended. "Maya is one of the heads of the only national Asian American magazine our country has right now; the leader of a direct action group working on a number of social justice issues in the Bay Area; and she's my second-in-command at the only supernatural sanctuary in the region. Maya's position is comparable to Maral's or Aahil's, albeit of a different kind. And compared to them, she's *very* visible."

Hunh, I thought. Monkey thought the same.

"Okay, so Chucha and Bu Bu and Justin weren't these

kinds of powerful people. And you're trying to say that they were targeted because they held the Huexotl?" Tez asked.

"It clearly enhances your essence," Ayo said. "I saw that when you came in with it last night. It makes it brighter and more visible, in a similar way. If the creature wanted to collect shapeshifter essences, like Maya suggests, it would want to go for the ones that are the strongest, the brightest. For Justin, a very young, lone wolf, with no connections, the enhancement of the Huexotl would have been his only appeal. But Maya tells me Bu Bu was previously a bit of a public figure, and with the magical enhancement, he would've been pretty tasty looking."

"And Chucha was coming into something of a leadership position among the San Antonios even before she took on the stick, so she would've been even more attractive," I said.

"I think the shadow creature found Justin by accident, and then stuck around to see what other creatures the Huexotl offered up to him. The fact that it didn't follow the stick to the 70s' werewolf, and didn't attack you immediately, supports Maya's theory that it's trying to eat a different kind each time."

"And it just tried to consume me because it needed a kill," said Tez.

"No," I said, thinking furiously. "It doesn't sound like it needs to kill. It could easily have knocked you unconscious and been on its way. No, I think it wasn't going after you, but you—a semi-active nagual holding the stick—were probably too tasty a dish to pass up, if you were going to lay yourself out on a platter the way you did."

"Why don't you think it needs to kill?" Ayo asked.

"Well, look at the timeline." I said. "It got Wayland

around October 10, then Justin on October 11, then Bu Bu on October 14, and Aahil, as far as we can tell, on October 15. Then it got Chucha on October 18. So far it didn't go for more than three days without a kill. But then, it waited four days to go after me. Why? If the previous killings were a pattern, going four days without a kill would have meant that it was hungry as hell.

"Assuming it's not from around here, by last night at the latest it must have had the lay of the land. And by last night at the latest it certainly knew where the sanctuary was—i.e. where the 31 Flavors of shapeshifters had its storefront—and could easily have lain in wait there for any shapeshifter it hadn't had before to leave. Then it could have followed it to a dark, quiet spot.

"But, if I'm remembering correctly, there were no alphas among the shapeshifters at Sanc-Ahh last night. So it waited for me. And when it didn't get me, instead of hiding nearby, it went *all* the way across the Bay and got Maral, another network-y leader type. It's clearly being choosy; and hungry creatures in need are opportunistic, not choosy." Suddenly I remembered: "Ayo," I said, "What about Dalisay?"

Ayo's eyebrows nearly hit her hairline. "Yes, you were thinking that maybe Dalisay was the first victim."

"It would fit, wouldn't it? She's a leader. And she disappeared only two days before Wayland was killed. Did you talk to the Hung For people?"

She shook her head, and I explained Dalisay to a puzzled Tez. "But I'm prioritizing this now," she promised. "I'll go down there tomorrow, first thing."

We were all quiet for a while after that. The logic was indisputable ... and rather terrifying. If it was being choosy, that meant that it might not give up on me. I didn't have the stick, but I started out more powerful than most ... okay, let's be honest, more powerful than *all* of the shapeshifters I'd ever met, including a pre-Huexotl Tez, if Chucha was anything to go by. And I apparently had that whole network-y leadership thing going, too. I was a yummy morsel.

Was that really how Ayo saw me? I had never looked at myself that way. Truth be told, it was Baby who led me into activism. I'd always thought of Baby as the leader, and myself as the follower. Hell, I was even managing editor to Baby's editor-in-chief. But then, that *did* make me Baby's second-in-command, and, as far as everyone else was concerned, they looked to me *or* Baby to take the initiative. And I *had* taken over the protest arm of the organization. I didn't do it by myself ... but I did all the organizing and ... shit, I was a leader!

I didn't know how to feel about this.

"What do you mean '*semi*-active'?" Tez said, with an aggrieved air. Oh, that's what *he'd* been spinning out about? Huh. While I was tripping on being called a leader, he was tripping on being called *not entirely* a leader. What a *man*.

"Tez," Ayo said in her "handling touchy men" voice, "we've talked about nagualism before. You know I've seen naguals at work, and they are completely embedded in their community life. You're not. That's all. No one's accusing you. This isn't exactly a village, and how you fulfill your responsibilities isn't as clear cut."

Tez didn't look at her, and I carefully avoided looking at her, too.

"What?" she asked, looking back and forth between us. "What happened?"

I refused to speak.

"Maya," Ayo said, "tell me. You two went to see Amo—*Amoxtli*—yesterday. I can tell you did. What did

311

he tell you?"

"It's not my story to tell," I said.

Her eyes narrowed, but those were the rules. Hell, we were the ones who enforced them.

"Tez," she said, but he got up and moved away. I got up, too.

"Tez," Ayo said, "supernatural problems *are* human problems. We're inextricably linked." But Ayo's philosophy wasn't gonna do shit in this situation. Tez kept walking down the green.

"Tez—" I started, but he held up his hand.

"I'm sorry, Maya, but I need some time. It's too—" he stopped. "I just need to clear my head. I'll call you later."

And he left, quickly, leaving me feeling cold all over, like a child who had fallen asleep in her mother's arms, only to be put down into cold sheets and left alone.

"Maya," Ayo said quietly, "You should come back to Sanc-Ahh and help me look for this shadow creature. I'm certain now that it's not after the Huexotl, but you and I really need to figure out what it is and what it wants." She paused, and continued gruffly, "And I'd like to get you behind some protective spells, too."

My spine prickled at the reminder. She was 1000% right, and I needed to stop thinking, so I got up and led her out of the maze of cyclone fencing that would soon be a waterfront high-rise.

CHAPTER TWENTY-NINE

SUNDAY, OCTOBER 23, 2011
ROSA PARKS LANE; MAYA'S APARTMENT, SAN FRANCISCO

FOR ONCE, MY delight in Ayo's library was dimmed, and hours of hard searching turned up nothing. Ayo even admitted to me that she had, after all, reached out to her communities yesterday, but nobody had heard of a shadow-monster-soul-sucker before now.

After an interminable BART ride home (I was afraid of running into Slim Shady on my own, and too tired to fly fast) I took a short cut through the Valencia Gardens Projects via Rosa Parks Lane, a short stretch of street that was always strangely deserted for this active part of the Mission, but especially so at this time of a Sunday night.

My bumpy reverie was interrupted when I was bowled ass over head from behind by what felt like a ... a concentrated shockwave. I barely had time to notice the shadow gathering, a sentient cloud of smoke, over me, before Monkey took over and rolled me away and onto my feet. I distantly noted that I hadn't changed form—good— and then Shady hit me again in the chest, throwing me across the lane onto the sidewalk beyond.

I turned to stone, instinctively, removing the pain from all the small bones he'd broken. That strike was definitely harder than ever before. Was he getting stronger?

Shady was on me so fast I didn't have time to think, and pinned me down with a pressure that just felt like the weight of the world on me. I turned to water, like I had done last time, but the shadow seemed to be prepared for this. It descended around me like a dome, and I had nothing to put between me and him. I couldn't run out from underneath him, and the pressure continued to press me down.

And then, I felt it.

I rarely felt heavy or substantial, but suddenly, I felt like the shadow was sucking away my weight, my substance. My ... importance. I felt myself growing light, and Monkey, panicking, took over. I shifted from a puddle of water to Monkey form, flailed my long arms and legs, but couldn't otherwise move. I grew lighter, less substantial, less meaningful.

Something was calling to me, telling me to just let go, to just let myself disappear. My chagrin and shame for ... for everything came to the fore ... and then were sucked away. I felt that secret shame for not belonging—that was sucked away. I didn't have to worry about Baby hating me because I was a violent freak—but that thought was sucked away, and I started to feel relief. I didn't have to worry about my sexuality— sucked away; I didn't have to feel disgust at my own violence—sucked away; I didn't have to feel uncomfortable with Tez—

Tez! Tez needed me! An image of Tez's dangerous, adorable face appeared before me. I still hadn't kissed him. He needed me to be strong for him! The thought galvanized me and I gathered myself up and gave a great heave. It barely made a dent, but I distracted and displaced Shady for a moment, and I felt the sucking sensation stop.

But it wasn't enough, and the shadow's weight settled over me again. I heaved again, but it wasn't enough. And again. Not enough.

And then, suddenly, it was. The weight was gone and I was lying in the clear air, gasping and feeling my body caving in around a hollow space in my center; part physical, part metaphysical.

Then I heard a grunt and a thud, and I sat up in terror.

A few yards away, in the middle of the empty street, Slim Shady was fighting some … thing.

Or … somethings. I couldn't tell; it was happening too fast. The shadow was a twisty, rapidly morphing mass of darkness, in the center of a whirlwind of motion. The whirlwind was … it was hard to tell. It seemed to be morphing, too, but I saw … some creature … some furry creatures, and bundles of … no bushes of … brownish … no blackish-red fur? Could that be right? I strained my eyes, since I felt strangely disinclined to move. The only thing I could see with any clarity were those bushes of reddish-black fur. They looked like … tails? What creature had a reddish, bushy, fur tail?

As if to answer my question, Shady hit out in all directions with his shockwave, and the whirlwind of sinuous, reddish fur resolved into a single creature, the size of a large mastiff, that flew towards me and landed, stunned, a few feet away.

It was an enormous fox.

I just stared at it with, I'm sure, WTF?-face.

Sure, I'd seen werewolves aplenty, and were-hyenas, and even, recently, a were-dog. (This thought gave me a sharp pang in my now-empty spot.) But I had never seen a ... were-fox? Is that was that was?

The fox opened its eyes, gave me a rueful, goofy look that was ringingly familiar, then leapt up and faced Shady again. It lashed its full, bushy tail ... s? Was that more than one tail I saw, or was it just an optical illusion from a fast-lashing tail? The question quickly lost interest when I saw a strange, bright energy growing and coalescing around the tail/s' motion. No, not an energy: fire!

The fox turned its body slightly, then drew back its lashing tail/s once more and struck forward with them, sending the hot yellow flame in an offensive streak towards the shadow.

Having had little impact on Shady myself—with all my strength and power—I didn't expect this fire streak to do much. But, shockingly, the shadow shrank back from it, and swirled frantically to get out of its path.

Of course! We'd been calling it a shadow creature for weeks, but I'd been thinking about it more as a solid substance. But it really *was* a manifest darkness— an actual *shadow*. And, of course, light is inimical to shadow!

The fox, evidently heartened by its initial success, was now lashing bright lines of yellow/orange fire all over Shady's general direction. I dragged myself to an upright position and plucked a hair off my arm. I turned it into a fireball; it didn't burn me, and I had no idea if it just cast light or actually had the power to burn others. But the light was the thing.

I threw the fireball, and it flew into the center of Shady's mass. The shadow shrank away from it on all sides, creating a hole in his center for the fire to pass through. Well, *okay* then. I began yanking clumps of hairs out of my arms and chest at random, creating strings of fireballs, and heaving them over towards Shady.

The shadow took on—somehow, I still don't know how—a posture of severe alarm, formed a random cloud shape, and flew off into a side street as fast as it could.

I dragged myself up, and galumphed on all four sets of toes a few yards down the street to the intersection. But Shady had already disappeared. It knew, apparently, when it was beaten ... and now, so did I.

I turned to look behind me at the fox, who was watching me intently. Time to find out what this creature wanted from me.

I walked upright toward the fox now with a deliberate, stompy pace, turning quickly back into human form as I did so. Changing shape while moving deliberately towards a target is as intimidating as changing size while doing the same. But the fox didn't flinch.

I stopped two yards away: a good tactical distance for me.

"Thanks for the help, but who the hell are you?" I demanded, in a firm, but not hostile voice.

The fox turned its back to me and ducked its head. It looked like it was ... throwing something up? Huh? I thought I saw, for just a split second, the fox placing something on top of its head ... but that was impossible. It didn't have any hands ... did it? And then, the next instant, it was morphing and growing quickly; its fur was disappearing, and being replaced by skin, covered by jeans and a red t-shirt. Its tail, or tails, were the last thing to disappear, as if they didn't want to go. Finally, I looked at its strangely familiar, triangular face and saw ... Todd Wakahisa, wearing a cautious, rueful grin.

I was strangely unshocked. Todd was a were-fox.

"Huh," I said. "Well, *that* explains a lot."

Todd's grin lost its caution and widened.

"A *were-fox*? Really? That's a thing?"

"Not a were-fox. Just a fox. I'm a kitsune."

"Oh, you mean like you're a fox who turns into a human? A fox-were?"

He looked around us uncomfortably.

"As much as I'd love to stand around in the middle of public street talking about our most closely held secrets, why don't we go somewhere a little more private?"

I nodded, suddenly feeling disinclined to speak, and turned to lead Todd back to my apartment a block away. At least, I tried to turn and walk, but the turn was apparently too much for me. I felt my knees buckle and was entirely unable to do anything about it. A strangely blithe feeling came over me as I thought, "Hey! I'm going to crumple to the ground! Oh well."

The expected blow on my backside from the sidewalk never came, however. Instead, there was Todd, holding me up.

"Whoa," he said. "Are you okay?"

I still didn't feel like speaking, and after an effort, realized that that was exhaustion.

"Sucked it out of me," I mumbled.

"What, that smoke creature? Sucked *what* out of you?"

"Essence," I mumbled, and my head started to loll. I couldn't do anything about that, either.

Without another word, Todd swooped me up into a bodice-ripper carry and legged it down the street in the direction of my apartment. Hm. How did he know where I lived? I struggled to put this into words, but Monkey, who was tiny and depleted, just leaned back in my head and told me to enjoy it. I'd always fantasized about being literally swept off my feet like this. I only wished it had been—

"I'm gonna have to set you down," Todd said. We were at my building's front door. He put me butt-first on the ground. I felt better, actually, and was able to hold myself upright while he swung my purse around his back and fished my keys out.

"Hey," I said, only slightly slurring. "How do you know where I live?"

He immediately looked shifty. "Oh," he said breezily, opening the door. "It was some meeting or retreat or something."

"We've never had a meeting or retreat here," I said. "It's too small."

"Huh." Todd said, silencing me by picking me up again and carrying me up the stairs.

Boy, being carried by a strong man was kinda awesome. And rare. I was unexpectedly heavy, like all beast-shifters; something to contain the power, Ayo thought. Guys would test my weight, and then never bother to try again. I'd actually carried injured or drunk guys far more often than the reverse. Hm. It had never occurred to me before to deliberately seek out supernats to date, but maybe that was the way to go. Too bad it wasn't—

"Okay, I think you can stand now," Todd said, propping me up on the landing outside my apartment door. He turned out to be right. He unlocked the door and went to pick me up again, but I demurred.

"I can make it inside, thanks," I said. My words were coming back, and the hollow in my center was shrinking.

He waved me in ahead of him, which is why I saw *Journey to the West* lying on the floor directly in front of the door. I hurriedly kicked it under the couch.

He had taken his shoes off before entering. "You're feeling better," he said.

"Yes, a lot."

"You're welcome."

I paused in taking my shoes off. "That was you?"

319

He bowed slightly. "Kitsune provide general benevolence and good luck. It takes many forms. Perhaps my presence called your ... essence? ... back from wherever it had been taken." He waggled his eyebrows. "Or maybe it just couldn't stay away."

I plopped down on my bed and hmphed. That was interesting. What was suddenly more interesting, though, was how soft my bed was. I decided to investigate with the rest of my back. Yep, that was surprisingly soft. I'd never noticed before.

"What *was* that thing, anyway?" Todd asked, sitting down on the couch. Oh, I had a guest.

"Would you like something to drink?" I asked, from my supine position.

"Uh ... sure," Todd said doubtfully.

"Okay, I have coffee, tea, soda ..." and I fell asleep.

CHAPTER THIRTY

SUNDAY, OCTOBER 23, 2011
MAYA'S APARTMENT, SAN FRANCISCO

ONLY TO BE jerked out of sleep a short time later by the blaring of Ayo's ring tone. I answered the phone, still half asleep, and woke up while telling Ayo the latest about Slim Shady.

"How did you get him away from you?" she asked. Apparently, she'd accepted Shady's maleness, too.

I glanced up at Todd who nodded approval. "Todd Wakahisa was there. He knocked the shadow off me and we were both able to drive it away with fire. Not sure if it was the heat or the light, but I think it was the light. I think this thing is literally a manifest shadow."

"Yes, you're right."

"Wait, what? Did you figure out what he is?"

Todd handed me a cup of tea and a plate of three sandwiches—neatly arranged into an overlapping row— instead of the usual single one that humans ate. Yes I really needed to start dating supernats.

"Yes. It was difficult. The creature is not behaving the

way it's supposed to. But I'm almost certain now that he's a nalusa chito. That's a Choctaw shadow creature; shadow, in this case, meaning malevolent, not necessarily made of shadow. But there's disagreement about its form: some saying it takes the form of a black panther, and some saying it's a big black shadow."

I remembered thinking I saw a black cat standing over Tez the night before, but didn't interrupt.

"This creature is interesting, because it's a literal representation of depression. It creeps inside you when you allow evil thoughts or depression into your mind, and then it eats your soul. I had always classed the nalusa chito as entirely mythical: a very direct story to explain depression or other mental illnesses. This is part of the reason it took me so long to find. My bad."

"What did you find?"

"Well, I was remembering how the San Antonios were so convinced that the shadow was employed by someone else, and I thought about how that actually mapped onto what Bu Bu told you about there being a creature with the shadow. And that got me thinking: what if this creature *doesn't* usually behave this way, but it's being constrained by someone else, or it's acting as an agent for someone else? Could a creature be magically forced to act differently than its nature?

"Then I remembered a story I'd heard from a Chickasaw medicine woman in Tishomingo, and I went and looked it up. She said she'd witnessed a foreign creature—she couldn't be specific about what kind of foreign; just not white, not Black, and not Indigenous—draw out a nalusa chito from a possessed young Choctaw/Chickasaw man, and then enslave it. She said she was the one who referred the afflicted man to the foreign creature. She said the creature had been in the guise of a man, but was radiating an unusual level of supernatural energy. That sound familiar to you?"

It did. That was pretty much exactly how Ayo had described me to myself the first time we'd met. But Todd was right there, had were-animal ears, and I didn't want him to know about this.

"You think this foreign creature might be the same guy Bu Bu saw with the shadow creature?"

"I wouldn't jump to any conclusions, but it's too much of a coincidence to dismiss out of hand. After all, stories like this, of mysterious supernats who enslave not-quite-corporeal nasties, are extremely rare. In fact, outside of sorcerers bottling djinns, I can't remember ever hearing any other such stories, which is why I was able to find this one."

We both chewed on this for a moment.

"When did the whole enslavement thing happen?"

"I got the story about three years ago, but the medicine woman was irritable and wouldn't be specific about when the story actually happened. And she was *old*. So … no clue."

"Okay, how do we … uh … defeat it?"

"I've never seen any stories of anyone defeating a nalusa chito—besides this one, I mean, and she couldn't give details. The stories are all cautionary, mostly about not giving in to evil thoughts or despair. But once the creature gets in you, it eats you up and then your soul is gone. What happens to the creature after that, I don't know. But you said light works."

"Drives it away. Hey! As far as we know, it's never been seen in the daytime, right? But I don't know if light destroys it. *Can* it be destroyed?"

"No idea. I'll make some calls tomorrow, see if I can get some more direct information. In the meantime, since it's clearly after you now, you shouldn't be alone."

"I'll stay the night," Todd volunteered, loudly. Monkey perked up.

"Todd said he'd stay here tonight. Any ideas for tomorrow night?"

"I'll get right on it. I might be able to gin up a protective spell for your apartment or something. Or you can always sleep here. Get some sleep." And she hung up.

I turned to find Todd unexpectedly close, and staring at me. "What?"

"Nothing. You're just, nothing I expected ... in a good way," he said, with his patented rueful smile.

Looking at him up close, I had to reinterpret the smile. Maybe it wasn't so much rueful as ... mildly amused at the world. Or maybe himself.

"Surely you knew from the first that I was ... something."

His unblemished brow wrinkled a little. Boy, was he good-looking, up close. Like a K-drama star, except less plastic and more ... um ... gritty? And he had a musky smell that was ... a little off from what I expected of a human man, but not unpleasant.

"It's true, your scent isn't quite ... right," he said, as if reading my mind. "But then, when I take a deeper whiff it's ... not wrong, either. I just assumed after a while that you were mixed blood and that was the deal. But you seemed so intent on passing for human that I didn't wanna out you, and I thought maybe you didn't even know ..."

I understood. Mixed blood people—people who were part human and part supernat—could be extremely touchy. They were very diverse: some with abilities and some not, some knowing their heritage and some not. And they had all kinds of ways to feel about it. We always had some of them coming into Sanc-Ahh, looking for a place to belong, and often being really difficult about it. It was understandable: supernats were all over the place about mixed bloods as well.

Part of me had always wondered if I was mixed blood, too. It would explain a lot. But the strength and extent of my abilities kinda kiboshed that notion. Human blood weakened abilities; magic was zero-sum like that. No mixie would be as powerful as I am ... unless my supernat parent was even more powerful. Scary thought. And my mixed-human-race features kinda suggested that I might be mixed in other ways as well.

Ayo had suggested once or twice that I might be mixed species—a mix of more than one kind of supernat—which was why my abilities were so multiplied in number and strength, and why I couldn't find accounts of creatures with my skill sets. Mixed species supernats—by all accounts—were extremely unpredictable in terms of appearance and abilities; there were stories of weak ones, ones with incredibly bizarre abilities, and unbelievably strong ones with abilities neither parent had. But mixed species creatures were so incredibly rare that Ayo couldn't point to single extant creature who was an actual mix. I'd heard many stories about them, but no one I knew had ever met one. So if I was one, I was a frakkin' unicorn.

Suddenly, I didn't want to talk about me.

"So, can you explain the whole were-fox, or fox-were thing to me?"

"Uh ... I'm not a were-anything. I'm a fox. Period. A *stone* fox ..." He waggled his eyebrows.

I just looked at him, confused.

"It's what people used to say to mean 'hottie' in the seventies ... never mind. Japanese foxes are just Japanese foxes, but some of us reach a certain age and we gain supernatural abilities."

"But you're a *huge* fox! Are Japanese foxes that big?"

He laughed. "No, no, not at all." He pulled out his phone and found a YouTube video. It was charming, and Japanese foxes were freakin' adorable—and fox-sized.

"It's part of the deal. If we reach a certain age we gain a whole lot of things, including the ability to change size, if we want that. I'm American, so I want it. We add new tails, and gain the ability to create fire-lightning, *kitsunebi*, and the ability to change form, including to become human."

"Okay, wait. 'Reach a certain age?' Todd, how old are you?"

He shifted slightly away from me. "Well, typically it takes one hundreed years to get shapeshifting--"

"You're one hundred years old?"

He shifted some more. "Um, well, more like one hundred-fifteen, if you must know ... but I was *only* a fox for the first hundred years, so I'm really fifteen in human years." He leaned back towards me and waggled his brows. "Which makes you a cougar right now—"

"Wait, when you were telling me about your grandparents being interned, you seemed kinda shifty. Does that mean that ... *you* were interned?" All the hair on my head felt like it was standing on end.

"No! No, nothing like that. But you're right, my parents were issei and *they* were the ones who were interned. They left me behind on the farm, actually, and—"

"So, is this anything like the Chinese evil fox spirits you told me about? I can't remember what they're called—"

"Huli jing, yes. There's a cross-over. Huli jing are related to us, a different breed of fox."

"But, and maybe I'm remembering this wrong, but, I

thought you said the foxes only turned into women, to lure men."

"But what should we turn into, to lure straight women?"

He leaned in closer, leering manically, until I laughed.

"It's traditional for kitsune to turn into beautiful women, but that's because men had all the power and mobility and agency in the old days, so they were more interesting. Also, back in the day the women were much more up on their old wives' tales and harder to fool. Nowadays, women are a lot more interesting than they used to be—and a lot more credulous—so we're branching out." He waggled his eyebrows. "Wanna be lured?"

I sat back from him and regarded him seriously.

"Stop smiling and look serious," I said.

He tried, but he could only manage to return to a mostly straight face with just a touch of a smile. Oh my. Yes, yes, I could see how this guise would lure straight women. And gay men. And anybody else who liked to touch men. A lot. Oh my. He was *really* good looking. Like, shirtless-Rain-in-*Ninja-Assassin*-covered-with-blood-and-sweat good-looking.

"So this is just a glamour? It's not your natural form?"

"I'm not restricted to one form, but all of us shifting ones have a form we tend to fall into, and it quickly becomes a default, and feels natural to us. This is mine."

"But you can look like other people."

He stood up, lifted his arms, and then faded for a moment. When he ... she brightened again, she was a stunningly beautiful woman with Resting Bitch Face. She looked ... in fact, she looked like Gong Li. She was wearing a red cocktail dress and her hair was down, and she was smiling ... that same damned smile that Todd always had on, except on a woman it looked more knowing, less deprecating.

She took out her phone—which had apparently survived the change intact—from a pocket in the dress and looked at herself.

"Gong Li, huh?" she said, in a voice that rang like a bell. I shivered a little.

"She's at the top of my freebie list," I said. I'd gone through a phase in high school, when I was exploring my roots, where I was obsessed with the films of Zhang Yimou, and had fallen in love with his actress/muse. "Hey! How did you know that?"

She smiled. "It's part of the whole turning-into-a-beautiful-woman-to-lure-men thing. You let yourself turn into the beautiful woman for the specific man ... or, in this case, woman. It's a skill."

I shivered again. "Dude, *please* change back. You're freaking me out."

She raised her arms and slid back into Todd form.

"So, are kitsi—"

"KIT—SOO—NEH. All syllables equally emphasized."

"... kitsune all pansexual?"

He laughed. "Most foxes are primarily het, for reproductive purposes, but you never know when a fox is gonna bat for another team just for fun. And when we get older and are able to change form we become whatever that form suggests. I've done the beautiful woman thing before ... I mean, when I'm in a woman's form, I'm a woman, and I guess if I'm a woman to lure a het man, I guess I'm a het woman ... and if I'm a woman to lure a queer woman I'm a queer woman ... I mean, I suppose ... Probably best not to put labels on it ... unless you're putting the label on with your own hands," he leered at me again, stroking his belly in demonstration.

"And ... are you a dude fox?" I hadn't really had a chance to check his undercarriage during the fight and he'd been moving too fast, anyway.

He raised his eyebrows. "Does it matter?"

Without even thinking, I turned into a pretty little Japanese vixen. I whisked my tail at him and then changed back. "You tell me," I said.

His face froze for a moment, the first time I'd seen him nonplussed. Suddenly, I was embarrassed. Monkey screeched a laugh. "Dude, what time is it?"

He looked. "Whoa, it's almost three. Bedtime."

"Lemme get you a blanket," I said, and started to get up.

He pushed me back down. "Don't bother," he said, stood up, and changed back into fox form. Wow, it was true, now that I could get a clear look. He *did* look like Todd in fox form. He was beautiful, with long, black legs, fluffy oxblood fur and two deliciously bushy tails—tail*S*, there were *two*—which waved a gentle smile at me. He opened his sharp muzzle in a grin, leapt up on the couch, circled a couple of times, and curled up—in just such a way that I couldn't check his junk. He didn't put his head down until I turned off the light, but he seemed to go to sleep right away.

Which was apparently my cue to wake up completely and start spinning out. Not about Todd and his thing (that was too fresh and I could spin out on that later) but about Slim Shady and his seeming invincibility. How do you defeat an embodiment of dark thoughts? I mean, this "foreign creature" had clearly found some way for him to operate outside of his normal parameters. Before, when he could only suck out the soul of someone who gave in to dark thoughts, there was a clear defense. But this guy? He'd been made immensely more powerful, able to attack anyone at any time—or any time at night.

But why *now*? Had it gotten loose from its captor?

Or had its captor sicced it on us right now? Was it hungry? Was it part of a plan? If it was being controlled by the foreign creature, to what end? I punched my pillow but it was fresh out of answers.

How could I fight it?

My brain was just circling, but the center of that whirlwind of thoughts kept resolving into a thought that I didn't want to think: Tez might have to go through with it. He might have to bond with the walking stick. I might not be strong enough to kill this thing and if *I* wasn't, no one else in the Bay Area would be. But the power he'd get from this thing—I remembered the shockwave that came after Tez struck the werewolf with that stick; he'd be *more* powerful than that, much more—maybe that would be enough. If he didn't bond with it, if he destroyed it, he might be destroying our only hope of killing, containing, or driving this creature away permanently. Would we just wait until it killed every powerful supernat in the Bay Area? Would we just let it get more and more powerful until no one could stop it? Would it eventually consume the world? Would it consume *me*?

... and ... I found I was reluctant to tackle this question, but it was a more deeply pressing one for me: who—or *what*—the hell was Slim Shady's captor? The "foreign creature"? Was that the "same kind of thing" like me that Bu Bu had mentioned? Was it a creature like me? Was it ... was it my ... parent? Was it an evil creature? A monster? Was *I* an evil creature; a monster?

It turned out, that was the thought that had been stuck like a thorn in my mind, keeping me from sleeping. And now that I had drawn it, the whirlwind turned into water swirling down the drain. My last thoughts as I fell asleep were of certainty ... and sadness ... and fear ...

CHAPTER THIRTY-ONE

MONDAY, OCTOBER 24, 2011
MAYA'S APARTMENT, SAN FRANCISCO

WHEN I WOKE up, the late morning sun was streaming full in the window, Todd was gone, and a piping hot cup of tea and an equally piping plate of double loco moco were sitting on my table, set with cutlery and a napkin. Where had all this food come from? I didn't have ground beef or eggs or gravy in my kitchen, I was pretty sure. Or napkins. Was this a kits ... kitsune ability? To gin up breakfast from thin air?

Not really caring about the whys that much, I devoured the whole in under five minutes. It was delicious and tasted homemade, down to the gravy. And I'd been really hungry. It was only when I was finished and taking the plate to the sink that I found the note he'd left under it. It read:

"Have appointment. Filled ur fridge. Pathetic. Must learn 2 cook. Free tonight. Call for bodyguard."

I checked the fridge. Yes, indeed, he had filled it: fruits, veggies, meats—so many meats—kimchee, cheeses, even bacon. I checked the cabinets: yup. All sorts of basics. Grains, cereals, nori, canned stuff. Not so much my thing, but he'd replenished my depleted fruit crisper, and that made him alright in my book.

Monkey screeched a sudden warning and I rushed to the freezer. Whew. No, he hadn't thrown out my frozen fruit pies and dinners, although he had left another note here:

"Stop eating this crap. Fresh food below."

I tried to take out one of the frozen dinners, but it was stuck fast to the one below it. I tried to take the whole stack out, but discovered it was all stuck together, and all stuck to the inner panel of my freezer. I checked everything in the freezer: all of it prepared food with lots of chemicals. Sure enough, it was all stuck to the freezer's insides. I looked more carefully and realized that Todd had poured water all over everything, including his own note about the crap, and frozen it all together. Now I'd have to defrost the freezer to get everything out, and the food would all be ruined in the process.

"Dammit!" I yelled aloud, while Monkey, in my head, nodded and said: *respect*.

Oh boy. He had already taken over my diet. I knew enough about weres—and he was a sort-of were, despite what he'd said—to know that feeding and sharing food was a big deal to the canids; it was the mixture of human and canine social behavior that made food so central. This was mating behavior.

And these groceries ... he must have spent well over $100 on these! He was a were, and Asian, so he'd never, in *ever,* let me pay him back. But he would definitely use it to push his way in. He was already doing so.

Hoo boy.

I grabbed my phone, found his number, and spent

$2 of my entertainment budget on a ringtone for him: "Twentieth Century Fox" by the Doors. I needed advance warning the next time he called.

Monkey noted my chagrin, tapped me politely on the metaphorical shoulder, and then screeched in my metaphorical face. Here was an *extremely* good-looking, *terrifically* ass-kicking (Monkey loved asskickers) would-be lover, who provided *food,* and was, astonishingly, interested in my hadn't-had-a-date-in-months ass. *What was the fucking problem*?

"The Eye of the Tiger" started playing on my phone and I literally ran to answer it. Monkey crossed my metaphorical arms and hmphed. Monkey was a proponent of the bird in the hand; the bush needed to get laid.

"Hello?" I said rather more breathlessly than I would have liked.

"Maya?" Tez asked, rather less confidently than I'm sure he would have liked.

"Tez! What's wrong?"

"Nothing. I just … um, I've made a decision, about the … you know what. I don't wanna say. I'm being paranoid."

"No, the you-know-who is definitely listening, and I have it on very good authority that they have a special division that watches us. So yeah, maybe avoid key words."

"Really? 'Cuz Ayo's been saying a *lot* on the phone …"

Ayo was able to magically obfuscate our phone calls, but I didn't know how to do that, and evidently, neither did he.

I paused to find a way to tell him this and then gave up "… I'll talk to her," I promised.

"Okay. Uh … I don't know why I'm telling you this.

... I guess it's because I wound you up in all of this ... tangle ... and I kinda feel like you have a right to know. I'm sorry about all of this, by the way."

He trailed off. I let the silence sit. He took an audible breath.

"Anyway. I've decided not to go ahead with the ... thing ... this week. I'm gonna try to destroy it instead. Maybe ... maybe that'll work. I don't know. I just know that I can't do it, and I don't think I should."

He stopped again and I just stood there, holding the phone to my head. I thought I'd left the possibility open for this decision, but I realized in that moment that I had been expecting him to take it on: the power, the responsibility.

I would have.

Immediately I felt unsure. Who was *I* to say what was right or wrong in this situation? Who's to say how much future *I* would sacrifice for the good of everyone else? Who was *I* to judge him?

But I *did* judge him. It was Monkey who judged him, but ... I judged him. And it was more of me than just Monkey, really. That terrifying, delicious, frustrating, gorgeous man, the one who had seen what I could do and still liked me, *that* man had disappointed us ... me.

I tried to think on the other side of the question: freedom! Longstanding dreams! Autonomy! An open book in life! But none of those things tasted good in my mind. I tried to be happy for him. But I couldn't in that moment.

And he knew, he *knew* that thing was after me.

I realized that the silence had gone on too long when he cleared his throat.

"Uh, so anyway, I just wanted to say that I'll probably be a little off line for a while, taking care of Amoxtli and dealing with the ... thing. So ... you won't hear from me for a while. But I'll see you around, later, when ... when things settle down. Okay?"

Yeah right. He'd chickened out in front of me. He was never gonna call me again. And ... had he forgotten that thing was after me? He must have. Yes, he must have. There's no way he'd just leave me hanging in the breeze ... Not that I needed him. I had Ayo, and ... and Todd. And we'd figure something out. And it was Tez's whole life. I had no right to ...

"Tez," I said, then stopped.

"Yes?" he asked after a moment. He sounded ... hopeful, as if he really thought I could say something that would make things better.

"Just ... watch your back, okay? ... And call me if you need help."

"Okay."

Another pause.

"Okay," he said again, "bye." And hung up before I could reply.

I wasn't sure if I *would* have said "bye," even to stay on rhythm. Because I didn't feel that this was an end. Or maybe, more precisely, I didn't feel that this was the *right* end.

I had barely had time to formulate this thought when "Oohh Child" went off.

"What?" I asked, impatiently.

She didn't comment on my rudeness, it had really been that kind of week. Month.

"You were right," she said. "They had her this whole time. Dalisay. Her body."

I wanted to hit someone. "I take it the culprit was our Slim Shady."

"I really wish you wouldn't call him that. He's killed

too many. It's disrespectful."

She was right, of course, and I didn't want to have to say aloud that Shady terrified me too much to be treated seriously. "What the hell happened, anyway?"

"Well, we were partly right. The Hung For Tong *were* the last ones to see her. Apparently the nalusa chito found her there and killed her right in front of them—right in front of Bu Bu, in fact. They were worried the aswang coterie would blame them for not protecting her. It was in one of their buildings so it really *was* their responsibility. And they were also worried that she was an accident and that it was really after one of them. But I facilitated a sit-down with them this morning and they came clean. They'd even kept her body, not sure what to do with it. Apparently, they weren't even agreed on the idea of selling her wings."

My mind was still a bit fuzzy, but one thing popped up clear. "Ayo, what did they say about the …?" I couldn't find the words, but she knew what I was after.

"I remember there was some confusion as to whether there was one creature or two. It seems that Dalisay came to negotiate and one of their lieutenants showed her to a sort of reception room and left her alone there while he fetched the boss. Apparently there was an extra piece of furniture in the room when they came in that nobody noticed. When the lieutenant returned with the boss, they found that piece of furniture gone, replaced by some sort of homunculus—"

"Or a large monkey—"

"Yes. And there was also a shadow creature attacking Dalisay. So they called for help, and focused on trying to remove the shadow creature from Dalisay, and by the time they thought to look for the homunculus, it was gone. Apparently Bu Bu came in and chased the shadow thing out of the room and up onto the roof, where it disappeared. I'm guessing that Bu Bu either heard about the homunculus later, or possibly encountered it himself up on the rooftop. But," she sighed, "I'm afraid we'll never know ... not from him at least. I'm thinking they might have happened on Dalisay in the street—she had parked several blocks away—and followed her there. And I'm guessing that since it seems that Dalisay was the first victim, the, uh, homunculus might have been there to direct the Nalusa Chito the first time, and thereafter was able to let it, uh, hunt by itself."

We sat in silence for a very long time. But I didn't make very good use of that time. I didn't really want to think about the implications of a thing *like me* siccing its soul-eating slave *on me*.

Finally, Ayo spoke: "Listen, Maya, I'm not trying to pry, or encourage you to break a confidence, but what the hell is going on with Tez and that damned Huexotl? *Is* it the piece that the Aziza mentioned in his story?"

I hesitated, my mind whirling with desire to get her take on it ... and, let's be honest, to offload this heavy responsibility onto a real adult. But if I wasn't an adult ... and if this responsibility wasn't *clearly* mine and mine alone ...

"Okay," she said crisply, "Let *me* talk, then. Nobody currently in a leadership position in the Bay Area's supernatural community is indigenous to the Bay Area."

"What does this have to do with the price of tea in—"

"Let me finish. This means that the Bay Area is, and has been for nearly two centuries, without strong supernatural guardianship. It's like this all over the United States, but mitigated in most places either by some continuity in various Indigenous peoples, or by the continuity built by settler colonist or immigrant communities who maintain a constant presence over a long period of time. Or both. But in ports of entry like San Francisco, where the Indigenous populations are so embattled, and where there are constant boom-and-bust cycles which bring new populations in and take old populations out, and where, now, all the old neighborhoods are being gentrified, stability is a much, much bigger problem. The slings and arrows that affect humans affect supernats just as much, and in the same ways. Because of what I just said, the Bay Area is supernaturally chaotic."

"Ayo, I always thought that *you* were the supernatural leader here. I thought that's what Sanc-Ahh *did*."

"It's not," she said flatly.

I felt like she'd slapped me in the face. I started to react, but held back.

"I ... I thought so too," she admitted, finally. "I thought ... I've been many places in the world—even in the U.S.—with strong supernatural guardianship, and ... it makes a tremendous difference. I'd been aware for a long time that the Bay Area hasn't had strong supernatural guardianship at all since the gold rush. The energy here is chaos, and has been my entire life. When I ... when I came back here, it was specifically to try to fix that. ... I was ... very arrogant ..."

I held my breath.

"There are sanctuaries like this in every place where there's a large concentration of supernatural creatures. Sanc-Ahh's become a locus, but we aren't leaders ... not in the way that you, for example, are a leader with your magazine, or with your organizing. We can't envision, or guide, or ... *lead*. All we can really do is comfort and clean up."

Ayo took an audible breath. "I thought I could change

our sanctuary into a center for guardianship, but humans can't be guardians. They never are, I've never seen it, and my attempt hasn't worked here. The energy here ... it's still chaotic, it's still wild and unruly and dangerous. And the true wonder of it all is that no one has tried to take advantage of it for such a long time."

"You mean, they *have* before?" I couldn't help breaking in.

"What do you think caused the Loma Prieta earthquake?"

I took that in.

"Maya, I've had a bad feeling for a while that we're vulnerable here. And I didn't want to believe that this shadow creature, this nalusa chito, could create a huge problem. But it's growing stronger, and we've been—without knowing it—throwing our strongest at it and y'all've barely made a dent. *This* is the thing I've been dreading. I have no idea what the end game is, if there even is one. But it doesn't have to have a plan. It can destroy us through sheer hunger, sheer malevolence. And we *have no guardian*."

"Ayo, what do you mean by 'guardian' then? If you're not one, what could ... what could Tez do that you couldn't?"

"Maya, you know when you said the power in Tez's walking stick felt 'alien' to you? And when I said how difficult it was for others to steal power from shapeshifters, because it wasn't *theirs*?"

"Yes ..."

"Maya, I have no inherent magic, except the Sight, and that's ... never mind right now. Human magic is a matter of learning the techniques to manipulate the ambient energy of the world. I thought a human could be a guardian of these energies because we can manipulate them, with adjustments, anywhere we go. But the magic isn't inherent; and it doesn't tie us to the land. Supernatural creatures have inherent magic, and it ties them to their location. They can live on land that is not in their region of origin, but the magic of that region ... it takes a lot of time, to become a part of a new land. Generations, and hard work, and adaptation. The loogaroo, for example, come from werewolves that were created from non-European humans, and adapted over several centuries to the magic and energy of the Caribbean, and the cultures they helped develop there. Now they're more vampiric than lycanthropic, and many of them have guardianship of pieces of the islands they live on. The Bay Area doesn't have anything—any*one*—like that."

"And you think Tez can just ... skip over all of that?"

"I don't know if I'd exactly call it 'skipping over,' but yeah. The Huexotl sounds like it was created for specifically that purpose. I mean, it's a *walking* stick, made for migration. If I had to guess, I'd say it was created during a time of migration or diaspora for the people who made it."

This was so on the money that I gasped a little. Ayo heard it.

"I thought so," she said. "Maya, you have to understand: Tez and Chucha coming back into contact with the Huexotl just as this strangely powerful nalusa chito shows up: it's not a coincidence, you understand? There are no coincidences like this when it comes to magic. A problem was created, so a solution was found."

"You're saying the ... the *Bay Area* is conscious and came up with this solution?" It had never occurred to me before that my fantasy of the spirit of the Bay Area might be something real ... until just this moment.

"Not exactly. There is a spirit of a place, but it's not conscious ... exactly. If it helps to think of the Bay Area as an entity with a consciousness, go ahead. What's really important here, Maya, is that if—when—Tez takes on this guardianship, I can help him, and so can you. This could be what ... what this whole region needs. I mean, not just to weather this crisis, but for many many reasons and purposes."

Ayo was landing every punch tonight and, for Tez's sake, I couldn't stand it.

"Ayo, I'm not trying to be a bitch, but you just said yourself, you're not a supernatural creature. I understand that you've dedicated your life to the supernatural and feel a stake in it, but you *can* walk away. It's not like chaos among supernats is going to cause that big a stir in the human world ... unless someone causes an earthquake, which I don't think Slim Shady can do."

"Maya!" Ayo cried, suddenly passionate. "Have you learned *nothing*? We don't *exist* in separation; we're entirely interdependent! We both draw from the energy of a place, and the place is ordered and affected by the energy of both! Why do you think we're in a drought? Why is violent crime on the rise in the Bay? Why are so many people living on the streets? This region is out of balance, both the humans and the supernaturals! *That* is why I'm here! *That* is why I do what I do! Because humans and supernats living side by side, in ignorance of each other, not caring for each other, inevitably destroy themselves!"

She stopped and I could hear her gasping. I was shocked. This was a familiar lecture, but it was one I had never really ... understood. At least, not in a visceral way. I had always thought of it more as Ayo's own hobbyhorse, her own little set of morals and ethics. I had never thought of it as something that controlled the big picture... or even my own little picture.

"It's true, what you thought about the stick," I said hurriedly, before I could change my mind. "It's all true." She started to speak. "—and I talk to it sometimes ... no, *it* talks to me: the spirit of the Bay. I think." She was silent. "I don't know. I don't know if it talks to me."

She paused for a moment, to see if I was going to say anything else. I could almost hear her tamping down on her desire to ask for more.

"And Tez knows this?" she asked.

"Not all the stuff about guardianship; not about the spirit of the Bay ... but he knows the stick stuff. Amoxtli told us the whole story. It's like you said."

"So he's going to go through with it," she said, sounding relieved.

"No!" I cried. "He just called me before you did! He's *not* going to go through with it! He's going to try to destroy It!"

"What? Maya, and you didn't try to stop him?"

"Ayo, don't you remember? Once he's performed the ritual, it bonds him to the stick and them both to the land, so he can't leave again. Ever."

She sighed. "So that part's true. I thought it was just ... an amplification of the story."

"No, it's true. Did you know ..." I felt like I was betraying him, but in for a penny ... "that he's always dreamed of traveling the world?"

She sighed again. "Of course he has. A young male beast shifter—a predator—not attached to any indigenous land. Of course he has wanderlust. He'll settle down once he's bonded with the land." She said it in a dismissive tone, but I didn't think that Tez's dream since childhood could be put down to just a biological imperative. "It'll be fine,

Maya, you just need to talk to him."

"*Me*? Why me? *I'm* not his elder. You should be the one to talk to him. You can tell him all about … what you just told me. It's a far better argu—"

"Maya, he doesn't listen to me."

"He came to you for help."

"He was desperate. But he wouldn't take any of my advice."

"Well, why should he?" I burst out suddenly. "You're not exactly trustworthy. *You're* the one who sold Juice the instructions for the stick!"

There was a dead silence down the phone, and I felt how unfair the accusation was. I opened my mouth to take it back, but then Ayo laughed bitterly.

"Jesus, Maya. I just gave you a lecture about the spirit of a place and how I'm not a guardian, but even *I* didn't get it. Ha!"

"What are you talking about?"

"All this time, *I've* been a tool of The Bay, as well. It used me to bring Tez to the stick. I'm just a pawn, as are you. I thought I'd passed him on to you as a last resort. Then later, I thought he might be persuadable to impress a pretty girl. But it worked better than I'd hoped. You've been a tremendous influence on him; and a tremendous support. Clearly, something else was at work here."

"He's not really listening to me about anything involving the stick, though. Not this whole time. And he's not going to listen to me now. He basically kissed me off earlier."

She smiled. "Oh, Maya, you'd be surprised. He's stiff-arming you because he feels somewhat ashamed of his decision. Go talk to him." She grew serious. "You can't let him destroy the Huexotl. We have no idea what will happen, how much power is bound up in that stick. If he releases it, it could be disastrous."

"How bad?"

"I don't know, but if it's more than a century old—"

"Try five. It's from the Conquista. From the fall of Tenochtitlan."

She was struck dumb for a moment.

"Jesus, five centuries of power, and God knows how many generations of naguals adding their blood to it? It might not be the cataclysm, but it won't be small ... and it *could* be Loma Prieta all over again."

I made an inadvertent noise of denial, but she rode over me. "Maya, do you really want to find out? Look—" and her voice became brisk, "I need to manage some things for the aswang coterie—help smooth over the transition of leadership. Go talk to Tez. Let me know if you need any help."

And she hung up.

CHAPTER THIRTY-TWO

MONDAY, OCTOBER 24, 2011
SAN FRANCISCO GENERAL HOSPITAL, SAN FRANCISCO

I WENT STRAIGHT to SF General and approached Amoxtli's room cautiously in case Tez had come here. But he was alone, except for his roommate, who was asleep.

He looked a lot better, although his skin was still somewhat faded looking, and the wrinkles that had seemed small when he was well looked deeper.

He brightened when he saw me. "Maya! Good to see you!"

"How are you feeling?"

"Much better," he said, touching his abdomen lightly and then wincing. "They've moved me off the serious drugs, so I'm feeling it, but it's not as bad as I expected. They're gonna release me tomorrow morning. I think Tez bringing the Huexotl around must've helped."

I wanted to ask about this, but the urgency I felt pushed all questions of curiosity aside. "Have you talked to Tez today?"

His face grew serious and cautious. "Yeah, he called."

"So he told you he's not going through with the ritual tomorrow?"

"Yeah, he told me," he spoke carefully, as if to betray no emotion.

"And you're okay with that?" My voice was rising, and I checked the roommate, who hadn't stirred.

"Maya," Amoxtli said calmly. "It's his life. It's his choice. I have no right to feel ... any kind of way about it."

"You're his too! You helped raise him! Of course you have feelings about it."

"Yes, of course I do, but Tez is a grown-ass man, and he can make his own choices without me butting in. And straight up: my feelings about it are none of your business." He didn't say "young lady" at the end of it; Amoxtli was too chill to say things like that out loud, but this was him pulling age-rank. And it worked.

I wasn't chastened enough to let it go, though.

"Are you just going to let your clan lose this treasure?"

"Yeah, of course that worries me, Maya. Tradition is important. But this is the 21st century. The very fact that we're living up here should tell you that we're no longer a people that is bound to the land. Our clan is scattered over millions of square miles on both sides of the border. We migrate, we travel, and nowadays, we do it several times within a lifetime: several times within a year. Tez is getting into a career that could send him all over the country—all over the world! Yes, we lose our connection to the land and that kind of power. But we gain something in exchange."

"Freedom," I said dully.

"Not just freedom. There's a power that comes from being mobile. Speaking two languages, living in two cultures. Combine that with an education and an important skill set: that's power! Those are the people who are going to rule the 21st century. Look at Obama's people: it's all folks like that, people who grew up moving between places. Hell, look at Obama! He's like that! And my Tez, he's like that, too. He's smart, educated, he's starting to be well connected, and he has mad computer skills. He's completely bilingual—a poet, in two languages—and right now, when Latin America is globalizing. Tez is gonna have the whole world at his feet! He could be anything, do anything. He could run a Fortune 500 company. He could be fucking president!"

He broke off, gasping, and holding a hand to his wound. I guess today was Gen-Xers-make-passionate-speeches-about-the-big-picture Day. He really should date Ayo. They'd make beautiful, declamatory babies.

"It frees you, too," I suggested, not judging.

"Maya, it's too late for me," Amoxtli said. "I was raised to do what I was raised to do. Clinging to the past has made my life what it is, and it's fine. But I won't have that for Tez or the kids."

He just breathed for a while, slowing down. "When Ome died, I thought he'd been irresponsible by not bonding with the Huexotl right away and giving our people a home. But I've had a lot of time to think about it, and I have to wonder, what good would it really have done? Ome felt the pull of the land and that magic. He felt what kind of responsibility it would burden him with. Our naguals have never taken on a city, much less a group of cities like the Bay Area. No, they've only ever taken over villages, towns, farmland. The kinds of places naguals used to be tied to naturally. Taking care of a land that so many different kinds of people lived on? People we didn't share language or customs with? Could he have done it? Would it have driven him crazy?

I don't know. And I don't think it's right to force anyone to find out. Not in this day and age, when there are so many better options."

I thought about bringing Ayo's guardianship argument to him, but really, what was the point? He'd made his feelings clear, and his perspective was a … good one. An interesting one. One I'd have to think a lot about … later. He obviously believed it, wanted it, and I didn't have the heart to argue an injured man out of his dream.

But he was dead wrong, I could feel it in my gut. My gut, unlike, apparently, other people's guts, did not speak to me often, nor did it speak to me clearly. But when it spoke, it was never wrong. And it was saying: Tez needed to bond with the stick. Period.

As I said my goodbyes and left the room this instant certainty was shaken again, as all my certainties were shaken. The usual: who was I to think I knew—

All these people were different from me, older than me—

The arrogance, to think that I could decide—

But unlike my usual, I couldn't quite dissipate that "certainty" in a rain of insecurities.

Then, in the middle of the hallway, a stronger thought arose: Amoxtli's view of the world was one that explicitly excluded me, wasn't it? I wasn't bilingual, or bicultural, despite being, possibly, biracial. I'd spent half of my growing up just trying to survive, and here I was, twenty-five years old, and barely able to make my way in the one culture I had. I was one of those ugly Americans being left behind by the Obama century, one of the ones that wanted a wall built on our southern border, to keep people like Tez out. Was that where my certainty of what was right came from?

I doubted Tez was thinking globally, or had anything

but the information at hand to decide with. But I had a little more info at hand—and a little more perspective—than Tez. What did I see? Really see?

I walked to the end of the hall and looked out the window there: it looked out over rooftops in the valley of the Mission district. But I didn't see the cityscape.

Because, for the first time, I was looking inward, looking out from my own limited life with my mind's eye, looking at the Bay Area, and beyond it, the whole, huge, confusing world. What I strained to see snapped into focus, and suddenly, with a dizzying inversion, I became aware that I was looking through a magical eye at not just the world of my imagination, but the world as it truly was.

This was a new ability. In that moment I could see the world at a glance: not the entire world, but the world of my awareness; not just places, but the things that were important. I saw San Francisco—the Mission, and SOMA, and Chinatown—I saw Berkeley and Telegraph Ave., from the University down past La Peña and Sanc-Ahh, to downtown Oakland. I saw Ogawa/Oscar Grant Plaza, spiky with anger and hope. I saw my friends, the knots of bright action and thoughtful power. I saw the supernatural world, overlaid, a parallel universe.

I saw the lights of Silicon Valley and the shadow its brightness cast; the creeping shadow of greed over the vividness of the City's clashes; I saw the dryness of the drought and the frustrated, dying life of the Bay; and creeping like a rat through this giant maze, the deep blackness of—somehow I knew—Slim Shady distorting and fading the light all around him—but not destroying anything ... yet.

And I could see all of this laid out like a three dimensional map, like a holographic diagram in a superhero movie.

I could see ... I could see their energies, their magic, in colors of light, bright and dim. And I understood, for the first time, that here, where I stood, on a 7-mile-wide spit of land turning a shoulder to the Pacific Ocean, was a powerful nexus of energy and magic. It wasn't the only one. I could see many others in the distance, some even brighter.

But this one, my one, the Bay we lived around, glowed white with combined colors, energy, and potential, jigged crazily with chaos and conflict and darkness, and sent its impact in rays outward, where it struck all over the globe. The energy of the entire world was tied into the Bay. What happened here, had repercussions everywhere.

I knew that would be cold comfort to Tez, because I could see—standing here with the world's light in my eyes—I could see the beauty, the difference, the enticement, of other places. There were other nexuses of energy shining brightly: major cities, islands, forests, deserts, rivers. Oh, to be there would be something! To bathe in those vibrations and smell those smells and taste those tastes! I felt a completely novel desire to move out, to travel, to explore, awakening in me. And I felt the irony as well: that I could now travel, and probably would, awakened to the desire by the closing of Tez's possibilities.

Because that was what this was. The Bay shone in my mind, and the shine grew brighter and brighter until I understood that this wasn't a new ability of mine, but a vision, a vision granted to me by what I could only understand as the Spirit of the Bay. It—my home—was showing me what needed to be done, and my home didn't care what I would be sacrificing, or that what I was sacrificing did not belong to me.

And, as if it had a voice, the Bay asked me: Are you

willing?

My mind was a jumble of ecstasy and confusion. Willing to what? Willing to sacrifice Tez?

Are you willing?

I didn't understand, and knew I didn't understand. Am I willing to do what?

And the "voice" seemed to change, as if I had answered: Are you ready?

And I understood that I didn't have to understand. This was not a choice of the mind. Was I ready?

I was ready.

The vision faded.

I spared a moment's grief for Tez, for all those shining jewels of cities and places that he would never see.

Then I got to work.

I knew in a flash that Ayo's hopes of pretty girls and jaguar boys trying to impress them were vain. He'd done all the impressing of me that he was going to do (and I'd been pretty impressed), but he'd also had no problem with disappointing me with his decision not to bond with the Huexotl. No, I couldn't be the one to convince him.

I searched the floor, and then the one above, until I found an empty room with a phone. I shut the door behind me, drew the blind, and changed, painstakingly, into Amoxtli. It took me a few slow seconds; I usually disliked taking on the form of actual people. Unfortunately, my imagination was being literal today: I was wearing nothing but a hospital gown, and boy, was Amoxtli hairy. I pulled out my phone, found Tez's number—I was still pretending that I hadn't immediately memorized it—and dialed out from the hospital line.

"Hello?" Tez answered after several rings. I had never heard him sound so ... scared.

"Tez," I said in Amoxtli's voice.

"Padrino," Tez answered. "Como estas? Are you all right?" His voice was anxious in a way I'd never heard before from him—but also annoyed in a way I'd never heard before, either. It kinda sounded like me, actually, talking to Ayo.

"Mijo, I need to talk to you. You need to come here."

He knew immediately what it was about. "But you said you supported my decision."

"I will support whatever decision you make. But I can't let this go without a proper discussion. It's my job to advise you, and I haven't done very well so far."

"You're not going to change my mind." He was dangerously stubborn now.

"I'm not trying to. You know how I feel. But there are some things ... things I haven't told you. Things I left out because I didn't want to influence you too much in one direction. You need to hear these things."

"I don't see what difference it will ma—"

"Please."

There was a startled silence. Uh oh. I was realizing now Amoxtli, like many middle-aged men, probably never said please or thank you to his ... uh, his kids. Well, maybe it would have an effect.

"All right," Tez said reluctantly. "I'll come right over. But I can't stay long. I have things to do today."

I decided to underline the effect. "Thank you. Oh, by the way, they've switched me to another room, I've been doing so well." I stuck my head outside and recited the room name to him, then we hung up.

The room was currently serving as a dumping ground for what looked like broken beds and gurneys. I shoved most of the detritus behind a curtained area, and laid three broken beds out in a row. A few of my plucked hairs turned into vague-looking machines—good enough to be in a hospital drama on tv, which should be good enough for Tez—a couple more into sleeping patients.

I put a little more work into the machines around my bed. One of them made a pleasant humming sound, and one attached to my finger with a clip. I wished I was more observant, because the details of these things escaped me. My bed was broken so that it wouldn't sit up, so I had to hold it upright with some invisible duct tape.

I'd barely climbed into the bed and arranged myself when Tez came striding in. I paused to admire the length of his legs.

"What?" he asked irritably. Oh. I was staring at his legs. Probably something his Padrinos wouldn't do unless there was something wrong. I needed an opening. I needed sympathy.

"Oh, sorry, mijo. I was just zoning out. I'm a little tired. I haven't napped yet today."

And just like that, Tez was all solicitousness. "Are you comfortable? Can I get you some water? Should I call the nurse? You need a pain killer, don't you?"

Monkey jeered in triumph. I couldn't help feeling satisfaction at my success. But I had to concentrate: Tez would never forgive me if he caught me out.

"No, no, Tez, I'm fine. Really. Just a little sleepy. Don't call the nurse. I need to talk to you."

He sighed, but gave in. He really was a Good Boy.

"I'm not trying to tell you what to do. But there's more at stake than just your own path, or that of our clan."

Tez frowned, and I couldn't tell if it was my words, or their content. I had to be careful to speak like Amoxtli, and not like me.

"Places of power, like here, the Bay Area, usually have a supernatural guardian watching over them, keeping things from getting too out of hand. I've talked to Ayo about this ... And she's just human, she can't do it. I've talked to other folks, too ... no one has watched out for the Bay Area, not as long as we've been here. Your father—"

Tez looked up intently.

"... he felt the chaos of this place. He knew. But he wanted to escape, just like you do. I don't blame you, but he didn't do what was necessary to save himself, his family, his clan, because he wanted his freedom. And, I have to admit, I wanted mine, too. I've paid for my failure. Everyone has paid for our failure. I hate that it all comes down to you to take on this burden that everyone else has refused. But there it is. This is real power. You can do some real good, good that no one else can do. This land needs a guardian, and you're the only one who can do it."

That was it. That was all I could say without going too far afield from what Amoxtli could know.

Tez's face was wretched, and he was looking at the ground again. "What about...what about the kids?" he whispered.

"Do you really think one of them could take over for you? Run this place?" It was a real question from me. I didn't know the answer.

But Tez did, and apparently he thought Amo did, too. He shook his head, as if in answer to an unspoken agreement between them. "But if I left," he said, desperately, "If I went traveling for a long time... for years..." He trailed off, still looking at the ground.

My certainty was shaken by this. What if?

"Walk me through how this would work, Tez," I said, as myself, and was startled to hear it come out in Amo's voice. Thank god for unconscious reflexes!

"I know!" he cried, as if in answer to a judgement I hadn't expressed, but probably Amoxtli would. "But they could learn! Manny used to look after the littles! He's inflexible, a little bit blinkered but… or Pronk could, Pronk could… I know, I know: nobody would listen to Pronk, because they think ze's flakey… a freak. But things could change. They could work together! They could… like…"

He trailed off, working it out in his head.

I'd grown up with a tendency to spin out into fantasies and just… live there. It took years with my foster— my adopted Mom working on me every day, to learn how to use my imagination to understand reality. I could see, in his face, that he'd learned this hard lesson much earlier, and harder, than I had.

After a very long few minutes, during which I held my breath and bit my tongue, Tez looked up at me. His shoulders were completely relaxed, as if he'd just let go. There was my answer. And I could see what it took for him to look me in the eye, and it felt like he was tearing off a part of his heart.

"I can't, Amo, I can't do it. Don't make me."

It felt like he was at a breaking point. I didn't want to push him. And I was afraid that if I did, he would really break, and then he'd be … useless. Yes, I actually thought that, and hated myself.

"I can't make you do anything," I forced myself to say dispassionately. "You have to make this decision yourself."

"I can't do it. I can't do it. I don't want to. I don't have anything left in me. I can't do it. I'm useless. I can't guard anything …" and all at once he was hyperventilating, sobbing without tears. The word "useless" struck me like a blow. God, I was doing this to him! After all he'd been through, how could I be so heartless?

"It's okay, Tez, you don't have to do anything you don't want to," I said, putting a hand on his head and stroking his hair. Monkey screeched at me in disgust, but I couldn't help it. I heard in my own voice every bit of yearning and ... love? Was it love? Whatever it was I felt for him, I heard it in my voice, and I was shocked and afraid that he would hear it too.

But apparently, he only heard avuncular love, because he bowed his head to rest on the blanket ... and then heaved himself away without looking at me, and left the room.

Okay, I had failed, and at the critical moment, too. It was my own weakness, though, and I wasn't going to let that happen again. Almost at the same moment, I hatched a second plan: one I wasn't going to botch.

CHAPTER THIRTY-THREE

Monday, October 24, 2011
Tez's House, San Francisco

I HAD SOME time to kill so I flew back over the Bay to the encampment for the general assembly. I found my friend Timmy Lu at the meeting. He was helping to organize the POC contingent in arguing for "Decolonize," and a less white-centered set of demands. But that didn't seem to be under discussion tonight.

"What's going on?" I whispered.

"The fire marshall took all the propane from the cooking tent," Timmy said. "They're talking fire hazards and health hazards, and word is that the encampment is likely to be raided in the next few days."

"Oh, shit."

Contingencies were being planned, but my mind was a whirl of other problems—Tez's intentions, Todd's expectations, Shady's threat, and general guilt—so I had trouble forcing myself to pay attention. After asking me things three times and getting "Mmm hmm" as an answer, Timmy finally asked, "Are you alright?"

"Sorry," I whispered. "My friend was killed last week and now there's all these logistical nightmares to deal with."

"I heard about that," he said. "Why don't you go deal with them? I'll text you about whatever actions are decided on."

I hated leaving early, but Timmy was right, and I wasn't being of much use, so I took off.

No question I was worried about facing Slim Shady by myself, but I had things to do that night that couldn't wait for safety, so I hid out at the sanctuary until after midnight—catching a quick nap, eating two dinners, and ignoring several texts from Todd—and then took a cloud back over the Bay to San Francisco, traveling as fast as I could.

I came in to Tez's apartment through an open window, changed back to human, and went invisible, just in case. I found their family photo albums and pulled out one from the middle, flipping through it in the light of the outside street lamps.

Tez's father had only been in his early thirties when he died, and boy, had he been a handsome man. Shorter than Tez, Ome had a kind of shaggy, rangy appearance and a clever, confident face that reminded me of a coyote. Tez and Chucha favored him in a way that made tears spring to my eyes.

I became visible again, and stood before the built-in mirror over the mantlepiece. I tried to turn myself into Ome, but it wouldn't come. My skin and features stretched and snapped back into Tez's face, over and over again. I'd never tried to become a person I'd only seen in pictures before. Not having a 3-D model to work from made it immensely difficult. But let's be honest: desperately not wanting to do it was what was really stymieing me.

I sat down on the couch. Last chance to change your mind, Maya. And I wanted to. Doing this was a point of no return, although it was hard to say return to what. Something more fundamental to who I was and what I did in the world. I didn't really have the time to think it through, here on Tez's couch. All I knew was that I was planning to force Tez to tie himself to all our futures, at the expense of his own. And that I didn't entirely have the right.

But I felt, from far off, like the clanging of a ... temple bell? ... the feeling of certainty, of clarity, that had come to me in my vision of the magical world. I could choose otherwise, but to do so would be to diminish my world, and with it—somehow—myself. And—I could feel it—to diminish Tez, too.

So I let Monkey out of her cage, Monkey, who was always up for fooling; Monkey, who was anxious to try this trick. I stood up, went to the mirror, and a complete vision of Ome's form came to my mind. I embodied it, then, upon reflection, changed the density of my form to that of a pale mist. It didn't matter how accurate it was. Tez only had to recognize it; he'd be half asleep anyway. My real problem was going to be that I'd speak to him in English, when, presumably, Ome had spoken to his children in Spanish. But I was relying on Tez's sleepy disorientation and lack of a conception of the afterlife.

Tez was sprawled across his bed with the abandon of a housecat in the sun. His face, despite its persistent halo of stubble, looked like a teenager's, for once. I wanted to touch him, to kiss him, to lie down in the crook of his arm and fold myself up in his warmth. And in that moment, I realized that I probably could do just that. If I dropped all this and curled up with him, he would probably wake up and ... let me, and we could be together and travel the world together and ... let the Bay Area and Ayo and the sanctuary and Baby and my friends and community and Occupy just go fuck themselves.

Right. Get to work.

I touched his face with my misty-cool hand and said his name, low, in a voice I had cast somewhere between Tez's own timbre and Amoxtli's accent and intonation.

Tez tried to swat my hand away from his face.

"Tezcatlipoca," I said again. "Wake up." This was a calculated risk. Amo had said he was named after the Aztec god of nagualism, but perhaps Ome had never called him that.

That one worked. Tez's eyes flew open and he sat up all at once. I backed away a few paces so he could see more of me.

"Papa?" He looked sleepily confused, exactly as I'd pictured. Ha! I'd done it!

"Listen," I murmured urgently. I didn't have much time before he awoke fully and started to question this apparition. Wait— did he even believe in ghosts? Argh! Too late to wonder that now!

"Pá ... cómo ... how are you here?"

"Listen to me now. You have to do it. You have to bond with the Huexotl."

"Pá, I can't. I can't ..."

"That selfish thinking nearly doomed our family, our whole clan. I'm sorry that you have to take on this burden with no help. That's my fault. But you can't make the same mistake I did. You are a Varela. You have to bond with the Huexotl."

"What if I destroy—"

"You can't destroy It!" I cried softly. "The release of magic will cause a disaster! It's too powerful! And you can't let It fall into the wrong hands! That would be another kind of disaster! Bond with the Huexotl tomorrow!" And with that, I tried to fade away through the door.

"Papa! Chucha is dead!" The anguished cry stopped me in my tracks. Was there anyone who could comfort him like his father?

"I know, mijo."

"Papa, I can't ..."

"You *can*. You *must*. You've done well enough for how little you were trained. You will manage."

He was starting to look stubborn. I had to close this.

"Mijo, you have to do this, for Chucha. Chucha has paid for my failure."

Tez's face drained of color. "But the kids ..." Tez choked out, then immediately looked ashamed.

"Do you really think either of the kids can do it?" It sounded like an accusation, but it was a real question. Maybe ...

Tez looked even more ashamed. "Maybe Manny ..." He trailed off, and his silence was enough. He didn't think either of his siblings could handle it, and he would know. Time to push down on it.

I hated myself.

"No. *You* are the ocelotl. *You* were made for this. If *you* run away, why should they believe in themselves?" I stepped forward and let my misty hand pass through his cheek. "You *can*."

Then I slowly went invisible before his eyes. Once he couldn't see me anymore, I turned into air and swept out through his window. But I hovered there, for a brief moment, watching his confusion and grief. My joy at a trick pulled off mingled with my ache, for Tez, for Chucha. And I whispered in my own voice, without knowing I was going to do it, "I won't leave you alone with this."

I flew on a cloud straight back over the bay to the sanctuary, and didn't take a breath the whole time.

CHAPTER THIRTY-FOUR

Tuesday, October 25, 2011
Downtown, Oakland

I WENT TO sleep in the protection of the sanctuary. Exhausted by the past week's emotional rollercoaster, I slept right through Timmy's texts telling me to get my ass up at 3 am and go downtown to protest the clearing of the encampments. By the time I woke up, around 9 am, the Ogawa/Grant encampment was gone, as was the one at Snow Park: the tents shredded, a hundred people arrested.

Ayo had opened Sanc-Ahh by herself, letting me sleep. I ran down the street to the donut shop and got us breakfast, and we sat, reading Twitter accounts and text messages about the morning's action. In my exhaustion, I felt vaguely as if I were responsible: my inattention last night, and my sleeping through this morning had somehow caused the raid and dispersal of the encampment. I knew this was ridiculous, but I kept getting up to go downtown, as if my presence could do anything. Fortunately, Ayo kept making me sit down again. There was a plan, after all, to gather and march at 4 pm. Until then, all I could do down there was confront police and get angry, and nobody wanted that, did we? Finally, she set me to inventorying the bar, then the storage room, just to keep me busy.

We didn't talk about Tez.

As morning turned into afternoon, members of my affinity group started trickling in, including Todd. His entrance made my heart simultaneously settle, and drop: what did he expect of me after Sunday night? It hadn't, exactly, been a romantic interlude. He'd spent the night on my couch as a friend.

But.

"When was the last time you ate?" was the first thing Todd said to me. Ayo's eyebrows went into her hairline; she knew all about canine weres and their feeding fetish. She moved immediately to the other end of the counter. Why was everyone conspiring to leave me alone with Todd?

"Uh … Hi Todd. How are you today?"

"That's what I thought," he said, producing a fresh onigiri, like magic, from his messenger bag. It was already wrapped in its nori sheet, but the nori looked fresh, like he'd just wrapped it. How'd he manage that? Jesus, was it homemade?

I meant, for a split second, to refuse it, but then the scent hit my nose and Monkey reminded me that I hadn't eaten anything since that single donut this morning, and was actually pretty ravenous. I seized and inhaled the onigiri—beef teriyaki, my favorite—then paused to realize the price attached when I saw the satisfaction in Todd's face.

"Uh, thanks for that. I spent the night here and didn't lay in any provisions."

"I figured. Here, put these in the fridge." He pulled

an unlabeled clear plastic bag full of equally unlabeled onigiri, all in their cellophane-wrapped nori sheets, out of his messenger bag and handed it over the counter. I fumbled the bag into one of the mini fridges, not looking at him.

"Thanks," I mumbled. "Uh, what time is it?" I called to a bemused Ayo.

"Quarter past three," she said. Thank god.

"We should start heading down there," I said, in Todd's general direction, then repeated it with a raised voice. While Todd had his back turned, gathering up our comrades, I surreptitiously slipped four more onigiri into my go-bag. I was still hungry and that one had been *delicious*. Todd didn't have to know.

As I ducked around the end of the counter, Ayo grabbed my arm.

"Do you think maybe you should sit this one out?" She asked, seriously, but somewhat expressionlessly.

I goggled at her. "What? Are you *kidding*?"

"You seem a little ... worked up. Things could turn violent out there. It's just been ... it's been a really rough week. The last thing this movement needs is a superpowered protester whaling on cops."

I rolled my eyes. "I promise not to whale on any cops. Let's go." And I stomped past her.

We straggled down to the meet at the library, and by 4 pm nearly a thousand people had gathered. We marched around downtown, disrupting rush hour traffic and getting angry honks; or maybe I chose to interpret them that way. Our mood was angry, but righteously angry, assuredly angry—*hopefully* angry. This wasn't the end of the movement; it felt like just the beginning, although no one knew where it would go from here. Todd marched at my right, Ayo at my left; Mari, who joined us at the library, marched next to Todd. We all fell into the same mindset, the same determined wavelength, for several hyperreal hours.

A few hours in, the sun had set and we approached the plaza again. We were given the order to disperse. I felt our energy rise to meet the opposition. Monkey was a soldier for Truth, and all parts of my mind pointed at getting back into the plaza. The cops had tear gas ready, gas masks on. Ordinarily, this would have concerned me; any smoke makes my eyes burn in the wrong way. But then the word went down the line to wet a scarf with vinegar to fend off the tear gas, and bottles of vinegar were passed around; and that gave me an idea. Todd pulled an extra cloth for me out of his bag, but I plucked a hair and changed it into a respirator. He grinned, and Monkey grinned back. I pulled out another hair and made goggles for myself, and then offered him a pair. He took them. I made Ayo a pair as well. I made a mental note to remember goggles in the future.

Colorful protesters and black-suited cops boiled in the intersection. A line of clear plastic shields approached; order bearing down on chaos. After another warning, the cops began firing tear gas and lobbing flashbangs. Monkey screeched and jumped up and down in my head. Fucking cops! People began running in every direction, screams and imprecations thrown. I found myself automatically guarding Ayo; she wasn't *that* old, but she had some arthritis starting and I just felt—

I saw Todd lift an arm to protect Mari—or was that Jenn?—from a flying tear gas canister, but the canister cleared all of their heads. Monkey screeched angrily.

A few yards away, tear gas flew, a white kid went down, and blood started streaming from his face. People dove in to help the injured protester, pulled him up and carried him out, screaming "Medic!" The fucking cops stood in a line, watching, throwing flash bangs, impassive, doing nothing to help.

Suddenly, my mood turned, from righteous anger to hot rage. Monkey began screeching incessantly in my head. I couldn't stand down here any longer, doing nothing. They wanted mayhem? I'd show them mayhem! I shoved Ayo towards Todd, who was partially shielding both Mari and Jenn, and cried, "Get them up past the the line on 15th!"

"Where are *you* going?" he yelled back.

I leaned in so only he could hear me. "I'm going up, to get a better view."

Ayo's eyes narrowed at me.

"Maya— " she started, but I was already gone, having used the smoke from the tear gas to cover the cloud I'd called down. Mari and Jenn were watching the injured man being carried away and Todd hustled them along after. I rose quickly above the level of the high-rises, ripping my mask down at the first opportunity to breathe freely. The fresher air was like oxygen to a fire.

The airspace above Ogawa/Grant Plaza seemed completely socked in by police helicopters and haze. Bring them down! I considered growing my fists large and just walloping the birds until they fell. Fucking cops! Then, when a fucking cop goggled at me out a helicopter window, I realized that, in my enraged, distracted state, I'd forgotten to go invisible. I corrected the omission, then stood back and glared at his craft. How to bring down his chopper, fast? Fucking cops! I tried to track the fuel line, but had no idea where that would be on a helicopter, or any other vehicle for that matter, and couldn't be bothered to study it in my fury. Maybe I could snap off one of the propellers!

From below I could faintly hear, among the rest of the hullabaloo, Ayo's voice calling my name. She sounded a bit … desperate. Maybe something was wrong. But I couldn't see her.

I looked consideringly at the chopper again. It was rimmed in red.

The cop pressed his face to the glass and his bug-eyes scanned the air frantically, for me. That was actually kinda funny. Monkey's screech turned to laughter. Fucking cop! I really wanted to smash his … I really wanted to make his eyes … I really wanted to *fuck* with this guy.

I moved in and rapped "shave and a haircut" on the window directly over his bewildered face. His eyes nearly popped out of his skull. While he eye-scrabbled the air for the source of the sound, I flew under and around to the other side of the chopper and pounded "two bits" on the opposite window. He must have shat his pants! High-larious!

The rest of the chopper's inhabitants were starting to cop to the strangeness and look around, puzzled. "Cop" to, get it? I screeched with laughter, not caring if they heard.

I flew over to the next chopper and considered. Idea! I pulled out a hair, turned it into an invisible bullhorn, which I placed directly against the glass, and, in a booming, sepulchral voice shouted, "The roof! The roof! The roof is on fire!" Instant mini-pandemonium, wild eyes looking around, guns pulled out. Hah! I flew under and up to the other side and placed the bullhorn against the opposite window. "LET THE MOTHERFUCKER BURN!" I loosed at the perfect moment. *Major* freak out! One cop even had to stop another one from firing through the ceiling.

I sat down on my cloud and gave in to a severe bout of guffaws. While Monkey was enjoying herself, and feeling the sudden rage blow off, my rational mind was able to insert a slim finger. Maybe, just maybe, scaring the crap out of cops who'd been out here for 16 hours and had already started injuring protesters wasn't the best idea.

Ayo! Where was Ayo? Where were Mari and Jenn and the rest of my crew? I stuck my head over the edge of the cloud. I didn't see them immediately in the chaos and darkness, but then I remembered, and scanned the mayhem at speed for a … there! Up near 15th St! A burning flash! That must be Todd!

I landed next to him and waited for a cloud of tear gas to blow past to drop the invisibility.

"Maya!" Mari shrieked. Jenn grabbed my arm.

"Where have you been?" Ayo cried, distressed.

"What did you do?" Todd asked, eyes shining.

Ayo grabbed my arm and pulled me away from Mari and Jenn and the handful of others who'd collected. Todd followed.

"What did you do?" she hissed.

I told them.

Ayo huffed. Todd guffawed.

"It's not funny," Ayo said to Todd. "The last thing we need is someone provoking the cops. Maya, you promised— "

"—not to 'whale on' any cops. And I didn't. I just shook 'em up a bit."

Todd snorted again.

"Todd, don't encourage her. I think you two have had enough excitement for the day. Let's put your strength to good use and shield people who are trying to get away."

And, ever so slightly abashed, but chortling occasionally at each other, we did, for the next hour or so. While the cops continued to hurl objects and smoke, and grab protesters, and make arrests, and use their nightsticks … Then, something in my eyes made Ayo wary again, and she insisted that I go back to the sanctuary, and that Todd accompany me there, in case Shady showed up.

I had a hell of a time getting Todd to leave me alone there, but I needed him to go; I had an appointment with Tez that night, although Tez didn't know it. I finally got him to go away by retrieving and scarfing the remainder of his onigiri, and letting him watch me eat them. Even then, he stood outside the door watching me lock it, and then watching me walk through the darkened cafe into the office. I don't know how long he stood outside there after I shut the door.

Probably not long, though, because Ayo came into the inner sanctum a short time later, fuming.

"I'm really disappointed in you, Maya," she started, "I thought you'd come a lot farther than—"

"I have to go, now," I said flatly.

"Don't try to duck out of this—"

"Tez is bonding with the Huexotl tonight and I have to be there to back him up, just in case."

She shut up immediately, and narrowed her eyes at me. She was too damned perceptive, was the problem.

"So … you convinced him …?" she asked suspiciously.

"Well, *somebody* did," I said bitterly.

She knew immediately what I meant. "What did you do, Maya?" she asked, hopelessly.

"What I had to do." I looked up at her tiredly, and she looked surprised at my attitude; I guess normally I'd just be defiant. "You said the Bay doesn't exactly have a spirit, but it does. And it spoke to me. And I had to do it." I pulled out a hair and made a windbreaker and pulled it on. She looked even more surprised. "And now's not the time to talk about it. Is the coast clear outside?"

Suddenly, she was all business, like she finally understood; not just what I was saying now, but my erratic and dangerous mood all night. "I'll walk out ahead of you and make sure."

And she did.

CHAPTER THIRTY-FIVE

Tuesday, October 25, 2011
Kite Hill Park, San Francisco

I MADE SURE I was set up, invisible, in a tree outside Tez's house by 10 pm. I watched as Tez watched tv with his siblings. Manny, the bigger, stockier one—way bigger than Tez—with the stubborn lower lip, looked like a mule … a mule on steroids. Pronk, the skinny gamer from last week, could not sit still, and sprang up periodically to get snacks as if zeir feet were spring-loaded. I watched as Manny put on a security guard's uniform and left for work; as Pronk went to zeir room and somehow instantly transformed from a quivering mass of springs to a facedown corpse, legs akimbo.

Later, I watched Tez making a call. He probably was talking to Amoxtli: he was taking copious notes. So I flew up to the nearest window and heard his side of an argument about whether they should use a cave and, once that was resolved in the negative, what greenspace is in the exact center of San Francisco: Dolores Park or Kite Hill. He was going through with it. Monkey hmphed in satisfaction, but the rest of me felt an unnamed anxiety.

He spent nearly an hour studying his notes. I guess if your training is incomplete you try to make up for it with studiousness—if you're Tez.

I followed him the mile or so to Dolores Park. He knew he was being followed; he repeatedly turned around and looked right at me, puzzled, before resuming. Probably thought he was being paranoid. We walked straight through Dolores Park, at 19th St., took the bridge over the MUNI tracks, and continued up the hill. We walked for a while through a nice residential area that I'd never explored, steadily upward, until Tez suddenly disappeared into the bushy darkness of what looked like someone's yard—or perhaps an overgrown empty lot.

I dove in after him and found a footpath that led behind the house next door, and followed the fence surrounding that house's backyard for a stretch, before turning and heading straight up a grassy hill that had been hidden behind backyards and tall trees, in the middle of the block. Halfway up, the overgrown slope opened out into a large empty space on top of the hill. Tez trudged to a flattened, open, dirt area near the top. I turned into an invisible mist so as not to leave footprints or make a noise, and floated up to a position behind him.

This must be the Kite Hill he'd been arguing with Amoxtli about, at or near the geographical center of the city. Behind us the hills of Twin Peaks cupped our promontory in their orange-streetlight-starred embrace, like we were standing on the pistil of a broad-petaled flower. From this flattened spot—like a dirt-floored stage—you could look out over the audience of Eureka Valley to the entire Inner Mission, up Portrero Hill, and, off in the distance, to the bay. The location was perfect: empty and dark, yet lit by the orange ambient light of a million streetlamps reflected back from the partial cloud cover; quiet, yet washed over with occasional traffic noise; protected from behind, yet open to the world that mattered most in this moment: the world of the Bay.

For a moment, the Spirit of the Bay rose up and the entire vista shone on me, almost like a face. It was a nod of acknowledgement. Then it was just a view again.

It was midnight. Tez set up at the center of the dirt-floored stage. As he began his preparations, his movements changed; gone was his general, relaxed readiness, and also the tense uncertainty and uncontrolled eagerness of the past week. Now he was all intention, direction, competence. He clearly knew exactly what he was doing.

He set down the paper with his notes on it, but didn't seem to refer to it at all. I remembered suddenly how he'd perform even new and rough poems from memory. He set out the Huexotl, first, then a knife that looked like it was made of a highly polished black rock, a bowl with a plastic bag stuffed into it, and a few other things I couldn't identify from this distance. Was that ... lipstick? No, he was using it to draw stripes on his face. It looked like ... black? Or maybe dark red? I couldn't tell in this light. And another one in a lighter color, maybe yellow or brown. He dumped the contents of the plastic bag into the bowl, and lit it with one of the unidentifiable objects, which turned out to be a lighter. Then he muttered something and waved the smoke around with his hands in a formal gesture.

Things really started hopping when he picked up the knife, which flashed like glass, and cut his earlobe with it, leaning forward and letting blood run thickly to the dirt ground before him. The moment the blood touched the ground, I felt a jolt of some sort of power, some sort of consciousness awakening and looking around, much as Tez had done last night: confused and incoherent.

Tez muttered more words, slightly louder now, so that I could hear that they weren't English, or recognizably Spanish. Probably Nahuatl, I thought to quell the mild panic I felt when I didn't understand language. That's what they would use, right?

He caught dripping blood in his hand, then reached over to the Huexotl with his bloody hand and dripped on It for a bit, then made sure the trick was done by smearing the blood all over It. I wasn't close enough to see clearly, but the darkness of the blood seemed to seep into the stick and disappear. Whoa, freaky. Then he held his hands out, facing palm upward, and I could see that the slice into his earlobe had already healed, and the blood had disappeared from his hands. Even with everything that was going on, I was able to spare a moment's jazz for the beauty and length of his fingers, his strong palms.

He began chanting a bit louder and more regularly, and I started identifying words. Was that ... Latin? As he chanted, I felt that power, that almost-consciousness, increase ... or focus, as if waking up more thoroughly. Its focus seemed to narrow in on Tez, although I could feel a tendril of it reach out to me, as if to sniff me, like a dog, or something less friendly. A sort of ... amoeba of energy appeared to coalesce above Tez's outstretched hands. His chanted lines began to repeat more quickly. I could sorta see where this was going now, I thought. I started to relax.

Then a familiar engine sound, followed by a familiar screech of tires, broke my concentration—and his.

Tez looked around behind him and muttered, "Shit."

I floated off in the direction of the noise, only a few

yards up the hill and through a small stand of trees to where a short residential street dead-ended into the empty lot of the hill. Sure enough, the 70s Arroyos' gorgeous green Mustang was parking, and even before its lights were out, spilling out a clown car's worth of gangbangers. Actually, after a moment I was able to see that it was only six. Six very purposeful Arroyos, but surely Tez could handle them?

I recognized the driver from the shooting at Tez's house—his face still a mess from the beating—and the braided shot-caller from the restaurant patio in Fruitvale, but the rest of the guys were either new to me, or ones I hadn't noticed before—Hey, I never forget a face, but I don't always notice the face, either, do I? They moved with purpose and confidence, filing one by one through the little wooden gate into the open space on the hill, skipping down to the flat area, and spreading out in a circle around Tez.

I remained invisible, watching closely, but Tez was the farthest thing from alarmed. He stood up slowly and grabbed the walking stick in his left hand, although he was right-handed. The shot caller nodded to a henchman to his right, who drew his pistol and pointed it at Tez. Did they not have enough guns to go around? Or were they being smart and keeping themselves from shooting each other? I didn't like the latter option.

"Give me the Huexotl," the shot caller said in a raised, peremptory voice.

"That's not going to happen," Tez said. His voice was quiet, but somehow penetrating. "Either I bond with it now, or I destroy it. So, given those options, how would you like to walk away? Intact, partially intact, or not at all?"

The shot caller drew his own pistol from his waistband.

He pointed it at Tez. "How you gonna hurt me, asshole?"

"You have a short memory," Tez said, an edge of impatience breaking through his calm. "Last chance: walk away."

"Hand it over," the shot caller said, raising his pistol a little for emphasis.

Then, moving faster than I'd ever seen him move before, Tez leapt in a high arc over the distance between them, and landed beside the shot caller, knocking him out with a single blow from his right fist. I noted that he was controlled enough to not use the stick.

The shot caller crumpled, dropping his pistol. Tez seemed in my perception to pause a moment, but he must have moved immediately, because the henchman fired, and Tez was no longer in the spot he'd fired into. Instead, he was behind the henchman, felling him with one blow as well.

The remaining guys were apparently better trained, or smarter, because none of them pulled a pistol—if he even had one—as that was clearly the pointless move. Instead, they broke formation and re-encircled Tez, who allowed this. I didn't hold out much hope for them, and settled into my invisible cloud as the fists and feet started flying.

But my complacency didn't last long. Just as Tez was most occupied with the four remaining attackers, Monkey noted the purr of a high performance engine approaching. I floated back through the little gate to the street just in time to see two black Escalades pull up and park: one next to the 70s' 'stang and the other crosswise behind it. I didn't know if either of the cars was the one from two days ago, but had little doubt who was occupying them.

Sure enough, all eight doors opened nearly at once, disgorging a virtual army of San Antonios, including, of course, Juice, Beto, and—after a short delay sliding out of the middle of the back seat—Juice's little brother Jimmy. Juice waited for him, put a hand on the back of his neck.

"Oye mocoso, stay with Beto. Don't fuck up," Juice said to him, low.

I counted 13 assholes. At least half of them were packing, and they all had the intent looks of people whose boss has threatened them within an inch of their lives, even—especially—Jimmy.

I decided to stay invisible. Why give up an advantage? And why let Tez see me, Monkey countered, when I might still get away clean?

Tez must have heard the cars in the background. He'd already dispensed with the remaining four 70s dudes, who were lying where he'd dumped them: in an unconscious pile at the back of the flat stage area, bleeding slightly. He stepped away from the 70s, back into the center of his stage.

Juice wasn't stupid enough to go in guns blazing. He lifted a hand to Tez as his boys encircled him.

"I see you got back what they stole from us. That's a good job." Juice's voice was a combination of admiring friend and loving pet-owner. You could almost hear the "good boy," underneath. That probably worked well with a doggish Chucha, who had accepted her subordinate status, and was probably half in love with him; but wasn't going to do anything but piss off a jaguar, particularly one smart enough to recognize a Chucha-managing tactic.

Sure enough, Tez's nose flared in disgust.

Juice saw that he'd miscalculated and tensed a little. "Just hand me my Huexotl, primo," he said, still friendly, "and all of this will be over."

Tez lifted the stick, and as he did, it grew to the length of a staff. He whipped it around almost unimaginably fast and elegantly, then set its heel on the ground again, and let it subside back into the length of a cane. I was torn between a giggle and admiration: yes, they were now almost literally measuring dicks.

"Not yours, primo," he said, almost unnecessarily.

"I disagree," Juice said gently. "I paid good money for It. My money, my Huexotl."

"My family made This," Tez said, lifting it. "It was stolen from my father and came back into our possession when you gave It to Chucha. It was her Huexotl, by right of magic, and now that she's dead, It's mine."

I was so surprised by this that I actually jerked, quite a feat for an invisible cloud of mist. I'd been so focused on how I thought the stick was an evil influencer that I hadn't actually considered that Chucha had had as much right to bond with it as Tez—and in fact probably would have done so if Slim Shady hadn't killed her. I couldn't imagine her being stupid or manipulable enough to hand the thing back over to Juice, even if the magic had allowed her to, which it wouldn't have.

My god, if it hadn't been for this almost-certainly-entirely-unrelated stupid stupid fucked up shadow stupid rat-shit-eating camel-cock-sucking wrinkled-knee-length-ball-sack motel-cockroach of a creature, Chucha could have solved everyone's problems by taking over the family business. She was clearly dominant enough; enough of a leader. Why had that never occurred to me? Guess I wasn't as much of a feminist as I'd thought. It clearly, so clearly, had occurred to Tez. In fact ... was that part of his desperation to get her back? Had he been grooming her to take over so he could be free?

"I don't recognize that," Juice said, just as gently.

"There's no law in the universe that would award the Huexotl to you," Tez said, confidently. "And, in any case, possession is nine tenths of the law."

"I can fix that problem easily, Tez," Juice said. "But for love of Chucha, I don't want to cause her family any more damage. You can walk away, and be with your brothers. There will be no more beef with us. Just give me back my property."

Tez sighed. It was the strangest exchange I'd ever seen, both interlocutors sad and reluctant, and about to become violent. "It's your use of the word 'property' that explains why you can never have This. It's not about property, or buying or selling, Juice. It's about guardianship, and responsibility, and leadership."

"Let's not bullshit each other, Tez," Juice said, a little angry now. "We both know how little you want that responsibility. You could be calling the shots at 23rd Street by now, but you've always said no. Chucha said you're stronger and faster than she was, but she could always beat you because you wouldn't use it. And that's how it's always gonna be with you. You look down your long nose at me, but I haven't just been taking care of my own family since I was fifteen, but all of these vatos." He gestured around him at his boys. "I keep them alive and fed. I train them and educate them. I make men out of them. And I'm happy to do it. I've never hesitated to step up. And you, chulo ..." he sucked his teeth and contempt crept into his careful voice, "... so powerful, you couldn't even keep your own family safe."

I winced, but Tez didn't react at all. I knew immediately that he'd been saying such things to himself all week, and had been expecting such an accusation. In fact—and I almost gasped when I realized it—Tez was negotiating with Juice because he felt... responsible?... to him for failing to protect Chucha. God, how complicated this had all gotten.

Juice held out his hand again. "Give me the Huexotl. I already got the leadership, the responsibility. Give me the Huexotl and I'll become the … what did you call it? 'Guardianship'? I'll become the 'guardian,' not just of San Antonio like I am now, but all of Oakland, maybe the whole Bay. I can feel that it might even go that big. Do you doubt it? Do you doubt I could do a better job than you?"

It was a real question, not a rhetorical one, and Tez answered seriously. "Juice, if you were a nagual, with my abilities, or Chucha's, and our training, I have no doubt you'd do a better job than me. But if you were a nagual, with our abilities and training, you wouldn't be a San Antonio." He dropped the hand holding the stick and stepped slightly towards Juice. "You got juice, but it's the wrong kind. I know your rep. I know you prefer diplomacy to war. But you're still too willing to use violence. There's doubt in my soul, but there's straight up coldness in yours. You don't have the magic to manage it, and if you bonded with the Huexotl, the cold would eat you alive."

Still with his hand out, Juice said, "I'm willing to take that chance."

Still not moving, Tez said, "I'm not."

Juice adjusted himself to readiness and said, "Last ch—"

And Tez was on him.

They'd been too close for Tez to take one of his devastating leaps, so Tez had gone directly for Juice, fists flying. But Juice dodged him easily—it was probable that Chucha had trained him—and cried "to me!" His boys instantly obeyed him, even Jimmy, and I saw four of them jump Tez, while the rest closed in. Shit.

Tez could handle them.

Couldn't he?

Time to get involved. I passed a still-reluctant Jimmy on my way to the scrum and decided to do him a favor. Changing back into human form, albeit still invisible, I smashed his nose in (What? I was gentle ... for some values of "gentle" ... and it would get nice and bloody, and he had the sort of nose that looks good broken; he'd get hella play from it), choked him out, then threw his unconscious body near the pile-up of mixed assortment gangbangers. When they sorted themselves out later, they'd think he'd waded into the fight and gotten knocked out. Jimmy: taken care of.

I couldn't see Tez in the middle of the pile-up, but they were all too close together for anyone to use a pistol, and I was sure he could handle it for a while. My best bet was to pick them off, one and two at a time, just to lighten his load. I tried to decide if I was worried about down-the-line issues from concussions, but Monkey mentally shook me, screeching: Gangbangers! Everyone's attention was on Tez, and they couldn't see me anyway, so I just took them out with punches to the jaw. One, two, uh ... three, uh oh, he's noticed... grunt... four...

Unfortunately, after number four went down for no apparent reason, the rest of the guys started noticing, and looking around themselves. One smart, if silly-looking, dude starting swinging punches wildly around him. Monkey, who'd been lying back, found this funny and came to the fore. I knocked out a fifth guy who wasn't paying attention, but that just made the remaining two go crazy. Easy peasy. I plucked out a hair, turned it into an (invisible) tire thumper and went to town. One went down with two broken arms, but, just my luck, the second had some martial arts training and immediately started defensive blocking.

I paused, to consider the situation, and was therefore perfectly placed to see the guy laid out by a graceful blow from a now-standing Tez's fist. I looked at him and he looked right back at me.

"I know you're there, Maya. You can drop the glamor."

"It's not a glamor," I said, complying. "It's invisibility. I know the difference is subtle—"

"What are you doing here?"

"I thought you might need backup. Turns out ..." I gestured to the landscape of unconscious bodies around us. I most certainly did not tell him that I came because I promised not to leave him alone with this.

Tez frowned more deeply. "How'd you know that I was going to do this?"

Utter airhead that I am, I wasn't prepared for this question. Monkey flapped and screeched in my head, but wasn't very good with rational answers. If I'd been prepared, I could have said something like:

1. I guessed; I've gotten to know you pretty well the past two weeks;

2. I didn't. I was just worried that those gangbangers would come after you for the stick;

3. I've been following you, dude. In case Slim Shady came after you;

4. [pretty much anything except guilty silence.]

But I hadn't been prepared and I was stymied for a second. I opened my mouth, and nothing came out. And Tez's face changed. Even at that moment, I could have pulled it out, but my own confusion confused me further. I couldn't speak. I couldn't think of a single, goddamn thing to say.

"You knew … you knew already … you …"

I could almost see the images inside his head, could almost see him remembering how, when I first met him, I'd turned into him for a second, spoken with his voice. I cringed helplessly.

He was shocked, down to his feet. He was frozen.

"You evil bitch," Tez whispered. "You crazy, fucked up …" He shook himself … no, that was a shudder. "That was you last night. Not my dad. That was you."

He walked a few steps away from me in a passion of disgust and bewilderment. I felt my skin crawling, a cold sweat climbing up my legs and arms. Tez immediately turned back.

"Who does something like that? What kind of a … what kind of an animal are you?"

I wanted to believe that he was overwhelmed by the stick, but the disgust in his voice was too calm, too real. Too mirrored by my own disgust. I opened my mouth to explain, and as I did so, I reached for that vision I'd had yesterday, the one that explained everything. But it was gone. It was out of reach, as if it had never been, as if I'd made it up. Even Monkey was gone, hiding somewhere. My mouth hung open, and I couldn't find the words.

So it was almost fortunate that the shadow chose that moment to attack.

CHAPTER THIRTY-SIX

TUESDAY, OCTOBER 25, 2011
KITE HILL PARK, SAN FRANCISCO

SHADY DIDN'T MESS around this time. He just descended on me all at once, like a bell jar, and sealed me to the flat ground with his impenetrable smoke. I was shocked and confused for a moment, and weakened by self-disgust; and he was definitely stronger now, stronger than he'd been even the last time I ran into him. So he was able to apply that horrifying, familiar pressure to me without encountering resistance, and I felt my energy, my essence, my soul, start to give immediately.

And why shouldn't I give? I was an evil bitch. I'd tried to fool Tez into doing something he didn't want to do. I had no right. I was disgusting—

Fire! cried Monkey. Light!

Right.

Not able to think very well, I changed myself into a Maya-shaped bonfire. Shady reared back immediately, but it didn't retreat like it had two nights ago. It still contained me, but more loosely. And it had a ...

(shudder) … considering air. Oh shit.

It started to move, only this time, instead of smothering me closely with its bulk, it created a larger bubble around me—one that allowed it to keep most of its bulk at a distance—and simply sent a finger of smoky darkness down to probe me.

Again I felt that despair, that sense of hopelessness and pointlessness begin to rise up in me. Tez knew what I had done, and I was going to die and he wasn't going to save me because he hated me. It was no less than I deserved.

Then, all at once, Shady's pressure disappeared and I was gasping for breath and feeling that hollow in my core, but clear. It hadn't gotten as much from me as it had two nights before, and sitting up quickly, I saw it fighting with Tez, walloping Tez with its shockwave, and Tez walloping right back with the almost-as-effective stick, which had grown again and flattened at one end until it was almost like a pizza peel. Monkey cheered at the sight.

But almost as soon as I had caught my breath, the shadow dealt Tez an angry blow that sent him heels over head a few yards down the hill, losing his grip on the stick. The victorious Shady leapt to cover him, carefully avoiding touching the stick right next to him, and began sucking his essence energetically.

Without even thinking, I threw a fireball at him.

"Hey! Shady!" I yelled. "Don't be greedy! *I'm* the one you want! Let him go!"

Maybe Tez and I really *had* discombobulated the thing, because he seemed confused. He … uh … *looked* down at Tez, and then looked back at me, undecided. Uuuaagghh.

I looked up and found a cloud, called it down to me, and stepped onto it.

"Last chance, Shady. If you don't let him go, you'll give me time to get away and I won't come back. *Ever*."

Shady hesitated again, so I ordered the cloud to rise and that decided him. The creature released Tez all at once and leapt over to me, almost appearing to teleport, he moved so fast. He walloped me so hard I left the cloud and flew backwards up the hill to the street entrance the gangsters had used, hitting a tree trunk full with my back and knocking the wind out of me. The cloud skittered away.

And then Shady was on me again.

He flipped me over so I was face-down on the ground. I shifted into a knife-thin wall of flame, reaching for the sky as high as I could go, my flames passing right through the branches of the tree and not catching them. Shady backed off again, but then stopped just short of touching me and looked at me with that same, creepy, considering air.

Then he walloped me with his shockwave, and—I couldn't help it—my wall of flame bowed in as if someone had punched it in the stomach. In fact, that's what it felt like. I rolled myself up into a fruit-roll-up of flame, and somersaulted down the hill back to the flat stage area. But Shady followed, and arced over me before I could re-form into a high wall. Through his smoky mass—now in the form of a smoky arch over my roll of flame—I saw Tez run up, take a stance, and then open his mouth. I expected some incantation to come out, but instead, like a dragon, Tez roared out a torrent of fire. Wow, I thought, remembering my research: I guess naguals *can* spit flame.

But, as cool as that was, it didn't work anymore. Shady shuddered, but didn't retreat. And, even while he walloped Tez again so hard that Tez staggered back nearly to the edge of the stage area, he sent a finger of shadow to probe me again, and that feeling of despair rose in me.

I changed back into human form, so I could have a mouth.

"Tez!" I cried, as loudly as I could. "It's too strong! You

have to complete the ritual!" And then I was overcome by a choking inability to breathe. I was overwhelmed by my own uselessness. Tez would never complete the ritual. And then the creature would consume me and him too, and would go on to eat every shapeshifting thing in the Bay Area. Then he would go on to consume the world. And it was all my fault. All my fault.

At a distance, through the smoke of the creature eating me, as if in a fading dream, I saw Tez reaching toward me, his face a picture of alarm.

And then the despair retreated *again*, although this time, I was too depleted to do more than lie there, wondering what had happened. Slowly turning my head, I caught sight of a familiar blur of reddish-blackish fur, followed by streaks of orange fire arcing toward the amorphous cloud that Shady had become.

How did Todd get here? I thought to myself. Everyone is here. It's a party. Then I noted the distant shrieking of Monkey in my head.

"Okay, okay," I slurred, sitting up. "I guess I can throw some fire balls."

Which I started to do from my head hair, slowly, and at first ineffectively. I felt a hand on my arm. I turned, too slowly, to look, and heard Tez's voice asking me something urgently. I was too depleted to try to understand him.

"No," I said. "No, you have to finish the ritual. We'll hold him off." And I gathered what was left of myself and started aiming fireballs at Shady more carefully.

I distantly noted that Tez was now kneeling upright, taking up the stick, and beginning to chant. I felt that attention—that conscious *in*tention—coalesce around him again, more quickly this time.

I turned my attention—so slowly—back to Shady, who was no longer avoiding Todd's kitsunebi fire-streaks, but bearing the strikes of them, seeming to absorb these strikes, and, with increasing frequency, hitting back. Was I mistaken, or were Todd's strikes growing weaker and Shady's wallops stronger?

I threw a handful of fireballs, then dragged myself to my knees—standing was out of the question—and threw several more. But Shady had clearly taken the measure of my strength and Todd's, and we were no longer a match for him. As I watched, too slow to react, Shady seized Todd by the tails and hurled him ... directly at me! I only had the energy to watch, not to get out of the way, as Todd crashed painfully into me, and we dissolved into a tangle of furred and skinned limbs, and bruises.

Wow, I thought, slowly. Todd sure is heavy. And his bones are *sharp*.

And then the now-familiar, and almost welcome, weight of Shady's despair settled in a bowl over both of us and I felt my joy in the world draining away at a faster rate than ever before.

Through the tangle of Todd's furred legs and Shady's smoke I saw Tez lift his arms and the stick.

Tez did something, said something—I didn't know and hardly cared anymore, I was more focused on trying to breathe, and then trying to figure out why I was trying to breathe—and the consciousness shot into the stick, and through the stick into Tez, and through Tez, downward into the earth and upwards towards the stars.

What was left of Monkey cheered.

Tez stood and walked toward Shady. I noted blearily that his eyes were lit up from inside with starlight, and his skin was the color of freshly turned soil. *How handsome*, I thought. *Tez is the whole universe.*

He took the Huexotl, now an enormous staff, barely containing all the earth and starlight within it, and planted the foot of the staff into the flat dirt. The pressure on us seemed to halt for a moment, and I could feel Shady's attention turn toward Tez. The dirt at the foot of the staff split open, like a fruit splitting its rind, or skin opening on a wound. The split ran along the ground a few feet until it reached the skirt of the nalusa chito's shadow. Then it stopped, widened, and ... seemed to surround the creature, to surround all three of us. Beneath me was still dirt, but inside the split it seemed more ... more essential, more elemental.

All at once the pressure stopped entirely, and the creature threw its bulk upward, trying to escape, becoming unformed in the process. But he didn't escape whatever was happening. A tail of the smoky shadow had become fixed into the dirt.

Tez said something in an unrecognizable, guttural voice, and the billows of Shady's smoky darkness began to flow downward into the earth. The shadow attempted to struggle, but the slow flow downward was insistent.

I lay gasping in the middle of Shady's dome, nearly desperate with the pain of hollowness within me, Todd squirming on top of me, trying to get up. I watched as the creature was drawn down into the soil, like an inky waterfall all around us, while I remained untouched.

"What is happening?" I cried at Tez.

But it wasn't Tez who answered me.

The voice came as a voice in my head—familiar, not alien—in fact, it was the voice of despair I heard whenever Shady touched me. The only thing that allowed me to distinguish it from my own thoughts, in fact, was no doubt the creature's desire to be understood.

I am being dispersed into the earth, Shady said.

"I'm ... sorry?" I gasped. It's hard to be antagonistic to someone speaking into your mind.

This is powerful magic. I do not belong here. This earth will end me. It sounded curiously unconcerned.

"Is there … is there anything I can do for you? I mean, not rescue you or anything …" I gasped for breath again.

I am content. You have released me. Now I can speak.

I felt a sudden surge of interest strengthen me. "Oh! So you *were* enslaved! By whom? And why? What were you eating souls for?"

Not eating. Collecting. You were eighth and last needed. But now they will be released. He will not get them.

It was going faster now. I needed to … I shuddered. "What were the souls for?"

Spell.

Half of the creature had been pulled into the soil. The remaining shadow was less dense, less dark somehow. I could see Tez more clearly. He muttered something and and settled into his stance.

"What was the spell for?" I asked, somewhat frantic now.

Power, the creature said, and its "voice" was almost sardonic. *What else? More power.*

It was disappearing now. I almost couldn't see it anymore.

"But *Who*?" I shrieked.

Someone powerful. Someone like you. He knows you now.

And then, just like that, the creature was gone.

All at once, the self-doubting voice disappeared from my mind like a bubble popping, and I felt all my stolen strength return. I scrambled backward out of the rough circle inscribed by the nalusa chito's dome. It felt tainted. Almost in the same movement, Todd leapt out of the circle as well, and took off running into the night, his two tails tucked between his hind legs. I didn't blame him.

And just as I stepped off that ground, an energy burst through: an energy, a light, a ... a soul. I couldn't see it so much as feel its presence, but somehow my mind translated its presence into a visual form. It resolved itself into a crocodile with a thick, fleshy seal's tail, which turned into a brisk-looking, dark-haired woman. I recognized Maral, the Nhang from Mission Bay. She nodded at us. Then she dispersed like smoke, rising as she went.

I was in too much wonder at her appearance to be prepared for who came next. The next burst of energy coalesced into a form: first a large, lithe doberman, out of which stepped a beautiful, familiar young woman.

I was still too out of breath to say anything, but Tez's anguished cry of "Chucha!" felt as if it came from my own heart. As if she heard me, she turned to me and gave me that perfect little sister smile, and it lit up the entire hill. Tez stepped forward and she turned that smile on him, reached out a hand I knew wasn't there, and touched him over his breastbone. The starlight in his eyes pulsed, then dimmed as Chucha, all at once, dispersed.

Tez slumped.

The next burst was Aahil, who smiled only at me, then Bu Bu and Justin, both of whom ignored us in their hurry to be released. Next, a white tiger stepped powerfully out of the ground, transformed into a distinguished-looking older man, nodded formally to Tez and me, and went on.

Finally, an impression of leathery flapping resolved into a rail-thin woman with a long nose and the ghost of bat wings on her back. Dalisay. She observed me, she observed Tez, acknowledging us both. Then she disappeared.

The tainted ground seemed to close, somehow. The soil

rolled back against itself, although the dirt was now a bit cracked and dry around the shape of the nalusa chito's dome. Tez's staff shrank back down to a baton size and Tez let it tip over onto the ground.

We both sat there, collapsed in on ourselves. All of my essence had been returned to me, but there was considerable wear and tear, and I was exhausted. Tez was no longer starry-eyed and earth-skinned ... he looked blank.

All at once, he heaved himself upright, swept up the Huexotl and bowl and accoutrements into his bag, turned around, and marched down the hill away from me, stepping over a few unconscious bodies as he went. He didn't indicate in any way that he was aware of my continued presence, and I was unsure if I hoped that he was faking it or not. I watched him until he stepped through the foliage in the yard below and back into 19th St., but he never once looked back.

CHAPTER THIRTY-SEVEN

WEDNESDAY, NOVEMBER 2, 2011
PORT OF OAKLAND, OAKLAND

IN THE DAYS following the raids on the Occupy encampments, the feel of the movement changed from the giddy joyousness of experimentation and initial success, to a more dug in, hunkered down, committed seriousness. The Spirit of the Bay didn't visit, and I was glad of it. I was, at the moment, pretty sure I preferred communing with It more distantly, through my community and through activism. Talking to It directly had caused me only trouble.

The kid we'd seen go down with a head injury turned out to be a veteran, and his wound was critical. The mayor apologized, the police backed off, and statements of support flooded in from all over the country, and as far away as Tahrir Square. We reoccupied the plaza the very next day, and voted nearly unanimously—and with a sense of purpose that was almost grim—to stage a general strike a week later.

My clan was more excited than I'd ever seen them, and

started showing up to the GAs and rallies in force, unlike the sometimes grudging trickle I'd seen during the first two weeks. I was still somewhat numb. I'd had to fake enthusiasm more than once to keep up with my folks.

Nevertheless, I got to the plaza early the day of the strike, and, as the day wore on, and more and more groups joined, I could feel my numbness start to break up like a fog bank in summer. Ayo joined around noon, bringing sandwiches and occasionally even smiling. Sanc-Ahh was taking part in the strike, of course, and my eyes flared at a few knots of magical critters that Ayo'd no doubt been the one to light a fire under.

Shortly before the march to the port began, two thirds of Cerberus arrived, as well as Baby and Mari and the marketeers.

"Is Todd coming?" Baby asked me.

"No," I said. "He emailed me that he's got a family emergency and he's not going to make it. He didn't specify what and I didn't want to bother him." Todd had emailed me that morning, actually, and had said nothing about the big fight the previous Tuesday night, or what the hell he'd been doing there. I'd figured that he'd probably never actually left on Tuesday night, but had hidden and followed me when I left Sanc-Ahh for Tez's, tho' how he'd followed me across the Bay on my cloud was beyond me. Magic, no doubt. My eye-flares were pretty potent, but I had to actually *look around* for deception if I wanted to catch it; and I'd been very distracted that night. I was grateful for his intervention, but I wasn't sure how much I liked the idea of Todd following me without my knowledge.

"Okay," she said and looked at me slantwise. "Is ... uh ... Tez coming?"

"I doubt it. It's all hitting him hard right now and I

don't think he's even capable of leaving the house."

"Did you … do something … wrong? Are you guys … okay?" she asked hesitantly. She knew me way too well.

"… I mean … I don't think he's okay … with me. But I don't wanna talk about it."

"Okay," she said again. She sounded actually relieved.

The march started and we focused for a while on keeping our group moving and together. The plaza and intersection were wall-to-wall people. Twitter was giving numbers anywhere from ten thousand to one hundred-thousand.

A chant went up and we chanted along for a while.

When it quieted again she said, with no preamble: "I'm sorry."

I sighed. "I'm sorry, too, Baby."

I was about to move on with my life, and the march, when something Baby had told me years ago echoed in my head. I didn't remember the words, but when she was doing the training in conflict resolution, she said that making active amends after a conflict was resolved was key, even if it was small, and even if you felt more sinned against than sinning.

I hefted my picket sign over the opposite shoulder and stepped closer to her.

"I'm sorry I haven't been helping with the fundraising, Baby," I said.

"It's all right."

"No, it really isn't. You're right that I've been spending way more time with Ayo's work. But you need to understand: I'm getting more deeply into her work and I … I think I kind of had a breakthrough … you know, while I was working with Tez. I've always been Ayo's assistant in … well, whatever she needs done: taking care of the cafe, doing research, being a spiritual guide. But with Tez, I was building a relationship *myself*, offering help and guidance *directly*. And it's not just because it was Tez, although it started out that way. I was doing it with Chucha as well, before she …"

Baby nodded, intent.

"Baby, I think there's really something in this work for me. I know I seem like the last person to be a spiritual guide for anyone—"

"No, I think you're perfect for it."

"What? Really?"

"You see people more clearly than most, Mai, even me. I pride myself on my people-wrangling skills—and they're *awesome*," she said facetiously, sweeping her hair back, "but you can look at people and cut right to the heart of their bullshit. It's intimidating, but when people need a spiritual surgeon, it's you they turn to, not me. They come to me to be validated, and to you to be … cleansed? No, that's not the word. To be … fixed, I guess. You're the mixie fixie."

I was astounded, and gawked at her, while our group took up another chant. I'd been using "spiritual work" as a euphemism for the supernatural shit I did, but Baby sounded sincere about me being some sort of spiritual surgeon. Could that even be true? I was able to cut through their bullshit because I knew, magically, when people were lying. And transforming. And … creating … Did that give me a special insight that was more than a simple lie detector? I marched silently for a time, turning that over.

"Anyway," I said, finally, "it wasn't how I did with Tez; the jury is out on that, but I suspect they will convict. It was more how I did with Chucha. I was starting to reach her. And it felt really— … no, I was helping Tez too, before I … before I shat the bed. It just seems like there's something here for me and I want to explore it, figure out where I am in all this. That means that I'll still be spending a lot of time doing Ayo's work. Only I'm going to be doing it more on my terms now."

"Good," she said firmly. "And don't get all guilty about the fundraising. I need to you *pay attention*, because this is your magazine, too. But I don't necessarily need to you start organizing fundraising or anything. I mean, we *all* have to fundraise, but ..."

"I will," I said.

"Good," she said again, and tucked my arm into hers. We lifted our signs again and marched on.

CHAPTER THIRTY-EIGHT

MONDAY, NOVEMBER 14, 2011
SANC-AHH CAFÉ, OAKLAND

I WAS MAKING up another endless round of free, relaxing mugs of herbal tea, when I felt a displacement of air, and knew instantly that Tez was there. I'd been waiting for him to come in for over two weeks. Knowing Ayo, there was no way she'd sent me out on Tez's errand without asking him for some sort of return. I knew he'd have to come into the cafe to make good sometime, I just hadn't expected him to show up when shit was going down (again) with Occupy.

I turned around just in time to catch him disappearing into Ayo's office. I was sure he'd seen me. I'd expected him to want to avoid me, but it stung anyway.

"Was that Tez?" Baby asked. I hadn't heard her come up to me. She'd taken off from work early when I texted her about the plaza encampment being raided and cleared, *again,* and we'd protested for a while before withdrawing with our contingent to Sanc-Ahh to rest and check our feeds for further instructions.

I gave her a meaningful look.

"I'm not gonna ask," she said, "but Mai, you can tell me anything, and at some point I know you're gonna wanna tell me what happened there." She went back to sit down with Mari, Romeo, and Han.

Yeah, right. Maybe.

Tez stayed closeted with Ayo for no more than five minutes before he came back out, looking down, as if he thought he could erase me from his world as long as his eyes didn't land on me.

"Tez," I said.

He stopped. He stood for a moment, and I thought he might continue as if he hadn't heard me. Instead, he stepped up to the bar, still without looking at me.

"I thanked Ayo for her help," he said. "I suppose you want thanks, too."

"No," I said, suddenly snappish, "I got paid for my time."

"Okay," he turned to go.

"Tez," I said. He stopped again. "Look at me." He did, and his look was, for a moment, full of resentment. A familiar look, but one that I'd thought—hoped—I'd never see from him. But this one wasn't resenting me for being strong, or fast, or smart—smarter, braver, more competent than he was. No, this one was resenting me for something I'd actually *done* to him.

I'd do it again. It was the right thing to do and I was sure he knew it. But, god, he was right, too. It had been his choice to make and I'd made it for him. I'd overstepped, unequivocally. Maybe all those guys who resented me for being who I was had actually turned out to be right. Maybe I *didn't* deserve to be loved.

But then he took his look back in, like a breath, and composed himself. He was taking it on himself:

everything I'd done, everything that had happened. Even though I'd forced his hand, he'd taken it on anyway. And he was trying to forgive me. Despite what Ayo had said about me, I knew that *this* was what made a true leader. Maybe it was time that I stopped thinking about myself and took a moment to try to save something for him.

"This doesn't mean you have to stop writing," I said.

He was surprised for a moment, but then he laughed, bitterly. It was the first ugly sound I'd ever heard come out of him.

"You don't get it, do you? I *was* writing again. I didn't write anything for three years after my Mom died, and I thought I'd never write again, but then, things just settled down and I was able to pick up a pen again. I was figuring out a whole new way of writing, and it was hard, yeah, but I was figuring it out. And I didn't tell anyone about it because … because it wasn't quite there yet. But I was doing it …"

"And now?"

"Everything is different! Half the time, my mind doesn't even recognize words. It's this … connection, this new connection to this land here. It's totally real. It's not metaphorical, it's not conceptual, it's not verbal. I can't break it down. The Bay is so complex, and so poisoned with … so many things. I can't observe it. I have to be *in* it, work it, be poisoned by it. … I have no fucking idea what I'm doing and I have to do it, on top of the job and the kids, and the 'hood. I'm exhausted and confused all the time. It's like right after Mom died all over again, only a thousand times worse. I'm so overwhelmed I don't even know if I *want* to write anymore."

"Is it really that bad?"

"Yes! … No. It's, it's just … *I'm* just … totally different. I never asked for this. I never knew it was possible to be like this. I don't know. ..."

"Maybe you just have to get used to it."

He looked at me in disbelief, then barked out a laugh that was so uncatlike, I almost looked around to see if the sound had come from someone else.

"You don't get it," he said again. "You don't have to be responsible for anyone but yourself. You don't understand."

And it was back, that flare of resentment in his face. But this time, it was matched by my own resentment. How dare he say that to me? He had no idea what a privilege it was to belong somewhere, to actually have people who knew you, and expected things from you, and depended on you. I'd had to create that for myself, and every moment it threatened to fall apart. But for him it was just a fact of life, as immutable as the wind.

I started to say exactly that, I opened my mouth ... and saw him brace himself for impact.

I hesitated. He was taking this on as well; whatever I had to say, he'd take it on board and make it his responsibility.

And didn't I just decide not to make this about me? And what about my promise, to stand by him, to not leave him alone with this?

I took a breath.

"You're right," I said. "And forget what I said about writing." His eyebrows went up, and, in spite of himself, his shoulders relaxed a bit. "I guess I just meant that you don't have to lose yourself in all of this."

"How do you know?" he sounded ... intent, as if he believed me.

I opened my mouth to answer, but didn't know what to say. The memory of that vision of the Bay, and of the world, was bright in my mind, but I still didn't know how to describe it, how to explain to him what the Bay had shown to me— had *promised* me.

I smiled ruefully. "I just ... *know*. I guess you could say ... I have faith." And in that moment, I did have faith, in the Bay and its light buoying him up, but also faith in Tez himself. If anyone could do this ...

He sighed, turned, and left, so abruptly that my grin went empty in the space of a breath.

"That was ... kind," Ayo said. I hadn't seen her approach.

"It wasn't anywhere near enough."

"Well, nothing you could *say* will fix things. He's got a lot on his plate right now. Give him time. He'll figure it out." And she went back into her office.

Scarcely had Ayo disappeared through the door, when I heard the bell ring again, causing a slight fizz of electricity to shoot through me. It was Todd, who had missed all the excitement at Occupy. Never rains; pours.

As usual, he was both unwelcome and welcome. Someday soon I was going to have to examine the fact that I resented him for standing in the doorway to the space in my head that Tez occupied, but that day was not today.

He made a beeline for me, his goofy masking grin spreading across his face and wiping out the faint impression of anxiety I thought I'd seen.

"Hey Monkey-Girl. How's tricks? I heard things got a little dicey today."

"Hey Foxy-Boy. We're just licking our wounds. How's your, uh, family emergency?"

"Oh, ongoing," he said evading my look. He looked off into the distance to let me know that was all he was gonna say on that topic. Then he looked back. "So, do you wanna have a little impromptu meeting about that article?"

"Good idea. Are we going to meet our deadline?"

"Honestly? I don't think so, unless you can help me focus. There's enough here to fill a book. I'm not sure how we're supposed to narrow this down to 1500 words or less."

"Yeah. Why don't you make it more literary, more critical? You know, like talk about the place shapeshifters have in Asian cultures and what fills that spot in American culture, and then how anime and urban fantasy and film/tv have sort of taken over hitting that spot with the death of traditional storytelling, epics, and theater. And you can just pick a few creatures to illustrate it. Or something."

"I think I've got a post on my blog that I can adapt."

"Yeah, that's what I was riffing off of."

"Oh. Well, I'll check it out when I get home, to see if I can make something of it."

"Cool. ... I'll give you a week to get me a rough draft."

We sat there for a moment.

"Is that our meeting, then?" he asked.

"Um, unless there's anything else?"

"Not on my end. You?" he charmed his grin back up. "Anything on your mind?"

"Uh ... well ..." I thought ... and then immediately decided to go for it. An Asian shapeshifter with a seemingly encyclopedic knowledge of Asian mythological creatures? I'd never had such a good chance. I looked around to make sure no one was within earshot. "Well, actually, maybe you can help me with something different."

"Hit me."

He knew I was ... something. He'd seen it all. But somehow, I couldn't bring myself to say the words

"I don't know what I am, can you tell me?" My old, practiced lie just flowed out of me like a river.

"Well, I'm kind of writing something. Like fiction, like a novel, or maybe it'll turn into a screenplay."

"Really?"

"... And well, um, I have this character who has these magic powers, and I've written a lot of scenes with her using them and it's important to the integrity of the piece that she maintains this particular set of magic powers."

"Okay ..."

"But now I really wanna make her into an actual mythical creature that actually exists in an actual mythology."

"That's three 'actuals'."

"That's two 'actuals' and an 'actually.' And shut up."

He shut up.

"So ... I'm wondering if there's a mythical creature that has this particular set of magical powers."

I looked at him. He stayed shut, watching me intently.

"Um, so there's shapeshifting, of course. Into animals: primarily a monkey, but any animal, really. And into objects as well." He gave me an extremely dry look. "And going invisible. And she can also shape-shift her ... um ... hairs. Each individual hair can become whatever she wants. And she can put them back on her head and body."

I checked him out to see how he was taking this. He hadn't changed posture or his "shut up" expression, his arms loosely crossed, his heels hooked on the foot rest of the stool making his knees splay out, one knee, as always, jiggling slightly. His eyes had started to feel like drills into my head.

"Okay, and um ... there's super strength, of course,

and super speed. And she can open any lock, but needs tools to do it. And ... um ...there's this thing with her being able to tell when someone is being deceptive because her eyes start to burn. And ... like, she can travel on clouds ..."

"Is that all?" he asked.

"Um ... for now," I said. "She might develop new ones as I keep ... writing."

He killed me softly with his stupid gaze some more. I was quivering inside, but also starting to get angry.

"Well?" I finally demanded. "Have you heard of a creature in mythology that does all that or not?"

He sighed.

"You are so. Full. Of shit," he said.

Succinct.

"Why didn't you tell me you didn't know what you are?"

"Why, exactly, would I have told *anyone* that?"

He rolled his eyes. "Maya, there isn't exactly a creature in *mythology* with those abilities."

I let go the breath I'd been holding. Of course not. "Nevermind."

"Hold on. There is, however, a *fictional* character with those powers, one based on a lot of different myths." He paused, presumably for effect.

"Who?" I almost shrieked.

"Well, Sun Goku— er, Sun Wukong. The Monkey King."

"Monkey ...? Who? *What?*"

"Well, he's a— actually, there's some debate as to what his mythological origins might be, but he's definitely a fictional character—"

"From what?!"

"It's this Chinese novel from the Ming Dynasty— have

you *really* not heard of the Monkey King? And you with all his powers? Is your Google finger broken?"

I didn't know whether to bash my head into the counter or snatch him bald. I took a deep breath.

"No." I said as calmly as I could manage, "*What's the novel?*"

"Oh," he said. "It's called *Journey to the West.*"

MAYA MACQUEEN'S BESTIARY

FROM MY OWN PERSONAL NOTES ON THE SUPERNATS I'VE
ENCOUNTERED AND/OR HEARD ABOUT SECOND-HAND.
YMMV.

ASWANG: Tree-dwelling Filipino vampiric shapeshifters, who infiltrate human communities by taking on the shape of an attractive woman and marrying a human man. They suck their husband's blood if none other is readily available, but prefer to use the husband as cover while spreading the blood-suckage around. They have an especial predilection for unborn fetuses and newborn babies, and also eat corpses. They have two other forms: a dog form, and a segmented, winged form, in which they separate the winged top section from the legs to fly around looking for victims, much like the Enterprise D with its saucer section and star-drive section, except way less cool.

AZIZA: Beneficent fairies from Benin, these critters are little and hairy and live in anthills and silk cotton trees. They hang out in forests when young, helping hunters and gifting people with fire. As they get older, though, they withdraw and hide, or go traveling, much like human retirees. Being fae-flaky, long-lived, and highly adaptable, they generally have a poor sense of time and space, and should not be referred to when you are lost, or taking a history test.

BAJANG: Malay shapeshifting weasel-weres (not really! They look like weasels but are really a sort of civet, which is another type of animal entirely. I just like calling them weasels because, well, the shoe fits.) Legend says that men who say the proper incantations over the newly buried body of a stillborn child can acquire a bajang of their very own. Bajang then use their magic to curse their master's enemies, causing convulsions, unconsciousness or delirium. In exchange, its master feeds it eggs and milk and keeps it in a bamboo tube. It'll attack anyone it's ordered to, but particularly likes babies and small children. Nasty.

BOUDA: Ethiopian were-hyenas. The term "buda" actually refers to the ability to cast the evil eye, and folks with buda were believed to be empowered by envy to shapeshift into hyena form so as to attack and kill those they envied without being able to be identified. This is hogwash, of course; "buda" was almost always attributed to outsiders, especially Jews. Bouda are an actual supernatural race of shapeshifters, like werewolves, that can be created from humans. Now, exactly how a bouda is created is a secret closely held by these giggling mofos, and yes, they do have a strong tendency towards both envy and jealousy. Do not date a bouda unless you wanna date their whole pack.

"CHINESE MONKEY SHIFTER": Me, basically. I might be the only extant specimen, if there is such a species. Some kind of shapeshifter, with monkey as the default form—

or perhaps human is the default form and monkey is the animal form. Very strong and fast—more powerful than the generality of supernats living on the Earthly plane; can change shape into pretty much anything or anyone— although specific people are more difficult and require more concentration; and can clone self using body hairs, or turn body hairs into any object. Natural martial arts skills only enhanced by training; almost unbeatable in a fair fight. Can detect deceit, transformation, artistry through burning in the eyes, and call down clouds and ride them, super fast. Vulnerable to smoke, contempt, and accusations of inauthenticity.

CHUREL: Indian spirit of a woman who died either pregnant, in childbirth, or by ill treatment at the hands of her in-laws. She comes back as a pretty little girl dressed all in white and seduces men away to have their life essences sucked out entirely, which is appropriate for men who can be seduced by little girls, ew! If she died of mistreatment she comes back to avenge herself on her male in-laws, starting with the youngest first. Very effective assassins. Can be identified by their backward-turned feet.

HARIMAU JADIAN: Malaysian/Indonesian were-tiger, a species born to it. Unlike most were-tigers, these are benevolent, and task themselves with protecting crops from marauding pigs and protecting their communities from outsiders. The Japanese know: they were always getting attacked by strangely intelligent tigers during WWII. Dudes get pretty beasty, though, and don't recognize their friends when in tiger form, so you have to call them by name. Don't cross these dudes: tigers. 'Nuff said.

KITSUNE: Tricksters, Japanese fox "spirits," are actually just foxes that attain magical powers by living to one hundred years old. Can cast tremendous illusions and shapeshift into any form they like, but usually stick to beautiful women (to lure men,) or objects (to pull pranks.) There are temple foxes, who serve the god Inari as messengers, and field foxes, who serve the god Foolishness as cattle prods. Both have kitsunebi, foxfire, which they cast from the tips of their tails, but only field foxes use it to lead travelers astray. Even field kitsune can be benevolent, but are just as likely to cast an illusion to make you eat shit, fall into a ditch and break your neck, or leave your family for three weeks, thinking you've lived with a beautiful new wife for twenty years. High-larious. Speaking of, kitsune frequently outsmart themselves by falling in love with their marks, and staying with them and having children. The children tend to be very talented, but have no magic.

LOOGAROO: French West Indian vampiric shapeshifter, that looks like an old woman during the day, but at night sheds her skin (which she puts into a mortar) and flies around as a ball of flame (so, basically a Caribbean Baba Yaga.) They can enter a house through any type of hole or crack and suck blood from their victims' extremities, leaving bruises. If they take too much, the victim dies and becomes one of them. Ayo claims they evolved through indigenous and African magic and culture from French werewolves, but I dunno ...

NAGUAL: Aztec (originally) magical creature and/or bloodline or magical propensity. Naguals can mate with humans to produce full-blooded naguals and are almost entirely embedded in human culture, serving traditionally as medicine people. They possess shapeshifter strength, speed, and beauty, the ability to shapeshift into an animal form (usually only at night,) their own power of invisibility and illusion, and can breathe freakin' fire; plus they can manipulate ambient magic, like humans, when trained. Are constrained to the sole animal form associated with their birthdate (common forms include jaguar, dog, donkey, deer, coyote, etc.) which is also similar to the concept of a tutelary spirit or *cringe* "spirit animal."

NALUSA CHITO/IMPA SHILUP: Choctaw "shadow-creature" that appears literally as a semi-solid shadow; also can appear as a black panther. This monster is a soul sucker: it arises out of depression, or dark or evil thoughts in a person, and eats that person's soul. Normally the nalusa chito is tied to the person who "called" it, and dies with them. Normally. Let's hope that stays normal because ... *shudder* ... when operated upon with arcane magic and separated from their "caller," the nalusa chito can eat at will, and grow in strength as it eats. The creepiest thing I've ever encountered, and that's saying a lot.

NHANG: (from the Persian word for "crocodile") the Nhang is an Armenian river-dwelling serpent-monster that can shapeshift into a woman (to lure men, natch) or a seal, in order to drag people underwater to drown them and then drink their blood (natch). Like any other mermaid creature, they're more comfy in the water than on the land, although they can pass easily for landlubbers. They're closely related to western-style dragons and—little known fact—like both eastern and western dragons, have an affinity for book learning, and a tendency to be know-it-alls.

Qori Ismaris: In Somali mythology, a man who can transform himself into a hyena by rubbing himself with a magic stick at nightfall, and by repeating this process can return to his human state before dawn. I've never seen this process and can't attest to its validity. The few qoris I've met (definitely all male, tho') tend to the usual canid predatoriness, but seem to be less pack-y than the bouda. Incredibly irritating laugh.

Vanara: Indian Monkey Shifters. Apparently the Indian monkey god Hanuman was a vanara who was gifted with superpowers by the gods. Ordinary vanara, however, can only shift between human and monkey, and have the usual shapeshifter strength and speed only. They're very cool, though, with good senses of humor, and loyalty, courage, and adventurousness in spades. Also? All the ones I've met are pretty hot, which is standard for beast shifters, but still: a winning combo. Monkeys rule.

Werewolf: human/wolf shapeshifters forced to follow the moon's phases, but can shift at will. Allergic to silver and feminism. Pack-up at the slightest provocation and can't—thank god—reproduce. As far as we can tell, it takes more than a bite or a scratch to turn someone, which, also, thank god. Because they are nasty creatures with bad manners and more aggression than sense, who kill their way out of whatever problem presents itself and ask questions later, if ever. Have the usual attractive, healthy, shapeshifter glow, but don't be fooled. Mostly straight, cis-het white bros.

ACKNOWLEDGEMENTS

THIS BOOK COULDN'T have been completed without the help of many people.

Love and gratitude to Barbara Jane Reyes for making her poem available to Maya and Chucha. Many thanks to Jaime Cortez, Patricia Wakida, and Marcia Ochoa, who helped with language, names, and concepts. Bryan Wu's expertise with manga and anime was invaluable, as were the Occupy Oakland stories and experiences of Timmy Lu and Jessica Tully, and Noemi Ixchel Martinez's research, translations, and notes on nagualism. Any mistakes in these areas are mine alone.

Noemi and Lynn Brown provided immensely helpful sensitivity readings, and I couldn't have shaped this story without the support and critique of Jim DeMaiolo and Lexicats Charlie Jane Anders, Annalee Newitz, Liz Henry, Emily Jiang, and Sasha Hom. Special shout-outs to Annalee and Liz for reading and giving essential advice on two drafts of Monkey; and MVP goes to Charlie for going above and beyond and reading three full drafts and pushing each one substantially closer to the goal.

I was supported and helped through the querying stage by Charlie and Annalee again, as well as Victoria Feistner and the Rejectarinos, Jenevive Desroches, Michele Bacon, Allison Pottern Hoch, Mica Scotti Kole and Luke Dani Blue. A million thanks to the best agent in the biz, Amanda Leuck, for taking me on, loving Maya and Monkey, and making this whole thing easy. Another million to Kate Coe for seeing something worth publishing in this book, and making the process so incredibly smooth and joyful. Sam Gretton provided an amazing cover that I love, Jim Killen the easiest copy edit in the history of print, and Hanna Waigh (with Rosie Peat) a sound publicity boat to keep me from drowning.

There are too many friends who cared about this project, and my writing in general, over the years to name individually. You all know who you are. Thank you for being my writing community. Finally, gratitude to and for my gloriously excessive extended family for being largely supportive, and somewhat confused, about my various careers. Thanks Mom and Dad for being very supportive, and getting down to brass tacks, about everything. This novelist thing really is the happy medium between the humanities prof and the gallerist.

ABOUT THE AUTHOR

CLAIRE LIGHT (writing as Jadie Jang) is almost as organizy as her characters. She started a magazine (Hyphen) and an arts festival (APAture) with a cast of Asian Pacific Americans even more magical, if less supernatural, than the ones she writes about. She also got an MFA, went to Clarion West, and compromised between the two by publishing a collection of "literary" sci-fi short stories (*Slightly Behind and to the Left*) that maybe 100 people read. After wrangling arts and social justice nonprofits for 17 years, her already autoimmune-disease-addled body threw a seven-year-long tantrum, leading our then-house-bound heroine into an urban fantasy addiction. A few years, and a dozen Euro-centric-mythology-dominated urban fantasy series later, Claire sat up and said "I can do this!" and Jadie Jang, the part of her brain that writes snarky-fun genre romps, was born. She posts about monkeys every Monday under @seelight on Twitter.

FIND US ONLINE!

www.rebellionpublishing.com

/rebellionpub

/rebellionpublishing

/rebellionpublishing

SIGN UP TO OUR NEWSLETTER!

rebellionpublishing.com/newsletter

YOUR REVIEWS MATTER!

Enjoy this book? Got something to say?

Leave a review on Amazon, GoodReads or with your
favourite bookseller and let the world know!